DOOON MODE

DOOON MODE

Piers Anthony

A TOM DOHERTY ASSOCIATES BOOK
NEW YORK

This is a work of fiction. All the characters and events portrayed in this novel are either products of the author's imagination or are used fictitiously.

DoOon Mode

A Tor Book
Published by Tom Doherty Associates, LLC
175 Fifth Avenue
New York, NY 10010

www.tor.com

Tor® is a registered trademark of Tom Doherty Associates, LLC.

ISBN: 0-812-57542-3
Library of Congress Catalog Card Number: 00-048834

First edition: April 2001
First mass market edition: April 2002

Printed in the United States of America

0 9 8 7 6 5 4 3 2 1

Contents

ONE

❈

Felines

Cat crouched on the stand, pondering. It was not given to the stresses of emotion, but did feel troubled. The situation of their trio was not good, and the Feline nulls were suffering. Something needed to be done, but the course of action that offered was not benign. Perhaps they would be best off if they simply waited out the negative period, trusting to time to ameliorate the problem.

Cat felt as if its tail were twitching nervously, though of course there was no tail. The course of action that offered had a limited period for adoption, and that period ended in one more day. Thereafter that option would be lost, and it seemed unlikely that it would be repeated. Cat suspected that it related to the Virtual Mode project; if so, it was of special interest to the Felines. Perhaps it should be mentioned to the others. Yet their emotions governed them unduly; it was their nature. They were too apt to react rashly.

There was one day remaining to decide. Cat put its head

down and napped, awaiting the return of the others.

There was no mistaking their arrival. Tom's extended toe-claws clacked against the floor, evidence of anger. Pussy was mewling, evidence of grief. Something ill had happened.

They burst into the chamber. Tom was a powerful figure of a human man, his only feline aspects being his head, retractable claws, and a certain furriness. Pussy was a lovely figure of a human female, with the facial features of her feline persuasion. They were really human androids with their features tweaked to make them suggest cats, exactly as was the case with Cat itself. Male, female, and neuter: the Feline nulls.

"Oh, Cat!" Pussy cried, stepping into Cat's reassuring embrace. "It was awful!" Now, in privacy, she felt free to let her tears flow.

"It was an outrage!" Tom snapped, striking the featureless dummy and raking it with his claws.

"Let me guess," Cat said, letting Pussy sob into its shoulder. "The Swine?"

"The Swine," Tom agreed. "We were just trying to dance at the null club. No one asked us, so Pussy addressed a Canine. Hound looked interested. They were about to dance, when Sow cut in and took Hound herself. The others laughed. They won't let us forget, even for a moment." He clawed the dummy again.

"Hound would have danced with me," Pussy said brokenly. "He liked me. I could tell. He would have taken me into the private stall and humped me. I haven't been humped in a month! And Sow knew it."

"And I can't hump any of the females," Tom growled. "They all look down on me, because I'm unemployed."

"Because *we're* unemployed," Cat said. "Remember, we are in this together."

"I wish we could get an assignment," Pussy sobbed, not much comforted. "Why can't we?"

"You *know* why," Tom said, clawing the dummy again. "The employers don't want us."

"But it wasn't our fault!"

"But they still blame us," Tom said. This time he actually gouged out a chunk of material.

"It's so unfair! We're good nulls. We never fouled up."

Cat was on the verge of deciding. He postponed it for a moment by clarifying their situation once agian. "We are good nulls, and it is unfair to make us pariahs. But this is the way the limited minds of the Swine work, and the others take their cues from them."

"Because the Swine serve Ddwng," Tom said. This time he punched the dummy, and it rocked back with the force of the blow. Because his hands were essentially human, he could do this when he chose.

"So *they* fouled up," Pussy said, finally disengaging from Cat. "So why aren't they blamed?"

Cat tried to find a way to explain it that she could accept. She was emotional, and that got in the way of her thinking. "It is the convention that the master can't make a mistake. So when something goes wrong, someone else must be blamed. I doubt that anyone could have protected Ddwng from that error, but it is the job of the Swine to facilitate his convenience in any way feasible, so the implication is that they failed. They can't accept that, so they suggest that we, as the nulls serving the alien visitor, must have been at fault. Therefore the blame falls on us, and we have no one to pass it along to. We have become the pariahs of convenience. Therefore unemployable, until the situation changes."

"Just what did go wrong?" Tom asked. "All I heard was that Ddwng was ready to go with the alien party, there in the palace. Then he changed his mind, and they were gone without him."

"There was a factor none of us in the DoOon Mode understood," Cat said. "Do you remember the horse?"

"Horse?" Pussy asked blankly.

"The young woman Colene came with a beast of burden, a horse," Cat explained. "A stallion who was immediately stabled. It seems that the animal was telepathic."

"Telepathic! You mean it could read minds?"

"Yes. That horse was in mental contact with the girl. It was able to receive and project thoughts. When Ddwng was ready to travel on the Virtual Mode, the horse sent him a thought: a command to free the anchor. Ddwng did that without realizing it until after the fact. I believe it was a very sudden, very powerful thought, striking at a time when the master was making an effort to be mentally receptive to the nature of the Virtual Mode. So he was ambushed, and the alien party escaped."

"But a horse—a literal horse, not an Equine null? They don't have human intelligence. How could a mere horse do such a thing?"

"Whether the animal was sapient at the human level I don't know," Cat said. "I suspect there are stranger things on the Virtual Mode than we know. But it may not have needed such intelligence. It merely obeyed the will of the girl. *She* was the key to the loss of the Virtual Mode. It seems that Ddwng seriously misjudged the situation, not realizing the power the girl had through the horse."

"So she tricked Ddwng, and he is angry, and the blame descends on us because we served her man, Darius," Pussy said, finally getting it.

"Yes. Perhaps we should have fathomed that aspect, and warned Ddwng. We did not, and could not, because it seems that Darius himself did not know of the horse's nature. The Swine should have fathomed it."

"It isn't fair," she repeated, her delicate whiskers trembling.

"If only we could fight back!" Tom said.

Cat decided. "Perhaps we can."

Both oriented on the neuter, knowing that it never made foolish or emotional statements. "How?" Tom demanded.

"It is dangerous."

"Anything," Pussy said.

So Cat told them. "As you know, I am undistracted by most passions of the flesh, so I have attention for intellectual pursuits. I track the releases of special projects. One is now available that I strongly suspect relates to the Virtual Mode."

"Where Darius came from," Pussy said. "Is he coming back?" She had on one occasion come close to seducing the man, and surely had a hankering to complete that business.

"Perhaps. I understand there are different Virtual Modes, with different travelers. But it seems likely, because Darius had the use of a Chip. I believe the Swine have been watching, and are aware when an anchor changes. I think they want to be ready the next time there is opportunity for our Mode to become an anchor. Since there needs to be an anchor person or persons, they may have in mind training suitable prospects. Of course this is mere conjecture on my part; I am surely mistaken on details, or perhaps on the whole."

"But you know something," Tom said.

"What I know is that there is an opening for volunteers to undertake dangerous training for an important mission. It may not be this one. But if it is, we may have an inherent advantage, because we have had contact with a man who has traveled a Virtual Mode."

"Darius," Pussy said dreamily. "I just know I can do him the favor of seducing him."

"I think not," Cat said firmly. "The aliens seemed to have different ideas about sexual relations. The man may have been amenable, but the young woman did not wish him to indulge with anyone except her."

"But she didn't indulge with him," Pussy protested. "I just know it."

"Different cultures, different foibles. It is possible that one reason the woman wished to escape our Mode was that she did not like your association with Darius."

She pondered that. "So I may not seduce him?"

"Not until we know his situation better. But this is academic; we don't know that we will see him again."

"Unless we take that opening," Tom said gruffly.

"Agreed. And it may be for something else entirely. The chance of mortality is listed at fifty percent. So this is not something to undertake lightly."

"But it would redeem us?" Pussy asked hopefully.

"I believe so, if we survive it."

"So we'll take it," Tom said.

Cat looked at Pussy. She nodded. "We'll take it."

Emperor Ddwng himself made the presentation. He was a man in his fifties, portly and with receding reddish hair, but with piercing black eyes. There was an intensity about him that would have alerted others even if he were not supreme. "Eight teams of nulls are competing. Your mission is to obtain this flag and bring it back here." He held up a silver banner. "When this one is taken, it will be replaced by a lesser flag; the team that brings that one back will be the reserve. There are no other rules." He paused, and they realized that this meant that they could cheat and kill if they had reason. "But there is a complication. You will be accompanied by two human nulls in the forms of our recent visitors from the Virtual Mode: a mature man named Dar and a young woman named Col. The man is trustworthy and knows the location of the flag. The woman can not be trusted, but she knows the route, and will do what the man wishes. She may have special powers. The man will not reveal the location of the flag unless persuaded, and the one who can most readily persuade him is the woman. Thus you will have to relate to these two people, as well as to the hazards of the course itself. The people will not cooperate unless induced. You will be issued pain controls that will work on nulls, but caution is advised because once you hurt them, they will feel free to hurt you. We judge the likely mortality rate to be fifty percent, but this is approximate; it is possible that all of you will die."

He gave them a moment to assimilate this, then spoke again. "The winning team will go into training for travel on a Virtual Mode. This is a mission of honor, and the team members will assume the temporary status of full human officers of my court, with the right to address me personally. If the mission on the Virtual Mode is successful, that status will become permanent."

All around them, the assembled nulls reacted. Human officer status! This was an unprecedented reward. Cat was not given to emotion, but even it felt the magnitude of this potential. Tom was staring, and Pussy seemed about to faint. The other nulls were responding similarly. All of them were awed. This was a prospect well worth the risk of death. Seldom did any null trio achieve such recognition.

"Your prisoners are in the eight scattered cubicles," Ddwng continued after a moment. "Proceed." He turned away, dismissing them from his attention.

There was a scramble to reach the cubes. "Let's wait a moment," Cat murmured. "We may profit from observing."

Tom had been about to launch toward the nearest cube, and Pussy was not far behind. But at Cat's words, they both drew back. They trusted its judgment.

There were eight trios and eight cubes, but in their eagerness to be first, three teams converged on the closest cube—the one that the felines would have gone to. These were Ovine, Bovine, and Equine. The Equine horse saw the problem and called off the stallion and mare; they galloped for a farther cube. But the Ovine ram and Bovine bull came together before the cube, lowering their heads. They were of similar size—human—and similar temperament—male—and similar armament—horns. But the use of the horns differed. The ram tried to butt, while the bull tried to gore. The contest was brief and inconclusive, as their neuters called them off and guided them to different cubes. The closest cube was left free.

"Wait longer," Cat said. "Watch."

So they did not approach the cube. Instead they watched the other nulls as they went to the cubes and opened the doors. This much was routine; the man and woman emerged when released, seeming amenable. The male was slightly taller than the male nulls, and the female was somewhat shorter than the female nulls; she was in fact small for a grown woman. Neither was particularly imposing; the man was not muscular and the girl was not buxom.

The Swine were the first to get on their way. They ran, and the prisoners ran ahead of them. "They are using the pain buttons," Cat said. It brought out the one they had been given. "The pain is generalized, but strongest nearest the button. So the prisoners are being caused to run by a lash at their backsides, as it were. That is evidently effective, but for how long?"

"Those buttons hurt," Pussy said. "They can hurt a lot."

She was thinking of the time the Felines had been assigned to be with a visiting woman of somewhat sadistic nature. Pussy had done her best to oblige, but the woman seemed to resent her sexy nature, and had burned her on any pretext. Cat had been unable to prevent this mistreatment. They had of course not spoken of it to any other human, but the other nulls had known, and soon the button was replaced with one whose pain was nominal. Pussy had known immediately to act as if the pain were its usual intensity, and so they had gotten by. The masters and mistresses were not normally cruel to nulls, but visitors could be.

"How do you think a willful human would react to being prodded in this manner?" Cat asked Pussy.

"He would be angry," she said immediately. "He would strike back, when he had the chance."

Cat nodded. "The customary arrogance of the Swine may be their own undoing."

Meanwhile the other teams were proceeding at a slower pace. The general pattern seemed to be a somewhat threatening posture by the male, so that the prisoners realized that it was safest for them to cooperate. They were moving out, but did not seem entirely happy about it.

"They're getting ahead of us," Tom said restlessly.

"Perhaps. Would there be an advantage to persuasion?" Cat inquired rhetorically.

Tom let his claws spring out from his right hand. "I can persuade as well as any."

"That is not persuasion," Cat said. "That is threat. How would you do it, Pussy?"

"I would seduce the male," she said.

"You tried that before," Tom reminded her. "And made an enemy of the girl."

"Meow," she said, embarrassed. "Maybe I should befriend the girl instead."

"I suspect that would be wise," Cat said. "Other teams are using force of one kind or another. That may indeed be the answer. But we were warned that there will be surprises. Some of them may be in the nature of the prisoners. I think we should set ourselves apart from the others by truly befriending the prisoners, if that is feasible. That may not be the winning strategy, but it would be different, and sometimes difference is the key to success. I suspect we would be well advised to try an alternate strategy."

"Befriend them?" Tom asked.

"You could befriend the man, Tom, and Pussy could befriend the girl, trying to help them and make them feel at ease with us. If that encouraged them to cooperate fully, we would not have to watch them, and might even prevail in the contest."

Tom shrugged. "I can try it."

"Will they believe us?" Pussy asked.

"Perhaps they will, if we give them the pain button."

Both stared at Cat. "But that would give them the power!" Tom said.

Cat faced Pussy. "If a Master gave you the button, would you still serve him?"

"Oh, yes, of course!" she exclaimed. "Gladly. Because I'm still a null."

"And they will still be prisoners," Cat said. "They will know that."

She nodded. "If they are like me, they will be grateful."

"But they could use the pain on us," Tom protested.

"That is the risk we take. Are you willing?"

Tom spread his hands in a human gesture. "If you think it will help."

"I think the chance that it will help is about one in three. But our chance of prevailing by acting as the other teams do is about one in eight. So, yes, it may help, though it is risky."

"So no sex appeal from me, no violence from Tom, and no smarter-than-thou words from you," Pussy said. "We put ourselves in their hands."

"That is essentially it," Cat agreed.

They approached the cube. It had a simple bar closing the door from the outside, so the prisoners could not escape. Tom was about to remove it, but Cat cautioned him with a gesture. Instead, he made a knuckle and rapped on the door. "May we enter?" he called.

There was a brief pause. Then a female human voice replied. "Who are you? What do you want?"

"We are a trio of Feline nulls. We want to be your friends."

There was another pause. This time a male human voice replied. "Then enter."

Now Tom lifted the bar and set it aside. He drew the door slowly open.

The inside of the cube was a residential containment cell, the kind used to house prisoners who were not being punished. It had a bed big enough for one person, and a table with a jug of water and a loaf of bread. There was barely room for the three additional bodies. The man was, as expected, taller than any of the Felines, and the woman was smaller, really a girl, just as they had seen with the other teams. He was ruggedly handsome, and she was rather pretty in her fashion. Both were clothed, he in brown trousers and a long-sleeved gray shirt, she in white blouse and black skirt reaching to her knees. She also wore a red ribbon in her hair.

"We have not been told what's going on," the man said. "But we assume that you are to be our keepers for the duration."

"I can clarify the situation if you wish," Cat said.

"Yes, we wish," the man said. "I am Dar, and my companion is Col. We are Human nulls."

"But no neuter?" Pussy asked, then put her hand to her mouth, realizing that she had spoken impulsively.

"No neuter," the girl agreed. "We are Special Purpose androids."

Of course they knew the Feline names, as all animal nulls were identified similarly, but Cat introduced them anyway. "This is Tom, our male, and Pussy, our female, and I am Cat, our neuter. This is the situation: eight teams of Animal nulls are competing to obtain a silver flag. The team that brings it back will qualify for a special mission on a Virtual Mode. There are no rules, which means that the competition may become ugly. We understand that one of you knows the best route, and the other knows the location of the flag, so we need your cooperation if we are to prevail."

"Why should we help you?" Dar asked.

"I will answer," Cat said carefully. "But first I must inquire what fate awaits you after this mission is done."

"It is unspecified, but we assume that we will be melted back into the pool."

Cat nodded. "If you would prefer to keep your present identities, we might be able to encourage that—if we win the contest."

"Why should we trust you?" Col demanded.

"Trust is difficult between strangers," Cat said. "But motives are more reliable. We are in bad repute, and wish to redeem ourselves. The mission for which we compete should accomplish that. We are prepared to do what is required. We believe that your willing cooperation is our best chance. How can we obtain it?"

"You can't," the girl said. "We don't care about your mission."

"Then perhaps you will at least trust our motivation," Cat said. "Name your desire."

"We want to go with you on the Virtual Mode."

Cat shook its head. "We can't promise that. It would be meaningless. Even our plea on your behalf may not be effective."

"Then let us go now," Dar said.

"We can do that. But we doubt it would help you. This is an established competition range, well guarded. I doubt you could escape it."

"We could if we had the pain button," the girl said.

Cat wore the button on a cord around its neck. It lifted it off and proffered it to her.

"It's a trick!" she said, shying away from it.

Cat offered it to Dar. The man took it.

"It's a dummy," the girl said.

Dar touched the side of the button with his thumb. Cat, closest to it, felt sudden burning pain across his front. His breath hissed inward as he stiffened.

"You're faking," Col said.

Dar swung the button toward her. Cat's pain eased, while the girl stiffened. Now she believed.

"Where's the catch?" she asked.

"We believe that just as our success depends on your willing cooperation, your success depends on our success," Cat said. "We ask you to help us, and tell us how we can help you."

"It makes sense," Dar said. "I think we'll have to trust them."

"Okay," Col said. "We'll risk it. At least this way we'll have a chance to avoid the melting pot."

"Then, perhaps, we should move rapidly," Cat said. "The other teams are already well on their way."

"We will accompany you without duress," Dar said. "But you are not yet ready. This is as much as I can say."

Cat hesitated. He believed the man. These two were surely programmed to react in prescribed ways, depending on circumstances. The effort to gain their cooperation seemed to be successful, but they remained limited. What was the key?

It was Pussy who caught on. "You want to help, but can't volunteer!" she cried. "We have to ask you."

"You got it, puss," Col said. "We can answer some questions, and I don't have to tell the truth. But we can't warn you of what you don't suspect."

Cat nodded. "If we want to be sure of truth, we must

ask Dar. But you are the one who knows the route. So we will have to trust you."

"I can lead you into disaster," Col agreed.

"But if we don't trust you, we will lose," Pussy said. "So we have to."

"Did we start right?" Tom asked Dar.

"Yes. There are other ways, but yours is the most likely to succeed."

"The first portion of the course is a deep forest," Cat said. "I doubt that it is safe to cross without preparation. What is its danger?"

Col's answer was surprisingly complete. "There are teams of null predators, one for each contestant team. If you defeat the beasts, you will not be attacked again within the forest; you will be able to move swiftly through it to the next obstacle. Each team consists of a raptor, a snake, and a bear. They will attack simultaneously, one to a Feline. We Humans will be ignored. If you die, we will be free to return to our base."

"Is this the outcome you prefer?" Cat asked Dar.

"No."

Cat wasn't quite satisfied. "You answer truthfully, but do you have to tell the whole truth?"

"No. Not unless asked."

"What is the whole truth?"

"If you abuse us, we would prefer to see you die. If you treat us well and keep the faith, we prefer to see you win. Thus the case will differ between contestants, depending on their treatment of their prisoners."

"But you aren't prisoners any more," Pussy protested.

"We nevertheless remain bound," Col said.

"We do mean to treat you well," Cat said. "We gave you the pain button."

Tom had a concern. "You say the predators won't attack you. So why do you need the pain button?"

"We don't," Dar said.

"What is the whole truth?" Cat asked.

"The pain button works only on human-based nulls. Since you have agreed not to hurt us, it does not matter who possesses it."

"It won't work on the predators?" Tom asked.

"True."

"So we have no use for it either," Cat said. "Keep it. If we die, you may be in danger from other contestants. It may enable you to escape them."

"You really *are* trying to befriend us," Col said. "May I kiss you?"

Surprised, Cat agreed. She embraced it and kissed it firmly on the mouth. Cat was of course not given to sexual feeling, but her gesture was pleasant. Had she kissed Tom that way, he would have wanted to hump her.

"Does this action have significance?" Cat asked Dar.

"Yes. It signifies Col's acceptance of your friendship. She will now help you actively, without deceit."

So they had achieved another level of cooperation. "What is the distinction between active and passive help?"

"Now she will be alert for threats, and advise you of what she sees," Dar said. "This may be helpful if you are distracted. But we still cannot assist you physically, or tell you how to handle threats."

The man's responses were becoming more helpful; evidently the girl's signal of friendship applied to him too. "Thank you. We appreciate your commitment." Cat turned to Tom. "How will we handle a raptor, a snake, and a bear?"

"We must have weapons," Tom said. "Raptors swoop down from cover and attack before the prey knows it. Then it is too late. The snake will likely be poisonous, and strike without warning. The bear will probably be our best warning, because it will have to charge us. Then we will know that the other two are about to strike. But maybe the others will strike first, diverting us while the bear charges. Each of us will have to handle one attacker. I think Pussy should take the raptor, and you should take the snake. I will take the bear, which will be the most dangerous attacker."

"But the bear will be too strong for you," Cat said.

"I will distract and delay it while you deal with the others," Tom said. "Then the three of us can handle it."

"I hope so," Cat said.

"How can even three Felines handle a savage bear?" Pussy asked. "That thing may mass as much as all of us together, and be able to dispatch any one of us with one swipe."

"The right weapons can do it," Tom said. "Together with a plan of combat. It will not be easy, but is possible. Have courage."

"I'm not strong on that," she said.

"Fortunately Tom is," Cat said. "Let's get our weapons."

Neither Dar nor Col commented, but Cat saw Dar nod. They were on the right course. How many of the other trios were?

They left the cube and walked toward the forest. There was a scream that sounded Equine. A team was under attack within the forest.

Tom took charge. Physical combat was his specialty, just as physical appeal was Pussy's. "Pussy, find a branch with foliage. That will foul the wings of the raptor, and then you can claw it to death. Cat, find a forked stick. That will enable you to pin the snake's head to the ground, and then you can throttle it with your hands. I will seek more formidable weapons."

They got busy, while the two human nulls watched. There were many fallen branches of different sizes, and soon Pussy and Cat had suitable implements. Meanwhile Tom gathered a number of sticks and stones and made a pile of them.

There were too many for the three of them to carry, especially if they had to be ready to fight at any instant. "You may not help us fight, but will you carry our weapons?" Cat asked Dar.

"Yes."

This time it was Tom and Pussy who nodded, impressed. Cat had found a way by using its mind. "Thank you." The Human nulls were becoming increasingly useful.

They set off into the forest. "Col, I would be grateful if you would help me watch for raptors," Pussy said with the niceness that came naturally to her.

"I will."

"And I would be similarly appreciative for help in watching for snakes," Cat said to Dar.

"I will."

That would leave Tom free to focus his full attention on the bear. Tom as the combat specialist would be aware of the creature before any of the rest of them were. It was the predators who would lurk motionless until striking that were the most immediately dangerous, as Tom had suggested.

They moved cautiously through the forest until they came to a glade. Tom paused, wise in the ways of the hunt. "This is dangerous; the bird has room to swoop, and the grass conceals the snake. We'd better go around."

But thickets surrounded the glade, and extended some distance to either side, into marshy regions. "We'll have better footing here," Cat said. "Maybe we should try to trigger their attack, and be done with it."

Tom nodded. "Maybe they'll go for a ruse." He threw one of his stones into the grassy center, hard.

It worked. A viper rose up and hissed, searching for its target. Cat leaped forward with his forked stick, trying for its neck.

Pussy followed him, waving her bushy branch. Col

cried out "Raptor!" Sure enough, a hawk came diving down, trying for the back of Cat's neck. Pussy intercepted it with her branch, foiling its attack. That gave Cat time to trap the snake's head with the fork of the stick, pinning it to the ground.

Meanwhile the bear appeared, as if from nowhere. Tom hurled a makeshift spear at it. His aim was good, but the wooden point was not sharp enough to do much damage. The bear shook it off and continued its charge toward Cat. Cat realized that their choices of creatures to fight did not match the assignments of the predators; the bear was coming after Cat, not Tom.

But that meant that Tom could attack it from the side. He did, running in close and bashing it across the head with a heavy wooden club. That had more effect, but still didn't stop the solid creature.

Cat had a wild notion. It pounced on the viper and hauled it up between its paws, clasping it by the neck. As the bear bore down on them, jaws gaping, Cat whirled and hurled the snake into its face. The viper hissed and wrapped part way around the bear's nose. Surprised, the bear bit through its body. The snake fell in two pieces, both twitching desperately.

Seeing that, Pussy pounced on the entangled bird, wrapping it in foliage. She shoved the package at the bear's snout. The bear lifted a paw and batted the branch so hard that it flew far across the glade. The bird fluttered weakly and did not fly again; it, too, had been taken out by its own ally.

Dar and Col, watching, both nodded.

Now the three of them concentrated on the bear. Cat danced before it, leaping backwards, so that it continued to orient on him. Pussy got stones from Col and hurled them at the creature's head. Several bounced harmlessly off, but then she got lucky and scored on its eye. Half blinded, it still came after Cat.

Then Tom scored on its delicate nose, taking out another important sense. Pussy circled behind it, got more stones, and aimed for the remaining eye. Soon she scored, for the range was very short and she had mousing reflexes. Now the creature was reduced to hearing. But it did not know its prey by that sense alone, and started going for anything that made a sound.

Cat called out to Tom. "I see little point in slowly killing this creature. I doubt it will be much further danger to us. Let's let it go, and be on our way."

Tom, in the throes of battle fever, didn't want to break off, but Pussy joined in. She could enjoy playing cat and mouse as readily as any Feline, but had a gentler temperament. "Please, Tom—we can save time."

Grudgingly, Tom agreed. He backed away, leaving the bear to snarl in one direction, then another, trying to locate something to obliterate. They threw stones ahead of it, and as it went in pursuit of their noise, quietly circled behind it and on beyond the glade. In the process they came across the tattered body of a Bovine null, a bull whose belly had been ripped open. A swipe of the bear's paw must have done it. There was no sign of the other members of that team. Obviously it was no longer in contention, even if the cow and steer survived.

"You handled that obstacle well," Col remarked.

"Our first requirement is survival," Cat said. "Our second is swiftness. We surely started slowest of all the teams, but your warning enabled us to survive well. We do appreciate it."

"You had the wit to make a fair deal with us," Dar said.

And evidently the Bovines had not, and had been caught unprepared. "Are you allowed to warn us of the next hazard?"

"Yes. Col knows all the geographical obstacles."

That was an interesting qualification. There would be

more than geographical challenges. But for the moment, those were what they faced. Cat addressed the girl. "What is it?"

"A raging torrent you must cross. There will be several means to pass it, but each has its liability. That is all I know."

They heard a vague sound ahead, and as they advanced toward it, it increased in volume, becoming a sustained roar. That would be the torrent. It was evidently a river crossing the full area, and there would be no feasible way around it.

They reached the bank, and were daunted. The stream was a good four man-lengths across, and its flow was ferocious. There were rocks in it making tiny islands, but in no pattern suitable for crossing. It might be possible to wedge or roll one stone to another place, to make a stepping stone, but that would entail struggling in the fierce current. Cat took a stick and poked it into the water—and a toothy fish darted in to bite at it. There would be no wading there.

They walked along the bank. A short distance downstream there were several large logs, possibly suitable for making a raft. "We could lash those together with vines, and pole across," Tom said. "The current would carry us downstream, but a few good shoves would get us to the far bank."

"That's a bit too obvious," Cat said. "I distrust it."

"Oh, come on," Pussy said. "We can do it quickly, and be across before any other danger threatens."

"Perhaps. Still, I recommend caution." Cat, covertly watching the human nulls, saw another slight nod.

Pussy shrugged. Guided by Cat's hesitancy, they concealed themselves in brush and watched the logs.

It was just as well, for soon a Canine hound appeared, carrying an armful of vines. Evidently the logs had been collected by the Canines, who now were scrounging for vines. If the felines had tried to take them, they would soon have been in a scrap with the Canines. The natural challenges were enough; it made no sense to fight with other trios.

The hound began tying the vines around the logs.

"I could distract him," Pussy whispered. "So that you could overcome him and take the raft."

Surely she could, for male nulls liked female nulls of any persuasion except their own. They were made that way so that there would be no sexual interactions within persuasions. But Cat did not trust this either. "Canines are not stupid. Hound may be aware of us. Note that their human nulls are not in evidence."

"Which means they have been parked elsewhere," Tom agreed.

So they waited longer. Then an Ovine female appeared from the down-river side. "Hello, Hound," she said in a dulcet bleat.

"Hello, Ewe," he replied, seeming nonchalant.

"I seem to have lost my way," she said, sitting on the edge of the raft. Cat, from the vantage of the neuter kind, noted how artfully Ewe's firm thighs parted toward the male and how firmly her breasts moved with her breathing. She was making sure she compelled his attention. And where were the Ovine trio's human nulls?

"You sure have," Hound agreed. He moved so suddenly it was a blur, knocking her backwards so that her dainty hind hoofs flew up. He pinned her beneath him, working his body around to get between her legs.

"But I would give you a hump willingly," she protested. "There is no need to rape me."

"I'm in a hurry," Hound said as he shoved into her cleft. Cat saw that she was not resisting at all.

There was the beat of charging hoofs. Ram appeared, evidently from hiding, his horns lowered. Hound heard him and tried to get out of the way, but Ewe held him in place with arms and legs wrapped around his body, not nearly as helpless as she had seemed. She had evidently set out to distract Hound, exactly as Pussy had thought to do, to set him up for Ram.

But even as Ram connected, Bitch appeared from a lair under the logs. She had a crude net of vines, which she threw over Ram, entangling him. She tried to bite him as he fell. It was a countertrap.

Sheep, the neuter Ovine, appeared. It grabbed Bitch from behind, hurling her to the ground. Counter-countertrap.

Then of course Dog appeared, swinging a club at Sheep. Sheep ducked down and butted Dog in the belly. Meanwhile Ram was working his way free of the net. Neither trap had worked perfectly; they were canceling out.

Now it was hand to hand. The carnivores were all fighters, of course, but so were the herbivores. They were fairly evenly matched. But because they were fighting each other, both were likely to be losers.

The action was brief but vicious. Hound bit Ewe on the neck, robbing her of coordination. Ram bashed Bitch's head against a log, knocking her senseless. The two victors leaped up, about to tackle each other. Dog and Sheep seemed evenly matched. They grappled, being able to get in neither a good bite nor butt, and rolled into the river. In a moment both screamed as the fish attacked.

Hound and Ram ran to rescue their neuters, for the moment forgetting their own fight. They reached down to grab hold of Dog and Sheep.

And three Swine appeared, armed with clubs. They quickly bashed Hound and Ram from behind, knocking them into the water. Then they focused on the two females. "Take one, toss the other," Pig said tersely.

Boar got down on helpless Ewe, while Sow hauled Bitch to the water and rolled her in. Then she joined Pig, using clubs to bash back any who tried to scramble out of the water. Meanwhile Boar finished with Ewe, hauled her up, and heaved her also into the water. In a moment she too was carried away by the torrent. If she didn't drown, the chances were that her teammates would. Both Ovines and Canines seemed to be finished. Their human nulls would be free to desert them.

After that the three Swine finished the work on the raft and got on it, poling it across the river. Their two prisoners were bound and hobbled, and made no resistance. The Felines merely watched.

"We could have taken them," Tom said.

"And maybe gotten ambushed by the next team," Pussy countered.

"Time to find out," Cat said.

They rose from their concealment and walked to the site of the mayhem. "Any other teams watching?" Cat called, not loudly.

After a moment there was a stirring in the brush, and the Caprines emerged: Buck, Goat, and Doe. All had horns, beards, and hind hooves. Along with them were two human nulls almost identical to the ones the Felines had. "What is your position, Cat?" Goat inquired.

"We suspect that cooperation is better than conflict," Cat said. "At least at this stage."

"We agree, Cat. Can we do each other any good?"

"We have useful information."

"We have another way to cross the river."

Cat glanced at the other Felines. "Shall we declare a truce, not to be broken until after fair notice?"

"We agree. What is your information?"

"What is your way?"

Buck walked to a hiding place, and lifted a sizable coil of rope. "Tie this to a bough, swing across," he said.

"Why haven't you done this already?"

"Our captives won't go."

Cat nodded. "Or rather, you can't trust them to go across, since they might run away if not immediately threatened."

"We didn't threaten them," Doe protested. "But they are reluctant."

"Our information will solve that problem," Cat said.

"We thought it might," Goat said. "We observed yours carrying weapons for you."

"Here is the key," Cat said. "Ours are not prisoners. They help us because it is in their best interest to do so. Yours will help you similarly, if you give them reason."

Goat looked at the Feline's Dar. "True?"

The man did not respond. "You are free to speak," Cat reminded him.

"True," Dar agreed.

"How did they persuade you?" Goat asked.

"They freed us," Dar said.

"Why did you not then run away?"

"We have no reason to run, and we do have reason to stay. We are better off with them than without them."

Goat looked at Cat. "We must talk," it said.

They walked a bit away from the group, and Cat explained about the agreement to speak for the Human nulls after the mission, and about giving them the pain button. Goat was dubious, but decided to try it.

"However," Goat said, "this does not settle the matter of the contest. We can't promise our Humans much if we do not win."

"The second finisher is the reserve," Cat reminded it. "That also should be worth something. The Humans should understand."

Goat nodded. "Perhaps so," it agreed. "And perhaps also, when we have privileges, we could request the services of those Humans as our nulls. We could then treat them well."

Cat hadn't thought of that. "This may be feasible. Perhaps we should extend the truce, and try to finish first and second. Second place would be better than death."

"Three teams have already perished," Goat agreed. "We would not care to do business with the Swine. That leaves only two in doubt."

"Equine and Fowl," Cat agreed. "With some luck we can avoid them and beat them."

"But the Swine will have to be dispatched."

Cat nodded. "No truce with Swine. Suppose we cooperate until we have the first and second places secured, then have an honest, nonviolent, fair contest with agreed rules to determine which team wins?"

Goat nodded in return. They had an understanding.

They returned to the others. "We have agreed to cooperate throughout," Cat said. "To take first and second places, then decide amicably which team wins. We will avoid other teams, but will try to dispatch the Swine. We believe that this will make both survival and winning far more likely."

"I will address our Human companions," Goat said. "The rest of you may get acquainted." Goat walked toward the two Human nulls who stood within sight.

"Oh, goody!" Pussy exclaimed. "Come here, Buck."

"Come here, Tom," Doe said, smiling.

The males were glad to accede. The two couples went behind trees, already embracing.

"That looks like fun," Col said somewhat wistfully.

"Are you permitted to interact sexually?" Cat asked, surprised.

"We are allowed to resist rape," Col said. "But the pain pills make that possible. You have freed us from that threat."

"But you may have sex if you choose?"

"Maybe."

Cat looked at Dar. "May I have a more complete answer?"

"We are permitted, if our controlling nulls wish it," Dar said. "But we are not permitted to seduce them."

"So you can accede, but not initiate."

"Yes," Col said. "You may have noticed that neither I nor my counterpart with the Caprine trio have acted at all seductively. But neither have we made ourselves ugly."

Cat was thoughtful. "We interacted for a time with the originals you emulate. Darius was interested in Pussy, but Colene did not approve. We concluded that sexual interaction was appropriate only between the two humans, though there was none. You differ?"

"We are nulls, like you," Col said. "We may not indulge with our own companions, only with nulls of other persuasions."

"What about with alternate Human nulls?"

Both of them looked surprised. "That didn't come up in our indoctrination," Col said. "I suppose we could. But since we can't initiate, it won't happen unless we are directed to do it."

"Is it something you would wish to do?"

"No," Dar said. "No more than your Tom would wish to indulge with a foreign Pussy."

"If we succeed, with the Caprines, in securing the two winning places, we believe that the second place finishers will still be treated well, because they will be held in reserve for the Virtual Mode mission. The winners will go with the real Darius and Colene, but the second place team will request to be assigned their human nulls as servants. That should secure your identities also. If you then wish to indulge with our males and females, they should be happy to do it. We believe we can make a good life for you, at least until the mission is concluded. Therefore you should find it worthwhile to cooperate with us even if we finish second."

"Yes," Dar agreed.

Goat returned with the other couple. "They agree," it said. "They have the pain button."

"Shall we call our Humans Feline Dar and Col, and yours Caprine Dar and Col?" Cat asked.

"Call them F-Dar, F-Col, C-Dar, and C-Col," Goat said.

The two couples returned from their copulations, and the ten of them got to work completing the rope, which was made from rolled wiry grasses the Caprines sniffed out. The four human nulls worked with them, satisfied that their personal interests aligned. Soon the rope was ready.

They found a tree with a stout branch leaning out across the river. Tom, good at climbing, went up to tie the rope to the branch, so that it hung down to the ground in a broad curve. They made a small loop for a foot. Then each individual held it and swung across, almost grazing the water, and letting go as it reached the far side. They had a set order: Tom, Doe, F-Dar, Goat, C-Col, Buck, Pussy, C-Dar, Cat, and F-Col. That kept the two teams thoroughly mixed, so there was no temptation for anyone to separate when across the river. There was no reason to suppose anyone would violate the truce, but Cat and Goat agreed to buttress agreement with caution.

When they were all across, Cat thought of something. "Do we want to leave the rope there?"

"Do we want to return this way?" Goat asked in return.

"If any teams remain behind us," Tom said, "they can use it and still be behind us." He was always aware of tactical situations.

"They will hesitate, fearing a trap," one of the Human nulls said. It was C-Col. Cat and Goat nodded; she was right.

Buck glanced at her. "I could get to like you."

"Want me to inhale or bend over, big boy?"

He was almost taken aback. "In good time, perhaps."

So the Human nulls could respond readily enough, Cat

thought. The girl was definitely flirting, teasing Buck about his combination of human and animal traits without suggesting that she found either objectionable.

They moved on. "The terrain opens out ahead, becoming hilly," Col said. "The flag is beyond the worst of it."

She was correct: the trees faded and hills formed, with gullies between them. They became increasingly steep, but the girl knew the best paths around the obstructions, generally following a contour. They saw no other teams.

They came in due course to truly challenging geography. It seemed as though a mountain had been riven by an earthquake so that the two halves of it wedged apart, leaving a chasm between. The far side was a virtual mirror image of the near side, because of the manner of its formation, but both were endlessly jagged and devious. It was hard to see any continuous path through this dangerous maze. "This is as far as my knowledge goes," F-Col said, and C-Col agreed. "The flag is in this region."

"I can show it to you," F-Dar said. "There is a place where a sighting can be made. That is the extent of my knowledge."

He led them up a path along a ledge cut into the nearer slope, until they reached a flat-faced boulder with a crevice of its own. Dar sighted through this. "There it is."

Cat looked. There was a silver flag perched on a spire of rock directly across from them. Now they knew where it was; they would have to find a way to reach it.

"We had better get going," Buck said, looking down into the chasm. "The Equines and Fowl are ahead of us."

Cat looked down while Goat peered through the slit at the flag. The two other teams seemed to be racing each other. "Not much hope of catching them," Tom said. "They have too much of a lead."

"We Caprines can catch them," Buck said. "We're adapted to climbing."

Goat looked at Cat. "This disturbs me. There's a smell in the air."

"I agree," Cat said. "It is too straightforward. We were warned of the unexpected. It shouldn't be a straight foot race."

"Well, it *is* a foot race," Tom said. "And every moment counts. Let's stop wasting time."

"Two things," Goat said. "First, the smell. It warned us of the attack of the beasts, so that the Bovines got slaughtered instead of us. It made us cautious when the Ovines and Canines fought. We had best heed it now, for it is when things look obvious that they may be most treacherous. Second, we don't have to be first to fetch the flags, merely the first to bring them back. The other teams will have to pass us as they return."

"And where are the Swine?" Cat asked. "They were also ahead of us, but aren't in the chasm." For everything was visible; the Swine were not ahead of the other teams.

"They're behind us!" Buck said. "Waiting to ambush us."

"So we have to watch behind as well as ahead," Goat said. It turned to Cat. "Suppose we Caprines outrace the others, to get the flags, while you Felines hunt the Swine so our return is safe?"

"I agree in principle," Cat said. "You can perform better on such a slope, and we can hunt better. But I remain suspicious. I think we are missing something."

Goat nodded. "I agree. For one thing, it might be a tactical mistake to divide our force; the two leading teams might unite against us, and the Swine are neither stupid nor scrupulous. We may yet need to fight together."

"But we have to get the flag!" Pussy cried, and Doe agreed.

"We have to be best prepared for victory," Cat said, and Goat agreed. "I think we should tarry and try to fathom the mystery."

"Sometimes you neuter intellects give me a pain in the udder," Doe said, smiling obliquely at Tom.

"True," Tom agreed quickly. He did not try to conceal his interest in the Caprine female. They had coupled once, but seemed to be developing more than a sexual relationship. "You spend so much time analyzing, you don't get much done."

"Nevertheless," Cat said evenly, "we believe we should consider a bit longer. We are not driven by sexual passions."

"However," Goat said, "those of you who are so driven may as well indulge yourselves while we ponder."

The sexed nulls needed no urging. Tom took Doe to a nook in the rocks, and Buck took Pussy to another. Because they had to be prepared for any likely degree of interest by masters or mistresses, nulls were almost indefatigable in this respect. In addition, Tom and Pussy had been long denied. Caprine males had a reputation for randyness, and Doe was an uncommonly lovely example of her kind.

"And you human nulls," Cat said. "I suggest you take a walk through the brush, spread out, and protect yourselves if menaced."

"But do not seek any quarrels," Goat said. "If you see anything of interest, you may inform us when you return, if you wish." The phrasing was careful, reminding them that they were being treated as associates, not servants.

"You have our approval, should you need to use the pain buttons," Cat said. "But it might be better to conceal them unless there is no choice. The Swine are arrogant and cunning; the former trait may prevent them from suspecting the degree of autonomy you have, but the latter should not be underestimated."

The two Dars and two Cols nodded and set out on a walk that would cover a fair swatch of territory. They understood that they were scouting for the allied teams;

they would try to locate the Swine without alerting them. Swine, being what they were, would probably try to rape them if they caught them. Not just the Boars with the girls; the sows could do weird things with males when they had the chance. It was not often that any null could get away with any such act against a human-seeming person.

Meanwhile the two neuters put their heads together and conversed quietly. "I believe the Swine are watching us, and will ambush us very soon after we get the flag," Cat said.

"But three should not fare well against six."

"Perhaps we should reduce it to three before they strike, tempting them into overconfidence."

Goat stroked his beard. "Mock fight?"

Cat nodded. "We can fetch the flag, and you can betray us and butt us into the chasm. The Swine will not question that; it is the way they operate. Then we can circle behind the Swine and counterambush them as they strike."

"This requires considerable trust on our part."

"We can lead the way, if you prefer. I merely thought we would be better at hunting and pouncing, once we are away from the rocks."

Now Goat nodded. "Without trust, nothing is viable. You will trust us with the flag; we shall trust you with our lives."

"To facilitate trust, we can exchange human nulls. I think ours will not serve you directly, if they distrust your motive, and vice versa."

"Agreed. Do you know where the flag is?"

"I suspect it is on this side of the chasm, not far from us."

Now Goat was surprised. "This side?"

"We need to be alert for surprises. This chasm setup is too pat. I think the far side is a reflection."

"Your mind is truly devious!"

"You differ?"

"No, I had come to a similar conclusion in principle, if not in detail. I thought the visible flag might be a decoy, but your analysis seems more apt. Very well, you fetch it, we'll betray you and head back, you circle behind. This will require some choreography."

"Each couple can plan its own," Cat said. "We can advise them quietly, then you and I can do a search for the flag. I think anyone who falls into the chasm can't be seen from the trail side."

"Understood." They separated, looking for the two couples.

Cat found Buck and Pussy, who had evidently finished one bout and were warming up for another. Cat suspected that Buck was flattered by Pussy's unusual ardor; she wanted all the humping she could get, after her drought. "We believe we know where the flag is," Cat said. "The Felines will find the flag, and be betrayed by the Caprines, who will take it back to be ambushed by the Swine. Then the Felines—"

"Got it," Buck said. "I'll do Tom, and Doe can do Pussy. Let's check sites."

Males were very quick to catch on to the possibilities for violence. The two moved off as Cat returned to the base of the crag where the sighting crevice was. It saw that the human nulls were returning. "Anything there?"

"Swine tracks," F-Dar said. "But we didn't see the Swine themselves."

"Is there a likely site for an ambush?"

"Several."

"The Felines are about to fetch the flag. The Caprines will betray us and hurl us into the chasm. But when the Caprines are in turn ambushed by the Swine, the Felines will ambush the Swine in a countertrap. We do not ask you human nulls to participate, except to this degree: you who are with us, go with the Caprines."

F-Col pursed her lips. "Clever, Cat. It will not pay us to let the Caprines take the flag in by themselves."

"Nor will it pay the C-Humans to let us do so," Cat agreed. "We buttress our trust in this manner. Are you amenable?"

"Yes," F-Dar said.

"Then if you would be so kind, clarify this matter with the C-Humans, and exchange places. We prefer the Swine to mistake you for the Caprines' guides."

"Got it," F-Col said. They moved off.

Then Cat returned to the crag. Goat met it there. "Are we in order?"

"We are."

Cat climbed cautiously up along the crag, while Goat checked the rock to the side. Goat would find a suitable place for Cat to land, when betrayed.

The flag was absurdly easy to find. It was on the chasm side of the rock whose split gave them the view of its reflection. Now Cat could see its own reflection, reaching around to catch the flag. So simple a ruse, yet it had fooled all of them except those who had paused to consider. Exactly as some aspect of the Virtual Mode might deceive those who trod it carelessly.

Cat took the flag and made its way down the slope in the direction Goat had gone. "I have the flag!" Cat called to the others.

Then Goat sprang out, head down. "Shrouded crevice to your left," it said as it charged.

Cat jumped into the crevice, holding the flag high. Goat leaped over the crevice, catching the flag as it did. "Mine!" it bleated.

In moments the three Caprines were together. "Come, Humans," Goat called. "We have the flag. We're going back."

F-Dar and F-Col joined them and the group set off for the return. Soon they were out of sight.

Meanwhile Cat, Tom, and Pussy were slinking from their hiding places and circling out. C-Dar and C-Col saw them but did not react; instead they began walking disconsolately in the direction the Caprine party had taken. There was no way to tell that they were not the Feline's guides, bereft of their company.

Cat remembered something, and hurried back to the spot where it had found the flag. Yes, there was a second flag behind it that it hadn't seen before, this one blue. Cat took that flag and tucked it into its pocket. The back-up position was important too.

Cat looked to where the Caprines had gone. C-Dar and C-Col were waiting. "I thought you had gone with the others, Cat told them as it caught up.

"Sneaking and pouncing is not in our program," C-Dar said.

"It is in mine," Cat said. "I must be there when my trio members join the action."

"We understand," C-Col said. "We want to thank you for enabling us to be well treated."

"We can't guarantee that beyond this contest," Cat reminded her. "In fact, only the winner will have any real input on your treatment thereafter."

"And who will that be?" C-Dar asked.

"I don't know. If both of our teams make it safely back, we shall have to decide on the winner. Perhaps by lot."

"And if you lose the lot?" C-Col asked.

"Then we lose the flag," Cat said simply. "I have no true betrayal in mind, and I doubt Goat does."

"If you lose the flag, and are second, will you ask for us as your nulls?" C-Dar asked.

"No. We will ask for the Feline Humans. They are the ones to whom we are committed."

"Yet you expect us Caprine Human nulls to help you," C-Col said.

"You are not with me to help me," Cat said patiently.

"You are here to ensure that I don't betray your associates, the Caprines."

"How can we do that?" C-Dar asked.

"You have the pain button. Use it when you see fit."

They nodded. Then Cat slunk into the brush, while they walked straight ahead.

The path passed between outcroppings of rock capable of concealing an ambush. Cat saw the Caprines marching innocently into it, with the two Humans. Cat got as close as possible without showing itself, ready for action.

But there was no ambush. The open party passed on through unscathed. Where were the Swine?

Then, in an open area, the ground suddenly caved in. Buck, walking ahead, fell into it, and Doe stopped just at the brink. "Pitfall!" Goat cried. "Seek cover!"

But already the Swine were charging in from the sides, bearing home-crafted spears. The Caprines, caught in a bad position, seemed vulnerable. The two Humans with them stood still, not acting.

Tom pounced from cover, landing on Boar's back. Boar squealed, but Tom's claws were already ripping at his throat. But Boar's hide was tough, and he tried to throw Tom off; the two fell to the ground in a tangle.

Sow turned around, surprised. Pussy sprang at her. "But you're dead!" Sow squealed, amazed.

"No, you are," Pussy replied, stabbing her in the neck with a crude stone dagger. But Sow, too, was tough; she knocked the stone aside and barreled into Pussy. They, too, fell to the ground, locked in combat.

Meanwhile Cat was bounding toward Pig. But Pig had too much warning, and was standing its ground, holding up its spear. This was heading for a standoff.

Cat halted, needing a way to get around that spear. Then Pig brought out its pain button. Cat backed up, trying to get out of range, but Pig was advancing, keeping pace. This was mischief indeed.

Suddenly Pig squealed in agony and fell to the ground, untouched. The spear fell and the pain button rolled away. What had happened? Was this a ruse?

Then Cat saw C-Col standing near Pig, holding forth her own pain button. The Swine had ignored the Humans as noncombatants, and never suspected that the pain buttons would be in their hands. That had been a fatal oversight.

Cat swept up the loose pain button, then the spear, and turned back to deal with Pig. Before Cat got there, Buck had scrambled out of the pit and stomped Pig with sharp hooves. It was no thoughtless rage; the hooves were precisely placed, cutting through the tough skin of Pig's neck. In a moment the life blood was flowing.

Cat veered off and went to help Pussy dispatch Sow. The spear and pain button made it easy. The two Caprine Humans went to join Tom with Boar, and in another moment Boar's squealing doubled. The second Human pain button was being applied.

It was an ugly contest, but no contest; the Swine were overwhelmed, and soon all three of them were dead. The counterambush had been successful. Their own losses were slight; Tom had been gored in one arm, and Pussy had been bitten on one knee. The three Caprines were untouched.

"You fought for us!" Cat said to the Humans, surprised in retrospect.

"You gave the right answers," C-Dar said.

"But you are the Caprine Humans," Pussy said.

"With whom the Felines are allied."

"It sure surprised the Swine when our Humans fought them with the pain buttons," Tom said with satisfaction.

"They thought our alliance was with only the Caprines," Cat said. "Not also with the Humans."

They left the Swine and moved on as a group. But Cat

was dubious. This seemed too easy, challenging as it had been. "Dar," he said.

Both Dars turned to him. "Yes?" they said together.

"F-Dar, is there something else we should know?"

"Yes."

"What is it?"

"There is a fifth obstacle."

Cat reviewed their encounters. "The vicious animals, the raging river, the mirror-chasm. I make it three so far."

"The ambush," Goat said. "We had to pass an animate threat, then an inanimate one, then solve a riddle, then handle treachery. Four obstacles, each of a different type. Those who set up this contest knew that there would be trouble between teams."

"So we may anticipate a type we have not seen before," Cat said. "Occurring in territory we have already traversed."

"So it is not terrain," Goat agreed. "Dar, are you permitted to tell us what it is?"

"We do not know its nature," C-Dar said. "Only that it is formidable."

The party halted. "Could there be something to intercept us?" Cat asked.

"That seems likely," Goat said. "I doubt we can avoid it, any more than we could the other obstacles. It may seek us out."

"Then perhaps it would not be wise to delay."

"Unless it is triggered by our approach to the finish."

"That does seem likely," Cat agreed. "What, then, should be our best strategy?"

"Perhaps we should consider it another ambush," Goat said. "One team can invoke it, and the other team can deal with it."

"Unless it is immediately lethal."

They looked at the others. No one commented. "Shall we agree on a strategy?" Goat asked.

"One team can take the flag and run for the finish," Cat said. "The other team watches. If the first team gets through, it is the winner."

"Agreed. Which team leads?"

"We will," Goat said.

"You will take the risk of ambush?"

"And of victory. We Caprines prefer to charge ahead when in doubt."

"As you wish. We Felines prefer to lurk and watch."

Goat took the silver flag and charged ahead, followed closely by Buck and Doe and the two C-Humans, now back with their own team. The Feline group moved more circuitously, as they had for the prior ambush, staying clear of the main path. The Feline Humans split, with Dar accompanying Tom and Col going with Pussy.

Nothing happened. The Caprines came within sight of the starting line, which was now the finish line, without event. Was the final hurdle a bluff, to make the credulous pause and lose the victory? Cat had not thought of that, which meant it was indeed unexpected. Had they casually thrown away victory? A deal was a deal, but perhaps the gamble had lost. Cat watched from the cover of a tree, seeing its strategy defeated. Well, at least they had given it a good try. The Caprines were certainly worthy.

Goat stepped over the finish line—and suddenly floated into the air with a surprised bleat. The other Caprines halted, amazed. Goat was flying!

But not under control. Goat was flailing its legs, trying to get a footing, but the feet were not touching the ground. There seemed to be a wind bearing it back toward the forest. The others were trying to catch Goat, but it was floating too high. It was borne back over the forest, still ascending—and then abruptly descended.

Goat struck the branch of a tree, then dropped to the ground. F-Col, closest to that spot, ran over. She bent over the injured Caprine, then looked up, horrified. "Goat's done for," she gasped.

Pussy ran over. "No!" She dropped down beside Goat's form. "Hang on," she said tearfully. "We can help you."

Goat stirred. It was alive, but at least one limb was broken, and probably internal organs were damaged. It tried to speak, then collapsed into unconsciousness.

"We can help," Pussy repeated. "Help me carry Goat to treatment."

"Goat said something to me," F-Col said. "Magic."

"Magic?" Pussy asked blankly.

"Yes. I'm sure that was the word."

Cat was looking all around, trying to fathom what had happened. Doe was running toward Goat, but Buck, evidently dazed, was stepping back to the line.

"Don't go there!" Tom cried. But he was too late: Buck had stepped across the finish line, and was sailing into the air. All they could do was watch helplessly while he was swept up and toward the forest.

"There must be some force," Cat said. "Something pushing up from below."

Tom ran under Buck, but encountered no resistance. The Caprine floated on over him.

"Or an invisible cord from above," Cat said. "He can't just float without support."

"Maybe he can," Pussy said. "What Goat said to F-Col—remember how Darius came from a Mode of magic?"

"Magic!" Tom scoffed. "That's impossible."

But Pussy would not be deterred. "Buck, I conjure you, come down," she called. "Slowly."

Buck descended, slowly.

"Land gently, and stay on the ground," Pussy called. "I conjure you."

The Caprine came gently to the ground. "You saved me!" he said, hugging Pussy as she ran to join him.

"Magic," Cat said thoughtfully. "It does exist in some Modes. We have to be ready for it too. So they arranged for an emulation of magic. That never occurred to me."

"Because you're too rational," Pussy said. "Magic makes more sense emotionally." She kissed Buck.

"A fitting test," Cat agreed.

"But we didn't figure it out in time for us," Doe said sadly. "We can't go on without Goat."

"Goat's alive," Pussy said. "You can go on."

"Not if there's a Virtual Mode soon," Doe said. "It will take time for Goat to recover."

Cat agreed. "Carry Goat across the finish line, with the silver flag. Conjure yourselves back to the ground. Be the winner. If there is a Virtual Mode too soon, the second team will take it. Otherwise it's yours."

"Thank you," Doe said, her lovely eyes moist.

"It was our deal. We did not seek to destroy you, merely to follow another strategy."

Buck, Doe, and their two Humans carried Goat across the line. They all rose into the air—and sank slowly down again, the victors.

"We could have had it," Tom said.

"Not with honor," Cat said. "Without honor, neither of our deals would have been valid."

"True," F-Dar agreed.

"And it was Goat who figured it out," Pussy said. "He told us, but it was the Caprines who deserved it. We couldn't steal it from them."

"Now we must take second place, before another team comes to grab our flag," Cat said. "We still have a plea to make on behalf of our companions. Considering the circumstances, I think it will be honored."

They moved ahead as a group of five, toward the finish line.

TWO

❧❧❧

Dragon

O h, no!

Colene stared at the Feline nulls. Tom, Pussy, and Cat: she remembered them. That meant that instead of discovering a new anchor universe, their party had returned to an old one. This had to be the DoOon Mode, from which they had escaped before only because the corrupt Emperor Ddwng and his henchmen had not caught on to the fact that a member of their Virtual Mode party was telepathic. They had taken her closest friend, the horse Seqiro, for a mere animal. Seqiro had sent a forceful thought to make Ddwng free the anchor, thus getting them loose and establishing a new anchor and a new Virtual Mode. In fact, that was when they had connected with the Julia Mode, where fractals ruled.

But this time Seqiro was not here. They had no other way to force the anchor free, and Ddwng would not be fooled a second time anyway. There was going to be hell to pay.

Cat, the neuter Feline, made a yowl. "Please step forth," a nearby hanging globe said. "There is a paralysis device attuned to you, to prevent your escape. We prefer not to use it."

Colene turned to Nona, her companion from the Fractal Mode. "Can you do magic here?" she asked. "We need to get away, instantly."

"No. Not without Seqiro to connect me to my home Mode."

"I was afraid of that. We're stuck for an awful time."

"You recognize this Mode?"

"Yes. We were here before."

"Please step forth," Cat repeated via the translator globe. "We do not wish to risk your health with the paralysis."

It was no bluff. Colene sighed and walked forward. Darius paced her. Nona and their fourth member, Burgess, hesitated, then followed. They were prisoners. Again.

"This way, please," another hanging ball said for Cat. The neuter Feline null led the way through the spacious chamber to a hall. The two other Felines fell in behind the party.

"What kind of a realm is this?" Nona asked, looking around. She was Colene's senior by three years, and excruciatingly lovely, with thick dark brown hair and a figure to make any man stare. She was also the most important person on her home planet of Oria, with phenomenal powers of magic there. But for all that, she was a nice person, and easy to like.

"What we call super science," Colene said wearily. "They do things here that seem like magic, but it's not. It's governed by the Emperor Ddwng, who is absolutely ruthless. He wants the Chip Darius used to set up the Virtual Mode. Now he's going to have it, though it ruin all the other Modes."

"But Darius won't give that away," Nona protested.

"Not if we manage to kill ourselves first, so they have no hold on him," Colene said grimly. "But they'll prevent that. We're in real trouble."

They came to a doorway. "The space ship," Darius said, recognizing it.

"Yes, the same one," Cat agreed. "But a different destination."

"I don't understand any of this," Nona said plaintively, hesitating at the entrance. Colene knew that she felt helpless when stripped of her formidable magical abilities.

"Tom, see to her," Cat said.

The husky male Feline stepped toward Nona. Nona shrank away. "It's okay," Colene said. "We're captives, but the Felines won't hurt us. They have to do us a favor each day, so he's trying to do you one. He will never act contrary to your expressed wishes."

"You're sure?" Nona asked.

"I'm sure."

"This way, lovely woman," Tom said.

Nona still hesitated, but Colene nodded, and the woman followed Tom into the ship.

Burgess was another matter. He was a floating creature unlike any seen recently on Earth or anywhere else. He weighed about 400 pounds and was shaped something like a weedy island with elephantine trunks fore and aft. He barely fit through the door.

"Cat, maybe you had better talk to Burgess," Colene said. "Touch one of his contact points—they look like knobs—and think clearly, and he will understand what you want."

Cat did so. In a moment Burgess floated on into the ship.

That left Colene and Darius with Pussy. "So what are you up to, Puss?" Colene asked. She was especially wary of the female Feline, for good reason.

"We must take you to Chains, where we will negotiate," Pussy said, showing the way into the ship.

"Chains?" Darius asked.

Pussy smiled at him, and this gave Colene an additional irk; the cat woman had tried to seduce him before, and might try again. "It is the name of our world. Decorative chains are worn to signal obligations, but they must be assumed by choice. When you wear a chain, we can go on the Virtual Mode to fetch the Chip."

"When *who* wears a chain?" Colene demanded.

"When Darius wears it. He will not break his given word."

They had that down pat. Darius had never broken his word to anyone. They had escaped this universe before because Colene had conspired with Seqiro to free the anchor; Darius hadn't known. He and Colene had had a row about it later. But she had done what had to be done, and would do it again, if she got the chance. But she knew she wasn't going to get the chance.

"So how are you going to make him give his word? By threatening to eviscerate me?"

"No," Pussy said seriously. "Our leader realized that that threat was a mistake. Neither will I try to serve him sexually. We wish to be your friends."

"Friends!" Colene exclaimed derisively. "You can do that by letting us go and freeing your anchor."

"We can't do that," Pussy said. "So we must find another way."

"There *is* no other way. Darius won't give you what you want unless you torture me, and then he'll kill you."

"We will find another way," Pussy repeated. "Do you wish separate cabins?"

"No," Colene said. "We are married now." She wasn't sure the DoOons had marriage, but was sure the translator would render it into a close approximation.

"I am glad of that. Here is your chamber."

Colene hardly noticed the chamber, being far more concerned with the larger situation. "You are glad? It means you have to keep your paws off him."

"As I said, I will leave him alone. I will serve you. We want you to be satisfied."

Colene retained considerable doubt, but didn't push it. "So you figure you can charm us into doing Ddwng's will."

"Yes, we hope so."

"And if you don't succeed?"

"We will be destroyed."

That set Colene back. "They'll kill you—for not accomplishing what can't be done?"

"Yes. We have no choice. But this is not your concern. You will do what you deem appropriate."

Colene wasn't at all sure of that, but the case was not worth arguing. She and Darius needed to figure out some way to get free of this universe, and they couldn't discuss it openly; the translating balls were ubiquitous, and while this made dialogue easy, it also meant that there was no privacy. Maybe they could find some on the planet of chains.

"Okay, go see to the others," she told the Feline female. "We'll settle in here."

Pussy nodded and left, closing the cabin door behind her. "Settle in?" Darius inquired.

"You know, take a shower together, whatever newly married folk do. Or does a spaceship have a shower?"

"It was a cleaning chamber, as I recall. No water."

"Oh." She looked around. "A picture window?"

He followed her glance to the wall with a picture of a rich forest. "That would be their magic mirror."

"But there's no magic here. Oh—you mean the video screen."

"Yes." He went to it and touched a button at the edge. The forest disappeared and a chamber appeared, with Pussy curled catlike on the floor. She was showing a good deal more flesh of thigh and bosom than Colene liked. At least she was halfway clothed, as were the others; this must be in deference to the foibles of their Virtual Mode charges. As Colene recalled, they had been clothed only in their slight fur before.

Pussy jumped up and faced them. "Yes, Master."

"Don't call me master," Darius said. "Call me—call me by my name. Darius. Same for the others of our party."

"Yes, Darius. What is your desire?"

"He's showing me how the video works," Colene said. "How are the others doing?"

"I will put on their chambers," Pussy said eagerly. She touched a button.

The picture split. On one side was Nona, standing with Tom, who was evidently answering her questions about the accommodations. On the other was Burgess, with Cat doing the same.

Nona spied them. "Darius! Colene! You said there was no magic here."

"I said that super science could seem like magic, but it's not," Colene said. "This is a video connection. Maybe you should clean up and change, and we will too, and we can get together to eat."

"Yes. Tom has been very helpful. I am much reassured."

"Sure," Colene said dryly. "The nulls are helpful. Tom will do anything you want." She gave Nona a hard look. "*Anything*. Just ask him."

"I think I still don't understand," Nona said. But a trace of a flush suggested that she did. The nulls were servants or slaves that could be used, abused, or loved. Colene wanted Nona to understand that what she said to Tom might be taken literally.

"Burgess also will join you," Cat said from its screen.

"Make it blank," Colene told Darius. "So we can strip."

Darius shrugged. The wall went blank. "They have no

interest in our state of exposure. But if you mean to remove your diaper—"

"That's panties!" she exclaimed, remembering that in his Mode women of all ages really did wear voluminous diapers; it was a symbol of their femininity. She had been there, and seen it herself, and even worn one. The folk of Hlahtar thought that a woman's nether bifurcation should be well masked, though they were not in other respects sexually repressed. She enjoyed teasing Darius about it, though actually she was the one who had the hang-up. She was trying desperately to get over it, without notable success. Not where it counted.

"If you mean to strip, I will turn away."

"You're my husband. You shouldn't turn away."

He just looked at her, and she felt herself flushing. Then he turned away, and she did not protest. They *were* married, but had not consummated it, because she freaked out at the very notion of actual sex. Still, she played the game, trying to fool herself as much as him.

So she stripped, tossing her clothing on the bed. Naked, she paused. "Where's the shower?"

Darius pointed without turning. She walked across the chamber, aware that she could be under observation from the other side of the wall/video, but schooling herself to ignore it. She had much more important things on her mind than how much of her was seen by whom. Like how to get free of the DoOon Mode! So the less she seemed to be thinking of that, and the more she was able to distract the minions of Ddwng, the better it would be.

She stepped into the cleaning stall. There was a faint flash of light. That was evidently it; all her smudges were gone. Even her hair was clean and flowing. This was almost frustratingly simple. When she had been in this Mode before, an Ovine woman called simply Ewe had bathed her in genuine water and dressed her in a silken robe. This spaceship cleaning was spare in comparison.

She stepped out and discovered a silken robe hanging close by, similar to the one she had worn before, together with underclothing. She donned it all, and it fitted her well. This was just one more indication that the folk of this Mode had prepared carefully for their visitors. They had to have been waiting for the anchor to become available. When it did, they had pounced.

"Your turn," she said.

Darius went to the cleaning booth, stripped, and stepped in. This time Colene turned away, unable to stop herself. She looked at the blank wall, and it became a mirror. She twirled, admiring her appearance. She was so pretty, this way. There was no sign of the rot that was her emotional interior.

"You are indeed lovely," Darius murmured, startling her. She had not seem him emerge or dress, but now he was in a robe of his own. "May I kiss you?"

"Idiot! You don't have to ask." Then she caught herself. "I mean, of course."

He held her and kissed her, and she felt as if she were floating. He was just such a wonderful man. While she was such a loss.

"I love you," he said, and she melted, her own love overflowing. This was a storybook romance. Except that she couldn't consummate it. Except that now they were trapped in a hostile Mode, and would be lucky to survive it, let alone escape it. Except a thousand meaningless excuses she wanted to be rid of.

"You know, I bet I could do it, if you forced me a little," she said, glancing at the bed.

"Never." And that, in their odd inversion, was reassuring. If she did it—*when* she did it—the act would be entirely voluntary on her part. Darius would settle for nothing less.

She kissed him again. "We'd better eat."

They went to the door, and it opened. Pussy was there. "This way, Darius, Colene."

They rejoined Nona and Burgess in a larger chamber. Nona was garbed as Colene was, and looked not pretty so much as beautiful. It came naturally to her. "Tom tells me this ship is sailing," Nona said. "Yet I feel nothing."

"A thousand light-years an hour," Darius said. "With inertialess drive." The terms were not fully comfortable for him, but he remembered them from his prior experience. "Swift progress."

"Too fast," Colene said.

"I don't understand," Nona said.

"Naturally," Colene said, trying not to be smug about this very limited area where she was more comfortable than her beautiful, magical, Old Enough friend. "A light-year is the distance a beam of light will travel in a year; it's equivalent to the distance between similarly sized worlds in your Fractal Mode. So a thousand light-years is a very far piece—and this ship sails that distance every hour. We'll never get back to our anchor without the help of the DoOon Mode authorities. Which is of course why they're doing it. And that's just the beginning. Without supernatural abilities, we're sunk."

Darius' eyes barely flicked in Colene's direction. He suspected that she had something in mind. And she did, but she was not at all confident it would work.

Ship servitors brought in platters of food that was evidently tailored to individual needs. Colene had what resembled meat loaf, mashed potatoes, milk, and chocolate pie. Nona had a plate of odd-looking vegetables. Darius had something that might have been magically conjured. And Burgess had a dish of rocks and sand. She knew that none of it was literal; it all came from the ship's food synthesizer. But it would do.

"So how are you guys getting along?" Colene asked Tom.

"Nona is a most appealing woman," the Feline replied.

"Duh! I mean when you're not just looking at her."

"Tom has been extraordinarily helpful about explaining the things of this strange Mode," Nona said.

"That's the idea," Colene said. "The Felines have to do a service for their masters each day, or suffer. They also have to do whatever you tell them." She glanced darkly at Pussy, who had once tried to do Darius a sexual favor. "So they're very helpful. Except when it comes to helping us escape this Mode. Then they're our captors."

"If I may," Cat said. That meant that it had a qualification to make.

"You may," Darius said.

"Colene's statements are imprecise. We normally must do a service each day, but for this mission we have been reprogrammed to be as completely obliging to you as is feasible, without any daily requirement. We are not your captors. We have been assigned to serve your party, and so our loyalty is to you as individuals and in the aggregate. Any of us will serve any of you in whatever manner you decree. Should you disagree with each other, we will defer to Darius, whom we take to be the leader of your party."

"Just as Tom and Pussy defer to you," Darius said.

Cat nodded. "We defer to whichever one of us is most competent. I defer to Tom in matters of combat, and to Pussy in matters of feeling. They defer to me in matters of intellect. It is not a matter of power so much as of rationality."

"But will you help us escape?" Colene demanded, foolishly irked by being considered less rational, though it was certainly true.

"Yes, if you require this of us. But though our immediate loyalty is to you, we can be reassigned by Ddwng. Should you attempt to misuse our services, reassignment would occur."

"So you won't help us get away," Colene said, trying to nail it down.

"We would help until reassigned. You would not be able to reach your anchor without being intercepted."

"It doesn't matter," Darius said. "Even if we reached the anchor, we couldn't stop you three nulls from following us into the Virtual Mode. What we need is to free that anchor."

"The anchor is under the control of Ddwng," Cat said. "Only he can free it—and he has arranged to be far removed from your presence. He was not pleased when your telepathic horse tricked him."

"Seqiro isn't along on this hop," Colene said dryly. But her flip answer masked her pang of separation from her closest friend. She needed Seqiro for more than freedom from the DoOon Mode.

Nona was new to this Mode, but she knew Seqiro. "How would you try to help us escape?"

"You have only to agree to fetch the Chip for Ddwng," Cat said. "Then you will be free not only to travel the Virtual Mode, but to remain there indefinitely."

"And there's the catch," Colene said. "Darius won't let you have that Chip."

"We hope he will change his mind."

"Fat chance."

Cat glanced at her. "This is an unfamiliar expression."

"Let's eat." Colene dived into her meal. The taste was actually pretty close. There was something to be said for super science.

Nona tried hers, and nodded, surprised; hers too was evidently edible. Darius of course had no problem. That left Burgess. The hiver was busily sucking sand in through his fore trunk and blowing refuse out his aft trunk, assimilating nutrients along the way. There was a refuse receptacle for his use; someone had evidently caught on rapidly. Eating sand was only the beginning of his abilities, but it seemed best for now to let Burgess be mostly a mystery to the DoOon folk. It was enough that he was getting along. Cat had evidently taken the trouble to discover the diver's needs, and to accommodate them.

As they finished the meal, Cat spoke again. "We have arrived at Chains. This will be our home for the duration."

"In chains, our prison," Colene muttered.

"Oh, no," Pussy protested. "This is our home planet."

Colene stared at her. "You come from a prison world?"

"No. From Chains."

"This is the world where the nulls are made," Cat clarified. "Chains is home to all nulls, and other genetic adaptations. It is not an advanced world, scientifically or culturally, nor is it ideal in its simplicity, but it is familiar to us. You, as privileged guests, should find it compatible."

"Privileged guests!" Colene exploded. "Let's cut the hypocrisy."

"If I may," Cat said.

"You may not!"

Darius smiled. "Let's disembark." Colene liked that about him too: he understood her passionate nature, and smoothed it over when that was best.

The ship's door opened on a lovely meadow. Colene stared, amazed. "What happened to the tech?"

"The technology is limited on our world," Pussy said. "But the nulls will serve your needs."

"I don't understand."

"Chains is classified as primitive," Cat said. "It is maintained at what I believe you would call medieval level. If you find this uncomfortable, we can apply for reassignment to a technological world."

"No. This will do." For Colene realized that if this was truly low-tech, there would be no spy devices. That could be a considerable advantage.

"I like it," Nona said. "We have grasslands like this at

home." She kneeled to touch a pretty blue flower.

"We have much wildland here," Tom said. "I can show you fields, forests, lakes, glades, rivers—"

"Wonderful!" she agreed, and kissed him on his furry ear. Tom looked startled, glancing at Cat as if in fear he had done something wrong.

"All of this world is yours to roam," Cat said. "But we felines will need to accompany you, or provide you with weapons, if you wish to explore unsecured areas."

"There is danger?" Darius asked.

"There are natural hazards," Cat said. "You will be able to handle the terrain, if you are careful, but in some regions the creatures are predatory."

"Predators?" Colene asked, coming alert.

"There are many types. But the most dangerous are the dragons. We will have to wear special chains to discourage them."

"Dragons?" Nona asked, looking not frightened so much as hopeful. Her Mode had many magical creatures.

"Yes. The flying ones are little danger to creatures our size, unless they swarm, but the landbound and water-bound ones can be formidable." Cat glanced at Tom. "By all means show Nona all she wishes to see, but guard her too. Consider yourself assigned to her for now."

Tom nodded, reassured. So did Nona.

Colene's mind was whirling. "This is a null world, you said. So the creatures here have been made, not evolved. You made dragons?"

"Nulls come in many types," Cat said. "Some are experimental. Some are deemed failures, but since they may have redeeming features, or be useful in as yet undefined ways, they are maintained here. Chains is in this respect a special world."

"I'll say! So are there any true natives? I mean, natural creatures and people?"

"The substratum is natural. The biological basis. The

bacteria that generate organic matter for the imported plants and animals. The lichen, the plankton, the fungus. We need them to maintain the atmospheric quality. But the great majority of the higher life forms are what you would call unnatural. This was an empty world, as far as advanced entities went, before it was colonized by the Empire."

So much for stirring up any native rebellions. This was an Empire world. "Thanks."

"There is no need to thank us," Cat said. "We exist to serve you."

"No," Darius said. "You represent the DoOon Mode. You three are now the entity associated with your anchor, and a member of our Virtual Mode party, until such time as you free your anchor. That gives you equivalent status."

"Only when we enter the Virtual Mode," Cat said. "Here on Chains we are your servants. Until we come to an agreement."

"That may take a long time."

"It may take a lifetime," Cat agreed.

"So that's it!" Colene said. "You'll hold us here until we agree to fetch the Chip—or forever."

"That may be Ddwng's intention," Cat agreed. "He does not appreciate being balked."

She thought of something else. "You say this is a low-tech world. That means no translator balls?"

"Yes."

"So how come we're still talking? We shouldn't be able to understand each other."

"The ship has not yet departed. The translators are associated with it. But soon we will not be able to speak to each other. That is why we need to understand our situation now. We will show you the signs for the basic general communication system, and in the coming days we shall build on that. We Felines also wish to learn your mode of speaking, so that we can converse when on the Virtual Mode."

More of the DoOon scheme was coming into view. Trap them here, learn their language, until in desperation they agreed to go for the Chip. The Feline nulls would be equipped to communicate by the time the Virtual Mode travelers surrendered. And if they didn't surrender, they would just stay here until they died. This was a gentler process than what Dictator Ddwng had tried before, but its object and tenacity was the same.

Actually, it also fit Colene's agenda. She would need time to develop her own scheme, and this would provide her with that. She regarded herself as being in a private battle with Ddwng. The emperor thought he held the high cards, but if Nona could recover her magic, that would change. "Okay."

Nona had finished admiring her flower. "What favor can we do for you?" she asked Tom.

Tom, stymied again, looked at Cat. Cat smiled. "Aside from agreeing to fetch the Chip?"

"Aside from that," Nona agreed, smiling.

"In the course of our preparation to meet your party, we made an alliance with a team of Caprine nulls, one of whom was injured. We should like to be sure they are well treated. It would be nice if they could join us here, nominally to serve."

"But actually to have a vacation," Colene said.

"We would not phrase it thus. They are worthy and compatible, and we value their association."

Colene nodded. She didn't know why Nona wanted to do the Felines a favor, but it couldn't hurt. "Do it."

Cat glanced at Darius.

"Yes, we wish to make this request," he said.

Cat faced the ship, whose door was now shut. "The Guests require the attendance of additional nulls. Summon the backup team."

The ship floated up silently. When it was some distance overhead, it suddenly shot forward, then vanished.

Colene touched Nona's hand. *Why did we do that?*

To win their favor. We can better trust them if they know we can help them achieve what they want.

Good point.

Cat spoke, but all they heard was a series of yowls. The translators were gone. The seven of them were alone in the field of flowers.

"Cat says they will be delivered," Colene said.

"You can understand their language?" Nona asked.

Colene hesitated. "Just guessing. What else would Cat be saying?"

Nona was not fooled. "Seqiro?" She was asking whether the telepathic horse had found their range and was connecting her mind to that of the Feline.

How Colene wished that were the case! "Not exactly."

Now Darius glanced at her, but did not comment. He knew that Colene had started to pick up some of the talents of those who had been around her, such as telepathy, precognition, and maybe magic. Her abilities were as yet fledgling, but she was working on them. Her hope was to be able to reach out across the Modes and find Seqiro's mind. That would not only restore her contact with her friend, but enormously increase her reach, and possibly enable her to restore Nona's truly formidable power of magic. If they could read minds and do magic here in the DoOon Mode, it would be a new ballgame. If. But it would be best if the Felines did not catch on.

Cat brought out several bead necklaces. It proffered them to the others. Tom and Pussy donned theirs, but Darius and Nona hesitated. "Is this a chain?" Darius asked. "Symbolizing agreement to seek the Chip?"

"No, it's the dragon repellent," Colene said. "But I guess I don't have any way to know that yet."

Darius nodded. He faced Cat. "What?" he asked, pointing to a necklace.

Cat was ready. It yowled to Tom. Tom withdrew a few paces, then lifted his hands, extended his claws, and charged at Cat. Cat held up a necklace—and Tom abruptly sheered off.

"Dragon protection," Darius said, as if just realizing. He took a necklace and donned it. Then he turned to the others. "These are protective devices, to warn predators away. Cat mentioned them before. We should each wear one."

Nona agreed, and took one. But Colene, true to her image, balked. "How can we be sure? Maybe it's a trick."

Darius drew himself up to his full height, frowning at her. "Take it, wench," he ordered.

Evincing extreme reluctance, she obeyed. Nona turned away to hide a smile, knowing how absolutely out of character their roles were. Darius was a competent but gentle man; it was Colene who could become imperious. But it protected Colene's secret.

Cat took the last necklace and went to Burgess. Cat set its hand on the hiver's surface, communicating. It wasn't exactly telepathy with Burgess, but contact did convey emotion, and the hiver knew when a person was to be trusted. Then Cat set the necklace around the base of the fore trunk.

Now they were all protected from dragons. What next?

Cat touched Burgess' surface again. Then Cat set off across the meadow, and the hiver paced it. That suggested that it was all right. Indeed it was; Cat was showing the way to the village where they would stay. But Colene waited for someone else to persuade her of that.

"Ask Burgess," Nona suggested.

Good idea. Colene ran to catch up with the floating hiver, and touched his aft trunk. The neuter Feline was a nice cat. That was Burgess' impression, coming through as her own thought, but she knew it wasn't. Maybe her nascent telepathy was helping, but she had to make a show of communicating with the hiver the same way as Cat did, to account for her conversion.

After a moment, she brightened. "It's okay," she said. "Burgess knows it's okay." Indeed, Burgess did know, and was satisfied. The manner Cat had related to the hiver was impressive. That, too, was worth noting: Tom and Pussy were straightforward in their male and female roles, but Cat was dangerously smart and rational.

The meadow gave way to a scrub forest of flowering trees though which wound a moderately worn path. Evidently there wasn't a lot of traffic to the spaceship landing area. Colene was also impressed by the manner in which the ship could travel rapidly between stars, yet land so gently as to do no damage to delicate foliage. A ship like that could revolutionize things back home on Earth. But it would never happen, because that was in another Mode: an alternate universe.

Not far along was the village: a collection of mud-brick houses with thatched roofs. Felines were coming and going, carrying bundles of sticks, baskets of fruits, strings of fish and the like. Evidently a subsistence economy. They took little note of the visiting party, except to get out of its way. But Colene did catch more than one of the sultry females eyeing Darius sidelong. Why were they so interested in him, when there were plenty of Toms available?

Her question must have intercepted a Feline mind, because suddenly she had the answer. Nulls were not allowed to breed with their own persuasion! Indeed, they did not truly breed at all; they were made as children, and given to formed adult trios to raise and train. All nulls were sterile; they had sex only with nulls of different persuasions, and never productively. It was literally impossible for them to form their own breeding communities.

These folk were existing in a kind of hell, as Colene saw it. Yet they did not seem discontented. They didn't know that any other way was possible. They did have some private satisfaction, though, and a lurking fear.

Before Colene could run that down, they came to a larger structure, buttressed by rough-hewn timbers. This was evidently the village guest house, able to accommodate their party. It turned out to have five chambers and a privy alcove: one for each person from the Virtual Mode, and the fifth for the three Feline nulls.

"We don't need separate rooms," Colene said. "Darius and I bunk together anyway, and Nona and Burgess don't mind sharing." But of course the nulls couldn't understand her speech now. So she demonstrated by choosing one room for the married couple, and another for the other two. As a matter of general principle, none of them wanted to be alone in a hostile Mode.

Once they had chosen their rooms, Cat gestured to show that it had something to convey. This was a sign language session, and the basic signs were obvious: when Cat beckoned, Pussy came to it, and when Cat made a push-away gesture, Pussy retreated. Danger was shown by covering the head with the hands. Sleep was laying the head against the flattened hands; food by a hand lifting something to the mouth. Simple enough, and the lesson was soon over.

"You know," Colene remarked, "This stay promises to be totally boring. I mean, after admiring the flowers, what's left to do?"

"That may be the point," Nona said. "Boredom is a great inducement to agree to their mission."

"Well, I want to do something. I'm going out to meet the people. Anybody want to come along?" Someone had to, or she couldn't go, per their agreement.

Darius preferred to rest, and so did Nona. But Burgess was curious about this land, so they started out together.

Immediately Pussy was there to accompany them; it seemed that the nulls had their own agreement. Pussy was Colene's guardian.

This turned out to be just as well, because Pussy was able to explain things to the villagers in their own language. The adults continued about their various businesses, but a number of children came up to admire Burgess. They ranged from about five years old to ten, though that was assuming that they had started as babies. They were made young, she gathered, but not that young. They had never seen a creature like him before, which was scarcely surprising, as there had never been a creature like him in this universe.

"Let's give them a thrill," Colene said, seeing potential in the situation. These were Felines of three genders, but they were still typical children. She touched Burgess, clearing it with him, then addressed the group: "Free rides, kids. Like this." Of course they couldn't understand her words, so she demonstrated. Burgess sank down to the ground and she climbed onto his carapace behind the fore trunk, grasping two of the contact points. The hiver blew out air under the curtain of leg panels, and floated just over the ground. Then he moved forward a body length, and settled back to the ground.

Colene climbed off. "Now who else wants to try it?" she asked, looking around at the impressed faces. She pointed to a little girl. "How about you, kitty?" But the girl, abashed, hung back.

Pussy stepped forward and spoke to the child. Then the girl stepped forward. She was clearly nervous to the point of fear, but had to do it.

Colene realized that further reassurance was in order. "We'll do it together," she decided. "Come on, kitty." She took the child's hand and helped her climb on. Then she climbed back on herself; Burgess could handle this much weight.

They made another float-and-drift forward. The child was frightened but thrilled. Then Colene helped her off, and put two other children on, this time without riding herself. They were less frightened, and just as thrilled. And Colene discovered something: she was good with children. At fourteen she wasn't a lot older than the larger ones, but she had seen considerable adult experience, on and off the Virtual Mode.

The adult Felines continued about their business, but Colene could tell they were watching. She felt their emotions, first of concern, then of pleasure as they saw that the monster was harmless. That pleased her; she and Burgess were making friends with the locals. This was something she wanted to do, because she suspected their stay here would be a lot more comfortable if the visitors were liked.

After all seven of the children had had rides, their little party moved on to explore the neighborhood around the village. There was a lake nearby; that was where the fish were being brought from. Burgess immediately floated out over the water, evidently startling Pussy, who had not realized the capacities of the cushion of air he utilized. Burgess loved it; he sucked water into his fore trunk and blew it out his rear trunk. This looked like sheer sport, but Colene knew he was also feeding, seining nutrients from the water as it passed through him.

A bell sounded. Colene glanced at Pussy, who made the eat sign: time to eat. Colene realized that the afternoon had passed, and she was hungry.

They returned to the village, where a large communal table had been set out and piled with assorted foods. The visitors had places along one side, together. Colene found that she was much more comfortable with the assembled Felines now. There were seven trios, or twenty-one individuals, and the seven children, one with each trio. Those were the family units. Father, mother, and what? There was more to learn about the social structure of these null people.

"Each trio has a child," Nona remarked. "And our trio has us."

That was one way of looking at it.

The food was basic but good, and there was plenty. There were no utensils; bare hands were used, then licked off. A saucer of water at each end of the table served for those who were thirsty; they took turns lapping it up. But cups were provided for the visitors, who lacked lapping skill. Their own trio used cups also; Colene wasn't sure whether this was in deference to their charges, or because they had learned more civilized ways at the capital planet.

Colene also saw that there were a few non-Feline nulls just arriving, joining the meal. A Bovine trio and Equine trio, each with one child of their persuasion. They must have been traveling, and had to stop here for the night. They seemed to be welcome.

As the meal ended and the sun descended, several villagers brought out gourds with holes and strings and began playing them. They were musical instruments, with odd but pleasant tones. Others danced, in sinuous patterns. "Oh, lovely!" Nona exclaimed, delighted, for she was a musical creature.

Cat spoke to Tom. Tom stood, faced Nona, and bowed, extending a paw. "He's asking you to dance!" Colene said, picking up the thought.

Nona needed no urging. She joined Tom, and in a moment was moving as sinuously as any feline. She did have the body for it. Colene tried to stifle her jealousy; why did the women have to be so damned *good* at being female?

"Perhaps we should join them," Darius murmured.

"You can dance?" Colene asked before she thought. There was still a lot she didn't know about him.

"I can do this," he said.

So they danced, emulating the feline motions, and Colene made another discovery: she loved this. Being social, doing social things—she had never really gotten into it at school, because the boys were mostly creeps and the girls were mostly clothes horses, even at her age. A dance had been a grope session with little art. But this was different, and great.

The Bovines and Equines were dancing too, not trying to emulate the Feline moves. Their style was more like tap dancing, and their hind feet were hoofs, good at it.

Then something horrible happened. A great dark shape slid into the group. Felines screamed in terror, and then in horror: a serpentine monster was among them, its huge awful jaws clamped about a male, bearing him away. In a moment monster and man were gone, leaving only a trail of fresh blood.

"What was that?" Colene half screamed. But already the answer was registering: it was a dragon.

"Maybe we can save him," Darius said, casting about for a weapon.

But Cat intercepted him, shaking its head no. They couldn't go after the dragon—and with burgeoning horror, Colene discovered why. *The dragons were a protected species.* They preyed on villagers, but could not be fought or hunted.

Colene turned away from the group, bent over, and vomited out most of what she had just eaten. It was not the death or the blood that got to her; she was on intimate terms with both. It was the realization that these feline people were not ordinary residents; they were prey.

She recovered in a moment; she had always been good at masking her feelings. Pussy was there to clean her face. "Here you are helping me, when it's your folk who got savaged," Colene said, feeling the irony. Of course the cat woman could not understand the words, but maybe the tone conveyed the essence.

Then Colene felt a shock of a quite different nature. *Pussy understood her words.* There was no doubt; the meaning came through clearly, and was appreciated. But the Feline gave no indication; instead she kept her face carefully blank and continued to minister to Colene.

For the moment this discovery blocked back the horror of the dragon attack. Pussy—and therefore surely the other Felines of her trio—understood her language, but were pretending not to. They had spoken freely when the translator balls were present, using their own language, and now were much more limited. But they understood. Why should they do that?

The answer was hardly obscure. They wanted to learn things about the Mode travelers, who might speak more freely among themselves when they thought they were not being understood by their captors. If the travelers plotted to get away, the Felines would know. So this ruse made sense. Nevertheless, it angered Colene. She never liked being played for a patsy.

But two could play this game, and Colene was good at it. She had had years' experience fooling her parents, teachers, and friends about her suicidal depression. The few times she had been fooled by others, she had regretted it greatly. Such as the time she had gotten raped. There was nothing like getting raped to sharpen the senses to small signals. And now that she was able to read minds, a little, she was not at all easy to deceive.

Time to get back to the role playing, which had a lot of genuine feeling. "But what's the point in talking to you, when you don't understand? You've got problems of your own. What are you going to do about that dragon?"

Pussy gave no sign. She just attended to Colene. But her mind confirmed what Colene had already picked up: they would do nothing about the dragon, because if they ever fought back, their entire village would be obliterated. Not by the dragon: by an Empire ship. In any event, the dragons were infernally smart, having been crafted by the same biological technology that made the nulls. They had virtually human intelligence. So trying to avoid them was useless; they could track any creature they chose. Only those creatures who wore the beads were protected; the dragons were conditioned to avoid them. And only the travelers and their three nulls wore the beads. All of the villagers were vulnerable.

Colene turned back to those villagers. They were clustered around a female, a neuter, and a girl: the family of the victim. The woman was in tears, and the girl looked stricken; the neuter was trying to comfort both, without success. Meanwhile Darius, Nona, Burgess, and the other two beaded nulls were standing aside, not interfering.

Something roiled inside Colene. "Dammit, this can't be," she said. But she had no idea what she could do about it. So she, like the others, just stood and watched.

The three surviving members of the family started walking. They went to the other larger structure at the far side of the village. The child entered it, and the woman and neuter walked away. The others dispersed, going about the business of cleaning up after the meal, or to their homes for the night. The visitors retreated to their lodging. The episode was over.

But Colene could not let it go. She knew she had to do something. But what? And what about this deception of language? She had to alert the others about that, but could not do it in the presence of the nulls.

Well, there was a way around that. She grabbed onto Darius' arm. "I need you!" she said, letting her tears come again.

Darius didn't speak. He merely folded her into the circle of his arm. She sobbed against his shoulder and suffered herself to be led inside. The others, sympathetic, did not speak.

They went to their bedroom and closed the door. They

stripped and got into the bed. She was the one who always insisted that they sleep together naked, maintaining her illusion that they might have sex. The bed was oddly high, with ceramic funnels facing down on each leg. She wondered why, until she saw something like a rat skittering across the floor. It couldn't be a real Earth rat, of course, but it was this world's equivalent: fast and sneaky. It couldn't climb past the funnel. Ugh. There were also big roachlike bugs, and they could get past the funnels, but seemed more interested in searching out edible debris on the floor. The sheet should fend them off, Colene hoped, so she could sleep halfway in peace.

Colene snuggled close to Darius, plastering her bare body against him as if ready to make love. But she wasn't fooling him. She could read his mind, and he knew it, so he was playing along. He merely lay there and waited for her to make known her concern.

She nibbled on his ear, and kissed it. "We're not being watched, I think, but play it safe," she whispered. "Make love to me."

Obligingly, he shifted to embrace her, stroking her back and buttock. She loved that, because she could afford to: she knew he would not have sex with her until she was ready, and he knew she was not ready. This was a half-structured play, action without intention. So the motions of love and sex play were safe; she could enjoy them without fear of consequence. She wished she could handle the complete sexual act, and she longed for mutual possession, but the specter of the rape still walled her off from any possible pleasure in it. She loved Darius for his understanding and acceptance of her liability. Someday, somehow, they would do it, and then it would be great. But not tonight.

"They understand our language," she whispered between kisses. "They must have learned it from the translator balls while we were away."

Darius turned his face to kiss her hair and then her ear. "To spy on us," he whispered, unsurprised.

At leisure, she worked her mouth back to his ear. "Yes. Spread the word. Don't let them know we know. We'll have to give up some 'secrets' so they don't catch on." He squeezed her thigh, once, in agreement. Then she continued: "They are prey for the dragon. Not allowed to resist. I want to help."

He caught a handful of her hair in his fist and gently lifted her head to place her mouth against his. He kissed her, firmly. He liked this aspect of her. She read his mind, and knew that this was no simple thing; he liked her to be feeling, and he liked her to be distracted from her obsessive depression. When she got involved in the problem of another person, her awareness of death retreated. He wanted her to be happy. This was not mere positive desire; he had a formidable kind of emotional awareness of his own, in connection with his business in his home Mode, and *needed* her to be happy for their relationship to work out.

"I need to learn more," she whispered. She caught his hand with her own and set it on her breast, and felt his pleasure. She liked giving him pleasure, but could tolerate this particular touch only when it was under her control. "Even if they're all spies, they don't deserve this. But I don't know how to handle that dragon, if we can't kill it. So if you can figure anything, let me know."

He kissed her again, and gave her breast the slightest squeeze. He would work on it.

Then they settled down to sleep. Colene needed Darius' strength and understanding; in the absence of Seqiro, she felt emotionally naked and afraid.

That reminded her: where was Seqiro? Could they connect? They had done so across the Modes before; why not again? She needed him.

She reached out mentally, questing for the mind of the

horse. *Seqiro! Seqiro!* But there was no answer.

She tried and tried, but her own ability was painfully limited. She could read a mind when she was right next to it, and that was all. Seqiro could read a mind across light-years. He could range between Modes. He could project a thought. He could even take over a person and make that person do things that were otherwise difficult or downright impossible alone. He could link several minds so that they could talk with each other regardless of language or species. Colene, in contrast, was a baby. She could read a mind, imperfectly, from up close—and only because she had associated with the horse long enough to start picking it up.

There was more. Seqiro was able to link Nona to her home Mode, thus restoring her full powers of magic. There was no seeming limit to what she could do then. She could fly, or move objects without touching them; she could heal a person's wounds or burn him with fire. She could change the size or shape of something, or its very nature, making a rock into a rose. She could capture a familiar, making an animal serve her or be her eyes and ears. And illusion—she could build whole landscapes with that, or make people seem invisible. With Nona's magic, no prison could hold them; they could forge their way to the anchor and depart despite anything Ddwng could do.

But Seqiro was out of touch. They had had to free his anchor in order to escape the Mode Monster that was consuming Colene's mind. It had happened so suddenly, there had been no time to plan. The new anchor, forming immediately, was the DoOon Mode. What a bad break!

Bad break? No, obviously Ddwng had been lurking throughout, waiting for the chance to establish another anchor. Training the Feline nulls to pounce. And it had worked. Here they were, prisoners. They had blithely walked right into it.

Darius reached across to lay his hand on her back. He could not read her mind, but he was aware when she was stressed.

She turned into him and wet his shoulder with her tears. He did not inquire; he was used to her levels and levels of depression. He wanted merely to comfort her, to the limited extent he was able. *Oh, Darius!* Her distress morphed into love, expanding like a nova. In that moment he could have taken her sexually, and maybe she would have survived it. But he didn't know, and she couldn't tell him, for that would spoil the fragile, fleeting mood. But the comfort he proffered was great. She soaked it up, and sank into sleep.

In the morning they joined the villagers for breakfast. There were only six trios now. The visiting trios were gone; they had faded away in the confusion after the dragon had struck. Colene asked Pussy, by mixed words and signs: "Where Dragon Family?" It was cumbersome, and she had to play it through long after she had the answer from Pussy's mind, to conceal both her mind-reading ability and her awareness of Pussy's knowledge of her native language.

It turned out that the two remaining adults were gone; they had departed immediately for a central processing station where they would be in effect melted down for parts or material to make new children. Their lives were over; they could not function as a partial family. Colene had to shake her head in bafflement. Pussy took this to mean she could not grasp the fate of the family, but actually it was her resistance to the idea of setting up intelligent people as dragon food and destroying the remnants of families after the dragon struck. Colene had thought of barbarism as brutal butchery of innocent people with swords and clubs; now she had a new definition.

The Feline child was easier. Pussy took Colene to the other large house. There was the girl, in a dormitory with four other orphans. Colene recognized her by the colored cowlick on the back of her head; the Felines were not identical, and they all looked alike only when first seen. She was about eight years old, physically.

"I want to take her out of here," Colene said. Pussy pretended not to understand, and Colene saw that the other Felines, both adult and child, truly did not comprehend her foreign words. Only Pussy—and surely Tom and Cat—actually knew her language. Pussy's understanding was a secret from the villagers as well as from the visitors. Of course Darius would find a way to convey what Colene had learned to the others, probably by touching Burgess and establishing a mind rapport. Nona could then get it from Burgess. They would have to set up a regular secret mode of communication.

So she struggled through with the signs and actions. "I want to take her out of here," she said, hugging the child, whose name was Kit—just like all the others here.

But it could not be, for several good reasons. A juvenile null could be raised only by her own kind, ideally a grown trio. Human beings were not her kind, and they had no neuter complement. So Kit had to be raised by the orphanage.

There was a trio in charge, and while this was not as good as a private family, it would do. When the children there came of age, they would match up with others, forming trios that would in turn become productive citizens and adopt children of their own. They would continue—until the dragon got them.

Colene strove to voice clumsily what she grasped all too well. "The dragon—eats everyone?" So it was: individual strikes were random, but in time the average Feline expected to be taken by the dragon or recycled as a leftover. New children kept coming to the village, and in time forming new trios, and in more time falling to the ultimate predator. Only those protected by the beads were safe, or those taken for work on other planets, as their own nulls had been. The Felines—and the other varieties of nulls, who lived in their own communities around the planet—were all food farms for the dragons.

Colene returned to her group, and relayed what she had learned. "The irony is that their life isn't all that great regardless," she said. "The village is overrun by vermin ranging from giant roaches to vicious rats. They have to fetch in new food every day, because anything left over is taken by the vermin. They're allowed to kill those, but the bodies are foul, and there are so many that more immediately move in. They don't have bug sprays. So these are cats who don't eat rats. I think there's a greater biologic mass of vermin than there is of nulls."

Nona nodded. "I have been trying to clean them out of the house, but it's hopeless. We would need an airtight chamber. I wish I had my magic; I could make a spell to keep them clear. But I'm lucky: Burgess finds them tasty. He sucks them right up."

Colene laughed. "There's the tiny bit of silver lining to this monstrous black cloud. Burgess is happy."

"What was that story you told me," Darius asked. "When I was on your world, learning your language? About the fiddler and the mice." They were speaking freely, in the presence of the nulls, but being careful not to say anything about their secrets.

Colene laughed, a social habit that hardly related to her real mood. "The Pied Piper of Hamlin. He piped his pipes and led the rats out of the town and into the river, where they drowned. Then the city fathers didn't pay him, so he played all the children into the mountain, where they disappeared. Served that cheating city right."

"I could do that," Nona said. "I could summon the rats—or the children. If I had my magic. But what would be the point? There are easier ways to eliminate vermin, magically."

"But it is an appealing story," Darius said. "And if you could get just a little of your magic back, that might be the best way to do it. So that the felines would understand what had happened."

"Actually, these rats don't like music," Nona said. She glanced across the room where a rat lurked, then broke into song. The rat scrambled away so desperately that it actually rolled over and looked dazed.

"So if you sing long enough, you can drive them out," Darius said, smiling. "That's a responsive audience."

The dialogue continued, but Colene's mind drifted. Vermin—children—magic—was there something useful here? There was no magic in the DoOon Mode, but there were dragons. If they could somehow be tamed—

Then in a flash she had it. Maybe.

"Where is the dragon?" she asked Pussy.

The feline looked blank. Colene made a mental note: Pussy was good. She never slipped and revealed her understanding.

Colene pantomimed, baring her teeth, pouncing, carrying something away. She got the concept across: dragon. Pussy took her outside and pointed to the craggy slope of a nearby mountain. The dragon's lair was there.

That was not too far away. Colene went to Nona. "Would you sing to the dragon?"

"That might not repulse it," Nona said warily. "It is a different species."

"That's what I figure. It might *like* music. I need to know. I want to talk with it."

"Talk with it!"

"Maybe it understands sign language."

"This is humor?"

"This is serious. Will you come with me to see the dragon?"

"The beads protect us," Nona said thoughtfully. "But would they if we actually went to its lair?"

Colene turned to Pussy. "Would they?"

Still no reaction, though Pussy's mind showed perfect understanding of the question.

Colene touched the beads she wore. "Dragon. Safe?"

Slowly, Pussy nodded. She understood the dialogue, but was as mystified as Nona about Colene's purpose. Maybe that was just as well.

"We'll also need some rats," Colene said.

They went along with it. Soon they had a small cage with three captive rats. They had gotten them by putting the cage across the closest escape route, then singing to the rats. Spooked, the creatures had blundered into prison.

In the end the entire party made the trek. Darius knew that Colene's notions could be worthwhile, however weird they seemed, and Burgess liked exploring. The three nulls had to accompany them.

It was a longer climb than it looked. Sweaty and bedraggled, they came at last to the cave that was the dragon's lair. It was an opening in the slope of a steep rocky outcrop, the peak of the mountain rising behind it. The creature was in front of it, well aware of them.

Colene suffered a fit of nervousness. "The beads really do protect us?"

Pussy nodded. Colene knew that she wouldn't deceive them on this, because they were valuable prisoners; no serious risk to their welfare could be tolerated.

But Pussy had her own concern. By signals she reminded Colene that they must not try to hurt the dragon. "Got it," Colene agreed. "I'm a pacifist. I just want to make peace."

Colene walked out before the dragon. It was like an enormous snake or lizard, with five sets of legs and a face as toothy as a crocodile's. It did not move, but its eyes were tracking her.

She stopped about twenty feet from it. "We need to talk," she said.

The dragon did not move. She wasn't close enough to read its mind, so didn't know whether it understood her. Why should it? Her language was foreign to this universe.

She waved her arms, making big sign language gestures. PERSON COME TRUCE DEAL.

Still no reaction. Had she even gotten its attention? Maybe it simply tuned out those protected by the beads.

She stepped closer, and signed again. TRUCE MUSIC.

The dragon's tail twitched. It had reacted!

Colene turned slowly and beckoned to Nona. Nona came to join her, looking distinctly nervous. "Sing," Colene said.

Nona faced the dragon and sang. She was good with music, far better that Colene, but so nervous that her normally smooth voice had a tremolo. Colene didn't recognize the song, but didn't need to; the question was how the dragon would react. She had a wild long-shot hope.

After a moment, astonishingly, the dragon joined in. It pursed its long lips and issued a surprisingly melodic note. No, not a note, a tune, a melody—a descant. Not that either; a counterpoint, a nether harmony, melding perfectly with Nona's song.

Colene glanced across at the others. Darius' jaw had dropped. So had those of the three nulls. None of them had ever dreamed of this.

So far so good. Colene thrilled to her victory of logic. She had figured that intelligent predators could have other qualities. Such as appreciation for the arts. That they might be starved for intellectual exercise. Exactly as she would be, if marooned alone with nothing but rabbits for company.

The song ended, the dragon matching the conclusion perfectly. Oh, yes, it understood music! But what else did it understand?

Colene took another step forward and signaled again. TRUCE DEAL.

The dragon watched, but did not react. Either it did not understand the signs, or it did not care.

Colene decided to go for double or nothing. TOUCH she signed. Then she walked slowly, the last few steps. Her heart was pounding; she was terrified, and was sure that the dragon knew it. But she had to make this gamble.

Still the monster did not move. "Touch," Colene said. How far could she push the protection of the beads, without getting chomped? The dragon might not hunt beaded folk, but would it think she was offering herself as a sacrifice? This was a horrible risk to take—and her very terror gave her a thrill. Deep down inside her depressive nature she *liked* taking suicidal risks; she had done it many times. But never one quite like this.

She stopped directly before the dragon. It still had not moved. She got down on her knees and bent forward. She reached out with her right hand. She laid it on the top of the dragon's snout. It was warm and dry.

Then she concentrated her mind and sent as strong a thought as she could, just as she did with Burgess. *Truce. Parlay. Make a deal. Do you understand me, dragon?*

And the dragon's thought returned. *Yes, alien maiden.*

Victory! She had established communication. *Will you negotiate?*

One eye swiveled to orient on her directly. *Yes. How do you do this?*

"It's telepathy," she said subvocally, concentrating her matching thoughts. "I learned it from a horse. But I'm not very strong with it. I can read my own kind from close by. Others I have to touch. But it bypasses the language barrier; you read me in your thoughts, and I read you in mine. I thought—I thought if we could talk, we might do each other some good."

Follow me. The dragon turned sinuously, breaking the contact, and slid into its cave. It hardly seemed to use its legs. In a moment its tail was disappearing.

Colene glanced back at the others. "It's okay," she said. "I gotta go in." Then she followed the dragon into its lair.

The ceiling was just high enough for her to walk upright. She tread cautiously, as it was dark. But in a moment there was light ahead. Then she entered a chamber whose upper reaches extended to daylight. No sunbeam spilled down, but the refracted illumination was enough.

The dragon was coiled at one side of the cave. In the center was the creature's nest. It was fashioned of humanlike bones, neatly interwoven. Within it was a cache of— scrolls.

"I thought dragons collected gems," Colene said. Then, realizing that her words were gibberish, she approached the dragon. She extended her hand. "May I?"

The dragon did not move. She set her hand on its snout. "Those look like books," she said.

They are. I read to pass the time between hunts.

A literary dragon! So her guess had been correct: this creature had been given human intelligence, and that meant that it had far more of a mind than the life of a simple predator demanded. It craved intellectual diversion.

True.

"I may have a way to provide you that," she said. "But there is a price."

Of course.

"The Felines have minds similar to mine, only not telepathic. Spare them."

They are my prey.

"But if you spared them, you could converse with them. You could play games of mental challenge with them. You could keep up with the news of the planet, without having to go wherever you go to encounter a mind like yours. That would save you trouble."

I must eat.

"Yes. But if you can eat something else, then you won't need to prey on them."

What else?

"Rats."

There was mental silence.

"I know it sounds awful. But there's probably a greater biomass of rats on this planet than of nulls. You would never go hungry."

The taste and nourishment of rats is good. But I am unable to catch them in sufficient quantity to sustain me. They are too small and elusive.

"Yes. But I may have an answer. Music confuses them. So that they can be caught. I brought some for a demonstration. You could probably stun them yourself, just by singing to them. We can try it, if you want."

This interests me. But would the nulls agree?

"What choice do they have? If they don't, you go on eating them. I think they'd rather make music and let you grab the rats. And if you stopped hunting the nulls, they should talk with you. I don't have your language, but they could learn it. You would have time to work something out."

Show me the rats.

They went back outside. Darius brought out the cage of rats. Nona took her place beside it. Colene opened the cage and the rats surged out and scattered, running across the ground. Nona sang.

The rats lost purpose. They scrambled in circles, rolled over, paused, and tried to hide under the cage. The music disoriented them.

Colene returned to the dragon, putting a hand on its rough neck. "Want to see if you can do it?"

Yes.

She signaled Nona. Nona stopped singing. The rats immediately recovered their bearings and fled for the nearest brush.

The dragon sang. The rats tumbled, confused. The dragon advanced so rapidly that Colene was almost knocked over. It snapped up one rat and swallowed it. That action interrupted the song, and the other rats scrambled away. But in a moment the dragon sang again, and they were helpless; one actually ran toward the huge mouth. It was soon gone, and then the third.

The dragon could as readily have snapped up any of the people. This was its lair, and it could move faster than they could. Only the beads protected them.

Colene rejoined the dragon. "If the Felines sing, and you are near, the rats will be easy prey. It is true that they are smaller than the cats, but there are so many more of them. A hundred small bites instead of one big one. You need not go hungry."

Yes.

"And this would open up the entire intellectual realm of the Felines for you. You know they are smart."

They will not trust me.

"But we can make the deal. Then they'll know."

I have preyed on them for decades. Other dragons prey on the other nulls across the planet. They will not believe.

"But you're not attacking us."

You wear the beads.

So they did. "Will you spare us if we remove the beads?"

Yes, for I know their identities. But if the other nulls do not agree. I will have to prey on them again.

Colene put her free hand to her necklace. "No!" Pussy cried, leaping toward her.

"The dragon will not eat me," Colene said, though she was quite nervous. "We have a deal."

"You can't trust the dragon without the beads."

"I think I can."

"You must not! If we lose you, all is lost."

This is interesting, the dragon thought, for Colene's free hand remained against its neck. *She has been deceiving you but you have known it.*

She does not know I can read her mind without touching her, Colene thought back. *Will you keep that secret?*

Yes.

"You are speaking in my language," Colene said to Pussy. "You pretended you did not know it."

Pussy looked stricken. Cat stepped in. "We were given a directive to conceal this from you as long as feasible," it said. "We serve Ddwng, and must learn all we can, so as not to be caught as he was."

"So you pretended to be our friends, to spy on us," Colene said coldly.

"Yes. We are not your friends. But we wish you no harm. Otherwise Pussy would not have spoken when you imperiled yourself. She does care for you, and is mortified to have your anger."

"I thought we were being honest with each other," Colene said, putting hurt into her tone. "How can we trust you now?"

You are beautiful, the dragon thought. *You are deceiving her while making her sorry for trying to deceive you.*

But you know my true mind, Colene thought to it. *I can't deceive in telepathy.*

Continue with your scheme.

"We apologize for not being candid with you," Cat said. "This was not our choice. We must obey directives."

Colene glanced at Darius. "Does this make sense?"

"Yes," he said. "They never claimed to be our friends. We never claimed to be theirs. Neither side should expect complete candor from the other."

And if Darius didn't question the ethics of it, she didn't have to. "Okay, we forgive you," Colene said. "Now I have to know whether we can trust the dragon." She drew the necklace up over her head. Then she set it on the ground. The dragon did not move.

"So is it something in the beads that repels you, or are they merely an indication of what prey is forbidden?" she inquired.

An indication. Our makers have ways to destroy us, and rogue dragons are abolished.

"So you know I'm protected, even when I'm not wearing the beads."

All of you are protected, the dragon agreed.

"So this proves nothing. We need to get some unprotected Felines to verify your constancy."

Yes.

Colene looked at the others. "The dragon says it will not attack any of us, because we have been marked by the beads. It would be destroyed if it ate a protected person. So we shall have to verify our deal by bringing in some unprotected villagers."

"What deal?" Cat asked.

"The dragon will eat the rats instead of the Felines, if you will associate with it intellectually. You'll have to help by stunning the rats with singing. You have to be right there with the dragon while it feeds. So there has to be trust."

"This is not credible," Cat said. "No dragon can be trusted to be other than what it is: a predator."

"Felines are predators," Colene said. "Do you eat humans?"

Cat gazed at her. "Point made. But we will be destroyed if we violate our strictures."

"So will the dragon. Since it is the stricture that restrains it, rather than anything in the beads themselves, why can't it also abide by its own stricture? It has much to gain, for it hates the intellectual isolation. Why not give it a chance? What do you have to lose?"

Lovely. You have phrased it so that they are unable to refute it.

Cat nodded. "If what you propose is feasible, this would have planetary significance."

"So let's head down to the village and make it feasible," Colene said, half dizzy with her success. She focused on the dragon. "You're amenable?"

Yes. What you offer is appealing. But the villagers will not agree.

"We'll see."

They set off for the village: the four travelers, the three Felines, and the dragon. The Felines did not try to conceal their extreme doubt. The others, touched by Colene's mind, were able to link to the dragon when Colene walked with her hand on it. They discovered no effort of sincerity on its part, but rather a straight acceptance of a better condition: intellect for a shift of diet. This was a significant net gain, therefore it would be honored. The mind contact made them believers.

Instead it was the dragon who questioned motives. *Why are you doing this?*

"We're captives from other Modes," Colene explained subvocally, so that the Felines would not overhear. "We want to escape. We'll have a better chance if we can win our guards, the Felines, over to our side. I think this deal with you could do it. I also am repelled by the way you prey on intelligent creatures, while I don't care at all about rats."

It would be good if your deal could work.

"I'll make it work, somehow."

Perhaps you can. You are an unusual creature. How did you come by your ability to communicate?

"My friend Seqiro. He's a telepathic horse. I picked it up from him. But he's a whole dimension better than I am."

Could you teach it to me?

"I don't know. It's something you just have to catch on to by yourself, if you can."

I think I cannot. Your mind is more complicated than mine. If this effort does not work, and I must still prey on Felines, will you still associate with me?

That made her pause. "If you make a sincere effort to establish the deal, and it fails because of the Felines, then I will associate with you. While I am here. You have to do what you have to do. But I want to leave this world and this universe as soon as I can."

I can understand why your horse liked you.

That made Colene choke up. She missed Seqiro terribly.

They came in due course to the village, and halted in sight of it. "Can we have an assembly, or something?" Colene asked. "So we can talk to them, explain about the deal?"

"Yes." Cat went to talk to the villagers.

He soon returned. "They are afraid. They will not approach the dragon."

This is the case I anticipated, the dragon thought. *They have reason.*

"Let me try," Colene said. "You come with me, Pussy. Translate." She walked to the houses.

"This will not work," Pussy said. "The dragon has never done us any good."

"I saw it take a Tom last night," Colene said. "I decided this had to stop. Now there is a way to stop it. They have to listen."

"If I told you that you could spread your arms and fly, would you believe it?"

Colene thought about that for a moment. Actually, in the realms where magic worked, Nona could do exactly that. She didn't even have to spread her arms; she could simply levitate. When Seqiro had linked her with her home Mode, she had even been able to do it on Earth itself. But Seqiro was no longer with them, and this was not a magic realm. "No."

"I might believe," Pussy said. "I saw you touch the dragon, and befriend it. But even for me, this is very difficult. For the others, who have never been away from Chains, who have never seen the wonders of civilization, it is too much. They are not equipped to accept it. The dragon has always been our worst fear, and will always be."

"Well, somehow I'm going to change that," Colene said stoutly. "I don't care what our own situation is, I can't just stand by and let people I can talk with be brutally eaten by a monster."

Pussy guided her to a particular house. "This is the head Feline of this village," she said. "He is the first who must be persuaded." She knocked on the door.

The Cat appeared, yowling. "You brought the dragon here?" Pussy translated for Colene.

"We can make a deal," Colene said quickly. "The dragon won't hunt you anymore." Pussy translated that to yowls.

"Please don't tease us with the impossible," the Cat said. "The dragon will always hunt us."

Colene tried to argue, but it was no use. The Feline's mind was closed.

"You see, they can't change," Pussy said. "I wish you could be right, and that they would give you a chance, but they won't. You are just a visitor; you don't know how it is."

"But to allow your children to continue to be orphaned, when there's a chance to save your people—" Colene broke off. "Why do they make children, instead of adults?"

"There is too much to learn. They would have to spend much time teaching new adults how to function. But with children, they go to families, and in the course of several years they learn. That's much more efficient."

"So the children's minds are open."

"For learning, yes."

"Then let's fetch the children," Colene said, heading for the orphanage.

"But they won't let—"

Heedless, Colene went to the house and pounded on the door. "We're taking the children out for a walk," she announced to the Cat who opened the door. "Now."

"But the dragon is near."

"The dragon's no problem. Bring out the children."

The Cat looked at Pussy. She nodded. That, coupled with Colene's insistence, sufficed. Soon the seven children joined them in the street.

"Now we're going to do something weird and scary and fun," Colene told them, and Pussy translated. "No one will be hurt. I guarantee it."

Considerably more adventurous and trusting than the adults, the children came along. They walked the length of the village, and out to where the dragon waited with the others. Colene knew that the villagers were watching. They had no direct control over the orphan children, so could not protest.

The others retreated as the party of children approached, giving Colene leeway. None of them looked confident, because the children had no beads. Even if the dragon wasn't trying to hunt them, could it resist snatching such tender morsels?

"Now watch this," Colene said to the children. She marched up to the dragon and put her hand on its snout. "I have brought the orphan children," she said. "They are more open minded. Can you stand it if they climb over you?"

I recognize what you are doing. Perhaps it will succeed. I can tolerate them.

"Okay. I'll demonstrate." Colene put both arms around the dragon's neck, as far as she could reach. The neck was massive and muscular, and the hide was rough, but

she was careful. Then she sat on the snout. "See?" she
called. "No harm." She saw that Pussy was translating.
"Now come up here and meet the dragon."

This time they balked. They were trusting children, but
not utter fools.

"We need stronger medicine," Colene muttered.
"Dragon, I don't want to insult you, but if you could see
your way clear to—"

Do it.

Colene climbed onto the dragon's back. "Dragon ride!"
she cried. "See!"

The dragon slithered forward, bracing itself with its
stout limbs. The feet planted themselves against the
ground, and the main body seemed almost to slide between them, as though they were posts. It was strange,
but effective. When one leg got behind, it would lift and
move well forward, and the sliding would continue.

The children stood fascinated as the dragon and dragon
rider approached them. They did not flee, either because
of reassurance or terror. The dragon halted. "Next ride,"
Colene said. She applied the technique that had worked
with Burgess. "You—come join me for a ride."

And it worked. The child came, and Colene helped her
get up on the dragon's back. Colene held her, and projected strong feeling of reassurance. She wasn't sure she
could do it, but emotional transfer was one of the things
Seqiro did, so she made the effort. Then the dragon slid
onward, carrying them. The child, at first nervous, began
to enjoy it. It was working!

After that it got rapidly easier. By ones and twos, the
children rode the dragon. Then, their fear abated, they
joined Colene in other games. They played games of X's
and O's by scratching in the sand, with the dragon making
the X's with a deadly claw. They sang, with the dragon
making the harmony. It became a regular party.

Colene looked out around. Most of the villagers were

there, watching. Their amazement was manifest. "You see it's safe!" Colene called, and Pussy hardly needed to translate. "Come match wits with the dragon." No one moved. "You!" she called, pointing out the chief Cat. "Come play a game!"

Thus challenged, and responsive to the voice of command, the Cat came forward. The dragon wiped the dirt clean and sketched a fresh diagram with one claw. The Cat crouched down and drew an X in the center. The game continued to a draw.

Colene knew she had won. "Here is the deal," she said, pausing for the translation. "The dragon will hunt rats. But you have to help it. You have to let it into your houses, and sing the rats crazy. And when it's not feeding, some of you will play games with it, or debate philosophy. Anything, so long as it's intelligent dialogue. Treat it with respect. And the dragon will never hunt Felines again."

Colene know that the battle was not yet finished, but the tide had been turned. She had shown the way. She would continue showing the way until the new order was established. Then it could continue without her.

And when Pussy approached her, Colene read her emotion, and knew that the ultimate loyalty of their three Felines had shifted. Nothing was said, nor should it be said, but now the Felines were truly their friends.

THREE

~~~~~~~~

Doe

Darius continued to be surprised by the things Colene came up with. She was a vessel of dolor, and that was significant mischief for his home Mode and their long-term relationship. But she had other assets that bid fair to compensate. She was learning telepathy, and perhaps magic also. She was young, but she was pretty. And, unfortunately, he loved her.

Now she had persuaded the dragon to make peace with the Felines. Nothing like this had been done before on this planet; that had become clear. What else would she accomplish, as her odd mind wrestled with their captivity in this dread Mode?

They retired to their chamber in the house in the feline village. They shared a bed, but not sex, to his regret. They were married, but she simply wasn't ready yet.

"What a day!" she exclaimed, lifting her face from the basin and toweling her wet hair. She was in dishabille, wearing a bra he thought unnecessary and panties he still found shocking. "What do you think?"

"You are lovely," he said.

She paused, glancing at her wild hair in the mirror. "I look a fright."

"But a lovely fright." Actually he found the wild hair appealing. Yet there was that dichotomy.

"I'm not going to wear a damned diaper!"

She was referring to the traditional garb of women of his home Mode: the voluminous adult diapers that masked the untoward aspect, so as to prevent lascivious notions on the part of men. Colene's culture confined diapers to babies; she found the costume demeaning. He had seen her world, and so had come to understand this difference in costume, but he still wasn't entirely used to it. She had the present aspect of a woman who was about to indulge sexually. Yet he knew she had no such intention.

She must have picked it up from his mind. "I'm sorry, Darius. I'll put something on."

"Perhaps that is best."

"You know I will do it, if you—"

If he forced her. She would not resist, but would be rigid with revulsion. It would seriously damage their relationship. "No."

"Well, we can still snuggle, can't we?"

"Yes." He knew she liked being close to him, in every way but that. He didn't know how to get around that last barrier.

"I don't think there is any *nice* way," she murmured as she came to him.

That was what he feared. He stroked her damp hair and massaged her back, and she melted. He kept his hand well clear of her bottom.

"But maybe if you did—"

"No."

"Oh—the dragon told me that the Caprines will arrive tomorrow."

"The whats?"

"The Caprine nulls. You know, the ones the Felines wanted to help."

He remembered. "We requested them as additional servants."

"Yes. But we won't treat them that way. Pussy says they are good creatures."

"You are getting along well with Pussy."

"Yes, now that I can read her mind, and know that she has no intention of seducing you. She's okay. Especially now that the felines are so grateful."

"But they serve Ddwng."

"Yes. But now they love us. Nona was sure right about that. They would do anything for us that doesn't conflict with their orders."

"Colene, we can't let Ddwng have the Chip."

She sighed. "I know."

But she wished they could find some compromise, so their party could get back on the Virtual Mode. She hadn't been able to reach Seqiro mentally, and without the powers of the horse, feared they had no chance to escape this Mode.

"Yeah," she agreed. "But meanwhile, we have to send someone to fetch in the Caprines. Because the ship won't land in the same place, this time. It's a two-day walk. They'll never find us, without guidance."

"Can't they ask the natives?"

"No. The different types of nulls don't necessarily get along on this planet. They don't have the protection of the government." Then she reconsidered. "Well, they do get along, but that would delay them interminably."

"I don't think I understand."

"I asked Pussy what the Bovines and Equines were doing here, that night. Turns out that there's some intervillage fraternization."

"I still don't understand."

"Yes you do. The nulls can't make out with any of their own persuasion. But it's fine with other persuasions. So when they want a hot time, they visit other villages, where they're in big demand. If the dragon hadn't struck and ruined the mood, those Bovines and Equines would have made out with the whole Feline village. They like recreational sex."

Now at last he understood. "So one of our Felines with the beads can go."

"We need our Felines here to translate for us. I need to stay, to keep track of minds; the villagers aren't really convinced the dragon's change is for real. So I guess it's you."

"I don't know my way around this planet."

"You don't have to. The dragon will take you there."

"The dragon!"

"It's like this, Darius. If the villagers see you go with the dragon, and come back with the Caprines, they'll know the dragon can be trusted when I'm not around. Not near it, I mean. That's important, because this deal has to last when I'm gone."

"And if the dragon can't be trusted?"

"It can, Darius. Honest. I know its mind. It wants an intellectual environment."

"Do you? How can you be sure the dragon didn't make up a story, to get some prey alone?"

"I wish you could read minds, Darius. Then you'd know. There is no deception in mind reading."

He wasn't sure of that, but did know that she would never knowingly put him at risk. "Then I will go with the dragon. But if I die before I possess you, I shall be most annoyed."

She laughed. "Oh, Darius, that's so nice!"

In the morning Darius walked out of the village. The dragon met him. He couldn't talk to it, but Colene had said it knew the score. That was her way of saying that things were in order. Belatedly he wondered how the dragon could have known about an arrival on a faster-than-light spaceship that hadn't yet occurred. Did dragons know such schedules? Evidently so.

The dragon slithered rapidly into the forest. Darius had to jog to keep up. But he was out of condition for this, and soon was puffing. They had to make a two-day trip in this one day? He would not make it.

The dragon halted. It looped around him, then abruptly flung its massive body against his legs. Darius, surprised, fell halfway across it. Then he realized that the creature was offering to carry him. He flung a leg over to bestride it, and lifted his feet.

The dragon moved forward, carrying Darius along. The huge body flexed, hardly needing the stubby legs, and made remarkable speed. Darius did not have to hang on; the ride was more like that of a magic carpet.

Now it was clear how they would traverse two days' distance in less than one day. The forest was fairly whizzing by. This was almost fun.

In due course the dragon paused at a river. Both of them drank, and Darius plucked fruit from a tree to eat. The dragon evidently wasn't hungry at the moment.

They resumed, crossing the river. If there were any water predators, they stayed clear.

In the afternoon they came to a large open field. The dragon deposited Darius, then undulated away.

Alone, Darius waited for the space ship to arrive. The dragon hadn't eaten him, but he did not feel comfortable. Suppose no ship came?

Then something appeared in the sky. It was the ship, floating gently down. It landed before Darius. A portal slid open. Three Caprine nulls emerged. They were in their natural state, without clothing. The portal closed, the ship floated up, then vanished into the sky.

"Hello, Darius," the neuter null said. "I am Goat, and these are Buck and Doe. I have not recovered from my injury, so my pace will be slow. Doe will go ahead with you, so you can arrive on schedule."

"But how will you find the way?"

"The same way Doe will: we shall sniff the trail you made coming here."

"But my scent won't be on the ground. I rode a dragon."

All three stared at him. Then Buck put his nose to the ground. "It is true," he said. "The trace of dragon is very strong."

"This will require some formidable explanation," Goat said.

Darius wasn't sure he should tell them about Colene's telepathy. "We made a deal. But the dragon's gone now."

"A deal with a dragon!" Doe said. Then her eye fixed on his necklace. "Ah—you have beads."

"Beads," Goat repeated. "That of course explains it."

That hardly explained the half of it. But Darius didn't want to get into the complications at this time. He lifted the necklace from his neck and proffered it to Goat. "The dragon knows me, but may not know you. Wear this for protection."

Goat accepted it. "Thank you. We shall follow, avoiding villages where possible."

Darius understood why: the null females would be after Buck to stay the night. The Caprine might enjoy the diversion, but it would take them much longer to reach the Feline village. "I will tell them you are coming," Darius said, turning toward the slight trail left by the dragon. This seemed abrupt, but the alternative was to wrestle with concepts he preferred to leave to Colene. Her telepathy was after all her business.

He set off walking, and Doe paced him. She was a well-formed female, but of course all the nulls were. Her legs terminated in solid hoofs, and she had pointed furry ears, nascent horns, a solid nose, and a small beard, but was otherwise human. Except for the light fur that was her only covering, evidently serving in lieu of clothing. It was smooth and fairly glistening, like a form-fitting gown, concealing none of her body features.

"As I think you know, we nulls exist to serve," she said. "But it will help me to serve as we travel if I am better acquainted with your situation and preferences. Do you prefer dialogue or silence?"

Darius hadn't thought of that. "Whichever you prefer."

She smiled. "You are from another Mode, so are perhaps not fully familiar with our ways. I therefore presume to clarify in the way Goat would that the preferences of a null have no bearing with respect to a master. There is no other way but yours."

He considered for a moment. "I am, as you say, from another Mode. There are no nulls there. Women do have a somewhat subservient status, but they are not servants. I have also traveled to other Modes, and seen other societies, so have perhaps been liberalized. Since we are alone, you have no need to be subservient."

"If I understand correctly, you prefer that I express preferences when they do not conflict with your own."

"Such expression would be meaningless. I would prefer to know that when you agree with me, it is a true reflection of your state."

"But that would require occasional difference, and that is not in our nature."

Darius was intrigued. "We have about two days' walk ahead of us. I would much prefer a good argument to automatic agreement."

"But master, I would never presume to—"

"Call me Darius. Goat did."

"Goat may be your intellectual equal. I am not."

"We don't know that. In any event, assume that you are."

"This is not easy, Darius, but I will try."

"Is there anything you would like to know about me or my situation, or any related matter?"

"Yes."

After a pause, he realized that she had answered his question literally, without presuming further. "Then ask me, and continue asking until you are satisfied."

"Why have we Caprines been summoned here?"

"You made a deal with the Felines, and they felt you would be better off here than wherever you were. You are nominally to be servants, but actually to be on vacation."

"Vacation? This term is not in that portion of your language we studied."

"You will have no assignment, and serve no people. You will be allowed to relax without obligation."

"But we have to serve! And to do a specific favor for our master each day."

"You are released from that obligation, as the Felines have been." But Darius remembered how it was with the Felines. "If you suffer by being unable to do us favors, consider that you are doing them constantly. You will be sniffing out the trail when I lose it. When we get there, you can help us work with the Feline villagers to promote their cooperation with the dragon. There will be plenty to do. You have no need to seek anything beyond that."

She nodded. "This is reassuring. But there is another aspect. We female nulls are normally at the sexual service of our masters. But we were cautioned during training not to do this freely. Does that caution remain?"

"Yes. I am married to Colene, and she expects my fidelity. Do not make any effort to seduce me."

"I will not," she agreed. "But neither am I capable of opposing any such desire on your part."

"I will try to behave," he said wryly. Colene's attitude in this respect was something of a burden on him, as sexual limitation was not a feature of a relationship in his home society. It was worse because he could not indulge with Colene, either.

"The dragon," she said. "We have always been prey to the dragons, and never allowed to oppose them. How did this shift come about?"

"A dragon took a Feline villager the first night we were there. Colene did not like it. So she talked to the dragon, and it agreed to spare the villagers and prey on rats instead, if they would provide it with intellectual society."

Doe walked for a time, evidently pondering. Then she spoke, hesitantly. "I do not wish to offend you, Darius, but this is not easy for me to believe."

"The villagers don't believe it either. That's why there is some work to do. But it is true. The dragon played with the children of the orphanage, and ate none, and today it carried me here."

"I would not ever say or imply that you are guilty of a confusion, but there must be some error in my understanding. No dragon ever behaved like this to nulls. Sometimes one of us would go out to the dragon's lair, as an act of suicide, and the dragon always consumed that one. There was never any intellectual communication. We nulls of all persuasions have always been prey for the dragons; this is the natural order."

"You could not talk to the dragon, and have it listen?"

"I believe it would listen, but then it always ate the talker. All it ever desired was our flesh."

Darius saw that Colene had done something special, something not encountered in this Mode before. Doe was right to be skeptical. He would have to tell her the truth.

"Doe, I think I must tell you something, but it is important that it not be told to others. Can you keep a secret?"

"I can," she said. "Are you asking me to?"

"Yes, so I can explain what happened."

She turned her face to him. Beneath the ears and beard and nose it was beautiful, and the eyes were especially large and lovely. Colene had mentioned something she had read in her Mode's literature, describing an ancient queen as ox-eyed. Oxen had large, placid orbs. So, it seemed, did Caprines. "I will keep your secret," she said. "Give me a chain."

"A chain?"

"On our world, the making of an oath is signified by donning a chain. When I take your chain, this signifies a private commitment which binds me apart from my duty as a null. It is binding until the giver takes it back. No one will question it; all will understand."

This interested him on another level. "I had heard about the chains, but had thought it to be more symbolic. It really is binding?"

"Yes. When you wore the bead necklace, that was another type of chain that committed you to Ddwng, thus protecting you from all possible enemies here. Anyone who molested you would be destroyed. Even the dragons; they know. You passed that protection on to Goat, a generous act. There are many types of chains, and they confer benefits as well as commitments. The taking of a chain is a serious matter."

"Then why should you take my chain lightly?"

She gazed at him again, and her eyes seemed yet more lustrous. Now he became aware of her hair, which was silky long and light. She was, he realized, strikingly beautiful, regardless of persuasion; her Caprine qualities could not mask it. "Darius, I do not do so."

"But I just suddenly asked whether you would keep a

secret, and you agreed you would. You did not debate it or think about it, you simply agreed."

Her level gaze was compelling. "This is not so. Do you wish further information?"

"Yes, I do."

"We studied you—the Feline trio and the Caprine trio, the two who had won the privilege of serving you when you appeared. We learned your language and customs to the extent they are known in our Mode. We learned that the girl, Colene, is devious and not to be trusted."

"That's not so!"

"Allow me to rephrase. She is true to her own friends and beliefs, but is not ethically limited when dealing with those she perceives as enemies. She will deceive others, and find ways to overcome them. Her loyalty is only to her own, not to any higher principle. Therefore her enemies cannot afford to trust her."

Darius gazed at her, impressed. This was indeed a fair description of Colene. "I apologize for my denial. You are correct. And what is your judgment of me?"

"You, in contrast, are unalterably honest. You will keep your given word regardless of to whom it is issued, even if it is given under duress. Therefore you can be trusted, and you are the one whose commitment we must have. Colene will betray others, but will not betray you. Your word will bind her too."

"But I gave my word when we were in the Mode before, and it was invalid."

"That has been analyzed. It was concluded that you kept your word, but that unbeknownst to you, the girl arranged to void it, and so caused the anchor to be loosed. She had never acquiesced, and was in opposition to your decision. But you may now, if you choose, clarify that: did you approve Colene's action?"

"I did not. We had a serious difference about that. I thought I could not love her, because of that dishonesty.

But the deed was done, and could not be undone."

"This was our conclusion. She betrayed us, not you. Therefore we cannot trust her, but can trust you. But now that you have broached that matter with her, she will abide by your decision. Is this not correct?"

Colene had actually won that argument, their first serious difference. But he knew she would not put him in such a position again. "It is correct. You have analyzed us well."

"And did you find you could love her?"

"Yes. I was wrong to crucify her on my standards, which were not hers. I have to accept her for what she is, not what I think she should be. That applies also to her dolor."

"This is another term we lack."

"It means sadness, sorrow, grief. She is a vessel of dolor, and that makes our relationship difficult."

"Why so? Many people are sad on occasion."

"She is more than sad. She is depressive. When left to herself, she does not wish to live. I require a vessel of joy for my employment. But that becomes complicated to explain."

"I should like to listen to the explanation, at such time as you wish to give it. But I suspect it is not immediately relevant. Something else perhaps is. You do love her, as she is."

"I do love her," he agreed. "And she loves me."

"This relates to my commitment of the chain. You love her, and therefore accept her. She loves you, and therefore will abide by your standard when there is a conflict. You partake of each other in a way you did not before. She has become trustworthy when you are integral to the agreement, but you will not make an agreement she detests. I studied you as a prospective master as carefully as I could. In the course of that effort, I came to love you."

"You what?"

She raised her hands, which were fully human and attractively dainty. "This confers no obligation on you, Darius. You may ignore it, except to this degree: my commitment to keep your secret, whatever it may be, is not lightly given. We have only recently met, but I know you better than any human man I have encountered before. I long to take your chain, for it binds me to you. This, I know, is all I can ever expect to have of your emotion."

Darius was solidly set back, if not actually stunned. "Doe, I don't know what to say. I had no suspicion of this."

"Nor need you take any note of it. Except to understand that the chain I take from you is not casually accepted. I love you, and will do your will absolutely, whatever it may be. Now, with that understanding, you may bind me with it."

Darius hesitated. "I understood that there was to be no effort to seduce me."

"That is true for Pussy, who is at this time part of the lead trio. We Caprines were to be the lead, but Goat's injury makes us secondary until it heals. Therefore the stricture was applied to her rather than to me. She is unable to love you; I am able." She paused briefly. "But I would not do anything counter to your interest. I will not try to seduce you unless you ask me to."

"I ask you not to."

She nodded. "But I will take your chain."

There were aspects of the nulls he had not before appreciated. But he liked this candid creature, and wanted her to understand his position. So he looked for something to make a chain.

All he found was a small box of paper clips that must have come from Colene's Mode. Colene must have put them in his pocket, and he hadn't noticed. There seemed to be no paper in this super-science, super-primitive

Mode, so no use for paper clips. He brought them out and hooked them together, one by one, making a circular chain. He gave it to Doe.

She put the loop over her head. "I accept your chain," she said, gazing into his eyes. "Whatever you tell me that is secret will remain so, until you release me from the chain." She looked away, then her eyes returned to his face. "May I kiss you? It is the custom, though not required."

What harm was there in it? "You may."

She stepped into him, embraced him closely, and put her mouth to his. She kissed him neatly, efficiently, and with surprising passion. Then, as neatly, she broke it off and turned away, blushing through the light fur of her neck.

Darius resumed walking, trying to shake off the formidable impact of her kiss. It wasn't just her mouth; her full breasts and soft belly had pressed against him, and her thighs. She was very much a woman in almost every part. Even her hoofs were dainty and clean. None of this was surprising, as the female nulls had been designed for sexual aptitude; but he had been taken by surprise by the force of her allure. Her emerging personality enhanced her appeal.

"I apologize for being too forward," Doe said, pacing him again. "I should have made the kiss chaste."

"It's all right," he said. Now he was aware of the manner in which her fine breasts quivered with her steps.

"You may tell me your secret now."

He had almost forgotten what had started this. "You doubt that Colene could have persuaded the dragon to give up its traditional prey. She was able to do this because she has an ability not known elsewhere in the Mode: telepathy."

"The horse!" she said. "It wasn't just the horse?"

"It wasn't just the horse," he agreed. "It started with

Seqiro, but Colene learned it from him. From constant association with him. Her mind was constantly bathed in his mind, because he enabled her to understand other languages, even other alien thoughts."

"In the DoOon Mode horses are relatively unintelligent animals, unless enhanced as nulls. That was why we were deceived."

"Seqiro has horse sense, not human sense. But he draws from the human mind he is with. So he gave Colene telepathy, and she gave him a human mind, while they associated. But she was able to learn some of it, to use when apart from him. Her ability is only a shadow of his, but it is enough for her to read human and null minds in her immediate vicinity, and to share her mind with the dragon when she touched it. Such contact is persuasive; I felt it when Seqiro shared my mind. There is no doubt, no deception. When she merged minds with the dragon, it had to believe her. This is what brought the change. Colene did it."

"Human telepathy," Doe murmured. "We never suspected. But if she could read null minds—"

"You had no secrets from her," Darius finished. "We knew that you knew our language. Pussy gave that away when she saw what was happening with the dragon. The Felines don't yet know about the telepathy. That is the secret."

"I will keep it. But the Felines will not be deceived long. They have studied you too well, as we Caprines have."

Darius shrugged. "That is up to them, and Colene. It is not my place to reveal it."

"I understand."

"Thank you." It was an odd relief to have shared it. "So now perhaps you can believe that the dragon has changed, and probably the other dragons will change similarly, as the news spreads."

"Yes, now I can believe it."

"Of course Colene will know that I told you. But she will also know that I required your silence."

Dusk was coming. "We can if you wish continue to walk in the night," Doe said. "But though I can still smell the path, I am not adept in darkness."

"We should make camp," he agreed. "And find something to eat. The dragon stopped by a lake with fruit trees, on the way over, but we aren't that far along yet."

"I can find such things," Doe said, sniffing the air. "This way."

He followed her through the darkening forest, and soon they came to a river. Sure enough, there were fruit trees there. They ate, and separated briefly for natural functions, then came together again. "I can make a lean-to of branches and foliage," he said.

"I will find ferns for a blanket."

He wasn't sure how that would work, but set about cutting branches. In due course he had a small but serviceable structure. Doe returned with a pile of large ferns, which she then expertly wove into an equally serviceable blanket. "This and my body will keep you warm."

"I'm not sure that is appropriate."

"It is not sensible to sleep separately, when we can be more comfortable together."

"But you are a lovely woman. I need to keep my distance from you."

She looked at him in the near darkness. "While I am not able to refuse your interest, either formally or by desire, I know that this is not your intent. You have told me. I will, as you put it, behave."

"My concern is that *I* may not behave."

"And this would be improper, according to your agreement with Colene," she agreed. She squatted, and he saw that her feet were not really hoofs, but human with virtually merged toes and heavy hooflike nails. Now that he thought of it, he realized that it would have been difficult for her to maintain her balance walking upright in the human manner, without the human heel and toe. But her feet seemed dainty rather than malformed. "Is there then some way we can share warmth without my body tempting yours?"

Above her feet, in her present position, were her muscular but well fleshed thighs. In this light he could see their form but not their fur. The sexual suggestion was maddening. "Well, you could don a diaper."

"That term is not in—"

He interrupted to explain the concept. She smiled, her teeth white in the darkness, and used more ferns to fashion a formidable diaper. She donned it, and his burgeoning desire faded.

They crawled into the lean-to and shared the blanket. It was surprisingly soft and tight; Doe clearly knew what she was doing. She curled up, animal fashion, and he curled around her warm body, wearing his clothing. He tried to relax.

"Am I interfering with your sleep?" she inquired.

"No, it's not you. It's me."

"Normally my master has his will of me, then sleeps. If you are accustomed to similar with your wife, our present situation represents a disturbance in your ritual. I do not know how to abate this aspect."

"It's not that," he said, dismayed.

"I am a fully female creature. I think the diaper does not sufficiently nullify that."

A fully female creature? That was a serious understatement! He had thought Pussy to be sexy, but this Caprine was more than her match in that respect. "Doe, you are if anything too willing to accept blame."

"Of course. A master is never at fault."

That set him back again. "In my culture that is not the case. Fault is determined by the situation, not the status of the participants. Certainly in this case there is no fault in you. I would be lying awake were I alone."

"It is my obligation to assist you in any way I can. If you are sleepless, it is my failure."

"No!"

She was silent, and he was immediately sorry for his outburst. "Doe, I apologize. I did not mean to hurt you."

"Darius, you did not hurt me. But you may do that, if that brings you relief." She uncurled, and the process brought her full breast under his hand. "Do what you need to."

He withdrew his hand. "I take no pleasure in hurting women. I have done enough of that to last me forever."

"I do not wish to inquire into what does not concern me, but if you should care to talk about this, I would care to listen."

He laughed without humor. "Is this your way of saying that you are obliged to listen to whatever I may say, but in this case you happen to be interested?"

"Yes."

"Then I will tell you how I hurt women. In my home Mode I am a Cyng of Hlahtar, which loosely translates to 'King of Laughter,' but it is no laughing matter. I do bring joy to the multitudes, so that their dolor is ameliorated. But because I lack sufficient joy in myself to do this without ultimately destroying myself, I must take a wife for a year and draw on her joy. I magnify it a thousandfold and send it to all the people around us, including her, but her restored level is less than it was originally. In time her level is too low, and I must divorce her and seek another. This is painful, even if I do not love her. I must leave her depleted, to recover alone, and that may take the rest of her life. It was to escape this necessity that I sought for a wife in another Mode, hoping to find one whose resources of joy were such that she would not be depleted by my action, and I could afford to love her and remain with her for life." He paused. "But I think I have said too much for you to understand, as this is no part of your culture or your Mode. I apolo—"

"Never apologize to a null," she said quickly. "I do understand to a degree, for I have studied you, and relate well to your concerns. But it is true that I have difficulty with the concept. You are saying that you can take the joy from a woman, and leave her sad?"

"Yes. Of course I return most of it immediately, but it can never be as much as she started with. We travel from village to village, delivering joy, but at her expense. I think there is no worse cruelty than this."

"I want very much not to seem to doubt you, but—"

"Were this my own Mode, I could demonstrate. But my kind of magic is not operative here."

"Perhaps if you could do with me what you do with women there, I would be better able to understand, even if the magical effect is absent."

"I can try," he agreed. "I can go through the motions. First I must embrace you."

She turned in place and lay facing him. He brought her in to himself. Again he was aware of her extreme femininity; he had never before embraced such an embraceable woman. Then he invoked his power and drew her joy from her—and felt a trace of the effect. It was after all working here, to a degree. He broadcast, and returned it to her. Then he nudged away from her, physically.

"Oh, Darius," she whispered. "I thought I would die."

"I did not think it would work in this Mode, but there was a slight manifestation of my power."

"Slight! You drained me of all delight, and had you not returned it, I would have drowned myself to abate the horror of my existence."

Apparently his impact had been greater than it seemed to him. "This is the nature of it. I will not do it again."

"Darius, I have no right to ask, but if you would be so kind as to—to—"

"To comfort you," he said. He had of course encountered this reaction before. He moved back and hugged her, stroking her hair. Her face was wet with her tears. "I am sorry, Doe. I thought it would not work at all. Had I realized, I would not have done it."

"No, I thank you for doing it. Now I do understand. I simply was unprepared." She spoke sensibly, but her tears continued and her body was shuddering.

"Of course. It is a terrible moment. And it is continuingly terrible for the women I marry. Yet when I sought elsewhere—" He broke off.

"If you wish to say it, I wish to hear it."

Surely true. She was recovering from the dreadful shock of his demonstration, but still needed context. Understanding helped a person to handle it. "I thought I had found a vessel of special joy, in Colene, but was mistaken. She is instead a vessel of dolor, generating grief instead of joy, the opposite of what I need. Yet I love her, and can not give her up. So it is my hope to compromise, to find another woman to draw from, so that I can be with Colene, as I am unable to be now."

"But at least you can enjoy her body."

"No. I can't. Because—"

Doe was silent, but he knew she still wanted to hear. Did he have the right to tell? "The chain you took—the paper clips—may I add to the secret?"

"Yes. Everything you ask me to hide is covered by the chain."

"Then this is added. I do not have sex with Colene. I thought at first it was because she was too young for it, by the standard of her culture, but later we married, changing the definition. Then I discovered the real reason. It is because she was raped before I met her, and is unable to accept with pleasure what was forced on her. So I am not accustomed to this form of activity with her, and we normally sleep much as you and I are doing now, touching but without sex. So you see, you are not disruptive in this manner."

"I am glad of that. But saddened by what you have told me. I did not suspect."

"It was not your business, no offense."

"You can't offend a null."

"I don't want a null, I want a person!"

She paused just a moment. "I will try to do better."

"Oh, I'm sorry again. I seem to have my own hang-up on this subject. What could you know of rape?"

"I do know of rape, Darius."

Again, his interest quickened. "Oh? I presume you don't mean that a master used you harshly."

"I will explain if you wish. Perhaps my experience is relevant."

"Yes, I wish—if you wish."

"My own wish has no—"

"Stop doing that!"

"I apologize for—"

"And that!"

Again, that small pause. "Is it permitted to request the same of you?"

"I'll try to stop yelling at you, yes. It is unfair."

"I mean the apologies. They put me in an awkward position."

Once again, she had set him back. "I am a person. You are a person. We shall neither yell nor apologize to each other."

"Yes, Darius. I was made and grew to adulthood here in Chains, in the manner of all nulls. I was thrilled to be chosen for select service to the emperor on the capital planet. There I learned of the advanced science that had before been merely theory and story to me. To serve on space ships, to use translator balls, to see far planets—

everything was a wonder to me. But one day when I was on an errand for the master to whom my trio was assigned, a boar waylaid me. I knew I was not supposed to give myself sexually to any but my master, and tried to avoid him, but the Swine hauled me into a private chamber and had his will of me even as I fought him. He simply hit me in the face until in the distraction of my pain I let my legs loosen, and then he completed himself at his leisure. Then he let me go, squealing with laughter. I was appalled and ashamed, for not only had I betrayed my master, I knew I could not report the boar, because the Swine are favored of the emperor. All I could do was bring blame upon myself, and on my trio, for my carelessness in allowing myself to be caught."

"You do know about rape," Darius agreed. "It was like this with Colene, only it was not a single man, but four who did it. She did not dare even fight—and blamed herself for that, too."

"This is the way of it," she agreed. "I stumbled back home to Goat and Buck, in great—you call it dolor. Buck of course was angry, but Goat was sensible. It cleaned me up and applied medication, and I was soon mended, physically. It comforted me and told me to forgive the assault, not because the Swine was worthy, but because it was the only way for me to recover my equilibrium. I tried, but couldn't do it. I was afraid the master would realize, but fortunately he was inattentive and used me without noticing my fear. It was—I lack the term in your language. An invisible creature that clings to one, bearing her down, emotionally."

"An incubus," Darius said. "That also has a sexual connotation."

"An incubus," she agreed. "Had I been in a relationship with another null—we are free to do that, between employments by masters, and we do enjoy it—I would have been, I think, the way you describe Colene, unable to do it with pleasure. Luckily it didn't matter. I kept thinking of that boar, hating him, unable to let go of the foul memory. It was affecting Buck and Goat, for we of a trio are very close. Something had to be done."

"Yes," he breathed. "But *what*?"

"That boar came to a sudden and brutal end. He had challenged a Canine and gotten his throat ripped out. Apparently this hound had received special training, and was a killer, unknown to the boar. So my nemesis was gone, and that Swine trio was finished; the sow and pig had to be recycled. I never inquired, but somehow I knew that Goat had arranged it. The neuters have ways; they are very smart and not driven by passion. As Goat saw it, it was an imbalance that needed to be redressed. But it was vengeance, for me." She paused. "*Then* I was able to forgive the boar."

"Vengeance—then forgiveness," Darius said. "I had not thought of that."

"I do not know whether this is usual or proper, only that it was so for me. We nulls are not completely identical; there are small differences between batches, and of course the circumstances of our adoption and maturing differ in detail. So perhaps my experience is not relevant."

"I think it is. Colene had fears and horrors, but she is no wilting flower. She takes suicidal risks, as she did with the dragon. She understands vengeance. And she had it on those rapists; Seqiro made them confess to the police, and they were punished. So maybe she is ready to forgive. May I tell her your experience?"

"You may, of course. Or if you prefer, I will tell her myself."

"Yes. All you have to do is get close to her, and have it in your mind, and she will read it. I think it will help her."

"I am glad, Darius."

He thought of something else. "But you, Doe, you said

you love me, because of your training. I shouldn't make you do this for Colene."

"On the contrary, I am glad to help you in any way I can. My feelings have no—"

"Stop it!"

She was silent, having been forbidden to apologize. Embarrassed and sorry, he was on the verge of apologizing himself, as he had done what he had promised not to. But that was no good either. So he caught hold of her head and kissed her, hard.

She met him with utter passion. He felt himself being swept away. "Stop me!" he gasped as he grabbed for her remarkable bottom, heedless of the diaper.

She twisted, and was suddenly clear of him. "I obey, against my will."

"You know why I must not."

"I know I must do your will."

That was not at all the same, but he let it pass. "I think I have recovered control of myself. Rejoin me, but do not let me remove any of my clothing or handle your sexual parts."

She resumed her curled position, and he pressed himself against her back and flank. His upper arm came across her folded arms, and his fingers touched her face. It was again wet with tears. He realized that he was being cruel in a new way, but he saw no alternative.

"If I had not forbidden it," he murmured, "you would gladly accommodate my physical passion. Similarly, if we had not agreed to avoid such expressions, I would sincerely apologize to you for tormenting you in this manner. But you must not, and I must not. Do you understand?"

"Of course." She kissed his hand.

He willed himself to sleep, and this time was successful.

In the morning they rose, washed, ate, and resumed travel. Doe removed her diaper; it was beginning to fade as the ferns dried. The revelation of her central portion stirred him as it had not during the prior day, but he stifled the urge. "If I understand correctly, you are allowed to indulge sexually with any male not of your own type."

"Yes. With any master or male null other than Caprine. But by choice I will not do so with a boar."

"I understand. But I am not your master."

"You are equivalent. Had Goat not been injured, we would have been assigned to you, and we remain assigned on a secondary basis. Certainly you may do with me as you choose."

"That was not the direction of my thought. You should be free to be with any of the Feline males."

"Not while assigned."

"If you are assigned to me, am I free to release you?"

"Yes."

But he had learned caution. "Do you wish to be released?"

"No."

"So the kindness I thought to do you is no kindness?"

"That is correct, Darius. I would prefer to indulge sexually with no other male while I remain in love with you. But—"

"But I could release you anyway. Your feelings have no bearing."

"Yes."

"Then I think I can't release you at the moment. But neither can I use you sexually. I am thus with you as I am with Colene."

"Perhaps she will change when she views my mind."

He remained unsatisfied. "What motivates you, with regard to sex—is it sexual desire, or the need to cater to a master's preference?"

She walked for a moment before responding. "It had not before occurred to me that the two could be distinct. While we nulls do enjoy sex between ourselves—we call it humping—it is not a compelling drive, other than a matter of status."

"Status?"

"We females wish to be considered desirable. Those who are not humped frequently are considered less so. The males do have desire, as this is required for performance, and some crave variety, as in the case of the boar who raped me. In fairness I must say that boars are not the only nulls with a taste for deviant sex. But this is merely among ourselves. Our need to oblige our masters, in contrast, is overwhelming. It is not possible for a master to rape a null; she inevitably welcomes his interest. So it is the latter."

"But suppose the master likes to rape?"

"He will tell her to pretend aversion, to resist and weep as she submits, and she will do so. He may also require her pain, or what among nulls would be considered unnatural acts. She welcomes it all, from the master."

"I find this horrifying."

"You are a nice man."

And she was a nice woman. "You oblige me best by your candor. You have helped me understand much that I need to, and I really appreciate it. I may not be allowed to apologize, but I think I am allowed to thank you. I do so, Doe."

"Oh, Darius!" Her tears were back. This time he was glad of them. Her emotions were genuine, but governed by her need to oblige. It would be the same with the Felines.

She wanted to kiss him, and he felt he owed at least that much to her. "I believe you understand why I should not express physical affection for you. But you may, if and only if you choose, show it to me."

"I understand." She turned to him as they stopped walking. He held his arms rigid at his sides, while she embraced him and kissed him. It would be treacherously easy to love her.

She held the kiss for a timeless moment, then withdrew. "I think I should not do that again, even when given leave," she murmured, once again blushing as she turned away.

She was surely right. She understood her impact on him.

They walked at a good clip, but the dragon had brought him farther than he had realized, and the terrain was more rugged than he had appreciated. Darius didn't want to admit it, but he was getting tired. Doe was having no trouble, however. That suggested the type of exercise she normally got, and the way she had been designed. She was accustomed to hard work.

"Perhaps we should pause for food," she suggested.

"There are no fruit trees nearby."

"I could go to a village and ask for food."

"While I rest my feet?"

"Of course."

"No way."

She was disconcerted. "If I have displeased you—"

"No. You're trying to give me a pretext to rest without hurting my feelings. You will face mischief in that village from males, and it may be unpleasant for you. I won't have it. I'm tired, not weak. Maybe there are fruit trees ahead."

"Surely so." She hesitated. "I can assist you in walking, if—"

"No." Then, aware that he seemed petulant, he qualified it. "We would have to walk with our arms around each other's waists. That could lead to awkward notions."

"The notions already exist." But she did not argue further.

So they went on. The route descended into a valley where a large river ran. This must be the one the dragon had swum. Well, he could swim it himself. He stopped at the bank and began stripping his apparel.

"Darius, you asked me not to let you remove your clothing."

"I meant when we were touching each other in the lean-to. Now I merely want to keep my things dry as I swim across the river."

"You must not do that."

"I won't touch you, Doe. You can swim well apart from me. You *can* swim?"

"I can swim well, but I must not be apart. Should you falter, I must be ready to bear you up."

Oh. "Very well, then. That sort of touching is permissible. Then I will dry and dress again on the other side."

She stood looking at the water. "No, you must not."

"Not dress again?"

"Not swim across."

"A moment ago you were going to swim with me."

"A moment ago I had not seen the plesiosaur."

Darius looked. A small but formidable head was rising from the water, perched on a long neck. The head rose so high that there had to be a formidable body beneath the surface. "That's a river predator? Capable of consuming us?"

"Yes. We nulls are not allowed to resist it, but we can avoid it by staying clear of the water when it is near. Sometimes it catches us by surprise, however. We must find another way to cross."

Darius considered the creature. "I think it could grab a person right off a boat."

"It can. There must be a ford at some point along the river, too shallow for the plesiosaur to swim. I can look for it, if—"

"We'll both look for it."

They started to walk upstream. Then Doe raised her nose and sniffed the air, alarmed. "Dragon!"

"The dragon won't attack us. It knows me."

She turned her great eyes on him. "This is not the same dragon whose trail we follow, Darius."

An ugly chill ran through him. He did not doubt her ability to distinguish between dragons by odor. He drew his knife, though it seemed a puny weapon. "Get clear, Doe. Maybe I can back it off." But it was bravado; he knew he was no possible match for the predator.

"No, you must not threaten it. This is not allowed."

Because the nulls were designated victims. "Then we had better hide."

"We cannot. It will take us if it wants us. Oh, Darius, I am sorry I did not give you pleasure last night, though you bade me not to."

She thought they were going to die, and he wasn't sure they were wrong. "Well, there is one other chance. I may be able to draw out its joy, as I did with you. If I do not return it soon, it will die."

"No, Darius! You must not hurt it."

This was firmly entrenched. "Doe, I am not bound by your conventions. You must do what you must do, but so must I, and I must try to survive."

She nodded, surprised. "I was forgetting. It is true: I must serve your needs, not mine."

"Maybe we can compromise. Signal it about my power. Maybe it will go away."

"I will try."

They waited, and in a moment the dragon appeared. Indeed, it was not the one he had ridden; it was slightly smaller, and looked older. But it remained huge and deadly.

Darius put his left arm around Doe's small supple waist, and they turned to face the monster. "Translate," he said. "I have the power to destroy life with my touch. I will use it to defend myself and you."

She signaled to the dragon. It watched, then flicked its

tail several times. Doe relaxed. "It is giving the signal of indifference," she said. "That means it is not hunting us. But there is more I don't understand. Something about hunger but not eating."

"The other dragon must have told it!" Darius exclaimed. "It wants to stop hunting nulls."

"Yes, that must be it. But then why is it approaching us?"

"It must have a reason."

The dragon slithered slowly toward them. Doe clung to Darius, still frightened. "It is showing no threat signs," she said. "But why is it coming so close?"

Then Darius had it. "The river! It will carry us across the river."

She remained highly uncertain. But when the dragon's body stopped beside them, its head at the edge of the water, Darius climbed onto its back, and half hauled Doe on in front of him. He held her in place, his hands against her belly. He could feel her breathing and pulses racing. "Go, dragon!" he called.

The dragon slid smoothly forward, carrying them along. Doe screamed, but did not move. Darius thought it was not terror that froze her, but his touch: she would not flee as long as his hands showed her that he wanted her here.

The dragon forged through the water. The plesiosaur swam close, looking as if it might like to snap them up, but the dragon lifted its head and emitted a musical note. The plesiosaur took warning and retreated.

They reached the farther bank, but the dragon didn't stop. It carried them on at a faster pace.

"It's taking us to its lair!" Doe said.

"I doubt it. It has another purpose."

They were borne swiftly through the forest. Then they came to a village. "Fowl!" Doe said.

The dragon halted outside the village. The Fowl were watching nervously, their routine activities halted in place.

"The deal," Darius said, finally putting it together. "The dragon wants to make the deal, but this village has not been told. That's why it brought us here."

"The deal," she echoed faintly.

"Come on." He jumped off the dragon, and lifted her after him. "I'll talk; you translate."

"But I don't speak Fowl dialect."

"Sign language. And demonstration. We'll get it across. Now here are the words: Dragon make peace."

He waited while she made signals with her hands, gesturing to the dragon. The villagers stared, hardly crediting it.

"Dragon hunt rats," Darius continued. "Fowl let dragon come into houses. Stun rats with music."

Still they stared, unable to grasp this.

"We must show them," Darius said. "Where are there rats?"

"Everywhere. Especially in the storage shed," Doe said. "They can't be kept out."

"Lead the way there."

She looked around, then walked toward a structure near the center of the building. Darius followed, turning to beckon the dragon. The dragon slid toward them.

Doe opened the shed door. She made a musical bleat. A rat scrambled out, confused.

The dragon sang. The tone swelled eerily. The rat rolled over on its back, helpless. The dragon reached it and snapped it up. Then the dragon put its head into the shed, sounding its note. The head snapped back and forth. Rats squealed, but none emerged.

Darius took Doe by the arm. "Tell the Fowl that all the dragon needs is their trust, and someone to talk to. Then it will not prey on them any more. It will eat rats instead. That's the deal."

Doe signed, but still the villagers stared, incapable of believing it. However, Colene had handled this too. "The orphanage," Darius said. "Fetch the children."

Doe walked to another building. It seemed that all villages were similar in layout. There were a Cock and Hen guarding the door. Doe signed to them. They drew back, horrified. Doe pushed past them, went inside the house, and came out leading two chick-children by their clawlike hands, a male and a female. A third, a neuter, followed; evidently they had bonded, and Chicken could not leave its companions to their fate.

Doe brought them to the shed where the dragon was finishing. It was licking blood from its jaws, and there were no rats in sight. "Get on its back with the children," Darius said.

But Doe was still too frightened to go that far. So Darius picked up the little Cock and set him on the dragon's back. Then he lifted the little Hen, and finally the little Chicken. "Follow me," he told the dragon, making a grand beckoning motion.

It slid forward. The children screamed with birdlike chirps. So did some villagers. But the slow ride continued. Darius walked in a loop around the central village square, followed by the dragon with its small burdens. "The dragon will not hurt any villagers," Darius said. "If you give it the rats. And if someone talks to it. First with signs, then with language, as it develops. *Tell* them."

Doe signed desperately, trying to tell them, while the dragon looped around again, carrying the children. But still they would not believe.

Darius looked around. He spied a young trio that looked less frightened than the others. He went to them. "You," he said. "Tomorrow the dragon will come again. You will meet it. You will talk to it. You will lead it to rats. You will get to know it, and show the others."

Doe signed repeatedly, making the points. They seemed willing to understand, a little. Then Darius led them to the dragon. "Tomorrow these three will meet you," he said, and paused while Doe signed to the dragon. "Make them trust you, and in time the others will."

Then he lifted the three children down from the dragon's back, and led them to the orphanage. He returned them to the proprietors. They would have quite a story to tell their fellows.

He returned to the dragon. "We must go," he said, and Doe signed. He faced the villagers. "Tomorrow—dragon—these three." He pointed to the dragon and to the selected trio as Doe continued signing. If they didn't understand by this time, they never would. He had started the process. He had done what he could.

He faced outward from the village and started walking. "Come," he said.

Doe joined him, and the dragon followed. When they were well clear of the village, Darius turned to the dragon. "Good enough?" he asked, and Doe signed. "Return to-morrow to talk."

The dragon blew a melodic answer. Then it slithered rapidly away.

Doe watched it go. Then she collapsed. Darius managed to catch her and bear her gently to the ground. This had been a weird, wonderful, and terrifying experience for her. "You did good work, Doe," he murmured. "A revolution is coming to this planet, and you did your part."

Her eyes fixed on him. "Is this a dream?"

"No dream, Doe." Then he kissed her, and drew away before passion had a chance to overwhelm them.

In a moment she recovered. "Darius, I forgot to get food in the village."

"*We* forgot. But what we did was more important."

She scrambled to get back on her feet. He helped her up, though she did not need it. Then they walked on, sniffing out the original dragon's trail.

As luck had it, they passed a fruit tree. They had food

after all. They paused to eat their fill, then walked on. Darius no longer felt tired.

He thought of an aspect he had overlooked. "How did you train?" he inquired. "So well that you came to love me, when I was not there?"

"Dar and Col were there."

"Who?"

"They are human nulls. Manufactured as we are, but with fully human forms. One crafted to resemble you, the other resembling Colene."

"Physically," he said, surprised. "But what of their personalities?"

"Those, too, resembled you, as closely as was known." She glanced sidelong at him. "But Dar did not do you justice. You have qualities we had not guessed."

This was increasingly interesting. "So you could indulge sexually with my image?"

"No. We understood that this would alienate Col, and make her more dangerous and treacherous."

Treacherous. He could not argue with their perception; Colene was the one who had deceived and defeated them. "So when Pussy almost seduced me, that alienated Colene, as you see it, and made her betray you and escape."

"Yes. So we were trained to be careful of that aspect. But when I came into your real presence, my defenses collapsed. You overwhelm me. Perhaps it is the drawing of my joy, and the returning of it. I have no power to resist you, other than by your command."

Darius nodded ruefully. "It has similar effect on the women we draw from. That's why they must be our wives. I had thought it would not work on you, as this is not my home Mode."

"Perhaps. So even as Colene has powers we did not grasp, so do you. This changes our situation."

That started another notion percolating in his mind. "Where is your ultimate loyalty?"

"We serve Ddwng. We have no choice. But in anything not opposing his purpose, it is to you."

"If you had a choice?"

"I would serve you completely."

That had been his impression. "These human nulls—where are they now?"

"When we competed for the honor of this mission, we made a deal with them to share our benefits with them, to whatever extent we could. That was why the particular ones with whom we had associated were chosen to join our training. There are four of them—two Dars and two Cols. They remain on the capital planet, awaiting the outcome here on Chains."

"What happens once the issue here is decided?"

"Those of us not used will be recycled."

"What is that?"

"Reduced to protoplasm and added to the store of substance from which new nulls are made."

"So it's death, once your mission is done."

"No, our material does not die."

"But your identities are lost."

"Yes."

"Isn't that very much like death?"

"This is not relevant to your interest."

He caught her by the arm and swung her about to face him. She met his gaze, and he saw the dolor in her. "Yes it is. How can we spare you that?"

"We will remain only if we have continuing relevance to the mission. Once you depart, there will no further need for us; our training made us unsuitable for other purposes. So it is better that we be recycled."

He shook his head. "Doe, I can't have sex with you, and I can't remain with you. But I do like you, more than I should, and wish to help you in some fashion."

"There is no—"

"I will see what I can do."

The rest of the trip was uneventful. By evening of the second day they reached the Feline village. Colene ran to embrace Darius. Then she drew back, looking at Doe. "Oh, Darius, you should have taken her. She earned it."

"It would have helped if you had told me that before I set out on this venture," he said. Then they both laughed.

Colene went to Doe, who stood somewhat awkwardly, not knowing her reception. Colene hugged her and kissed her. "I know what is in your mind. But do not tell. Ah, I see you won't." She looked again, physically and mentally. "You wear a chain—of paper clips!" She laughed again, and this time Doe laughed with her.

The village had made progress in the past two days. It seemed that the dragon was systematically cleaning out the rats from the houses of the first families to trust it, and with each house, the remaining Felines were reassured. A trio from the orphanage was now assigned to accompany the dragon, learning to communicate with it more effectively, and to play new intellectual games. "Soon they will be able to handle the process without me," Colene said.

They joined the villagers for dinner. Doe hung back, uncertain of her welcome, until Cat beckoned her. "Join us," Cat said, indicating Burgess, with whom Cat was keeping company. "Tell us of the state of the Caprines, and your journey here."

Doe accepted gratefully. Darius knew that she did know Cat personally, from their training, and that she answered to the authority of a neuter null, in the absence of her own. Soon they were eating and had a dialogue going. They were speaking Colene's language, learned for the mission, but surely they had had a common language before, when they were assigned to the capital planet.

"So tell me how it was with you and that sexy Doe," Colene said brightly. It was necessary for her to ask him openly, lest she give away her ability to learn it from his mind. Actually her mind reading was as yet minimal, so he normally either spoke his thoughts or phrased them in silent speech for her benefit. She would have only the barest gist of his relationship with Doe.

He presented the physical highlights of the walk, but omitted most of the dialogue they had had. The neighboring Felines paid close attention as he described the encounter with the other dragon, and the manner in which the Fowl village had been started on the cooperative deal.

"So the news is spreading among dragons," Pussy said thoughtfully. "And they are willing."

"Yes," Darius agreed. "The dragon came to us, wanting to make the deal with the villagers. Once the word spreads among all the villages, the process should accelerate."

"It seems impossible. Yet here it is happening."

"Sometimes all that is necessary is a new perspective. Colene has that."

"Yes, she does. This goes beyond our study."

There was an increasing levity among the villagers as the meal progressed. "They are truly starting to believe," Colene murmured. "I'm getting the background feeling."

"Maybe our report on the Fowl village helps," Darius said. "They understand that it's general. You have started something that will free all nulls from the fear of early death."

"Yeah, maybe." He did not need to be a mind reader to pick up her deep satisfaction. She had indeed accomplished something significant.

After the meal the Felines set up an impromptu celebration, making a bonfire. They began to dance, in trios. Darius watched, intrigued by this new glimpse of Feline culture. The attack of the dragon had interrupted their prior dance before it really got going. The neuter was the center of each, with the male and female whirling around, clasping hands, spinning out, and returning in a developing pattern.

"Oh, mistress, may I go?" Pussy asked excitedly.

"Sure," Colene said. Obviously the relationship of the two of them had progressed; the Felines had been committed to Darius before.

Pussy glided out to join Tom and Cat in the dance. Doe was left sitting by Burgess. Darius glanced their way, then turned to Colene.

"Why not?" she asked rhetorically. She ran to Doe. "Come on—you'll have to be the neuter. Sorry about that."

They joined the dance, as a trio. The basic movements were simple enough, and it was evident that they weren't fixed, so that they could improvise as convenient. Darius held hands with Colene, and turned her about, and let her go. She spun away from him, then spun back to hug him. She was smiling, and he realized with a pleased shock that this was the first time he had seen her truly happy.

Then the trios started to mix. Darius saw Pussy spin out and tag Nona at the sideline. Nona took her place, dancing with Tom and Cat. She danced well; it was natural to her. When she swung with Tom they looked as if they had done this before.

The Bovines and Equines were back, their prior visit having been balked by tragedy. They too soon mixed, and it was evident that both their males and their females were in much demand. Darius understood why; this was sexual relief for villagers who were otherwise inactive.

A neuter came to Darius' trio. It took Doe by the hand and drew her out, then stepped into the center. They now had a genuine neuter for their trio. Doe started to walk to the sideline, but a male feline caught her and swung her around, bringing her into his trio. She was being accepted by the Felines.

The changes continued. Darius found himself dancing with a village Pussy as Colene went to a feline trio. All the Pussies were very similar, but the villagers wore no clothing. Then he danced with Nona, followed by Doe as a female. She was glowing, becoming yet more lovely in her motion and joy. As she swung with him, she looked at him. "Darius, perhaps—"

Ordinarily she would want to go with a Tom, but he knew this was not the case now. What did she want? "I release you to do what you wish," he said.

She drew in close and kissed him, as if it were part of the dance, but with special flair, then moved on. Colene returned. "I saw that."

"Your turn," he said, and kissed her.

She melted. "Oh, Darius! I love you!" And she did; he felt her emotion.

"You're projecting," he whispered.

Her mouth dropped open. *I am?*

Yes you are, he thought back.

"Oh!"

He shared her wonder. It was the first time she had done that. It meant that her mind powers were growing.

The dance dissolved. Darius saw the cow walk into a house with a male feline, and the bull with a female feline, while the neuter stayed to watch the fire. It was similar for the stallion and mare. But when a Tom approached Doe, she touched her chain of paper clips and shook her head: she was committed to a master. Now he understood why she had made a production of kissing him, with him accepting it: she was demonstrating her commitment as his null.

"Now that's interesting," Colene remarked. "They can't do it with their own kind, so Doe is in great demand. Why doesn't she want to?"

"She loves me."

"Oh, that's right. Too bad."

Darius did not comment. The last thing he wanted was to have Colene jealous of Doe.

"And you really like her."

He made no attempt to conceal it. "I came to know her well. But I did not do anything with her."

"I know. Let's turn in."

"What, and not warm ourselves by the fire?"

"We won't be cold." She squeezed his hand. She was breathing hard, her breasts showing beneath her shirt, and her hair was wild.

Darius suddenly caught her drift. Was she hinting that she was ready to fulfill their marriage?

"Yes, I think so," she said, hauling him inside. "If I won't let you do it with Doe, I'd better do it myself."

They shut themselves in their chamber, stripped, and got into bed. He embraced her. She pressed herself against him—and froze.

"Damn!" she swore. "Damn damn damn!" Then the tears started. She wasn't yet ready.

Resigned, he held her, disappointed but not really surprised. Her reticence was too firmly entrenched to be abolished by the events of a single night.

"I thought I could," she said into his chest. "The dance—maybe you should fetch Doe."

"She understands that this is not allowed."

"It is if I say so!"

"No. You do not wish this."

"Because I should be doing it myself!" she flared. "If only I could forget. I still think that if you forced me a little—"

"No."

"But, Darius, I may never get past it on my own."

"The time will surely come."

"Say—maybe if you imagined it, and I read your mind, then it would be okay."

"I'm not sure it would. The barrier is emotional, not physical."

"Well, try it anyway. I've got to know."

So he started a train of imagination, picturing her nude,

coming to him, lying beside him, spreading her legs. She was actually in that position. Then he pictured himself naked, embracing her, as he was doing, seeking to make the sexual connection.

She rolled out of the bed as if propelled and fell on the floor. "Damn!"

"Now you know," he said sadly.

"Now I know. But it isn't fair of me to—I mean, I may be hung up, but you're not. So if Doe—"

"No." She was trying so hard to be fair, by her pained definition.

"She loves you." Her emotion was bittersweet. Colene loved him too, but could not do what she knew Doe could, if given leave.

"I know. It's not the same."

She sighed. "I guess not." She returned to the bed, and hugged him. He kept his thoughts away from sex. "But some day, some how, I'll find a way."

"Some day," he agreed.

"Darius, we've got to get back on the Virtual Mode."

"To do that, I must take the chain."

She laughed. "How about a chain of paper clips?"

"Whatever it's made of, its meaning remains. I would have to take the Chip to Ddwng."

"And you can't do that," she said. "I understand." She forced a laugh. "You know, Ddwng's the one person in this universe fouled up worse than I am. I read his mind; it's a cesspool of conflict. He can never be satisfied. That's why he's so dangerous."

Something about that changed his perspective, but he wasn't sure how.

"Well, tell me about your trip," she said. "I mean the parts you didn't tell the villagers. Especially about how it was with Doe."

She could read his superficial thoughts, but not his deeper ones, and memories were beyond her reach unless specifically called to mind. But when he did call them to mind, she could pick up pictures and feelings as well as words. She was indeed jealous of his association with Doe.

"You bet I am," she said. "She could do it with you, if you let her. I can't. She's a whole female, even if not quite human."

So she resented Doe's capacity, rather than her physical appearance.

"Yeah. Only I'd kill to have that shape, too. She's actually as lovely as Nona, in her fashion."

"Your shape is not inferior."

"You're only saying that because you're stuck with me. The vessel of dolor."

That was a problem. If only there were some way to change her from dolor to joy.

"You're right, Darius. I'm bad for you. I should get out of your way. Then you could—"

He caught her head and kissed her.

"You know it really irks me when you think that you can shut me up with a kiss. As if I have no mind at all."

He patted her bare bottom. She stiffened, then relaxed, knowing that he had no intention of going farther.

"It irks me worse when it works." She was smiling. She liked the semblance of lovemaking when it was no more than that. She couldn't handle the imagination of sex, but could handle its touch—to a degree. Each night he was able to do a bit more with her, as long as his intention was negative. They both hoped that one night they would be able to take it farther, but progress was slow. "It works because it's true; I can feel your real desire when you touch me like that."

He stroked her buttock, and she was silent. He reviewed the dialogues he had had with Doe, summoning salient images, then moving along to others, in sequence. This was faster than words, because of the detail of the images.

Soon he had caught her up to the present, his hand still cupping her.

"If Doe loves you, but knows she can't have you, why did she kiss you so openly?" she demanded suddenly.

"She's pragmatic. If she can't get what she wants, she'll take what she can get. In this case, it is protection from the sexual interest of others."

"I think she did it for me," Colene said. "To show me she's not sneaking around, but is damn well available if I don't want you. And it almost worked. I was determined to do it. Damn!"

"Nevertheless, I think I had best stay clear of her."

" 'Cause you like her too well," she agreed.

Then his elusive thought coalesced. "Yes. I have reason to depart this planet."

"But you can't, unless—"

"Yes. There is risk either way. But the Virtual Mode is dangerous; anything might happen there. If I stay, a null will get me, for they are feeling creatures, more human that they realize. You would not like that."

"I know how I can stop it." But her body tightened as she spoke.

"Knowledge is not the same as feeling. You must have time to handle your feeling. You may not have that time if I continue to be exposed to temptation of this nature. In my own culture I could indulge without prejudicing my relationship with my wife, but you are not like that."

"I am not like that," she agreed grimly.

"I will take the chain."

"But Darius, this is crazy! I'm not asking you to do that."

"Because you love me."

"Yes. But—"

He patted her bottom, and this time she did not flinch, even unconsciously. "And I love you. And one day we shall be together, truly making love instead of pretending.

But I think not while we are captive in the DoOon Mode. If we remain here too long, injured Goat will recover, and the Caprines will resume their position as the primary team to accompany us."

"And if Doe hasn't seduced you by then, she'll have endless more chances," Colene agreed.

"There is that risk. I do like her, partly because she is honest about her feeling. I am more guarded with Pussy."

"I have come to know Pussy. She is catering to me so that I will know she is not catering to you. I—like her. And I think I trust her. She will not try to seduce you. Of course if you came to her and demanded sex, she'd do it. She couldn't help it. But I'd rather have her along than Doe."

"Yes. They are very similar in that both are female-nulls, but I was tempted by Doe more severely than I was by Pussy. The difference is in me. I was prepared to resist Pussy, but unprepared for Doe. So I think I had better take the chain now."

"Darius, I can't argue with you. I'm feeling your feeling as we touch. You are blocked from me and from Doe, but you could have sex with her without hurting her. So if it were *her* bottom you were feeling, instead of mine—"

"The urge would be severe," he said. "Because I love you, I want you to know the threat."

"Which I could abolish just like that, if only—damn, damn, damn!"

She kept coming back to that. The threat was real. "I will take the chain tomorrow."

"No! Maybe we can salvage something from this. Let me tell them that I think I can persuade you to take the chain, but there are some things they have to do in exchange."

"I am not making demands on them."

"But *I* am. And you won't take the chain if I tell you no, will you?" She didn't need his answer, reading his mind. "So it's not a lie, just a qualification."

She was right. Her definitions of truth were not his own, but he had learned before that compromise was necessary. She was what she was, and did what she did, following her own rules, and he had to accept her as she was.

Yet it was too bad that when the Chip first oriented on her as a potential multiplier of emotion, it had not identified the problem: that her power multiplied dolor, not joy. He had never anticipated that. Colene was a woman of considerable potential, and her growing ability with telepathy was only part of it. But how were they to reconcile her fundamental wrongness for his purpose? He wished he had understood this problem before falling in love with her.

"Yes, I am definitely bad for you," she said. "And you can't even use me and throw me away. We are a disaster in progress."

"We are," he agreed. Then he kissed her.

"I know you want to help Doe and the other nulls, including those human ones that look like us. So let's put that price on your chain."

"Oh, Colene, I hadn't thought of that."

"I know. But it's a way I can please you, and I do want to do that." This time she kissed him. He knew she felt his special pleasure in her generous gesture, and in her kiss.

They relaxed. He did believe that they were making personal progress, and that at some point Colene would conquer her sexual demon. But the dolor—how was that ever going to be handled? He could not resume his business at home without a suitable source of joy.

Colene suddenly came alert. "The nulls! Do they have joy? Maybe you could use them."

"No. I drew from Doe, as a demonstration. She was ordinary in that respect. That means all of them are."

She went tense, then expressed her notion. "How about Nona?"

"She also is ordinary in that respect."

"Sure, without her magic. But what about when she has it? Why couldn't she turn her powers to multiplying joy?"

That was disturbingly interesting. Nona's powers of magic were formidable. If she could magically restore her joy, it would indeed be an answer. But even so, there were problems.

"She's beautiful, nice, and Old Enough," Colene said. "The perfect match for you."

"Except for two things," he said. "She's not interested, and I'm not interested."

"So you turn her down. Which does two things: it saves me, and ruins you. Darius, you need her for your job."

"I am not sure of that."

"The weird thing is that you really *aren't* sure," she said. "But you had better test her."

"When she has her magic," he agreed reluctantly. And what would he do, if Nona turned out to be the one? She was in all respects the ideal woman—and he wasn't interested in getting interested in her. Because it would surely cost him Colene.

"If I didn't love you already, I would love you for that."

"It's a good thing I am not a liar," he muttered. "Because—"

"Because I'd read your mind," she finished. "Oh, Darius, you really are my ideal man. If only I could have been what you need."

"If you raise this subject again, I will tickle you."

"Well, it's true. I'm not only too young, I'm a vessel of—"

Then she screamed as he ticked her bottom. She writhed around, trying to escape, but his fingers pursued her, catching her in most intimate regions. She grabbed a pillow and whammed him on the head, but finally collapsed into helpless giggles.

"God, Darius, this is sex play," she gasped. "Maybe if you tickled me enough—"

"I think not yet," he said regretfully. "But I did get an illicit thrill touching your parts."

"It's not illicit!" But they knew there was no future in that. Not till she could follow through.

Then at last they slept.

In the morning they approached Cat. "I think I can get Darius to take the chain," she said. "But there are terms."

"Of course," Cat said, knowing that the key to Darius' agreement was indeed Colene.

"The Caprines—they won't go on the Virtual Mode, but they have to be treated right."

"This is not something you need to do," Cat said. "I assumed you would demand concessions for yourselves." But it seemed gratified.

"And the—the Human nulls," Colene continued, evidently reading Cat's mind to verify what she knew. "Them too. All four of them."

"This is your true desire?"

"Look, Cat, the revolution on this planet could fizzle out if it isn't properly guided. What happens if we go now? I figure the Caprines and the Human nulls can take over."

"This planet is not the responsibility of the nulls on this mission."

"It is if we say it is," Colene said evenly. "Bring the human nulls here, we'll brief them, and Darius will take the chain if Ddwng will take it too."

"Ddwng cannot be bound by any chain!"

"Well, he'll have to give his word. Three Caprines, four humans, working on this planet indefinitely. No recycling."

Cat looked at Darius. "While I do not question Colene's

word on this, I need your stated confirmation."

"You have it," Darius said.

Cat turned and walked back to the house. "Cat has an interspace communication link there," Colene murmured. "It is very pleased to be thrown into this briar patch."

"Are not briars painful?"

She grabbed his hand and projected an explanatory thought. The expression derived from her local folklore about a fox and rabbit.

Pussy and Doe approached, near twins in body and nature beneath their superficial distinctions. Pussy hugged Colene and Doe hugged Darius. Both were bursting with the joy of the moment. He was glad to have done it for them, despite his considerable misgiving about taking the chain.

FOUR

❧❧❧

Travel

Nona was amazed by the suddenness of the settlement. Darius had gone with the dragon, returned with the lovely female Caprine called Doe, and now was ready to accept the cruel Emperor Ddwng's mission. What had happened? She knew that Darius had an iron will in matters of conscience, and Colene could not have charmed him into it.

Well, she would doubtless learn the story in good time. Meanwhile, she was satisfied with the settlement. The nulls were good people despite their dedication to an unscrupulous regime, and the other members of their party needed to get back on the Virtual Mode.

Darius had an unsettling surprise for her. "I drew joy from Doe, and returned it," he said. "I thought I could do this only in my own Mode, or when connected to it by Seqiro, but I do seem to have a portion of my ability here. I need to know whether you can handle such drawing without suffering erosion. Your powers of magic in the Fractal Mode suggest that you can."

"This is not something I know about," Nona said uncertainly. Actually he had drawn from her once, and spread her magic to others, but that had been on the Virtual Mode in Seqiro's presence. Without the powerful connecting telepathy of the horse, that seemed impossible. "I know you have magic in your home Mode, but it is not the same as mine."

"I draw joy from a woman, multiply it a thousandfold, and broadcast it to the throng. But the level is always slightly less than my subject starts with. It was my quest for a vessel of joy who could maintain her level that brought me to Colene."

Nona was familiar with that problem of theirs. She did not want to interfere with their relationship in any way. "She has special talents."

"But she is a vessel of dolor. That destroys the prospect."

Which was their tragedy. The two had fallen in love, and were diametrically ill-matched. Nona wanted no part of that complication, either. So she remained wary. "What exactly are you asking of me?"

"I want to draw joy from you, and return it—and discover whether you can maintain your level."

"That is not the type of magic I ever practiced. But I am without my magic now, so this can not be ascertained."

"I have a little of mine. Colene has a little of hers. You may have a little of yours. Enough to test."

Could that be? She still did not trust this. "And suppose I test positive. That I hold my level of joy. What then?"

"Then I would ask you to return with me to my Mode and be my wife."

Just like that? Nona knew better. For one thing, Darius was already married. "And what of Colene?"

"She would be my mistress."

"So you want both of us?"

"No. I want Colene. But I can not use her as my vessel of joy, which must be my wife. For this purpose, a wife is a business partner, not a lover."

It was beginning to come clear. Darius could love Colene if he didn't have to draw joy from her. Nona would not be coming between them. This had its appeal, for Darius was a man whose power of magic perhaps matched Nona's, in his separate fashion. But the idea of serving him in this manner without being his lover had much less appeal. He was aware of beauty in women, and she was beautiful. There would inevitably come a physical attraction between them. They could not allow that. Should he lose Colene, Nona could afford to love him. As it was, she could not.

Maybe the drawing would not work, in this Mode without magic, or she would be depleted. That would solve that aspect of the problem. "Try me."

"I think you need to have your magic, for the trial to be valid."

She was relieved. "Then it must wait for another time. Perhaps on the Virtual Mode. Perhaps in range of my home Mode." Regardless, it would postpone the problem.

Colene appeared. "No. We can try it now. I think I can connect you to your magic, a little."

Nona looked at her, surprised on more than one level. "You can do that? And you wish me to succeed?"

"Yes and yes. It would solve our problem. And we could remain together."

Nona did prefer to remain with the group, or the hive, as Burgess considered it. She liked all its members, and they understood her situation. Still, this was too chancy. "But to have me that close to Darius—"

"It's a hell of a lot better than the risk of losing him."

One thing about Colene: she was a vessel of realism.

But also of suicidal risk. She knew that Darius might fall in love with Nona—and was putting him into that danger. Now more than ever, she hoped the test failed. "Try me," she repeated.

Colene came close and took Nona's hand. Nona felt the power of her rapport. She was evoking the memory of Seqiro, trying to reach out across the Modes to connect to the Fractal Mode.

Then Darius embraced her, while Colene still held her hand. He held her close—and then she felt herself sinking into an impossibly deep well, truly down into the point-lessness of life and welcoming of death. It was awful. She found it, struggling to hold on to her joy, but his power was overwhelming.

He released her and stepped back. Then she felt a blast of psychic energy that restored her. She was herself again, shaken but all right.

"You retained your joy!" Colene cried. "And now I have a share of it; I'm much happier than I was. Oh, Nona, you're the answer!"

Nona knew that it was true. She *had* restored some of her own joy, so that she was not depleted. That meant that their plan was viable, if they escaped the DoOon Mode and got to Darius' home Mode. Now they had an answer.

So why was she still in doubt?

She did not comment. Instead she smiled vacantly and walked away, hoping that Colene was not reading her mind. She would try to sort out her true feelings at another time.

The next few days were busy. Their purpose was to establish the dragon deal in as many villages of as many types of nulls as possible before departing. Other dragons came and carried individual members of their party to-gether with translator Felines to the closest villages of Equines, Bovines, and Canines, and they made their dramatic case. It was clear that the news was spreading rapidly, for the villagers were ready to watch and listen.

Nona went with Tom to see an Ovine village. They rode the dragon of that region, and Nona spoke while Tom translated, using mostly signs. The Rams, Ewes, and Sheep understood, but were extremely doubtful. They had never known anything but terror of the dragons. Nona went and fetched lambs from the orphanage and put them on the dragon, and gradually the tide of disbelief turned. The Ovines wanted very much to be free of predation, and this promised that. They knew that similar demonstrations were being made at neighboring villages. They wanted to have the new order, if only it wasn't some awful hoax.

What a revolution Colene had fostered! The entire planet would change in the next few months, becoming a far better place for all its inhabitants. If the emperor did not act to prevent it—and Darius' stipulation went far to prevent that. Ddwng evidently was satisfied to let the planet change, in return for the coveted Chip.

And with that Chip, Ddwng would savage the neighboring Modes, raiding them ruthlessly for supplies and genetic material. Their inhabitants would be executed or enslaved, their cultures destroyed. How could Darius have agreed to that? She knew he would not break his given word, but he was giving it, it seemed, entirely too readily.

So she was distracted as she made the presentation to the village. But the Ovines seemed to be convinced. They would be increasingly satisfied as time confirmed the deal.

The next day they went to a Swine village. As they hiked toward it, the Feline become sullen.

"What is it, Tom?" she asked.

"Nothing that need concern you, Nona."

"Tom, we have to work together, so what concerns you does concern me. But if it is a private matter, I don't mean to pry."

He turned to her. "I must not keep anything from you that you wish to know. But I think this is not something that you would care to know."

"Then let me experiment. Tell me, and if I wish I had not asked, I will heed your warning next time."

"It is that a Boar raped Doe. We learned of this when we trained with the Caprines, and came to respect them. We never liked the Swine much, and now like them less. I dislike having to help them escape the dragon."

Nona walked in silence for a while, considering that. She knew that Tom liked Doe, and had as the nulls put it humped her many times, before she encountered Darius. Colene had picked that up from their minds, and told Nona. That had obviously been entirely voluntary; Nona had seen how joyfully the female Felines related to the visiting males of other persuasions. The visiting females were just as ardent, and none had been forced. Nona wasn't sure, but she suspected that a single mare had managed to have sexual relations with every tom in the local village in one night. But when a cow had declined a tom's invitation, he had not insisted. Later in the evening, the cow had asked the tom; it was her preference to take the initiative. It was always a matter of mutual choice. "I think your anger is justified. Rape is objectionable in our culture too. Was the boar punished?"

"In a manner. The Caprines could not make a formal protest, because the Swine are favored by the Emperor. That is why they are so arrogant. But Goat made a private arrangement, and the boar ran afoul of a hound who was specially trained, and the Canine killed him."

"We understand vengeance too. So then it should be all right with you."

"It should be," he agreed.

"But it's not?"

"Do you understand that we nulls may have sex only with nulls not of our own type?"

This had been obvious, but a null never presumed that a master or mistress was already fully informed. "Yes, I had gathered that." Now was her chance to obtain information openly, so as not to give away Colene's power of mind reading. "So you and Doe—"

"Yes. Because our association was extended, and during training we did not associate with other nulls, she and I had considerable intimacy. I—came to have stronger feeling for her than I have known elsewhere."

"This is romance, Tom. There is nothing wrong with that."

"It is discouraged between nulls, because we must serve our human masters. We can love our masters or mistresses, and Doe does love Darius, but that is another matter. So Doe and I do not love each other. But her pain of memory—it hurts me. It was caused by a Swine."

"That *is* romantic, Tom! I see no evil in that."

"Sometimes directives were relayed to us by Swine. Doe tried to hide it, but I felt her aversion, and my anger renewed. She is a good creature."

"I am sure she is. Your feeling is understandable."

"But I could not help her. When we humped, sometimes she cringed. She always denied it, and masked it well, for nulls are not supposed to have sexual reservations, but I knew it was that memory. I learned to avoid whatever manner or position reminded her of that boar. I hate the Swine!"

"And now we are going to help Swine make peace with their dragon," she concluded. "I wish I could help you, Tom, but I think I am as helpless in that respect as you were with Doe."

"It does not matter. It is right to help the Swine too, and I will do it."

"Despite your aversion," she agreed. "That is commendable."

He was grim. "It is necessary."

Their dialogue lapsed, but not her thoughts. Tom's attitude impressed her favorably, and reminded her of someone. It did not take her long to identify the comparison: Darius. Darius put honor and duty before all else, and was in her estimation an ideal man because of it. The kind of man she had not discovered on her home world of Oria. But of course Darius was taken, and she would never try to change that. Unfortunately he had set a standard in her fancy, and this left her unable to truly appreciate other men. Not that she had had much chance, during their travels on the Virtual Mode. Her main hope was that when they finally reached Darius' home Mode, there would be other men like him.

Yet even so, she knew it would be wrong. Nona was the ninth of the ninth, and supposed to govern her world and guide it into the new order where women had magic and men did not. But she had found another way, and left it, not wanting to be royal. And felt guilty for deserting her destiny.

Where, then, was the solution to her life? She was in her fashion as unsettled as Colene—and Colene was badly disturbed.

"We all must do what is necessary," she murmured.

They reached the Swine village. A dragon came out of the forest to intercept them. Both Nona and Tom paused nervously, but the dragon gave the signal of peace by averting its gaze as it approached. It was ready.

Boars, sows, and pigs were gathered in the village square, looking frightened. They had evidently received word, but hardly trusted it. Nona did not blame them; however arrogant the Swine on the capital world might be, these here were innocent.

The demonstration proceeded in the pattern they had established, with Nona speaking, Tom translating, and the dragon cooperating. In due course they had piglets climbing over the dragon's huge body, and the case was being made. Rats were routed.

While they were watching the progress of the Swine villagers' trust, a sow approached Tom. She spread her knees slightly in invitation. She was of course sexily human, except for her pert snout and hooflike feet. The Swine tended to be more heavily fleshed than the Felines, and this one's breasts were very large and full, and her bottom impressive.

Tom hesitated, glancing at Nona. She knew that he did not wish to hump a Swine, but also did not want to annoy the villagers. Normally any visiting non-Swine male would be in considerable demand. He needed a pretext to decline.

"Eyes on me," Nona snapped, as if jealous.

Tom obeyed with alacrity. The sow apologetically retreated. She had not realized that Tom was committed to this mistress. No other sows came forward; they had gotten the word, and of course no boar would ever dare approach a full Human woman. Nona knew that if she should signal any boar to come to her, he would obey immediately and gladly, but she had no such interest. Thus Tom shielded her as much as she shielded him. This was a convenience she hadn't thought of before. Thereafter she made more of her supposed relationship with Tom.

"We must go," Nona concluded as the day declined. "But tomorrow the dragon will come again. Let it hunt your rats, and have folk to converse with it, and all will be well. Assign a villager, perhaps an intelligent pig, to befriend it with information and entertainment."

They left, but were later than expected, and darkness caught them before they were more than half way to the Feline village. "I think we had better camp, and complete our return in the morning," Nona said.

"As you prefer," Tom said. "I will make a nest for you, and guard it."

"No, don't expose yourself to danger unnecessarily."

"It is my duty to protect you."

"Yes, of course, and I do not question your competence. But we can share whatever protection we have."

He hesitated. "Normally we nulls are completely at the service of our masters, and your party is our master. But we were instructed not to indulge our masters or mistresses, because of complications."

"Indulge?"

"Normally masters make sexual use of nulls."

Nona laughed. "Tom, I wasn't suggesting anything like that! I merely meant we could share accommodations, as it were, for convenience."

The Feline looked embarrassed. "I apologize for misunderstanding."

"Don't. I should have been more careful in my expression."

Tom sniffed out a suitable spot, with fruit trees and a streamlet nearby, and fashioned a kind of treehouse from branches and leaves. He worked efficiently and well, while Nona ate and went briefly aside for urination. The structure was a nice job, rounded like a large covered nest, and looked comfortable and safe.

"I will find some large leaves for blanket covers," Tom said.

"Tom, it is now almost completely dark. Is it safe for you to be out in the forest at this time?"

She saw the vertical slits of his eyes narrow. "Yes. We Felines are hunters of the night."

She realized she had made another mistake. "Of course you are. How silly of me; I was thinking of my own limitations."

"I will return soon," he said, and disappeared.

She settled into the nest. But she was not quite comfortable. She needed a cushion for her head. In her home Mode she had been able to conjure a pillow, or transform any handy object into one. She had gotten out of the habit of planning ahead for such things.

That made her wonder. Colene was learning to read minds, and sometimes even to glimpse spot scenes of the future, though her interpretation of those could be confusing. At one point she had thought that Nona was marrying Darius, when actually Nona had been a proxy for Colene herself. So Colene's vision of Nona at the altar with Darius had been correct, but the meaning was quite different. But here was the prospect: if Colene, who originally had no supernatural powers, could slowly develop them, what about Nona herself, who originally had extremely strong magical abilities? She had been deprived of those when she left her Fractal Mode and encountered other fundamental forces of nature. But the Mode-crossing telepathy of the horse Seqiro had connected her to her home, and on occasion restored her powers. Then Seqiro had freed his anchor, to save Colene, and they had been stranded here in the dread DoOon Mode. But Colene's limited magical power remained. Could Nona herself have some?

There was one way to find out. She would fetch a stone or dead branch and see whether she could transform it to a pillow. If she couldn't, nothing was lost by the effort. But if she could, why then her prospects and those of their party would be significantly enhanced.

She climbed cautiously out of the nest and lowered herself to the ground. She cast about in the darkness with one hand, and found a small rock. She held it before her and focused on it, willing it to change its form and nature.

Almost, she thought it was transforming. But her effort collapsed, and the rock remained a rock. So if she had any magic here, it was too slight to do more than perhaps soften the surface slightly. She dropped the rock, disappointed.

Something loomed suddenly before her. It was a huge pale monster face with glowing eyes and glistening fangs. She screamed.

There was a pounding in the forest, coming rapidly closer. The face bobbed, the eyes flickering. Nona screamed again and backed up against the trunk of the tree.

Something bounded in from the darkness. "Mistress!"

It was Tom, and in a moment his strong arm was around her. The sound had been his response to her screams, as he charged back to help her. Her relief was great. But the fanged monster remained. "Tom! That thing!"

He looked. And laughed. "That's a moth," he said.

"A what?"

"A radiant night moth. That's protective camouflage. To frighten potential predators. It will fly away in a moment; it's just curious about you."

Sure enough, the fanged face turned away and fluttered on through the forest. She had been terrified of nothing.

She drew away from him. "It certainly works. I'm ashamed of my ignorance. I shouldn't have interrupted your search for leaves."

"I should not have left you alone," he said, refusing to let her take any blame. "You have no way to know the features of this world." He hesitated. "I have not yet gotten the leaves, but do not wish to go again."

Nona still had the shakes. "Then stay. We can sleep close for mutual warmth. The night is not that cold; we can get by without a blanket."

"As you wish," he said uncertainly.

"Is there a problem?"

"There should not be."

"I'm not sure that's a straight answer."

"I prefer to avoid such an answer."

She considered. "Let me see whether I understand. A male null does not normally embrace a human woman unless she has directed him to be sexual with her. You find the prospect of being close to me unsettling."

"Yes, mistress," he agreed faintly.

There was an irony in the term "mistress" but she doubted that he was aware of it. He meant that she was the one in command. "I regret putting you in an awkward situation. Perhaps we should simply continue traveling in the night."

"No, Nona. That would not be safe. You lack—you would not find it comfortable."

"I lack the night vision and knowledge to avoid blundering around and bringing mischief upon us," she said.

"I did not mean to imply—"

"My feelings are not hurt, Tom. I merely stated the reality you are trying to spare me. So we must remain here, where you have made a fine safe haven. I am sure I will be safe in your embrace."

"I will protect you with my life," he said.

"I certainly hope it will not come to that."

They climbed back into the nest. Tom curled into a near ball in a remarkably Feline manner. Nona curled up beside him—and remembered that she still lacked a pillow. She needed some sort of support for her head.

She tried to find a suitable position, lifting her arm, but nothing was right. In a moment Tom's head lifted. "There is a problem?"

"A really stupid one. I have always slept with a soft pillow under my head. I find myself unable to get comfortable without one."

"My shoulder is soft. But—"

"Oh, I wouldn't want to impose."

"There can be no imposition. I mean that I should have to be closer to you than perhaps is suitable."

"Tom, you are such a gentleman! Get close to me."

He uncurled and moved over to join her. He stretched out his arm, and she put her head on his furry shoulder. He closed his arm across her. This was much better.

But he did not relax. She could feel the continuing tension in his body. She knew why: they were too close, and he had a conflict between physical and intellectual signals. So she was gaining her comfort at the expense of his.

"Maybe this won't work," she said with regret.

"I apologize. I thought my shoulder would be soft enough. But I am too tense. It is my failure."

"No, Tom! Your shoulder is perfect, and marvelously muscular. But it bothers me that you can't relax too, especially when it's my fault."

"There is no—"

"Yes there is. Let me speak bluntly: I am a beautiful woman. I am acting physically as if I seek your sexual service. But you know I am not. So you have a conflict."

"It is true," he murmured. "But I am supposed to adapt to whatever you require, so the failure is mine. Please sleep; I do not need to."

Was there any way out of this impasse? "I will sleep," she decided. "Then maybe you will be able to relax and sleep yourself. I hope so."

He did not respond. She closed her eyes and felt the faint strong pulse in his shoulder; it was indeed comforting. And in due course she felt him relaxing also, as he grew accustomed to the proximity.

Then suddenly he tensed again, much worse, rousing her from her lassitude. What was it?

"Mistress," he whispered. "There is danger."

Nona sat up. "Can you handle it?"

"No. We must flee immediately."

She felt her heart beating hard. "Show me the way."

He looked rapidly around, sniffing the air. "I fear it is too late."

She neither saw nor heard anything. "What is it?"

"You would call it a flytrap. A predator plant."

"Flytraps are little plants that catch insects."

"This one is big. It has spread its strands around the nest. It will slowly close in, having cut off escape. I should have been alert!"

"I told you to relax," she said, distressed. "If it moves slowly, can we charge past its strands?"

"No. They are triggered by touch, and are extremely sticky with digestive acids." He turned, feeling the nest. "But maybe I can attack it with sticks from the nest, and make an opening for you to pass through."

"And you," she said.

"No. It will entangle me the moment I attack any strand. If you get free, get well away from here. It will not pursue you once it has me to digest."

"Tom, I can't do that!"

"You must do that, or die horribly. You must not die." He wrenched at a stick, and the nest began to come apart. "I will throw stick after stick at it, hoping to engage enough strands to enable you to pass. It is a very efficient predator, but not intelligent. I should be able to fool it for a while. When I call to you, go without hesitation."

"Tom—"

"Mistress, I will save you if I can. May I kiss you before I die? It will help me endure."

She knew he was serious. Now she smelled something faintly sweet, faintly awful. The flytrap was closing inexorably in on the flies. "Yes."

He paused in his wrecking effort, caught her in his embrace, and kissed her passionately. Suddenly she knew that there was more than a question of mistress and servant, or any question of sexual engagement between them. He had feelings for her. It was the way of any null with a mistress or master; Doe had feelings for Darius. But suddenly it was embarrassingly personal.

Then he let her go and returned to the demolition of the nest. "Down through the bottom is best," he said. "Prey normally flees upward or outward. I am making a hole. I wish we had light so you could see the strands; then you could better avoid them."

Light. Her magic had been inadequate to soften the stone, but what about illusion? That was so simple as to require very little magical energy. She concentrated, and made the image of a lamp.

Light eked out, providing dim illumination. Her magic was slight. But it was working!

"What is that?" Tom asked.

"Light," she said. "I have just a little of my powers of magic. Just enough to make a little light. Is this enough?"

"Can you make a fire?"

"Not a real one. Not here in your Mode."

"A pretend one. That looks as if the nest is on fire."

She caught his drift. "Yes!" The glow disappeared. In its place appeared a little flare of light, as of a twig being ignited. A tiny flame licked up, and began to spread.

"Yes!" Tom echoed. "The flytrap hates fire. Fire dries up its substance and wilts its strands."

"Got it." She focused, and the tiny flame spread. But as it grew larger, it grew paler.

"Brighter," Tom said tersely. "Hotter."

"I can't. I have only a trace of magic here."

"Then I must fight it," he said grimly. He was not exaggerating; now the strands were coming into view, thin dangling green tentacles covered with translucent ichor.

Nona remembered her experience with Darius: how he had drawn her joy, and returned it. She had been meaning to sort that out internally, but had been too busy with other things. But if the principle could be applied elsewhere, they might have a chance.

"Tom, there may be another way. I lack sufficient strength of magic to make the flame bright and hot, but I might be able to do it if I drew strength from you. I don't know whether this will work, and it might not be pleasant for you—"

"It must be better than being dissolved in acid. What must I do?"

"Just let me draw from you. If I can."

He remained still while she embraced him. Then she applied the feeling of the power she had felt in Darius— and felt it drawing into her. Suddenly she had all the illusion she needed.

The tiny pretend flame leaped up. It spread into the surrounding twigs of the nest, and they crackled audibly as smoke billowed up. Nona felt the heat on her skin.

The strands of the flycatcher quivered and retreated. The flame climbed higher, reaching out. The strands jerked back. Still the flame increased, engulfing the entire nest, the two people included. But the heat did not burn them; it was radiating outward, pursuing the strands.

Soon all trace of the strands were gone. The flycatcher had been driven away. They were safe.

Nona let the fire die out. None of the nest was burned; all had been illusion. But what an effect! Light, sound, and heat. She had never made illusion that thorough before.

Her companion sank down. He fell face first on the nest.

"Tom!" she cried. "Tom! Are you all right?"

He was not all right. Suddenly she knew why: she had drawn too much of his life force, and not returned it. She had squandered it on the fantastic illusion, reveling in her sudden power. *Tom's* power, dwindling, ebbing, fading, leaving him with almost nothing. She had left him almost without joy.

"Oh, Tom," she said, taking his inert form in her arms. "I didn't realize. I didn't mean to do this to you. Tom, Tom, I'm sorry." She hugged him as closely as she could.

He stirred. "Let me die," he gasped.

"No! You must live. I did this to you thoughtlessly. You must recover. You must!"

He did not reply. His body was limp, and starting to feel cold. "Tom!" she cried again. "Don't fade." But she knew he was sinking.

How could she undo the damage she had done? She had to restore him quickly, or it would be too late. But she lacked her powers of magic; even simple illusion had wasted his life force horribly. How could she make him better?

She could give of herself. She had magic; the illusion had proved it. The most fundamental magic was healing. She could draw on her own life force to try to heal him magically. "Tom, I'm going to make you better," she said.

She found his face and kissed him. Then she held his head close to her bosom and focused on healing, or restoring his joy, his life force. She felt the power of it flowing from her body to his, strengthening him.

He stirred again. "Oh, Nona, I love you." Then he passed into sleep.

She held him firmly, feeling his body slowly recover. But now she was getting tired herself, very tired. She did not have enough life force to sustain them both. But she could not give up the struggle. She had to restore enough to him so that he would survive away from her.

And if he did, what else had she done? She had taken his joy and given back some of her own, and bound him in love. He might have had feelings for her before, but she had, she feared, inadvertently intensified them.

Maybe Colene would be able to help, by putting some other thought into Tom's mind. It was all Nona could think of at the moment. She sank into sleep.

In the morning Tom was up before her, and foraging for food. He brought her a pear-apple. "This isn't the best," he said apologetically. "But I would not go far from you, after what happened last night."

"Because I would get into mischief," she said wanly.

"That, too," he agreed, with a rueful smile.

She roused herself with difficulty. "How are you feeling?"

"Rather weak and disoriented. But I will manage."

"I drew your life force from you, to make the illusion. Then I returned some of mine, so that you would not die. But this has left both of us weak."

"I understand. It was kind of you to help me."

"Tom, I want you to understand that I did not comprehend what I was doing to you. First I almost killed you. I am so sorry."

"For you I would gladly die. Take anything you want from me."

"I fear that is part of it. When we exchanged life force, in effect, I may have made you love me. That was most unfair."

He shook his head. "I understand that you did what you had to, to save us both from the flytrap when my ability was not enough. Then you did what you did not have to, to help me. You have been most generous, and never unfair."

"But—" She was unable to find words.

"I understand that you are the mistress, and I the null. My feelings have no relevance."

"Yes they do! I never meant to hurt you this way. I would reverse it if I could."

"I am glad that you can't."

She looked at him, trying to mask the horror she felt. He regarded himself as a servant. Now he was a love slave. He refused to blame; her. "I think we must get back to the Feline village," she said after a moment.

"Of course."

She ate the fruit, and then they set off. It was apparent

that Tom was not strong, though he tried to conceal his weakness from her. If any danger threatened, they would be in real trouble.

But it was day, and nothing interfered. They managed to maintain a fair walking pace, despite unrelenting weakness, and finally stumbled into the village, where Darius and Colene met them.

"What happened to you?" Colene cried. "You both look awful."

And their minds were surely too confused for the girl to read with any precision. "We encountered a flytrap," Tom said. "Nona enabled us to escape, but we are—are—" He pitched forward, fainting.

"Very tired," Nona finished for him, and collapsed beside him. She was not unconscious, but she was too weak to get up again. They had both hung on until the reached the safety of the village, then relaxed and discovered how little strength remained.

"Darius, I think we need some joy," Colene said.

"We have no donor," he said. "You can't do it."

"I will do it," Pussy said.

Nona tried to protest, lest Pussy suffer as Tom did, but was unable to speak. She saw Darius embrace the female Feline.

Then suddenly Nona's mind cleared, and her body recovered much of its strength. Beside her, Tom was rising. They had done it.

"But Pussy," Nona asked. "What of you?"

Pussy looked stunned, but smiled. "I—will be—better in a moment," she gasped. "I—did not expect such a draining."

"Yes," Darius said. "I was able to multiply and broadcast, at least to the four of you. Pussy's level now matches yours, only slightly depleted. She will hardly be aware of the difference."

"This is magic," Tom said, awed. "We rehearsed for magic, but did not really believe it."

"I'm glad it worked," Colene said. "Because we expect the ship to arrive at any time."

Both Nona and Tom were blank. "Ship?"

"The one bringing the four human nulls—and taking us back to the anchor world."

"How do you know it will come here?" Nona asked.

"Cat signaled it when Darius took the chain. Also, while you were gone, Goat and Buck arrived, and Goat received a signal too. The Caprines and human nulls will take our places here on Chains, and continue the good work."

Now Nona saw the others: the two remaining Caprines, standing with Doe. "Hello," she said.

"Hello, Nona," Goat said. "We are glad to meet you. Doe has spoken well of you."

Nona had hardly interacted with Doe, but let it pass.

Buck looked a lot like Tom, being large and muscular, but had a beard and hoofs. Goat reminded her eerily of Cat, until she realized whwhy: both were neuters, and the intelligent leaders of their trios. "I'm sure we'll get along."

Tom and Nona had had their life forces restored, but were tired apart from that. "We must rest," Nona said. "Come with me, Tom." She wanted him with her because she was afraid he would otherwise be put to work and not get needed rest.

They lay on her bed. "Now we can complete the rest we did not fully achieve last night," she told him.

"I thank you, Nona, for helping me hide my weakness."

She wasn't sure what kind he meant, and didn't inquire. She held his hand and closed her eyes, and soon felt him relaxing into sleep. He was indeed tired, and had been hiding it. Then she allowed herself to sleep also.

The afternoon passed. Nona felt much improved when she got up, and Tom looked better too.

Then it was time for dinner. Tom rejoined his trio, and Nona sat beside Colene. "This is weird," Colene murmured when the attention of the others was elsewhere. "You have more dolor than I do, right now."

Suddenly Nona felt the weight of her situation. She had made Tom love her! But maybe Darius' superior power of emotional transfer could change that.

"No," Colene said. "He can draw and give back joy, but love is something else. That's part of why he's stuck with me. But you're right: Tom loves you. He is barred from loving me, the way Pussy is barred from loving Darius. But that didn't apply to others. The officials of DoOon just didn't think there would be another young woman with our party, or that we'd ask to have the Caprines here. So now Doe loves Darius, and Tom loves you. We'll be leaving soon, so neither Doe nor Buck will be a problem, but the Felines will be going with us. Maybe when you get your full magic back you can change his feeling."

"No. The making or dissolution of love is not within my power either."

"Maybe something will work out."

That was all she could hope for.

The meal dissolved into another dance, for the Felines were still exhilarated by their newfound freedom from fear of the dragon. Indeed, the dragon came, and immediately several villagers joined it, assisting in routing out rats, and talking to it. It seemed the dragon understood their speech, and could respond with twitches of its tail; dialogue was feasible and expanding. This was the course other villages would be following as they gained confidence in the new order.

Tom and Cat came to dance with Nona as a trio, and she could not refuse them. But she felt continuing guilt for what she had inadvertently done. They might be nulls, committed to lifetime service to human beings, but it simply wasn't right to inflict such a burden on them. She suspected that this would interfere with the internal rapport of the trio.

After the dance they retired to their chambers. But Nona couldn't settle down and sleep. She needed a better answer than she had. It had never been her way to torment others. She left her room and walked outside.

There she met Doe, who was also alone. She still wore the chain of paper clips Darius had fashioned for her. "Buck said you might wish to talk to me," Doe said.

So Doe's presence was no coincidence. "Yes! I need to know what happens when a null loves a person."

"Nothing. Nulls have no rights with respect to Humans. In fact, some masters and mistresses prefer to have their nulls love them. It makes for more passion, and better sexual experience."

"But that's cruel! What about when the Humans move on to other nulls?"

"Nulls are constantly reassigned. Our feelings are not relevant."

"Yes they are!"

Doe shook her head sadly. "You sound much like Darius."

"I may marry Darius." That gave her an internal shock. She had meant to sort out her feelings with respect to that, and had not yet done so. Darius was a fine man, but that arrangement lacked most of what she desired in a relationship.

"When neither loves the other," Doe agreed. "So both of you would be like masters, without passion."

They were walking past the dying bonfire, away from the village. Nona found the darkness oddly reassuring. "What does love mean to you? Within the trio."

"We understand each other. Our passions, like our bodies, are entirely at the disposal of our masters."

"I think Tom was saying something similar to me. In fact he said that he would not want to have his love for me abolished if it were possible to do so."

"It is true. My love for Darius gives my life a meaning it never had before. I live to be used by him, in any way that he might wish."

"But true love is not a matter of using! It is *shared* passion."

"Not for nulls. We may love, but can not expect to be loved, other than within our trio."

"Soon Darius will go from this world, this Mode, and leave you behind. What then, for you?"

"Oh, I wish I could serve him longer!" Then Doe recovered control. "I apologize for being emotional. Buck and Goat will support me, and in time my passion will fade. This is the way of it, with nulls. I am glad to have had even this brief association with Darius. He is such a fine man."

"You have no grief, no anger about the situation?"

"Grief, yes."

"And you never had sex with him."

"He bade me not to. Colene would not have appreciated it."

"But if the choice had been yours?"

"The choice could never be mine. I would have been glad to indulge his passion. As it happened, I was glad to refuse, because that was his choice."

The nulls really were different. They seemed to have no proprietary feelings with respect to humans, only the desire to serve. Nona realized that many humans would find that quite compatible. She did not. "What of Tom? He will be with me until the mission is done, then will no longer be with me. How will that affect him?"

"He will be your most loyal supporter and defender

throughout. When you are done with him, he will make no objection."

"That's a significant part of what bothers me. I don't want to do any of that to him. I'm sure Darius doesn't want to do it to you, either."

"You are both very kind to be concerned for us."

There seemed to be no satisfactory answers here. "Thank you, Doe. You have helped me understand."

"I am glad."

They turned around to walk back toward the village. The light of the bonfire caught Doe's face, and Nona saw that it was glistening wet. Oh, yes, this Caprine woman had feelings, though she would not let them interfere with her duty.

Nona returned to her chamber, and was able to sleep, though her dreams were troubled. She still had no answer she could abide.

In the morning she discovered she had overslept. She had indeed been tired, and the prior afternoon's nap had not been enough. She had missed breakfast. She hastily got herself ready and stepped outside.

Tom was there. "I have fruit for you, Nona," he said.

"Why, thank you, Tom. That was very thoughtful."

"Cat suggested it."

Cat had suggested a way for Tom to better serve Nona, and Tom was not taking credit. But what use to argue? "Join me in some fruit," she said. "What else have I missed?"

He joined her, obeying her whim without question. "The ship arrived before dawn. The others are there now."

"The ship! I should have been there."

"Colene said to let you be. You will not be left behind."

"No, only Doe will suffer that."

He did not reply, probably because he did not understand. That meant in turn that Doe must not have spoken to others of their dialogue in the evening. The nulls were discreet about the concerns of humans.

They walked out toward the ship, eating the fruit. Nona soon saw it, a huge vessel lying on the sward not far beyond where she and Doe had walked. There was a crowd around it, and she realized that the villagers probably seldom saw such a ship, and never before right at their village.

Cat and Pussy came from the throng to meet them, followed closely by Darius and Colene. "The human nulls are here," Pussy said brightly.

Nona saw the Caprines and two sets of other people who looked astonishingly like Darius and Colene. "Perhaps we should be introduced," she said. Her strength had returned, but so much had changed that she remained somewhat disoriented.

Darius and Colene exchanged a smile, and Nona realized how seldom she saw Colene smile. She was in a temporary state of joy, thanks to Pussy's donation. It would of course soon wear off, but was surely nice for a while.

In a moment there were six people standing before them, three men and three women. Then they clustered together, did a little dance with swinging and exchanging, and separated into three couples. "Can you tell us apart?" one Colene asked. "Which couple is original, and which two are nulls?"

They had arranged to wear similar clothing, so that there was nothing to set any couple apart from the others. Nona could not tell them apart. Except—

Except that their expressions differed, subtly but definitely. One man and one woman were, well, dominant. The others were submissive. But the two dominants were not together.

Nona marched up and took one Darius by the hand, pulling him out of the line. "Hello, Darius," she said. Then she fetched a different woman. "And hello, Colene."

They laughed. "How did you guess?" Colene demanded. "We thought sure we'd fool you by mixing up the couples. Did you use magic?"

Nona explained about the expressions. "But you would have fooled me, if you had had more time to prepare. You look identical."

"We're supposed to. The human nulls were made to emulate us as exactly as possible, and they were updated when the real ones appeared." She paused, eyeing the emulations. "You know, I sort of like my look. But that's probably because the joy I got from Pussy yesterday hasn't worn off yet. But when we get to Darius' Mode his magic will keep me mostly happy, and that will help."

"But meanwhile we need instruction," one of the other Colenes said, sounding just like her. "What are we supposed to do on this backwoods planet?" Evidently the Human nulls had not been raised on Chains. They were probably a special issue, with no neuter component.

"You're supposed to help the Caprines manage a revolution," the real Colene said. She launched into the explanation, forgetting Nona.

"You have given us positions of real responsibility," Doe said to Nona. "We certainly appreciate it."

Nona looked at her—and suddenly found herself in tears. Doe, responsive to implied as well as direct wishes, embraced her comfortingly. And of course that was backwards. It was Doe who loved Darius, and would soon see him leave forever. While it was Nona who would go with him and in due course marry him—when she didn't love him.

And that was it. Darius was a wonderful man, one well worth loving, but it was not her place to love him, and she was not going to. She would never do that to Colene. That being the case, she didn't want to marry him. Which meant that she didn't want to follow this course. Yet she seemed to be locked into it. What was she to do?

"Oh, Doe," she whispered. "I wish you could go in my stead."

"I wish so too. But that is not possible. I could never leave my trio for such a selfish reason, and you would not like it here without your magic." Doe toyed absently with her chain.

How true. Darius' Mode might not be the place for her, but neither was the DoOon Mode.

By the day's end things had been organized and they were ready for the change of guard. The Caprines and Human nulls would continue the conversion of dragon relations, and be allowed any social relations they wished. That would be a good situation for them all. Except for Doe, who would be left without the man she loved, only the paper clips to remember him by. There was no help for it.

They did not spend the night. They bid parting to the villagers, and Doe hugged Darius with momentary abandon, then turned away, not letting him see her tears, not making a scene. Nona couldn't help herself; she pursued the Caprine female and hugged her too. No more needed to be said.

The seven of them entered the ship. There was no sensation of motion, but Nona knew they were gone; Planet Chains was light-years away. She judged that the trip out had taken about two hours, and the velocity was about a thousand light-years per hour, so even one minute was something like sixteen light-years. From the Feline villagers, from the Caprine and human nulls. From Doe's futile love.

They went to their cabins, the same as before, then had dinner, as before. There was dialogue, but Nona did not retain it. She was suffering pangs of separation from Chains, though it was hardly a planet she liked. She was also in continuing dismay about her own situation with

Darius. Increasingly her position was coming clear: she did not want to marry him. But neither did she want to spoil his chance for happiness with Colene. The two women were ironically linked.

She saw Colene looking at her across the table, and hastily changed her thought. The girl would know soon enough, but Nona was not eager to share her misgivings yet.

The ship arrived at the capital planet as motionlessly as it had departed Chains. They walked into the elegant palace with its omnipresent translator balls and were conducted to Emperor Ddwng.

Then man wasted no time on amenities. "You have taken the chain," he said to Darius.

Darius showed the fine metal chain he now wore around his neck. "Yes. I will deliver the Chip."

Ddwng nodded. "With you there is no question of evasion or trickery. You will do your best to complete that mission."

Darius looked at him with something akin to contempt. "There is however a question with you. A condition of delivery is that Planet Chains be left to complete its social revolution. The three Caprines and four Human nulls with whom we interacted will be left there without interference. Should this not be the case when the Chip is delivered, the Chip will be destroyed."

Ddwng smiled. "And neither do you bluff. The Chip is worth more than a hundred such planets. It is hard to believe that you sold it for such a pittance."

"I am not selling it. I am exchanging it for the freedom of my party, in the belief that you will be unable to use it effectively, if it is delivered at all."

Nona was shocked. "But if you agree to deliver it—"

"Be not concerned, lovely lady," Ddwng said. "He merely means that he may die before delivery can be effected. The Virtual Mode can be dangerous. I know that if he lives, and is not prisoner elsewhere, he will deliver it to Cat, who will bring it to me."

"To Cat?"

"Darius will not care to enter the DoOon Mode again. He will allow Cat to take that final step. I am amenable to this; it is the Chip, not Darius, I want." He paused, then spoke again. "Correction: I do want Darius, because he is an exceptional commander. But he comes with dangerous baggage." He glanced at Colene.

"You got that right, rectum," Colene retorted.

"Charming creature that you are," Ddwng said pleasantly. "I think we are much alike inside." He glanced at the others. "Do you wish to enter the Virtual Mode now, or suffer our hospitality for a time?"

Nona was tired, and by the schedule they had been on, it was now night. She could use a good night's sleep in a comfortable physical environment. But she wanted to get well away from the DoOon Mode while she could. She was sure the others felt the same.

"We're outa here," Colene said.

"Of course." The emperor showed the way to the anchor spot. It was not visible, but Nona could feel its presence.

"We shall require supplies," Darius said.

That was right; Nona had almost forgotten. The neighboring Modes were barren, and though others had life, it was not wise to eat their substance. They had to carry all their food with them, and whatever other supplies were essential.

Ddwng had known this. There were full packs for all of them. They were heavy but necessary, and they would lighten as they used them. No one complained. Then they returned to the anchor.

They walked through it. First Darius went alone. He disappeared, then reappeared, signaling them to follow. Then Colene stepped across with him, followed by Pussy.

They vanished. Then Burgess and Cat crossed, vanishing similarly. Finally Nona and Tom went.

Abruptly Ddwng and the palace were gone. They were on a barren plain. Burgess and Cat were waiting for them.

"What happened?" Tom asked, startled.

Nona was glad to enlighten him. "The Virtual Mode changes every ten paces. Usually adjacent Modes are very similar—so much so that they seem indistinguishable. Their boundaries are marked by the fact that folk vanish or appear when they cross." Ahead of them Burgess and Cat vanished again.

He nodded. "Yes, now I remember. We were told. But I thought there would be another palace." They stepped across the invisible line, and the two ahead of them reappeared.

"The Modes next to DoOon are vacant," she explained. "We believe it was done to prevent DoOon from using them. To isolate it. Because it has traditionally been unkind to its neighbors."

"And will be again," he agreed. They were alone again. "How is it that I can see across this entire plain, forward and backward, yet can't see anyone else?" But as they crossed, their companions reappeared.

"Each Mode is a different universe," Nona said. "We see all of each that is in our line of sight, yet we are crossing a section of each only ten paces across, but infinitely wide."

"Infinitely wide?"

"Think of a layer cake. Cut a slice across the layers and lay it flat. We are like ants walking across the thin edges of those layers. Each seems narrow, but extends to the side to the edge of the cake. The Modes have not been literally cut; the Virtual Mode merely intersects them without damaging them. But we are the only ants that can walk it; the folk of the intervening Modes can't."

"But I understood that we of the DoOon Mode could do so."

"That's because the DoOon Mode is now an anchor Mode. There are five anchors, each fixing a different real Mode. But it's not safe for inexperienced people to travel a Virtual Mode, and they can't gain much, because all the neighboring Modes are barren, as you see. So Ddwng needs the Chip, so he can make his own Virtual Modes. Then he will be able to make far more productive connections."

"It is becoming intelligible as I experience it. But I would soon be lost by myself."

"Exactly. Only the anchor people have any awareness of their location. You are an anchor person, but lack experience. Soon you will be more comfortable here."

"I am glad of that."

"There is something else," Nona said. "Do not try to transport anything from one Mode to another."

"Why not?" Tom asked.

She smiled. "Try it and see."

He stooped to pick up a stone. They crossed to the next mode. The stone was no longer in his hand. They crossed back, and it was on the ground at the edge. "It didn't go," he said, surprised. "I held it, but it vanished."

"Yes. The same goes for food. If you eat and cross, you will lose what you just ate. That's why we carry our own supplies. There are exceptions, but you see the underlying problem."

He nodded. "Our training did not make this clear."

"You had little way to know."

They crossed again—and there were all the other members of the party, spread out to the sides. "Ddwng will be sending a party to track us," Colene said. "Now we will lose ourselves, so the trail gets confusing, then goes dead."

"A tracking party?" Tom asked. "How can you know that?"

"I read his cesspool mind."

"But your telepathic horse is not here."

"I have developed a bit of telepathy of my own." Now that they were safely away from the DoOon Mode, Colene evidently felt free to let it be known.

"But only anchor people can cross the Modes," Nona protested. "Remember, when we conveyed Slick and Esta to Provos' Mode, we had to tie them to us so they would not get lost."

"Provos," Cat said. "I remember her. But not the other names."

"They were an uncle and a niece who were in an impossible situation on Earth, my home Mode," Colene said. "We took them to another Mode, where they had a new life." She glanced at Nona. "You're right: only anchor persons, which all of us here are, can use a Virtual Mode. But Ddwng is devious. He arranged to have a whole group of anchors: the six Feline and Caprine nulls in training, and four others they didn't know about. Those four will be able to take the hands of nonanchor people, and enable them to cross Modes. We'd have been patsies, if I hadn't read his foul mind. But without competent guidance or prior experience, they won't be able to do much, because all the adjacent Modes are barren. That's why they'll be following us, because they know that we know the way to healthy Modes. That's also why we have to lose them. They'll have a hell of a time finding anything useful on their own."

"What objection do you have to being followed?" Cat asked. "These are not your Modes, and you will be unlikely to suffer any harm."

"We don't want harm to come to *any* Mode," Nona said. "They all have a right to live in peace."

Cat nodded. "Now I understand."

"Darius agreed to deliver the Chip," Colene said. "He did not agree to provide a map to the Virtual Mode, for all that it changes every time an anchor changes. So we will make our own way to his Mode, fetch the Chip, turn it over to you, and see that you get safely back to DoOon. Until then, we want no interference by Ddwng. Can you live with that?"

Cat considered. "Yes."

"So will you help us lose the pursuit?"

Cat considered again. "Yes."

Pussy clapped her hands. "Oh, good!"

Nona was surprised. "You want us to foil Ddwng?"

Pussy looked at Cat. "How can I answer that?"

"With your feeling," Cat said. "Which is separate from your duty."

Pussy looked at Nona. "When Colene saved our nulls from the dragon, now and in the future, we became emotionally loyal to her and to your party. We love you in our way, and want to help you in any way we can. The Caprines feel the same way. We can't go against our mission, but anything else that pleases you pleases us. We—" She looked again at Cat, who nodded. "Can we tell you something in private?"

"We will not betray your secrets," Darius said. "We hope never to see Ddwng again."

"We don't much like Ddwng ourselves," Pussy said. "He is merciless. The dragons ate us—ate all nulls— partly to show the emperor's absolute power over us. And the Swine reflect his attitude, brutalizing the other nulls in turn. What you did, and how you enforce it, with the promise of the Chip—maybe you didn't do it for us, but we do love you for it."

"I did the dragon bit for you," Colene said. "Darius took the chain for me. But it was also partly because we knew you would be loyal to us. We value that. Our lives may be dependent on you, as we traverse unknown aspects of the Virtual Mode. There is something else you need to know: there is a danger to me alone. Some kind of Mode Monster is after my mind, and when it orients on me, I'm helpless. All the others can do is get me off the Virtual Mode in a hurry. That's why we landed so suddenly in the DoOon Mode: I had to get off the Virtual Mode. It can't follow me onto a regular Mode. So when it orients on me again, we'll have to get off again, wherever we are, and if it doesn't go away, we'll have to free another anchor. Don't worry about yours; only you can free that. So the Virtual Mode will change, but you will still be able to get home. So chances are at some point, maybe soon, we'll have to get off, and I'll be helpless, so we'll need your help to manage. We wouldn't want to risk it if you hated us, but as it is, you're okay."

"We will help you," Cat agreed. "We did not know of this."

"We didn't want you to. But most of our personal secrets will come out, during this trek. We need to trust each other."

"We shall do our best to be worthy of that trust," Cat said.

"We know you will. We all need each other, and we may not all survive." Colene smiled without humor. "If I die, one of you may have to marry Darius, or be his mistress."

"One of us?" Pussy said. "I am barred from—"

"I said if I die. Then you would not be barred from doing anything with him, because it would not complicate his loyalties. He would still fetch the Chip. But he would need a woman, and it may not be Nona."

Nona felt a chill. So Colene did know that she didn't want to do it. Her telepathy made concealment impossible.

"If that were the case," Pussy said carefully, "then I would do whatever he wished."

"Actually he would prefer Doe to you," Colene said. "But no doubt you would do."

Nona saw that the girl's dolor was returning. She was teasing them with thoughts of her demise, and tempting fate. It was her way to take suicidal risks, and pushing Pussy at Darius was exactly such a risk.

"Do not tease her," Darius said. "It is a woman for the drawing that I need."

"The drawing?" Pussy asked, blanching.

"The drawing of joy. As I did with you to restore Nona. In my own Mode I must take a wife not for love but for the drawing."

Pussy visibly stiffened her resolve. "I would do whatever you require of me."

"But he would never require that," Colene said. "It is necessary but cruel. He would find some other woman for that."

"I hope you do not die," Pussy said to Colene. "But I will do what is required of me regardless."

"You would do just fine as his mistress," Colene said.

Nona wanted to stop this treacherous dialogue, but didn't know how. The girl's dolor was becoming poisonous.

"But while you live," Cat said firmly, "we Felines will do all in our power to serve you, and Pussy will not be available to Darius in any such capacity."

"I know it," Colene said. Cat had evidently seen the need, and done what was required. "Now let's mix up our trail. It's late, and we're getting tired, but this is something we have to do first. We need to find water or something that will mess up our scent trail, and see what else we can do to erase our traces. Once we give them the slip, chances are they'll never find us again. Any ideas?"

"On occasion we have played with mazes," Cat said. "When I was young, I was for a time deceived by one that consisted of concentric circles with barriers and apertures. We had to start at the outside and make our way into the center. The key was that sometimes it was necessary to proceed outward, not merely inward."

"Got it," Colene said. "I've seen that type. You figure they'll be looking for us forward, and if we duck backward toward DoOon it may fool them."

"It may," Cat agreed. "However, I would be wary of using an idea I suggest, because I am of DoOon, and others of my Mode are likely to think similarly."

"Still, it's a good idea," Colene said. "We'll start with it, and then see what else we come up with."

They proceeded sidewise along the Mode segment, so that all of them were in sight, then crossed back to a prior Mode, forward again, and back. Their party snaked in and out of view as they maneuvered; Tom showed his continuing surprise as they winked on and off.

"One becomes accustomed to it," Nona said. "Also, one learns never to take a Mode crossing for granted. These have all been what we call continuous: very similar to each other. But sometimes there are sharp breaks. Those can be amusing, or deadly. Stay close to me until you are accustomed to it, and your caution is automatic."

"May I comment?"

"Of course you may, Tom! You don't need my permission."

"I will of course obey your slightest stricture. But I find your directive to remain close to you appealing."

That reminded her. Tom loved her, and it was her fault. He might be just a servant in his home Mode, but this was something no servant should have to endure. What was she to do? Some other person might just ignore it, but she was unable to do that. "I wish I could free you of that emotion, Tom. You know I do not return it."

"There is no need for you to be concerned. You are the mistress."

But she *was* concerned. She brooded as they crossed

Modes, but came to no suitable conclusion.

They crossed to another Mode—and there were Cat and Burgess, with the others to the side. "We have discovered a discontinuity," Cat said. "The following Mode is a seemingly endless sea. We believe that Burgess can carry us across it, singly, leaving no permanent trail."

"Singly," Nona said. "That means that some of us will have to be alone in a Mode while waiting our turns for transport."

"This is true. I will go first, and will wait alone while Burgess returns for another."

"Why you? Surely it should be one of the experienced Virtual Mode travelers."

"I lack the emotion the gendered folk have. I can handle it. The question to be decided is who will be last. That one will also have to be alone for a time."

"I'll do it," Tom said.

Nona wanted to protest, but she knew why he was volunteering. If he were lost, she would have no problem about his disposition. It was a cruel equation, but perhaps valid. So she remained silent, and hated herself for it.

Cat climbed carefully onto Burgess, and the two disappeared forward. The others waited. "You know, when we were in DoOon the first time," Colene said, "I didn't like you nulls at all. But now I know you better, and you're real people. Good people. I think you'll be a real help on this journey."

"Thank you," Pussy said. "But so far we have not helped enough. We need to do you favors every day."

"I thought that was turned off for this mission," Nona said.

"It is," Tom said. "But we still feel better doing it."

"Well, crossing first does it for Cat, and crossing last does it for you," Colene said. "And I guess Pussy did it by being so nice about what I said before. I shouldn't have said it. But there'll be plenty of times we need each other's help."

They waited, looking across the barren plain. It was hard to imagine water being so close.

Burgess returned. "I'll go," Pussy said.

Darius shrugged. "All of us will go in due course. The order doesn't matter."

Pussy got on Burgess, and they disappeared. At intervals, Colene and Darius followed. Nona felt increasingly nervous when it was just two of them remaining. The Virtual Mode was eerie at the best of times, and this was definitely not that. Suppose there was some problem ahead? What would they do?

Tom put his strong arm around her shoulder. Nona discovered that she really appreciated his proffered comfort. "Thank you, Tom."

Burgess returned, and Nona went. She looked back at Tom, standing alone, and felt a pang. It simply was not kind to leave him isolated. Then he disappeared, and she found a great sea beneath them. Burgess was wafting across it, unhampered by the water; airborne, he could handle most terrains, provided they were fairly level and he had sufficient room.

She gazed ahead, and spied a bare island. She hoped they were not headed for that, but they were. As they drew close, suddenly the others appeared, standing on it.

Nona dismounted, and Burgess turned back. "This is a way station," Colene said. "We'll jump from here to another, to make it harder to trace. The pursuit will need boats, and they won't know where to take them."

"It will be hard to hold hands while managing a boat," Nona said.

"Yes. Between that and our hidden trail, they won't get far."

Soon Burgess returned with Tom. Pussy hugged him. "Was it lonely?"

"Yes. I didn't dare move, lest I be not there when Burgess returned."

"Oh, you can move around some," Colene said. "Burgess won't desert you on a technicality."

"Then maybe I will explore while waiting."

They made the next jump, to a larger island crossed by several Mode divisions. Cat was the first, again, and Tom the last. Then they jumped to land, having crossed the sea.

But this time Burgess returned without Tom. The Feline had not been there, and had not appeared. Burgess had looked, but not found him.

Nona felt a thrill of alarm. "We must find him!"

"We'll go back and search," Darius said. "He must have stepped across a Mode, and lost track of the one Burgess came to."

"I'll go back first," Nona said.

No one argued. She was Tom's closest companion, apart from the other Felines.

Burgess carried her back. The island was empty. "Tom!" she called. "Tom! Where are you?" But of course he was not in the Mode, and could not hear her.

She walked across the island. It was almost level and barren. She could see that Tom was nowhere on it. Had he somehow fallen into the water and drowned? Yet she knew he could swim.

"Burgess, let's circle the island," she said, trying to keep her voice calm. There was little in the universe quite so final as being lost on a Virtual Mode. "We must be missing something." How could he have disappeared?

Burgess carried her in a loop around the island. Its shoreline jumped back and forth slightly as they crossed Mode boundaries, showing that it had not weathered evenly in adjacent Modes.

They completed the circuit of the island. Tom never

appeared. Nona's nervousness increased. What could have happened to him?

She had a horrible thought. "The DoOon pursuers, could they have come and gotten him?" She wished she could communicate directly with Burgess; he could understand her, but his thoughts were opaque to her. She didn't have Colene's mind-reading talent. "No, that's impossible; even if they are following, they could do it that fast—and why would they give themselves away? They want Tom with us."

What were they to do? She couldn't just leave Tom here, yet neither could she find him. She just couldn't accept the idea that he had drowned. He wouldn't be that careless.

"Go around again, closer," she said. Burgess obliged, floating right at the edge of the island, so that the land was on their right, the water on their left. The shore flickered under them as they crossed Modes, never varying very far.

Then, suddenly, it changed. They were over land, extending as far as she could see. "It's a discontinuity!" she exclaimed. "But how could it be here—with no sidewise extension?" Yet it was the case, for in a moment the water returned.

They explored it, and found that it was a mere patch of a Mode, an island of its own, entirely surrounded by sea Modes. It had no sidewise extension. "So the layer cake analogy is not completely correct," she said. "Modes can overlay intermittently."

Tom was still gone, but now she had a hint of how he could have gotten lost. He could have walked around the island—and suddenly found himself here. And if there were another Mode of this type—"Cover every part of this island Mode," she said. "There must be another discontinuity."

Burgess floated in a pattern back and forth, canvassing

the spot Mode. Each time he passed back into the sea Modes, he turned around.

Then he spun around so suddenly that Nona almost slid off. "What's the matter?" she cried, grasping one of his contact points.

The thought came back: a picture of an abyss.

"Oh, another Mode. A discontinuity!" She climbed off, then got on her belly and crawled toward the place where he had balked. It looked like an endless plain, but as her head crossed the Mode line, she found herself peering down into an abyss. No, it was a landscape set significantly lower than the one they were in. That was why Burgess had balked: his forward sensors had picked it up, and he had reversed before plunging into it. Because he could not fly; he floated, on a roiling cushion of air trapped between his body and the ground. He might have cushioned his fall somewhat, if he landed upright, but then would not be able to return.

She angled her head so that she could look back. There was a mountain rising in the direction pointed at by her now-unseen feet. Its peak was at her present level. Too bad that mountain didn't quite coincide with their island; then they could safely step from one Mode to the other.

Then she realized that this new Mode might be the same, only without the water. That mountain *was* the island, near but not identical. If Tom had fallen here—

"Nona!"

She turned her head again, orienting on the sound. There was Tom, coming into view about twenty feet below, carrying a stone. "Tom!" she cried, enormously relieved. "Are you all right?"

"It was a hard landing, but we Felines are good at landings. I fell, and could not return. The neighboring Modes are rock or water."

And he could not simply step into deep rock. He might step into water, and swim to the top, but then he would fall again when he tried to cross back to this Mode. He might have been able to swim around it—but not if it was a regular one, with infinitely extending sides. He had to cross *here*—and couldn't leap high enough to reach this level of land.

"What are you doing?" she asked.

"Piling rocks from the sides, to make a mound high enough."

That made sense. Then he could jump from the top of the rock pile to this Mode. "It will be easier to pull you up with a rope," she said. "Darius has one. It has to be an anchor Mode rope, to reach across Modes."

"That sounds good," he said.

She drew her head back across the boundary. "Burgess, leave me here. Fetch Darius back. We need his rope to rescue Tom."

Burgess floated away and disappeared in a moment. She turned back to Tom, poking her head across. "How did this happen?"

"I was walking around the isle, then found myself in a land Mode, and then suddenly fell. I had never suspected something like this."

"Neither did we, and we're experienced Virtual Mode travelers. An island discontinuity connecting to a waterless section of a Mode. We've never seen this combination before. Oh, Tom, I'm glad you weren't hurt!"

"Thank you, Nona. I regret being a nuisance."

"It was an accident! Not your fault that you fell."

He paused. "That, too," he agreed. Then he laughed, and she realized that her statement had indeed had a double meaning. He had fallen in love, and then physically, but both were nuisances to her.

Soon Burgess returned, carrying Darius. Darius wore a coil of rope around a shoulder, for just such occasions. Normal rope from a nonanchor realm could not cross the Mode boundaries by itself. It could be carried across, but became discontinuous, and could not be used to haul farther than whatever Mode it was in.

Darius lay on the ground beside her and poked his head across. "This is interesting," he said. "This route is by no means obvious. Perhaps we should take it instead of the one we have been using. The DoOon folk may never find it."

Nona hadn't thought of that. "But can we reach our anchors from here?"

"I suspect we can. Any route will do; the problem is with the discontinuities, physical hazards, or living threats. The island Mode section serves as a link to another normal Mode segment that should return us to normal land at some point."

"All right," she agreed. "If the others care to try it."

He withdrew his head to talk to Burgess. "We'll be back in a moment," she called to Tom, then followed him.

Burgess was already going, leaving Darius behind. "He will ferry the others here. If they don't agree, we can haul Tom up and continue island hopping."

"That's fair," she agreed.

He looked at her. "Nona, while we are alone—you don't wish to marry me?"

"Colene told?"

"Yes. When I thought about it, I realized that your aversion is natural. You need a man who will appreciate you for yourself, not your magic or your joy."

"That's true. No offense to you, Darius; you're an ideal man. But I would not take you from Colene if I could, and would not wish any ill to her to make you available. I think I must go my own way."

"Have you considered Tom?"

"Tom? He's a null."

"When I traveled with Doe, I came to realize that the nulls are fully human inside, and worthy of fully human relationships. Tom has qualities I think you should appreciate. He loves you without concern for your magic, which he has never seen, or your joy, which does not relate in my absence. I doubt you will find another man who is not conscious of these things."

She was amazed. "But you need a vessel of undiminishable joy, so you can love Colene."

"Not at the price of your happiness. I could marry Pussy in the normal manner of my profession, and provide her with a normal retirement thereafter. I think that would still be better for her than what she faces in her home Mode."

"But Colene doesn't want you with Pussy!"

"Colene suggested it."

She stared at him. "Mind reading must be very liberalizing."

"It is. Colene is a realist, and she likes Pussy. But if Pussy does not return to DoOon, that leaves the Feline trio incomplete. If you cared to take Tom—"

"What of Cat?"

"He will carry the Chip back. He can do that alone. Then he could return to join us in my Mode."

"So we would all be together at the end," she said, seeing it. "That does appeal."

"Colene would like us to be together. But we are missing Seqiro. That is the complication."

"That is the complication," she agreed. "I will consider the matter."

Then she put her head back to talk to Tom. "We're bringing the others here," she said. "We may follow you though this Mode."

"This is feasible?"

"We think so."

Then a hand touched Nona's ankle. She recognized Colene's touch. She drew back.

"Seems good to me," Colene said. "I see Darius talked to you."

"He suggested Tom."

"You sure don't have to. We're just trying to patch things together for when we finally get off the Virtual Mode. Maybe it's a bad idea."

"I don't know. I just never thought of Tom in that manner."

"I know. But if it weren't for Darius and my hang-up, I could see being with Tom. So I figured you might too."

Nona was still trying to orient on the idea. "I will consider the matter," she repeated.

The others arrived. Then they used the rope to lower themselves down one by one to join Tom. Nona was first. When she reached the ground, Tom caught her, to steady her. She turned into him and kissed him.

He was astonished. "I do not understand."

"Neither do I," she said. "Consider it your reward for not getting killed. You must promise not to get lost like this again."

"I will try," he said humbly.

Burgess was the anchor for the rope. When it was his turn, they worked together to build up the rock pile Tom had started, so that it formed a rough ramp to the other level. Burgess was able to jolt slowly down that, with their help.

They considered whether to remove the ramp, and decided not to, because they might need it themselves if they had to return this way. It would be a giveaway of their passage here, if the DoOons found this site, but probably the DoOons would already know.

They followed the new Mode's side extension, poking at the boundaries every so often. Sometimes there was water, and sometimes impenetrable rock. But in time this slice rose, until they were able to cross to the shore of another. Thereafter they proceeded normally, crossing from Mode to barren Mode.

The first vegetation appeared. Nona made an exclamation of delight. "We're getting beyond the ruined Modes!"

Colene paused, looking strange. "Are you all right?" Pussy asked.

The girl's eyes were dreamy. "I think I feel Seqiro."

"He's finding us?" Nona asked, thrilled. For the horse's powerful mind was able to link them all together telepathically, and to provide them with each other's powers, to an extent. His return, even if it were only mental, would make a phenomenal difference.

"Yes, to a degree. He hasn't located us specifically, but he's orienting on our party, and the rapport should get stronger as we go. At first we'll just be linking minds, but as he closes in it will get stronger. Oh, Seqiro! How I missed you!"

Now Nona felt the faint touch on her mind, and knew it was true. It was like hearing a distant melody, but it was definitely Seqiro, and she liked him too.

"This is the telepathic horse?" Cat asked. "The one who foiled Ddwng before?"

"Yes," Darius said. "But I will honor my commitment. Seqiro will help us get safely through."

"This telepathy," Pussy said. "Will we Felines feel it too?"

"You may," Colene said. "I may be able to project to you; then you'll know. When it becomes complete, we'll all be able to know each other's minds without speaking."

"Is this necessary?" Tom asked.

Nona believed she understood his reticence. "You prefer that I not receive your thoughts?"

"I fear they would embarrass you."

Colene glanced at him. "I doubt it. But you can ask Seqiro to cut you out of the circuit. Mind sharing brings tolerance."

They walked on, crossing the Modes, orienting on an anchor. Nona wasn't sure which one. That was the nature

of traveling the Virtual Mode: they had an awareness of
anchors, but couldn't necessarily distinguish between
them until they got close to one. But they were definitely
making progress.

FIVE

❦❦❦

Earth

Burgess felt it the moment Seqiro's questing mind found them. He liked the horse, because he made communication and understanding easy. Burgess had felt isolated when they lost the horse in the DoOon Mode. Only Colene's faint telepathy and the good will of the others had sustained him. Fortunately he had come to understand their auditory utterances well enough to get along, and when one of them touched one of his contact points he could answer to a crude degree. But there was no substitute for the oneness they had had before. Now he was coming back into their hive, and it was wonderful.

They were crossing Modes, and Cat was with him. Cat had made a special and continuing effort to relate, and that had helped. Cat had become his companion when the others were busy, and now Cat was almost as easy to relate to as Colene. But none of them could match Seqiro.

They had traveled far, and were increasingly tired, so when they came again to the living Modes, they sought a place to rest. Burgess was good at odors, and soon found a region that was clean and healthy. It was by a pond in a river, where fish swam, and there were no large predators. There were fruiting trees and edible plants, but the others did not eat them, because either they would lose the sustenance when they crossed Modes, or would digest it and have it become part of them, eventually complicating their ability to return to their anchor Modes. Burgess, however, had no choice; he fed constantly on tiny debris in the air. Still, their time in the DoOon anchor Mode had restored him considerably, and he was in no immediate difficulty.

He searched around and assembled a pile of small spherical stones. If anything did attack in the night, he would blow those out his aft trunk with sufficient force to discourage further intrusion. If that did not suffice, they could all move across a Mode boundary, and the threat would be gone. A boundary was always within about one human body length, so it was not hard to do.

The others made a temporary shelter of local materials and settled down beneath it. That was all right, as none of its substance was crossing the boundaries. They had to place it carefully so that it did not overlap a second Mode, because the extra would simply vanish.

Burgess let his air subside to subsistence level, his carapace coming to rest on the ground. Cat came to join him. The others paired off, Darius with Colene, Pussy next to Colene, and Tom with Nona. All of their thoughts were slowly growing louder as the ambiance of Seqiro's mind slowly coalesced. Darius and Colene loved each other; this was a concept Burgess had slowly come to know as he associated with them. But their love was as yet imperfect, because she had had bad prior experience and could not banish it from her memory. Tom loved Nona, but Nona did not love Tom. She was however intrigued by him, and considering whether he would make a sufficient match for her. She was tempted to indulge him sexually, but was afraid he would take it too seriously.

There was something else. They were in the weak ambiance of Seqiro's mind, but that was not the only questing force. A more distant, hostile, deadly mind was also searching. It was the mind predator that had fixed on Colene. It wanted to consume her. It had been pursuing her when they entered the DoOon Mode and won reprieve, for it could not range into an anchor universe. It was a thing of the Virtual Mode. Each time that shifted, as it did when they changed an anchor, the predator lost its orientation and had to begin again. But as Colene's mental powers slowly increased, she was becoming a stronger beacon for the predator. Now with Seqiro's mind enhancing hers, she would be a brighter beacon. There was trouble coming.

But that was not immediate. Perhaps they would complete their journey and be off the Virtual Mode before the predator found her again. Burgess hoped so, for he liked Colene best of his fellows in the hive.

He relaxed, and let the night pass.

In the morning the party roused itself and performed its ablutions. The females, particularly, preferred to wash themselves periodically. That was why they chose to camp beside a lake or pond or river: it was a ready source of water for immersion.

"Who's for a swim?" Colene demanded as she stripped away her clothing. She had a danger-seeking nature in certain respects; women were not supposed to allow men to see their bodies, except in the case of their committed partners. That meant that Tom Feline should not gaze on Colene's body. Therefore she arranged to show that body. It was her way of daring fate.

Nona joined her. She was not danger seeking, but neither was she as much concerned about social proprieties.

She had a remarkably appealing face and form, as the minds of the two human males indicated.

Pussy also came. Her lightly furred body required no clothing except when the environment was bad, though she normally did wear some.

The three of them plunged into the water. Colene screamed: it was chill. But she was game. "Come on, men!" she called.

Darius and Tom accepted the invitation and joined them. "You too," Colene called to Cat and Burgess. So they too came. Burgess always enjoyed such hive games.

The six of them splashed in the water, getting clean. Burgess floated just above the surface and dipped his trunks. He sucked water into his fore trunk and jetted it out his aft trunk, soaking them all. The screams doubled, but they liked it. They could readily escape it by ducking across a Mode boundary, if they chose; the jet of water would not follow them. As it was, they remained in a confined section of the pond, so as to remain in a single Mode section.

Soon, thoroughly chilled and clean, they left the water and ran along the ground. Again the three females made an impression on the two males, as they intended to. Something about the way the flesh on their chests and lower hind torsos moved. Burgess enjoyed feeling their minds as they played this game of show and see. The females pretended not to be aware of the attention, and the males pretended not to be paying it. Both knew better, especially since they were all sharing each other's minds to an increasing extent.

"And now you Felines know what it's like on the Virtual Mode when it's good," Colene said as they dressed. "We have no secrets from each other, especially when Seqiro is near."

"It is a remarkably relaxed scene," Cat said. Cat, being

neuter, had no sexual inclination, but did appreciate social interaction.

They ate from their packs, and stepped in turns across a Mode line for elimination of bodily wastes. Unlike Burgess, whose processes of assimilation and elimination were continuous, they stored their wastes inside their bodies for a time, then expelled them in liquid or solid masses. Only their breathing followed Burgess' way, constantly taking in a vital nutrient and passing out a waste gas. Life had many mechanisms of processing.

They resumed their trek. Because they were now traversing living territory, their route was irregular, in contrast to the straightforward progress across the barren Modes. They had to go around trees and brush, and were wary of wild animals. In time they came to another discontinuity: suddenly the next Mode, instead of being a land, water, and vegetation scene, was something else. Something new to all of them.

"What do you make of it?" Darius inquired of the others as they put only their heads through the boundary and gazed at the confusion before them. Burgess put an eye stalk through. The scene was so different as to be difficult to assimilate.

"Something must have come and chopped up this landscape and scrambled the pieces," Nona said. "It reminds me of something."

"An avalanche?" Cat asked.

"That should be a pile," Darius said. "This seems to be suspended." He poked a hand through and touched a segment of vertically standing ground, and it moved. There was no sky above it; instead there were irregular segments of sky in the jumble.

"A jigsaw puzzle!" Colene exclaimed. "A Three-Dee puzzle, with the pieces scrambled."

"Please clarify," Cat said. Burgess appreciated that; the

girl was nice despite being a vessel of dolor, but her concepts could be confusing.

"At home on Earth, we have puzzles that are pictures, and they are cut up into a bunch of little curvy pieces and mixed up. The challenge is to put them together so that the picture is there again. Some are easy, some are so difficult they can take weeks. Each piece fits in only one place, but dozens of pieces look almost the same, so it's hard to figure out. Some of them are in three dimensions, so that when you put them together they form, oh, maybe a castle standing on a mound. Those can be real bruisers."

"How are we to pass this?" Pussy asked. "There's no path."

"There's no *scene*," Nona said. "The very substance of this world seems to have been taken apart."

"Maybe we have to make a path," Colene said. She put her hands on a piece of tree, and brought it toward her. It was about the thickness of her body, and part of it was green. She stood it up with the green at the top, and it remained in place.

"A puzzle Mode," Pussy said. "This is interesting." She took a piece of sky and pushed it up over her head.

"It seems to be malleable," Cat said. "We shall have to make a path for Burgess." From the start of their association, Cat had been attuned to Burgess' nature and problems, perhaps because the two of them were different from the others, albeit in different ways. Burgess was completely alien, physically, and to a significant degree mentally. Cat differed by being genderless and unemotional. Both were accepted by the others, but their differences would never abate.

"Maybe we had better see how many of these scramble Modes there are," Colene said.

"I may be able to explore ahead," Nona said. "I am recovering a bit of my magic, so may be able to levitate, and to move segments by telekinesis. If you can read my mind across the Modes, perhaps I can find a way through."

"Seqiro's connection is getting stronger," Colene said. "Maybe you can."

"I'll go with you," Tom said.

"Thank you." Burgess felt the woman's turmoil of emotions. She liked Tom, but did not love him, and love was important to her. So she was treating him politely while she considered whether there was any prospect for more. Meanwhile, she could not have a more ardent protector. That was important, here on the Virtual Mode, because danger could strike as readily as surprise.

Nona and Tom pushed their way across the boundary, and found themselves in the middle of a truly confusing disarray. Segments of ground, forest, river, and sky were intermixed, oriented different ways. It was indeed like Colene's concept of a cut-out puzzle, except that this was reality. When Nona touched a piece of ground, her body oriented to stand on it as if vertical, though she wasn't. When Tom reached into a section of sky, he oriented so as to be standing below it, though that meant that he was not aligned with Nona. Each piece of the puzzle had its own alignment to impose on those who touched it.

They moved pieces, getting skies aligned above, trees beside, and ground below, slowly forming a path. They stood on that path and reached for other pieces to extend it, and suddenly were at the next Mode boundary. This Mode was similarly scrambled, so they were able to continue. They passed through several, gaining proficiency.

Then they faded out. "I can't heeear you!" Colene called, stepping onto the path behind them.

They heard her, and turned back. But they had accomplished a fair amount. The path was not broad enough for Burgess, but it made the traverse easier for the others. It was a feasible way to cross the puzzle Modes, in time.

Nona and Tom returned, and the hive consulted. "It is

evident that we can cross," Darius said. "But it will be tedious—and what of the pursuit? Do we want to leave a clear path for Ddwng's men to follow?"

"We'll have to mess it up behind us," Colene said.

"But we need a way back to deliver the Chip."

"It is perhaps academic," Cat said. "When I deliver the Chip, they will know my route, and will be able to make new ones."

There was something devious in a mind, and Burgess was surprised to discover that it wasn't Colene's, but Darius' mind. But it was quickly suppressed. "True," Darius said. "If they find their way to this region, it may not matter."

"So let's widen the path Tom and Nona made, and start crossing Modes," Colene said. "The puzzle can't last forever."

Tom and Nona went back to the end of their path, while the others went to work broadening it. Burgess was unable to help with this, as the pieces were too large for his trunks, and he was able to follow only when the path had been broadened. So he maintained a rear guard, watching for any danger behind.

It took them several days to cross the puzzle Modes, but they came to enjoy working together on the challenge. Tom was a hard laborer, and quick to respond to Nona's cues, and she liked that. She was able to use a little magic to move pieces, but it was as easy to do it by hand. Seqiro's mind was still orienting on them, slowly closing on their specific presence. But so was the mind predator. Colene wasn't aware of it yet, but she would be when it found her.

They had to get into the vicinity of an anchor Mode. *Any* anchor Mode. Because that was Colene's only respite, once the predator caught up with her.

At last they made it through the puzzle—only to encounter another challenge. The following Modes were explosive. They resembled a war scene, but there was no fighting, indeed no large creatures—just continuing explosions.

They stood just beyond the boundary, contemplating the devastation. Every few minutes there was another blast, but without seeming cause. The surface of the lake detonated, spraying water in a sphere, and subsided. What was doing this?

"I will check ahead," Tom said.

"Not alone, you won't," Nona said. "We don't know how much worse it may be in the following Modes."

"We don't want to risk any members of the party unnecessarily," Darius said. "We have not encountered actual danger so far, but it may be ahead."

Burgess could do a limited exploration, and return quickly, so they would have information. He was less subject to physical changes than the others were, because he could float over water or thick vegetation.

Cat caught his thought, in the growing ambiance of Seqiro's mind. "Burgess and I will make a quick check, while others study the local situation." Then, before a consensus against it could develop, Cat climbed onto Burgess, and Burgess jetted into the next Mode.

It was much the same, with explosions near and far in an otherwise placid scene. The third and fourth Modes were similar. They looped back before chance could produce an explosion in their immediate vicinity. In a moment the remainder of their party reappeared.

"Similar," Cat reported. "I think we had best cross these Modes rapidly, because the explosions seem to be random."

But Burgess was picking up on something else. He analyzed the material that passed through him on a continuing basis, in order to assimilate its nutritive elements. There was rich food here. Of course it couldn't do him much good, because whatever he imbibed was gone the moment he crossed a Mode boundary, unless he lingered long enough to assimilate it into his substance. Even that wasn't ideal, because the more substance he assimilated on the Virtual Mode, the less of an anchor Mode remained, fudging his identity. Too much, and he could lose his ability to cross the boundaries. That was true for all of them. So they did not want to take in more than they had to. Air and water they could not avoid, but anything more they tried to minimize. So the very richness of this food was dangerous in its fashion.

That was only part of it, however. The food consisted of microscopically small particles that were living entities. "Plankton," Cat said, interpreting the concept for the others. "Microscopic algae and protozoa, the foundation of life for many realms. The water and air here are suffused with tiny creatures, like the plankton of the seas of our home worlds."

Not the variety any of them had known before, however. There was something special about what was here. Burgess was taking in great numbers of these creatures, and ejecting greater numbers.

"What?" Cat asked, thinking it had misread.

Burgess focused on the ongoing process. He seemed to be ejecting twice as many creatures as he was taking in. This did not seem to make sense, yet it was so.

"Step on it before it reproduces," Colene said, smiling. Then she paused thoughtfully. "*Could* they be reproducing?"

There was the key. They were fissioning, dividing into parts. Each part was smaller than the original, but a fully functioning entity. Also—and this was odder yet—they seemed to be releasing energy as they fissioned.

"Nuclear fission!" Colene exclaimed. "Back home on Earth we make bombs that do that." To her the only real Earth was her origin world, though most of the Modes they passed through were similar. If they were not, the air and gravity would differ too much to permit the travelers to survive.

"That might explain the explosions," Cat said. "Clumps of plankton fissioning together. Perhaps if we can understand the system, we can navigate these Modes safely."

"That seems apt," Darius agreed.

"Maybe I can help," Nona said. "I feel my magic increasing. If I can make them familiars, I will better fathom their nature."

Burgess remembered the process. Nona could reach out with her magical mind and infuse the mind of some wild creature, taming it to her will. She could then perceive through its senses. This could be quite helpful on occasion, such as when she used the eyes of a flying bird to spy out the surrounding territory.

"Thank you," Nona murmured. She was indeed getting her magic back, for now she was understanding his thoughts without touching him.

"No, that's me," Colene said. "Seqiro is enhancing my ability, and I'm linking you. Nona's talent is magic, not mind reading. What she's recovered is only a tiny sliver of her full power."

"But let's see what I can do," Nona said. "I must first identify with you, making you a familiar. Then, through you, I'll see what I can do with the plankton." She took hold of two of Burgess' contact points and focused her mind. He felt her merging with him, identifying with him so that his senses became hers. It was pleasant, for she was a nice person, and she was doing this with his acquiescence.

As she took hold of his senses, she enhanced them. He was able to orient on the plankton passing through his system with increasing focus. Now he saw that it was not a conglomeration of mixed species, but a single type of creature, an amoeba of a type unknown on any of the worlds the members of their party had known. It leached energy from the environment and converted some of it to mass, growing larger. Some it stored in its tissue. But when it got crowded, it fissioned, dividing rapidly into two or more fragments with the release of the extra energy in a burst that flung the parts far away.

"Just like nuclear fission!" Colene said. "Only this is living fission."

"It must be a survival strategy," Darius said. "The new entities get hurled out to new territory to colonize."

"But what sets them off?" Colene asked.

Nona and Burgess explored further, and discovered the trigger: when the amoebae were crowded beyond a certain point, they fissioned. The crowding they got being sucked into Burgess set them off so that their number doubled and was rapidly ejected. This also accounted for the explosions: whenever the amoebae got too crowded, they fissioned, flinging their offspring out around the neighborhood. That guaranteed that they would constantly land in less-crowded places, where they could absorb more energy.

"So what we need is to avoid concentrations of amoebae, and we won't be caught in an explosion," Colene said. "We should be able to do that by going carefully. Meanwhile we can relax for the night."

They relaxed, eating and settling for the night in the last of the puzzle Modes, where there was no risk of explosion. The scrambled pieces around them turned dark around their path.

But in the morning there was trouble. Colene was breathing hard. "The mind monster," she gasped. "It's found me!"

That was apparent, for they shared her mind and felt the horror of it. The thing was drawing her into its dark center, seeking to digest her very being.

Pussy went to her and put her arms around the shuddering body. "I will shield you."

"You can't do it physically," Nona said. "It's her mind, her soul it's after."

"But she's helping," Colene said. "Pussy *is* shielding me some. The mind predator's not as bad now."

"Yes, I am helping," Pussy said. But now she too was hurting; Burgess could feel it. She was taking some of Colene's pain on herself, diluting it by sharing. But it would get worse, and in the end overwhelm them both.

"We have to get her to an anchor," Darius said urgently.

"We've been moving toward one," Nona said. "But we still have a fair way to go—many Modes to cross."

That was true, but there might be a way to enhance their progress. If they could harness the plankton creatures, Burgess might be able to move much more rapidly than normal, and carry them along.

"This might work," Cat said. "We would need to funnel more amoebae in to you, so that you could condense them faster and make them fission faster."

"I can do that," Nona said. "I can use my telekinesis to haul them in from the surrounding volume and squeeze them together." She focused, extending her recovering magic, catching the plankton. She herded it together, so that it formed a cloud around them.

"But we can't transport it across a Mode boundary," Darius said. "So it won't do us any continuing good."

"Does inertia carry across the boundaries?" Cat asked. "If so, could he catapult through several at a time?"

They paused. It was a new question. "Assuming that it does," Darius said, "How could our bodies withstand an explosive start?"

"I could make a stasis spell," Nona said. "That would hold everything inside its range in place."

"With your full magic, you could make a telekinetic shield," Darius agreed. "But do you have enough magic now?"

"I am not sure."

But Colene and Pussy were suffering the siege of the mind predator. They couldn't wait. "We'll have to try," Nona said. "I will do my best."

First she formed the cloud around Burgess, and he tried sucking it in and launching himself with the released energy of the plankton. He shot along the sideways extension of the Mode, and coasted to a stop some distance from the others. Then he returned far more slowly. That aspect worked.

Next they tried it with his normal power, and the others holding on to his carapace. Colene sat on his back, and Pussy joined her there. He moved only slowly, but carried them along; the stasis spell held them all in place.

Then they went for it. Nona fetched in the plankton for Burgess; then, as he sucked it in and concentrated it inside his body cavity, she invoked her stasis spell. The amoebae fissioned, and Burgess jetted out a powerful stream of them. He launched across the Mode boundary, carrying them along.

Inertia carried them through five or six Modes. Then Burgess stopped, Nona gathered in more plankton, he passed it through, and they launched through another group. It was working!

The mind predator did not relent. Instead its hold on Colene slowly intensified. But their increased rate of travel was not intended to leave it behind, but to bring them closer to an anchor Mode, where they could escape. The sooner they reached it, the faster there would be relief.

Suddenly they were out of the energy-fissioning Modes. They were in familiar-seeming Modes. "We are coming to Colene's anchor," Darius said, recognizing the type.

The power of the plankton was no longer available. The others let go of Burgess, but Colene continued to ride, being largely insensible of her surroundings. He felt the continuing horror in her mind, ameliorated only by Pussy's protective contact.

They hurried on, past houses and streets and people who stared at them briefly, until they crossed the next boundary. They didn't care about attracting attention; they had to keep moving, because the mind monster was still gaining on Colene's mind.

Then they were there. It was a grassy yard. Colene threw herself down on it, kissing the turf. "I never dreamed I'd be so glad to see home!"

"The monster is gone," Pussy said, half in wonder.

"That is the way of it," Darius said. "It has power only on the Virtual Mode. But now that it has found her again, it will be lurking when we go on it again. This is mischief."

Burgess knew it was. He had carried Colene during her prior siege, and felt some of her pain. That pain had returned. How was she going to travel the Virtual Mode again?

Colene got up and hugged Pussy. "I love you," she said. "You made it bearable."

"I must do all I can for you," the Feline female replied. "I would take it all, if I could."

"You can't. But you helped." Colene looked around. "You have your magic?" she asked Nona.

Nona experimented, generating a small flame in air, then lifting a stone without touching it. "Yes, increasingly. Seqiro knows this location. But my powers remain relatively slight. There are a number of things I can't yet do."

"But can do you do illusion?" Darius asked.

"Yes. That is very easy magic."

"Then you can conceal Burgess. And the rest of us. Make your illusion of nothing."

They all disappeared, unable to see themselves or each other. "But that won't last when I'm not here to invoke it," Nona's voice came.

"Make us be of no interest, then," Colene said. "So passing folk won't notice us."

"That is easier yet," Nona agreed. They all reappeared, looking the same. "I believe that spell will last for a time after I depart the scene."

"Come on," Colene said, heading for the house. "Time to meet my parents."

Her parents had problems of their own, Burgess remembered. Her mother was addicted to a liquid beverage, and her father was often away from home with other females. But they had been shocked by their daughter's disappearance, and had done their best to improve. They had come to understand the reality of the Virtual Mode, and to support her ventures on it.

They walked as a group to the house. "I'll have to introduce you Felines," Colene said. "But they'll accept you too. Mom will cook up a big meal for us. We'll have to rustle up some money, though; they don't have a lot."

"I could conjure some," Nona said.

"Nuh-uh. It has to be legitimate. Maybe Amos can help."

"Who is Amos?" Cat asked.

"He was my science teacher. He helped save Burgess, last time we were here. He's a good man. I had a crush on him once. But we'll have to earn whatever he gives us."

"Earn?"

"We'll have to do something for him in return for the money. He's almost as honest as Darius. We don't want to go public about the Virtual Mode. He's already seen Nona's magic. So I'm not sure what we can offer."

"Should I offer?" Pussy asked.

"No. He's not into temptation."

They had stopped at the back door to the house. "We must first meet your family," Darius said.

"Yeah. I'll figure something out for Amos." Colene put

her hand on the doorknob. "Let me do the talking at first, okay? They're not much used to travelers like us." Then she opened the door.

The travelers entered, but Burgess was too large to fit, so he waited outside. However, Colene's power of mind reading was still increasing, and Seqiro's larger compass was with them, so Burgess was aware of what was happening.

The house was empty. But not unoccupied. Colene's parents were merely away at this hour.

"Okay," Colene said. "Maybe it's easier this way. Let's make a shed in back for us to camp in, and Darius and I will meet them when they come back and break them in easy. They'll help as well as they can, I know. They're not bad people, just fouled up." She smiled. "Like me."

They rejoined Burgess outside, and set about making a shelter. Nona used her returning magic to form planks and boards from clods of earth, transforming them, and Darius and Tom pounded them into the ground and fastened them together in workmanlike fashion. The males worked well together, and knew what they were doing; the edifice was soundly constructed. Then it was female time, and Nona transformed other clods into what Colene called foam plastic for Colene and Pussy to shape into pillows and blankets. By the time they added a chamber for Burgess, the structure filled a fair portion of the yard. But Nona's spell of unnoticeability kept it private.

"Know something?" Colene asked rhetorically. "We make a nice family group. I could be happy like this, if I could be happy."

"My little vessel of dolor," Darius said affectionately, squeezing her hand.

There was a flare of rapture from her that suffused them all, like a fire starting up and fading. She loved him, and now it showed mentally as well as physically.

"Oh, God, Darius," she said. "I've got to find a way to be with you."

"In time," he said, with an involuntary mental image of her shedding her clothing. Burgess knew that these folk, who habitually wore covering, tended to regard the removal of it as an invitation to copulate, or at least to consider that process.

"That too," she said. "I mean as a vessel of joy."

"That too," he agreed. "Yet there is that about your dolor that appeals."

"Because it's part of me." She paused, her feeling swirling like a multicolored cloud. "Awful thought: suppose I could get rid of it, and it turned out that I wasn't me anymore? That I am made of dolor, like that woman in Edgar Allan Poe's story who was made of poison?"

"What happened to her?"

"Her boyfriend gave her a potion to nullify the poison, so he could kiss her without dying. But then she died, because the potion nullified *her*. She just couldn't be what she wasn't, even for love."

"The first Chip oriented on you, from all the Modes," he said seriously. "That meant that you were the woman I needed."

"Except for one teensy detail," she said. "My joy setting was wrong. You should have gotten a more accurate reading."

"It does seem to have been mistaken. I don't see how that could have happened."

She looked around. "Here we are musing about it, yet again, while the others wait. We need to get them comfortable."

But the others were already comfortable. The hive had come together, with the joining of Seqiro's mind. Burgess loved the feeling of belonging, and knew that the others did too. Because now their feelings were one.

"Well, at least we should eat," Colene said.

"I will conjure food," Nona said.

That alarmed Cat. "Isn't that the same as Virtual Mode food? We need to obtain food from an anchor."

"This *is* an anchor," Nona said. "What I conjure here is substance of this Mode. It will endure."

They shared Cat's process of assimilating that clarification and filing it in its orderly memory. That was one of the things Burgess liked about Cat: its rational organization. It was much easier to understand human events when they were filtered through Cat's perspective. The neuter null liked to make sense of things. "Thank you."

"What would you like?" Nona asked the others collectively.

"Perhaps it is best not to tax your magic unnecessarily," Darius said. "If you focus unduly on inconsequential things, the important ones might be diluted. You do not as yet possess your full powers."

"True. I'll conjure undifferentiated edible solid and liquid."

Colene laughed. "That sounds like garbage!"

"Garbage is merely the unused residue of wholesome food," Cat said. "It is a stage in the development of alternative processes."

Exactly. Now Burgess understood what garbage was. He himself had none.

The food appeared in the form of a brown lump and a bucket of yellow liquid.

"That's worse," Colene said with a giggle. Her mental image was of one of their defecation trenches.

"I thought it was chocolate and orange juice," Pussy said.

"You have such a clean mind."

Nona smiled. The lump turned green, and the liquid turned blue.

"Now it's like cabbage and detergent," Colene said, unable to stop laughing. But she reached out and pulled off a chunk of solid. She bit into it. "Like hominy—not much flavor."

Nona concentrated again. Burgess tasted the substance in Colene's mouth, because of the shared sensation. It turned sweet. Burgess did not eat in that fashion, but it was interesting sharing her experience.

They all ate of the solid, and drank of the liquid, using cups Nona transformed from more dirt. It was what Colene pronounced a vanilla meal: bland but satisfying. Cat even sprinkled some crumbs and poured a few drops into Burgess' trunk tip so that he could taste the food directly. That enabled him to align the received mental tastes with the chemical reality.

They shared company, enjoying the freedom from the dangers of the Virtual Mode. Here they could relax without being concerned about straying across a boundary. Colene was right: they were a compatible hive.

Darius stretched out and slept. Colene lay beside him, reviewing in her mind what she should say to her parents when they returned. It should be all right, but such things could never be taken entirely for granted. She was also concerned about how long they would have to remain here. It was her fault that they had to interrupt their travel, because of the mind predator.

"It is not your fault," Pussy said, receiving the thought as they all did. "No more than it is the fault of any victim of any predator."

"You always take my side," Colene retorted. But she wasn't annoyed. "By the way, thanks for shielding me from that predator. You really helped. I know it was painful for you."

"I will help you in any way I can, to any extent I can," Pussy said. But there was looming horror in her mind; she had felt the dreadful power of the mind monster, and was terrified of it.

"Maybe if all three Felines joined with you, we could shield you more completely," Tom said.

"You shouldn't have to shield me at all! It's my own problem."

"It is *our* problem," Cat said. "We are here to facilitate Darius' delivery of the Chip, and understand that your safety and well-being are integral to his functioning."

Colene nodded mentally. "I hate to say it, but you may have to help, as Burgess did before. Because once the mind monster latches on to me, it doesn't let go. We tried to escape it on Nona's Mode of Julia before, but then it came back again and Seqiro had to free his anchor to change the pattern and lose it. Now it's found me again, and maybe the only way to lose it again is to free another anchor. And we don't have any left to free."

"We will do what we can," Cat said.

Then they heard something. "My folks!" Colene cried. "They're coming back!" She squeezed Darius' arm, and he woke. "Come on, Nominal Husband. We have to make a call."

Darius sat up, and she brushed him off. They stood and walked to the house as one of the mechanical things rolled up to the front. The others waited in the shelter.

"Mom! Dad!" Colene called as the two older humans emerged from their vehicle. "We're back!"

The mother was closer. She stared at the two without moving. Her feelings were a peculiar mix of hope and dread.

The father came to stand beside her. "It's them!" he exclaimed.

Now the concern and joy of the parents flared. Colene's mother hugged her, and her father eagerly shook Darius' hand. "We were afraid we would never see you again," the mother said.

"Almost, Mom. Maybe not after this. But we're here for now. With some new company."

They walked as a party around the house. "I don't think I remember that shed," the father said.

"We just made it, for a camp," Colene said eagerly. "Nona's here."

Nona stepped out of the shelter, and the mother hugged her. "I remember you! The magic woman."

"Yes. I said we would visit again."

"Where is the horse?"

"Seqiro couldn't make it this time," Colene said. "But he's with us in mind."

"In spirit," the father said, not properly understanding the allusion.

"And Burgess is here. I don't think you ever quite met him, before, but he was with us."

Burgess floated out. Both parents stared at him, astonished. But Colene put a vague thought into their heads, that they took as a memory, and they nodded. They found him very strange, but familiar.

"And three new ones," Colene said. "The Felines: Tom, Pussy, and Cat." The three came out.

"Why you're in costumes," the mother said.

"Permanent ones," Colene agreed with a smile. "They are good people too. We'll be staying here a while, but then we'll have to move on. No one else will notice them."

"Perhaps not," the father said a bit doubtfully.

"You must come inside," the mother said. "Your room is still as you left it. You—" She hesitated. "And your young man. You *are* married."

"Yes, mother, we are," Colene said with mixed feelings. Her mother naturally assumed they had been sexually active, and Colene wished that was true. Burgess had learned that these human folk set great store by the state of their reproductive activity, even though they often took much trouble to see that the activity was not effective. He did not quite understand that aspect, but accepted it. He wondered what it would be like to have human drives and participate in human sexuality. But that was something he would never know, except vicariously.

They entered the house. "It is better that the rest of us be forgotten," Nona said to the others. "This is not our Mode."

"Her parents seem nice," Pussy said. "Did they adopt her at age eight, to form a trio?"

"No, they did it the human way," Nona said. "They conceived her through sexual activity, birthed her, and raised her from babyhood. But they had problems. The father was interested in other women, and the mother was alcoholic."

"Alcoholic?"

"She imbibed too much intoxicant, and became bad company. So Colene's father was usually away, and her mother was in no state to take care of her. Colene became independent, of necessity. But also very unhappy. Since she left, her parents have done their best to restore their marriage, but Colene remains independent. That may be one reason she so resents her dependence on us when the mind predator attacks her."

"But we exist to help her," Pussy said.

"She prefers to need no help. She learned to survive by being independent, hiding her true feelings. So this is a difficult adjustment."

"We will nevertheless do our best for her," Cat said.

"Perhaps we should just listen to her dialogue with her parents, so she does not have to repeat the details later to us."

Cat nodded. "We will listen."

The people inside the house were just settling down. It was apparent that the parents simply wanted their daughter in their presence for a time, on any pretext, so as to become accustomed to her return. They were in their fashion strangers to her. Burgess had not realized this during the prior stay in this Mode, but he had been very ill, and hardly aware of anything around him. Colene had stayed with him, though that caused her to miss her own marriage ceremony, and her friend Amos Forell had finally discovered the nutrient Burgess required for recovery. So he hardly knew more of Colene's family than the Felines did.

There was an awkward silence. Burgess realized that the family members wished to converse, but were uncertain what to say. There was much they wanted to share with each other, but they were having trouble formulating it. Their lines of family communication, Nona understood, had never been good.

"So how have things been with you, Mom?" Colene asked, trying to establish the dialogue.

The mother had much she wished to convey, but couldn't organize it. So she fixed on the most recent detail. "You know I—I have a problem with the—the—"

"You're alcoholic," Colene said. Her statement was followed by a wash of regret: she was being brutal, and she hadn't come here for that. But it was too late to take it back.

"Yes. But I am on medication for it. I have not—not—not as long as I take those pills. But they have—have—"

"Side effects," the father said.

"Yes," the mother said gratefully. "Side effects."

There was another silence. "What side effects?" Colene finally asked.

"They make her hallucinate," the father said. "That's why she wasn't sure she really saw you, until I saw you too."

"Hallucinate!" Colene repeated. "Delirium tremens?"

"No, I never had those," the mother said. "I just got—got drunk and passed out. Eventually. Before. But the medicine stopped that. I can't stand to touch a drink; it makes me violently sick. So I'm sober all the time. It's hard. But Garret has been a big help."

"We have a deal," the father said. So he did have a name, like others of his species. "She stays sober, I stay home. We both gave up what was destroying us."

"Because of you," the mother said to Colene. "When you left, we—we—"

"We lost it," Garret said. "We realized that the biggest thing in our lives was gone. So we made a bargain with God, Morna and I, and swore to reform if only we got you back."

"Or at least knew that you were safe," the mother said. So her name was Morna. "We never dreamed that—what happened—this Visual Model—"

"Virtual Mode," Colene said. She was having trouble maintaining her composure. She had thought for years that her parents hardly cared about her. Now she knew they did, and this evidence of their sacrifice made her want to cry. She had misjudged them so badly, she was ashamed. But what could she say?

"Yes, that's it," Morna agreed. "That place you disappear—at least you are happy there. So we stay reformed, to keep you safe."

Colene believed them. It was painfully touching. They thought she was happy as she traveled, and how could she disillusion them? So she changed the subject back to them. "What about hallucinating?"

"I see things. I hear things. Sometimes I feel things. But they aren't there. Sometimes they make me so—so— I just want to die."

An ugly shock ran through Colene; Burgess felt it right through his carapace. "To die?"

"I've had to hide the knives," Garret said. "So she won't cut herself."

The shock was worse. Colene had cut her wrists to make the pain of her existence go away; a little physical pain banished the emotional pain, to a degree, for a while. That had been her guilty secret. But her mother was doing that too? "Mom, you're depressive!"

Morna nodded. "That's why I drank, dear. It made me forget, or at least not care."

"And it's why I strayed," Garret said. "The excitement of illicit love—that banished the melancholy. For a while."

Colene stared at him. "You're depressive too?"

"Yes. I didn't know it, until I got into therapy, after you left. Fortunately counseling and medication have been effective for me, and I am now in equilibrium. But it has been harder for Morna." He glanced at his wife. "What a pair we turned out to be!" He looked again at Colene. "Thank God you didn't inherit it."

Colene couldn't speak. All this time she had thought she was alone—and it was from her parents! She had concealed her own case so well that they didn't know it. And she hadn't known of theirs. They had all been perfect at one thing: keeping secrets from each other. To paraphrase her father: what a family they had turned out to be.

"So they put me on this other medicine," Morna continued. "And it worked. It made me feel better, or at least tolerable. But then there was a change in doctors, and they gave me different prescription, because they say the ones I was on weren't on the approved list, only these ones are much worse. I become—Garret can tell you."

"Wild," Garret said. "At times I hardly know her. Sometimes she thinks I'm a rapist."

Colene froze again. Rape! They had just touched the last base.

"I do know better," Morna said. "Garret may have strayed, but he was never violent. But these medications distort my perceptions so that I don't know what's real. I think someone's reading my mind, or performing magic, or chasing me—it's all so crazy."

"Crazy," Colene agreed weakly. People *were* reading her mother's mind, and doing magic. But what the woman actually perceived was indeed hallucinatory. How could so much irony collect in one place? "But if it's because of the wrong pills, why don't you tell them? The doctors?"

"They say they're not allowed to deviate from the list," Garret said. "For all that the right medicines were on it before. I think they cost more, so they were banned. I even went over the doctor's head and went to the supervisor. I told him that these were wrong for Morna, that they were tearing her up. And do you know what he said?" He paused a moment for effect. " 'I can live with that.' That's what he said."

Colene's astonishment was shifting into something else: anger. Burgess felt that deadly emotion. There was going to be trouble. "You told him, so he knows—and he doesn't care?"

"That's right," Morna said. "It's awful. We can't afford to pay for the pills ourselves, so we're at their mercy."

"And the bureaucracy is merciless," Garret said. "Sometimes I think the administrators literally don't care whether you live or die, so long as they can save a buck."

Colene's anger found a sudden focus. "Maybe we can do something about that," she said grimly.

There was a weird exhilaration in that emotion, because it was justified. Colene had once turned her horrors inward, destroying herself, but this was anger for an external situation. Someone *else* would suffer.

Garret shook his head. "That bureaucracy's immovable. We shouldn't have bothered you with this. It's our problem. How are you doing, Colene?"

"Never mind about me, Dad. Mom's the one with hallucinations. Give me the name and address of that idiot supervisor."

"Colene," Darius murmured warningly. "We don't want to attract attention."

But Colene's ire was now in full swing. When she got something into her head, she went after it with suicidal intensity. It was her way. "So I'll take Nona along to mask us, okay? Mom needs help."

Darius rolled his eyes, more for the parents' benefit than Colene's, so that they would know he had tried. "At least get some local currency first."

He had a point. They could get around better without using magic if they had a bit of spending money. "I'll get some."

"Legitimately," he said firmly.

She made a face. "Awww." Then she blew him a mental kiss and left the house. He would reassure the parents that she would be all right, and wasn't as wild as she seemed. He was a good man. That was Nona's thought. She would have loved Darius if it were not for Colene. She appreciated his qualities without having any designs on him. She was as good a woman as he was a man. That was Cat's thought.

Colene went out back. It did not make much difference, as far as Burgess' awareness of her thoughts went; they were all in constant touch. It was wonderful having the ambiance of Seqiro's telepathy again.

Pussy came forth to greet her. "You want to assist your mother," she said. "How can I help?"

"I don't think you can, in this. I need Nona."

"I will come too," Pussy said.

Colene didn't want to argue. "Okay." Then, as Nona joined them: "We need to get some money, so it's time for Amos. I'll call him. What day is this?"

No one understood her context, so she returned to the house. "What's the day?"

"Tuesday," Garret said.

"Thanks. I need to call Amos Forell."

"He's the junior school science teacher," Morna said, as if Colene did not already know that.

"Yes, I had classes with him. He'll be at the school now, but maybe I can reach him." Colene went for the telephone. Burgess could not make sense of that, until Cat clarified it: the device was roughly similar to mechanical telepathy.

"What does she want with the science teacher?" Garret asked Darius.

"He saved Burgess," Darius said. "She is grateful." But that was not the whole of it.

Colene was lucky. She caught the teacher in his office. "Hi. I forgot to take that book."

Burgess could not receive the man's response, as the telephone was not really telepathy, but some kind of distance conveyer of nothing more than his voice. But he understood from her reaction that the man was surprised. It seemed he had recognized her voice.

"No, I won't be needing it now," she said. "Nona and I are here. Yes, the lovely one with the magic. Can we see you?"

There was another pause. Then Colene spoke again. "Okay, we'll be there soon. But you know, we won't look like us, at first. Not until we're alone with you." She replaced the instrument, separating herself from the distant man. She looked at her father. "We need to go to the school. Can you take us?"

Garret looked at Morna. "Go ahead, dear. I'll be all right."

Colene made a spot decision. "Yes you will, Mom. Go out back and talk to Burgess and Tom and Cat. They'll catch you up on everything that's been happening. It's interesting. But I guess you know better than to talk about it elsewhere. They would think you were hallucinating."

Morna winced. Colene was immediately sorry. "I didn't mean that the way it sounded. I wasn't trying to make fun of you. I mean nobody in his right mind would believe anything about the Virtual Mode. But you and Dad know it's true."

"I will go with you," Darius said quickly.

Morna was reassured. "You are a nice young man. Colene has done so much better since she met you."

Colene, Nona, and Pussy followed Garret to the vehicle, while Darius led Morna to the yard. "Colene's mother would like to learn what we have been up to. Why don't we step into an adjacent Mode and tell her?"

Colene's mother had seen the closest Modes before; Nona had shown her. But she still found it difficult to accept. She paused before stepping across the boundary. "These other worlds—they extend indefinitely?"

"Yes," Darius said. "Each one is different. Some are completely different." He went on to explain how different some of them were, and to give a brief summary of their travels. "So the mind predator was after Colene again, and we had to return to an anchor Mode immediately," he concluded.

"She never said a word about that," Morna said.

"She is not used to confiding in you. She couldn't tell you everything herself. But she does want you to know. And she will try to help you with your medicine."

Cat stepped close. "One of us must take your hand to enable you to cross. Will you take mine?"

She shrugged. "All right. You seem like a nice cat." She extended her hand. Cat took it, and they crossed, with Darius, Tom, and Burgess close behind.

They crossed several Modes before pausing. All were very similar to the anchor Mode, but not identical. There were flowers in the yard of one, and a different type of house in another. "And there is a monster here?" Morna asked.

"Not here specifically," Darius said. "It lurks on the Virtual Mode, and seems to prey on dolor. So it has not touched the rest of us, but has been very bad for Colene."

"Dolor," she said. "Quaint word."

"You said you suffer from it too."

"Yes. Sometimes I almost wish a monster would carry me away and end it all."

"No. This thing is not nice. It ought to be abolished."

Burgess felt the same suicidal urge in the woman that Colene sometimes had. "How could I find it?"

"It is not wise even to think of it," Cat said. "I believe we should return to the anchor."

"Monster, where are you?" Morna called, looking around.

"Cat is right," Darius said, becoming nervous himself. "We must return."

But Morna walked forth alone, following the street. Darius went after her—and disappeared into the adjacent Mode.

"She is not an anchor person," Cat said, alarmed anew. "She can not cross boundaries without contact with one of us. She remains in this particular Mode."

Darius reappeared. "I can't follow her!"

"None of us can," Cat said. "She must return to us herself."

Darius turned and faced the departing woman. "Morna!" he called. "You must return! You do not wish to be trapped in this Mode."

She heard him. "I wish merely to see this monster that pursues my daughter."

"That is unsafe! Please return. We can not follow you there."

"But you are right here."

"No. We are on the Virtual Mode. You are in this individual Mode. If we try to follow you, this happens." Darius stepped toward her, vanishing again.

She was surprised. "He disappeared!"

"He crossed to another Mode," Cat said. "We can not do otherwise. You cannot cross alone. You must return to us. Colene would be most annoyed if we lost you."

Morna laughed. "Am I now in my daughter's charge? This is an interesting exploration. But where is this monster? I don't see anything threatening."

"It is a mental predator," Cat said. "None of us have seen it physically."

"Very well. I will seek it mentally."

"Please don't!" Pussy said. "It will hurt you."

"Worse than I hurt myself?" Then she froze. Her face assumed a look of wonder, then of horror. "Oh!"

Darius returned. He looked. "That's how Colene looked when the mind predator first came after her!"

"Morna is another vessel of dolor," Cat said. "It has found her."

"Morna!" Darius called. "You must come to us! Immediately."

The woman looked at him. "The thing is awful," she gasped. "It's drawing me in."

"Emotionally," Darius agreed. "Not physically. Come to us. Walk to us! We can help you."

She gazed at him, her eyes staring wildly. "I can't!"

They gazed helplessly at her. They could not go to her, and she could not come to them.

Seqiro, Burgess thought. The horse's thoughts could cross the modes. Could they reach the woman? *Seqiro! You must help!*

Burgess felt a distant response. Seqiro had heard him.

The horse's mind reached out to the woman, not limited to the Virtual Mode. Morna felt the touch on her mind, despite the siege of the predator. "The horse? I must walk?" She seemed to be trying, but remained where she was. "I can't."

The predator was stopping her. Colene had also become

immobile when under siege. What could they do?

"Set your right foot before you," Cat said.

Almost mindlessly, she obeyed that simple directive.

"Set your left foot before you," Cat said.

She did so, hardly seeming to understand it.

Step by step, Cat brought her in. Finally she crossed the boundary. "Tom!" Darius said. "Put your arms around her. Shield her!"

Tom did. "Oh, that helps!" Morna said. Indeed, Burgess felt her agony diminish. The Felines did seem to have some power of resistance. But it had a price: Tom was now suffering too.

"Cross back!" Darius said.

Cat put a hand on Tom, guiding him, and Darius helped. They urged the others across the boundary, toward the anchor. But they stumbled and fell; Tom could not support the woman when attacked by the same predator.

"Burgess!" Darius said. "You must carry her."

They lifted her onto Burgess, and held her steady. Then Burgess floated across the next boundary, and the next as they kept ragged pace. There seemed to be more boundaries than they had crossed, but that was only a seeming.

Suddenly they were back in the anchor yard. The awful power of the predator was gone.

Morna looked around. "What am I doing here?"

"Burgess carried you back when you fell," Cat explained. "Tom was shielding you, but then he suffered too, and could not support you well."

"We're safe now?"

"Yes. The mind predator can't reach into an anchor Mode. We don't know why."

Morna climbed off Burgess. "That's what's chasing Colene?"

"Yes."

"Now I understand. She must not come here again."

Darius shook his head. "She will do it, because she

wants to join me in my home Mode. You know she will not be stopped."

Morna sighed. "I know." She looked around. "Tom, would you hold me again?"

Startled, Tom looked at Cat. "For the shielding," Cat said.

Then Tom put his arms around the woman. "Yes," Morna said. "There is something about you that pushes away the depression. You did this for Colene?"

"Pussy did," Cat said. "We Felines are here to help as much as we can."

"Do you know, I hid my own depression from Colene. Now I learn that she hid hers from me. How could neither of us have suspected?"

"I believe the term is 'denial,' " Cat said. "Neither of you wanted to know."

"But now that she does know," Darius said, "she is trying to procure better medication for you."

Morna shook her head. "She can't prevail against that bureaucracy. It is impervious to human suffering."

Darius smiled. "I think it has not encountered her like before."

"They won't care what she's like. She can't even get in to see anyone. Not without waiting months."

Darius smiled. "I love Colene, so perhaps am not objective, but she does have special powers. She is learning to read minds, and to do magic."

"I understand that in other realms, other rules apply. So maybe magic is possible where you live. But this is Earth. There is no such thing here."

"Nona is able to do some magic here, and probably Colene can too. They will use it on those officials. I suspect they will get results."

"I do need something. Tomorrow I will think this is mostly a dream or a vision." She glanced down at Tom's furry arm. "You can let me go now; I am feeling better."

Tom let go, and Morna faced the house. "Thank you for clarifying so much." She walked to the door.

She would be all right. Burgess felt her calmed mind; the brief siege by the predator, followed by Tom's reassurance, had settled her. At this point she just wanted to rest.

The rest of them settled down similarly. But now Seqiro's mind was a stronger presence. *You are on Earth.*

We are on Earth, Burgess agreed. You have found us.

I have found you, Seqiro agreed. *I had not quite located you before.*

Burgess reviewed the problem: the mind predator had found them again. Colene could not go on the Virtual Mode without being under siege. The Felines could shield her somewhat, but not enough. How were they to complete their journey to Darius' home Mode?

You must free an anchor, as I did. That disrupts the predator.

But if Colene freed her anchor, she would never complete her journey. Either Colene alone, or all of them would be trapped here. She would never agree to that.

She would never agree, Seqiro thought.

But meanwhile Colene was trying to help her mother. She needed mind reading and magic. Could he help there?

Yes, now, to a degree.

"Then find her!" Darius said.

They felt the thoughts ranging out, questing for Colene in this Mode. In a moment Seqiro found her. He gave them the scene.

They were approaching the school building. Garret remained in his car; Colene, Nona, and Pussy were walking to the section where the science teacher's small office was.

Abruptly their images changed. Now they seemed to be garbed in the manner of the schoolgirls. Nona had used illusion to change them.

They reached the office. Amos Forell was expecting them. "Come in, girls." He glanced at them in turn. "You I would know anywhere, Colene. And you too, I think, Nona; you remain lovely as ever. But I do not recognize the cat woman."

"Pussy Feline," Pussy said. "From the DoOon Mode."

"And I presume you are not speaking my language, but using mind translation."

"Gotcha," Colene said. "Pussy is using it. But Nona needs translation."

"And where is the horse?"

"Seqiro had to return to his own Mode. It's complicated. I really miss him."

"Then how are you able to do your tricks?"

"Seqiro is with us mentally. He was looking for us before, and now he has found us. That enables us to share minds, and to do some magic."

"And what of Burgess?"

"He's here too. You made him better, and now he's fine."

"I would like to see him again."

"You can, Amos! When you get off here."

"I shall." Forell considered for a moment. "Now why are you here?"

"We need some money," Colene said. "Nona can make gold, but we want ordinary grubby used bills and coins. My folks are broke. I figured we could make a deal with you."

"I will give you what you need, within reason."

"No. We have to earn it. We may be here a while. We won't need a lot, but we want it straight. What can we trade for it?"

He shook his head. "You have nothing I need or want, apart from information about your fantastic adventures, and I think you would not charge for that."

"You have to want something," Colene said. "Do you mind if I read your mind?"

"That daunts me. Can I prevent you?"

"Sure. By saying no. Anyway, minds are complicated, and I'm new at it. Seqiro's help makes a big difference. You have to think hard, or vocalize, for me to get it. But if you cooperate, and run through all the things you'd really like, maybe I can find something we can provide."

"Are you not afraid of what a man might think when confronted by three lovely young women?"

Colene glanced to either side, at her companions. "We're sort of used to it by now. It's *my* mind I don't want read."

"As you wish, then. Read my mind."

Burgess felt Colene concentrate. Buttressed by Seqiro, she oriented on Amos Forell's mind. At the surface was exactly what he had implied: pictures of three lovely young women in somewhat less clothing than they were wearing. But close beneath was his real passion: biology. He was fascinated by living processes, and followed all the latest discoveries in the technical journals. It was his fondest dream some day to discover an animal or plant unknown to science, that might then be named after himself. But he lacked the resources to mount an expedition to any obscure corner of the planet, so it was no more than a dream.

"Got it," Colene said. "Suppose we help you find a weird new bug?"

"It is true that about half the unknown species are thought to be beetles," Forell said. "But at the rate the rain forests are being depleted, they'll be gone before I get there."

"In your own backyard," Colene said. "Or ours; Burgess can help. You know where my house is; come over after school."

"I do want to see Burgess," he agreed. "But the chance

of finding any undiscovered species locally is remote. I will be there." He brought out his wallet. "But in the interim, here is what cash I have on me."

Colene accepted several ten-dollar bills and assorted coinage. "Thanks, Amos," she said. "We'll repay you soon, one way or another."

"I think the story of your adventures in hyperspace will have to do."

"That's free," Colene said.

They left the school and returned to the car. The mental contact faded as Seqiro's attention focused on the group in the yard. *What has happened?*

Darius mentally reviewed the DoOon Mode sequence and the ensuing trek across the Virtual Mode to Earth. "It took the mind predator about the same time to locate Colene as you did," Darius concluded aloud. "Pussy and Burgess were able to shield her somewhat, but we need something better if we are to venture on the Virtual Mode again."

I am unable to sense the mind predator directly. It seems similarly unable to sense me.

"We believe it orients on dolor. That is why it fixes on Colene, the vessel of dolor."

"It must require dolor the way you require joy," Cat said. "Ordinary people are soon depleted, but Colene is a renewing source."

"That must be it!" Darius exclaimed. "It feeds on dolor, and needs a constant source. What makes her wrong for my use makes her right for it."

"Suppose it got her," Tom asked. "Would it deplete her of dolor, leaving only her joy?"

Darius considered. "If it is a form of my magic, I fear not. When I deplete a woman of joy, she will soon die if it is not returned. Even too low a level is dangerous. That is why it is rare for a Cyng of Hlahtar to keep a wife more than a year; he doesn't want to kill her. That is also why he must have a mistress; his wife cannot accept his touch as pleasure. I sought a renewing font of joy, but found a renewing font of dolor. I fear Colene would die if stripped of her dolor."

"But she can be your mistress," Cat said.

"Yes. But I want her as my wife throughout."

That has always been clear, Seqiro thought.

"So your problem is dual," Cat said. "You need to get her safely past the mind predator, and then find a way to draw joy from her without killing her."

"Exactly."

"And the only renewable font of joy you have found is Nona," Tom said sadly.

"Whom you love," Darius said.

"My emotion has no relevance."

"That is where you are wrong. It matters to Nona. I think that is why she does not wish to be my wife. It matters to me too, as I will not take a woman who does not wish to be used in that manner."

"I will be removed from your scene when the Chip is delivered," Tom said.

"Not necessarily." Darius looked at the Feline. "Suppose you went with Nona to her home Mode of Julia. What would happen to the rest of your trio?"

"It would be destroyed," Cat said.

"Is that because you can't function as separate individuals, or because Ddwng doesn't allow it?"

"It is not allowed," Cat said.

Now Darius looked at Cat. "When you deliver the Chip to Ddwng, what will be your fate thereafter?"

Cat considered. "Our trio might be reassigned to another master or mistress."

"Considering how much you will know about the Virtual Mode and the Chip, wouldn't you be assigned to Ddwng himself, for your expertise?"

"No. He prefers the Swine."

"Rather than allow that knowledge to be available to others, wouldn't he simply have you destroyed?"

"That is his right."

"So you face the prospect of dying after your mission has been fulfilled."

Cat nodded. "Yes. That is the most likely course."

"You must fulfill your mission," Darius said. "I understand that. But would you save Tom and Pussy if you could?"

"Yes."

Darius looked at Tom again. "So you might as well stay with Nona, wherever she goes."

Tom was surprised. "But what of Pussy?"

"I could take her as my nominal wife for a year, drawing her joy, and then retire her in my Mode. I believe she could find a normal man once she recovers. She is quite attractive physically, and her docile nature would appeal. It would be better than being destroyed."

Tom looked at Cat. "This is a reasonable course," Cat said. "I alone need die."

Darius nodded. "I am glad we have this understanding. I would save you, too, Cat, if I could, but I think I cannot."

"That is true."

"In fact I wish I could save Doe and her trio, but I cannot. I fear they and the Human nulls are all doomed."

"This is likely. Nulls are not retained after their usefulness diminishes."

"Do you have feelings about this?" Darius asked.

"Intellectually I do," Cat said. "I believe that Ddwng's reign is not beneficial to DoOon, and will not be beneficial to the other Modes he invades."

"Colene would say it sucks," Darius agreed. "But I appreciate your position. You must complete your mission. But are you obliged to go farther than that?"

"Yes. I must do my utmost to safeguard my ultimate

master, Ddwng. My opinion of his nature is irrelevant."

"But you understand that others in our party lack that particular commitment."

"I understand also that you will not seek to undermine the success of my mission," Cat said. "You wear the chain."

"And Doe wears my chain. She loves me, and is bound to me. You may feel that the obligations are all hers, but they affect me too. I will not lightly let her be betrayed, though I do not love her." He turned to Tom. "And Nona will not lightly let you be destroyed, though she does not love you. Colene will not let Pussy be destroyed. In our frames, love is not a one-way commitment. It brings return obligations."

"But I do not seek to bind Nona!" Tom protested.

"You have nevertheless done so, to a degree. My point is that should she ask you to remain with her, rather than returning to DoOon with your trio, you have the option to accept."

Tom looked at Cat. "Do I?" he asked in wonder.

"Yes. The likely destruction of our trio generates this option."

Tom remained amazed. He had never thought of leaving his trio.

Cat was bemused. "There is something devious in your mind, Darius, but I am unable to fathom it."

"Be assured that I will deliver the Chip to you as agreed, and enable you to bring it to the DoOon Mode. Ddwng will have it."

"I am so assured. But now you seem satisfied to do it, and that I do not understand."

"Then I will clarify this aspect. It is that I believe the Chip will destroy Ddwng, so the Modes will be rid of him."

"I must not take a dangerous or flawed Chip to him."

"The Chip will be perfect. It is Ddwng who is imperfect. That will destroy him."

Cat shook its head. "This smells of treachery."

"The treachery lies in delivering the Chip. If you wish to save Ddwng, you should remain with us and not deliver it."

"That I will not do."

"I understand. You must complete your mission, just as I must complete mine."

There was the sound of the vehicle drawing nigh to the house. The women were returning. There was something interesting in their minds.

"Okay, Burgess," Colene said as they approached. "We need to find a rare bug. I read somewhere that maybe half the species of life on Earth have not been discovered, so I figure there must be some unknowns around here. I think you can find one, if Nona and Seqiro help you."

Burgess was not sure how this could be. He could identify the nature of the material that passed through his system, but he did not know which of that was known and unknown to the human kind.

"Right, Burg," Colene said. "Nona doesn't know either. But Amos does. I figure you can fix on something, and Nona can make an illusion image of it, and Amos can decide whether it is known. Seqiro will link you all together for the survey." She looked around, mentally. "You can do that, can't you, horseface?"

I can, girlface.

"So we got us a plan. We'll find Amos his bug, and earn our keep. That will take care of us for now." She paused. "Now if I could only figure out how to get me across the Virtual Mode without getting eaten by the mind predator."

They oriented on bugs. Burgess sucked in many small creatures along with the nutrients of the air, and normally assimilated them. Now Nona coordinated with him, as she had in the explosive plankton Modes, and generated illusion pictures of the bugs that others could see. They appeared just above his carapace. Her power was strengthened by the presence of Seqiro's mind, which linked her to her magic home Mode. They practiced, trying to get the sharpest possible pictures in the shortest time. There were, Burgess discovered, a great many tiny creatures in the air and on the ground, so it would take time to check them all.

"That's great," Colene said. They could all tell that her dolor was less when she was actively engaged in something. But whatever she did soon passed, so that effect could not be depended on to help her cross the Virtual Mode. "Can you sort them so you don't show the same bug twice?"

That set them back. They had to recognize a bug to tell whether they had seen it before, and that took time. But it was true that they were seeing the same ones over and over, with only occasionally a new one. They needed a way to eliminate the repeats before processing them.

Amos Forell appeared. That meant that time had passed while they wrestled with the problem. "Hey, Amos," Colene called. "Come into our house so we can kiss you."

"I did not come here for anything like that," the man said, smiling.

"It's a joke," Colene said. "We just want to show off what we made with magic and muscle." But her mental image was of a human hand with two of its fingers crossed. Burgess wasn't sure what that meant.

So Forell stepped into the structure, out of sight of the neighbors. Colene flung her arms around him and planted a sloppy kiss on his mouth. "I lied," she said.

"I suspected," he said.

Then Nona kissed him also, and Pussy. "You can't fool us," Colene said. "We can read your mind. You like getting kissed by wild girls."

"I trust you won't bruit that about," Forell said ruefully. "It would wreak havoc with discipline in my classroom."

"And every girl in your classes would like to kiss you," Colene said. "But you never give any of them the time of day, no matter how much they hint."

"Or how much flesh they show," he agreed. "I do believe that ninth-grade girls are better endowed than they were a generation ago."

"It's the pesticides in the air," Colene said. "They mimic female hormones, and make us mature faster."

He looked at her with feigned surprise. "Did you actually pay attention in class?"

"Some," Colene confessed, looking down as if embarrassed.

Burgess found this to be a fascinating insight into the human species and culture. They were doing what was termed flirting with each other. The man did like the girl, and the girl did like the man, but their situation was such that neither could ever allow that to be generally known. Only now, in the ambiance of Seqiro's mind, was it being expressed openly. Nona and Pussy were similarly intrigued by Forell. He was, Burgess had learned, a handsome, intelligent, and decent man: exactly the kind teenage girls got crushes on.

"Now let me see Burgess," Forell said

"He's right here, Amos." Colene showed him toward Burgess.

Forell sat on the ground so as to place his eyes at the level of Burgess' optic stalks. "How are you doing, bug-eyed monster?"

Very well, thanks to this man. Seqiro relayed the thought to the man's mind immediately.

"I am glad of it. Also glad to see you again. You have had adventures I'd give anything to share."

Now they should show Forell the pictures. Perhaps he

could discover how to eliminate the duplications, and how to tell which ones were new.

"You have pictures? I didn't see a camera."

"Do we get to kiss you every time you say something stupid?" Nona inquired.

"No. I don't want to be kissed to death. My wife would not understand."

"Awww," Colene, Nona, and Pussy said together, keyed by the shared thought. Burgess enjoyed this continuing flirtation because they did; it was not possible to avoid the ambient mood. Darius, Tom, and Cat were enjoying it also, and remaining silent so that it could continue. Darius especially appreciated feeling Colene happy; she so seldom was. She really had had a crush on Forell, a year before, and loved having him treat her like a woman instead of a schoolgirl. She loved calling him by his first name without offending him. Such things buoyed her immensely.

Burgess oriented on a bug, and Nona projected its picture. Forell stared. "Illusion! I forgot you could do that. Lovely."

"Thank you," Nona said, adding the semblance of a blush to her face.

He glanced at her. "I was speaking of the image." But he paused, for Nona was truly lovely, with or without illusion. At the moment she was kneeling beside Burgess, and leaning slightly forward so that the upper portion of her flesh-covered chest showed. Burgess knew from the prior reactions of Darius and Tom that this was an extremely compelling view. "All right: you got me on that one. But I remain impressed by your magic. We don't see very much of that here."

"You don't see *any* of that here," Colene said, frowning as she glanced at Nona's chest. But she couldn't hold the frown. "Magic, I mean."

"That, too," Forell agreed.

It seemed to Burgess that this dialogue did not make complete sense, but that didn't matter. They were all having a good time.

"Here's the problem," Colene said. "They can make pictures of the bugs, but none of us knows which are old and which are new to science. Also, how do they eliminate the repeats, so as to show you new ones each time?"

Forell shook his head. "That is a task for a computer database. I'm afraid magic can't address it."

"The hell it can't, Amos! Let's bring a computer out here and tie it into the system."

"Colene, magic and science don't mix."

"Why not?"

Forell paused. "What would we do with a computer out here?"

"Set it up with a camera and feed the images into the database. Check them against the known bugs. When we get a mismatch, maybe we've got it."

He shook his head. "Photograph illusion images?"

"Why not, Amos?"

He reconsidered. "I suppose if we can see them, so can a camera. Very well, that might work. As for eliminating repetitions—if Nona can fathom the sorting and filtering mechanism of the computer, and teach it to Burgess, that might be effective. It seems just crazy enough to work."

"Got it," Colene said. She kissed him on the cheek.

"I will fetch a computer system," Forell said. "You will have to set it up, as I can't return until school is done tomorrow."

"Can do," Colene said. "See you tomorrow, Amos."

He smiled. "Tomorrow, Colene." He departed.

"He is amused by you," Darius remarked.

"So?"

"I am not conversant with that ploy, 'so?' "

"It means what's your point? Of course Amos is amused by me. He also finds me innocently sexy. If Nona and Pussy weren't here, I could impress him a whole lot more."

"That is fortunate for me."

"That's the trouble with you," she grumped. "I can't make you jealous."

"Not while I can read your mind."

She relapsed into dolor. "I wish I *could* be innocently sexy. But that's forever gone."

"It was nice to see you happy, for a time."

"I can't manage it for very long."

The day was getting late. They decided that Darius and Colene would join her parents for the evening meal, and the others would share a magical meal in the yard.

"Tomorrow," Colene announced, "we set up the computer. And I'll go see about getting Mom better medicine. Because Amos won't be here with the machine until later. We have lots to do."

It had, nevertheless, been a good day. Burgess was satisfied.

SIX

Julia

Tom woke early, as he normally did. It took him a moment to orient, for the woman beside him was not Pussy but Nona. Pussy slept beside Colene, and Cat beside Burgess.

Darius had suggested that they break up the trio so that two of them could remain with the party, and Cat alone would face recycling once their mission was done. That required considerable emotional adjustment, for trios normally never separated. But perhaps it did make sense.

He looked at Nona. She had conjured a nightslip to sleep in, and it was pink and frilly. Dawn had not yet come, and it was dark in their camping structure, but of course he had good night vision. Part of the blanket had turned back, and the woman's right breast pushed firmly against the thin material of the slip, outlining itself. He wished she would ask him to stroke her there, to kiss her and indulge her sexually, but of course that was irrelevant. He had been crafted, like all male nulls, to be continuously potent, so that a mistress could have sex as long and hard as her whim dictated. Because desire was a significant component of performance for a male, he did have desire. That was why unassigned nulls humped dissimilar nulls; the males desired, and the females often liked to stay in practice. Lack of experience was no excuse for failure to please a master. They understood each other perfectly, and of course sexual relations between nulls were of no account. But he could never ask a mistress; it had to be solely at her command. No matter how much he might long to.

Nona's eyes opened and she looked at him, though she could not actually see him in the darkness. She knew where he was by his mind. And she knew his mind. She had caught him thinking, desiring her. He was chagrined; he should not have allowed himself to think those thoughts in her presence. It was akin to asking.

Seqiro, she thought. *Please give us a closed loop.*

Tom's chagrin worsened. She was annoyed and was going to rebuke him, and it was justified. How could he have been so careless? He had allowed himself to forget his place. In DoOon, with no telepathy, it would have been permissible, but here it was not.

"No, Tom," she said. "It is permissible. You are being true to your nature, in a situation for which you were not designed. You cannot be faulted for that." She spoke aloud to focus her superficial thoughts, and the closed loop meant that no one other than Tom would hear either voice or thoughts. The mental power of the horse was phenomenal.

"I am culpable," Tom replied. "I knew my thoughts could be read. I thought you were asleep, and I became careless."

"I was asleep," she said. "Your thoughts woke me."

Still worse! He had disturbed her repose. "I should be punished."

"Tom, you must understand this. I traveled with Seqiro before we came to your Mode. I became accustomed to the linkage of minds. I came to know directly what I had always known indirectly: I am sexually desirable to men. Some have imagined quite thorough handling and penetration of my body. Colene has encountered that too, but she blocks it out because of prior bad experience. She can't tolerate it, even in thought, but I can. I can give myself sexually when I choose, and it is my hope one day *to* so choose, when I encounter the right man. So I am neither annoyed nor embarrassed by your desire. It is normal."

"But I must not indicate it to you!" Tom protested. "It must always be suppressed, unless you command that it be expressed, and then only to the degree specified."

"In the DoOon Mode that is the case; I understand. But this is a different realm, with other conventions. Here, you are a person, with personal rights."

"I am a null. I can be nothing other than that."

"You are also a human being."

"No. I am merely a null."

Her thought was of amused impatience. *Kiss me.*

He got down and put his lips to hers. He would have obeyed such a command regardless of his personal feeling. Her arms came up and caught his head, drawing his face into her face. She kissed him, deliciously hard.

She let him go. He lay beside her, his pulse racing, his eye slits involuntarily dilated.

"You are a human being," she repeated. "A human male. Your creation and your culture have set severe limits on you, and made you catlike, but you are a man."

"I am a man," he agreed, still stunned by the kiss.

"You therefore owe no apology for your man thoughts. Your actions are controlled, and that's what counts."

"You are kind."

"Tom, you're a good man. I believe I would enjoy sex

with you, because your lust is buttressed by genuine love. The reason I do not indulge is that it is in my nature, fostered by my gender and my culture, to regard sex as a form of commitment. Were I inclined to commit to you, I would take pleasure in indulging your physical passion for me. In fact I am more than casually tempted, but I restrain myself lest I imply such commitment. Do you understand?"

"No. You may do with me what you wish, without commitment. Past mistresses have used me intensely and discarded me at their convenience. This is your prerogative."

"I know you believe that, Tom. I could tell you to have sex with me, and then to go away forever, and you would do your best to obey. But this is not the way I am. I will not have sex with you unless I am ready to commit to an extended relationship with you."

"There is no need!"

"Yes there is need, Tom. I must treat you as the human man you are. Therefore I say, think your thoughts in my presence, without embarrassment. I am as I am and you are as you are, and we must both be satisfied with that."

"Thank you, Nona." He was profoundly grateful for her tolerance.

"Now let's get up and see what we can do for the morning." *Seqiro, we're done.*

They got up and went to the section of the structure reserved for sanitation. Nona dissolved her nightdress, conjured water into a basin, and used a cloth to clean her lovely body. Then she conjured a daytime dress and went out to conjure food for them all for breakfast. Tom watched all of this with amazed pleasure; he had not before seen this extent of her magic. She was a phenomenally gifted woman.

"But you loved me before my magic returned," she said. "You would love me if I lost it all."

"Of course."

"In my home Mode I could not be certain any man would love me merely for myself. I have too much power. That's one reason I fled it."

"I don't care about power."

"I know that, Tom. I value that in you."

The others got up, and all of them ate except Burgess, whose eating was continuous. Then they organized for the morning's task: helping Colene's mother. Colene and Darius emerged from the house, being the "house guests," and the others gathered around.

"Amos won't be here till afternoon," Colene said, "so that gives us the day to get this done. We'll get a taxi to the med office and see the supervisor. I figure he'll be a tough nut, so I think we'll need Nona for some special effects."

"I don't think I'd better ask what you are going to do with that supervisor," Darius said wryly.

Colene turned a mock-innocence look on him. "I won't do anything to him—if he doesn't make me mad."

"He has already angered you."

"But he can pacify me, by doing what I want."

"Better take Tom too, to as a rearguard."

Colene looked at her posterior. "Why, is it sagging?"

He spanked it. "No. It remains firm."

"Brute." But her pleasure in indulging in such borderline sex-play was clear. Also her associated regret: that play was as far as she could take it.

The taxi turned out to be one of the wheeled vehicles, operated by a surly man. Colene gave him some of the money she had gotten from Forell, and he drove them to the building where the office was. Earth was rather spread out and haphazard compared to the civilized planets of DoOon, but it seemed to function well enough for its level.

"Here's the thing," Colene said as they rode. "I want

to get better medication for Mom and get it approved once and for all, so she doesn't have trouble after I go. But I don't know exactly what she needs. So I need to pick the brain of that supervisor to find out what's the very best, then make him approve it. I figure I can put a thought into his mind that it's been approved, but he might renege when he thought about it later. So I figure to shake him up some, to take his mind off the approval. How's that sound?"

"I hesitate to comment," Nona said. "This is not my culture."

Colene turned to Tom. "You're male. You know how to fight, right?"

"Yes."

"Think of this as a battle. Is it a good approach?"

"No."

Colene smiled. "You're trained to answer only the question, and not to presume. Okay. What's a better way?"

"First reconnoiter. Ascertain what medications are available without revealing your real purpose. Then, armed with that knowledge, approach the supervisor and require him to approve the best one in a manner that can't be readily reversed."

"Spy, then strike, right? I like it. How's it sound to you, Seqiro?"

Tom Feline has a reasonable strategy.

"You males always back each other up. But how do I spy?"

Tom considered. He liked being asked for advice. "Perhaps if you indicated that you were a patient in need of medication—"

"Won't work. This stuff isn't voluntary. I can't just walk in and ask for it. But maybe Nona could play my mother, and that would do it."

They worked it out. Then, at the front of the building,

they walked in. As they walked, Nona clothed them with illusion. She became an older woman, somewhat severe of feature, and Tom became a similarly older man, somewhat portly. They were to be Colene's parents. Colene did not change, other than in expression: she put on a dark, willful face.

They went to a desk, guided by Colene's knowledge of the way things worked on Earth. "We need help for our daughter," Nona said. Her command of the local dialect was not perfect, but Colene and Seqiro translated it into perfection in the mind of the woman at the desk. "She's out of control. She tries to kill herself."

"Are you covered by our policy?" the woman asked.

"Yes." Colene projected a thought: they had just shown the woman the policy, and it was in order.

"She will have to be tested."

Another projection: the testing had been completed, and the diagnosis was Severely Depressive. "We have tried her on medication," Nona said. "But it has side effects, such as hallucination. We need a change."

"I will make an appointment for Dr. Danforth." The woman checked her listing. "He has an opening next month."

"Next month!" Colene flared. Then she recovered, and focused another thought. *Cancel that outburst; it didn't happen. Our appointment is for right now.*

The woman blinked. "You are just in time for your appointment," she said. She gave them the office number.

They took the elevator, which was another interesting if archaic device: a mechanical lift. They were alone for the moment. "This isn't as smooth as I thought it would be," Colene said. "But maybe we can get what we need from this Danforth character."

Tom had to marvel at the way she was cutting through the evident bureaucracy of this establishment. She was finding her way rapidly.

"Thanks, Dad," Colene said.

He kept forgetting about the mind reading! Which was ridiculous, since they were using it constantly.

Dr. Danforth was a harried-looking man of indeterminate age. It seemed that he had to see so many patients, so rapidly, that he could not keep track of them. He did not realize that this one was out of turn. That was perfect for their purposes. "What seems to be the problem?" he asked.

Nona described the symptoms, which were Colene's own, with her mother's hallucinations added. The doctor hesitated, but Colene impatiently cut through this too. "Just tell us the very best treatment available," she said, projecting a compliance thought.

Faced with this command, the doctor did comply, in his fashion. "Your description is not sufficient to identify the specific form of depression, and this makes a difference in treatment. I am not clear whether it is melancholic or atypical or one of the others. What is proper treatment for one is not necessarily so for the others."

Tom caught Colene's worried thought: despite her own depression, she had no idea how it might be classified, and didn't have time to figure it out. "That first one—what's the best treatment for it?"

"Melancholic depression. That is associated with hyperarousal in the brain, perhaps a chronic stress response that can't be turned off. That makes it hard for the patient to eat or sleep. RTMS seems most promising, though it remains experimental."

Colene nodded. "Close enough. Give me that one."

He looked at her. "My dear, this is not a pill. The letters stand for Rapid Transcranial Magnetic Stimulation. Put simply, a powerful magnet delivers an electric jolt to the brain. This causes many neurons to fire at once, and this seems in turn to reset the rate at which the brain releases the chemicals involved in depression. Two weeks of RTMS treatments significantly help the vast majority, and the effect seems to be long-lasting. However—"

"I'll try it."

Tom, Nona, and the doctor all tried to protest, for different reasons. It was Colene's mother she was supposed to be inquiring for, not herself.

Colene turned back to them. "I need it too," she said. "If this big magnet can make me happy, I can maybe get across the Virtual Mode. And if it works on me, maybe it'll work on my mother too. So I'll test it for her."

Then she faced the doctor. "Thanks, Doc. You've been a big help. Now forget this session ever happened." She sent a forceful thought.

Dr. Danforth looked bemused as they left his office. He might not forget completely, but since they had been unscheduled and had left no record of their visit, he would find it easy to assume that his memory was confused.

"Now for that supervisor," Colene said. "What was his name—Gollins. Dr. Gollins. In another office on this floor." She set off for that office, and they followed somewhat helplessly.

Again, they had no appointment. Again Colene crashed through the social or procedural barriers, and they came to stand before Dr. Gollins. "I want RTMS," Colene said. "And my mother after me, assuming it works on me."

"But this is preposterous!" Gollins protested. "That is an expensive, experimental, unauthorized procedure not covered by our program."

"Authorize it," Colene said, sending a command thought.

But the supervisor's resistance to expense merely because of need was formidable. "This is impossible!"

Colene studied him. "I had hoped you would say something like that. You're the one who can live with a patient's hallucinations brought on by the side effects of wrong medication. Now I have an excuse to show you what that means."

"I have no idea what you are talking about."

"Nona, show him the Virtual Mode."

Nona was ready. Her power of illusion manifested, making the office walls disappear. In their place appeared a scene from the trek they had recently made, barren wastes through which a group of people walked—and disappeared, one by one. Then reappeared as the viewpoint person crossed the boundary behind them. And disappeared.

Dr. Gollins rubbed his eyes. "This is impossible."

Suddenly there was a restless sea. A truly weird creature—Burgess—floated across it, carrying a person. Then there was a drop-off, and a quick trek to the puzzle Modes, and the power plankton Modes, with their erratic explosions.

The doctor lurched to his feet, trying to escape what he saw. He collided with a wall he couldn't see. "This is impossible!" he exclaimed, looking wildly around.

End, Colene thought to Nona. The illusion vanished. The office was back.

"You look as if you'd seen a hallucination," Colene said sweetly. "I can live with that."

Tom, receiving the context from her mind, labored to suppress his laughter. Colene was getting back at the man who had been callous to her mother.

"What happened?" the man asked wildly.

"It doesn't matter," Colene said evenly. "All you need to know is that it will all go away once you approve those RTMS treatments and they are done. If you don't, you'll be seeing more hallucinations."

But Dr. Gollins was recovering his equilibrium. "Ridiculous."

Colene lifted her left hand in a signal to Nona. A scene on Planet Chains appeared, with the dragon pouncing on a Feline and killing him. It was so astonishingly realistic it made Tom recoil. That was the way it had been, before Colene made the pact with the dragons.

At the same time, Colene sent another compliance thought. "I'll do it!" the supervisor said desperately.

"Good," Colene said. "If you do, you will never see us again. Now make out the papers for these names and dates." She gave the key information, and the supervisor made hasty notes.

They left. "But won't he renege later?" Nona asked. "After all, there will be questions, if that treatment really is unauthorized."

"He's not stupid. If he even tries to tell anyone about what happened, he'll lose his job. He'll keep his mouth shut—and will make sure we're satisfied. Or else. He knows how to do it."

They returned to the house. Colene walked into Pussy's embrace. "I'm going to have an experimental treatment. I'm scared."

And she was. She had carried through without flinching, but now that it was arranged, she was frightened.

Nona conjured food for lunch. It was fancier than prior meals had been, because the increased presence of Seqiro's mind enabled her to draw on more of her magic.

When her parents returned, Colene explained things to her mother, who was astonished but gratified. Then Forell arrived with a portable computer and camera.

They got busy. It took time to connect the computer in the backyard, and to set up the camera on its tripod, and to integrate the software. But Forell knew what he was doing, and in due course succeeded in making the first video photograph of the illusion picture of a tiny insect. "This is an entirely common and ordinary bug," he said, pleased, "but it proves the technique. Now I must train one of you to operate the system, so that you can continue the survey during my absence."

"Tom can do it," Colene said.

"Me?" Tom was startled.

"You can pick it up by mind transfer from Amos. Nona and Burgess have other jobs, and Cat's helping them orient on the bugs. Darius and Pussy will be gone to Oklahoma City to steady me through my magnetic treatments. That leaves you."

"I will do it, of course, if I am competent."

"What is this about magnetic treatments?" Forell asked Colene.

"RTMS. I'm hoping it will make me happy."

Forell clearly knew what she was talking about. "How on Earth did you get approval for such rarefied treatment?"

"Amos, you don't want to know. Let's just say it's magic."

He nodded. "And telepathy. You can project thoughts as commands?"

"You catch on quick."

"You're right: I don't want to know. I think I don't ever want to be on the wrong side of you, Colene."

She sent him a wash of the remnant of her schoolgirl crush. Tom felt it too, as they were all linked. He wished Nona could feel that way about him. "You could never be that, Amos," Colene said.

"Even your right side is dangerous," Forell said. "Do you have any idea of the mischief a friendly girl can be to a teacher?"

"I sure do. But you never let me get that far."

"Fortunately." He turned to Tom. "Why don't you give this a try?"

Tom squatted by the computer and camera, and the information about their manipulation flooded into his mind. Each step brought it to Forell's forefront of consciousness, and Tom assimilated it. He photographed the second bug, then checked the computer screen to make sure it had been properly recorded. The process was straightforward,

as he came to understand it. This was not science of the
DoOon level, but it was adequate to the need.

Forell left it to him and worked with the others. "Can
you mind read a database?" he asked Nona.

"This is not something I have had experience with."

"I haven't had experience with photographing illusions,
but it's working."

"See if you can mind read the computer," Colene said.
"If Seqiro can connect you to what passes for its thoughts,
you may be able to use its database."

"If I can make it a familiar, perhaps so," Nona agreed.
She concentrated on the machine. "Yes I am attuning to
its memory. I am seeing through its eye."

"Now see if Burgess can connect," Forell said. "So that
he can know instantly what bugs he has seen before. That
way he can present you with only the new ones."

Tom had a problem with this. "May I speak?"

"Of course you may," Nona said. Then, to Forell: "Tom
comes from a culture where his kind are strictly responsive servants. He hesitates to initiate anything."

"There are cultures like that on Earth," Forell said.

"I do not understand why you wish to have Burgess
know which bugs he has checked before," Tom said.
"Why not have him check what he sees directly against
the database? His attention should focus on those that are
not found in it."

"You're right," Forell said. "We don't care what Burgess has seen before. We care what Earth science has seen
before. Any nonmatches we should check in case they are
originals, uncatalogued."

Nona smiled at Tom. "You see your thoughts are worthy."

It made no difference to his feeling: he already loved
her.

They worked on it, and soon Burgess was mentally
connected to the computer and able to check what he was

finding against its listing. Soon thereafter he found a mismatch, and Nona made an illusion picture of it.

"That's a variant," Forell said. "I'm surprised it's not listed. Make a file of all such cases; we can use it later to update the database."

Tom photographed the bug and entered its image in the file. But now it was getting dark. "I have to get home," Forell said regretfully.

Nona looked at him. "Can't we persuade you to spend the night with us?"

The science teacher put on a look of nervousness. "I hope you don't try."

They laughed together, and Forell departed. Tom envied the appeal the man evidently had for all three women in their party.

Nona took his hand. "It is because he is safe," she said. "We can flirt with him because we all know it means nothing. I can't do that with you."

They continued selecting bugs as darkness closed, because Burgess did not need light for this. They found several more nonmatches, then stopped for the evening meal.

"If there's an unclassified bug here, we'll catch it," Colene said with satisfaction. "Meanwhile confirmation has come in: I'm going in for treatment tomorrow."

Thereafter three of them were away, while four of them searched for bugs. The work might have been dull, except that Tom was glad to be interacting meaningfully with Nona. He would do anything for her, and this was something that she considered useful. The list of "new" bugs grew. Most were microscopic, but that didn't matter; Forell would be happy with a creature or plant of any size that was new to Earth science.

But finding a new bug turned out to be more of a job than Tom had anticipated. Forell checked their growing list of nonmatches against larger university databases on what he called the Internet, and found them; the list in this computer was incomplete because it was not possible to list every variant of every subspecies that existed without overflowing the local capacity. But the Internet had no such limit.

Burgess caught up to the purely local bugs and began surveying the passing ones, lifting his foretrunk to the breeze. This brought in samples from a wider compass. But still all were matched, in the little database or the big one. It began to seem as though they were not going to discover a truly new one. Tom felt Nona's growing sadness as the prospects became rarer. She wanted to reward Forell for his help during their prior visit to this Mode, and so did Burgess. It was in one sense a little thing, but it was important to the man, and therefore to Burgess and Nona, and therefore to Tom.

He did his best to cheer Nona, not by any words or specific thoughts, but by training his mind to the belief that success was likely if they continued long enough. She spoke of this one night as she lay beside him. "I know what you are doing, Tom, and I appreciate it. Your emotional stability is helping me to continue."

"I wish I could do more."

"I know you do. But you are doing enough." Then she took his hand and kissed it, and he felt as if he could continue this work for a century with no more encouragement than this.

"I know you do," she repeated with a feeling of warmth.

"You are tired. I can help that."

"What were you thinking of?" she asked, bemused.

"A massage. My mistresses have used me for that."

"I'll try it."

So she lay on her stomach, and he massaged her shoulders and back, then continued to her legs. "Oh, that's heavenly," she said. "You are so good at it." Her nightslip faded away, leaving her body bare, so that he could work directly on her skin.

"I was trained to be."

"I love the warm strength of your hands."

"Thank you," he said, foolishly flattered.

Then she chose to reverse it. "Now let me do you."

"But there is no need."

"I have the need."

That was a command. He lay down, and she massaged his shoulders and back. She was not trained in this, and did not know the most evocative techniques, but it was very nice. Her very touch was his pleasure. There was magic in her hands, even when she wasn't doing magic. He had never dreamed of a mistress doing this with him.

"You have nice muscles."

Again, he was foolishly flattered. He was of course as all male nulls were, equipped to work and fight and do whatever else a master or mistress desired. He could take no credit for his body or his mind. But the continuing touch of her hands was pure delight, and her words intensified it.

"Now don't get up," she said, and lay down against him. "I like the nearness of your strong body when I sleep."

It wasn't until some time later that he realized that she had not thought to magically re-form her night clothing, and had at some point during the massage dissolved his, so that they were lying together naked. He would do or refrain from doing anything she directed, of course, but what joyed him the most was that she had done this without thinking.

She woke. "Why so I did," she said, mildly surprised. Then she embraced him from the side and returned to sleep before he could express embarrassment at having again been caught thinking.

The work continued. A storm came, not a bad one, just

a turbulence in air and light falling of water. But it bore a number of bugs from far regions, and their prospects increased. Tom covered the computer and they continued working, for the rain itself brought down more prospects. But these failed to pan out.

Something tickled Tom's nose, and he sneezed, violently and suddenly. He didn't have time to turn his head, and the puff of air from his sneeze crossed the region that Burgess was sucking from. "My apology," Tom said, embarrassed.

Then Burgess found another prospect, and Nona made its image. It was a tiny disease agent from Tom's sneeze. It did not match.

Forell smiled and fed its picture into the Internet. It still did not match. He checked the databases across the world. Nowhere was there a match.

A suppressed excitement formed in him. They all felt it. "I wonder," he breathed.

"But it's only a germ from a sneeze," Tom said, embarrassed. "It may not even be native to this Mode. It is probably from the DoOon Mode."

"A foreign microbe," Forell said. "*That* would be new to our science."

"But you need a new local one."

Forell shook his head. "My dream is to discover something new to science. It doesn't have to be local. I just didn't think I'd ever have a chance to find an alien one."

"But this is perhaps a disease entity."

"They can be among the most interesting. We study their DNA."

The excitement spread to Nona. "Then this will do!"

"It certainly will. Can Burgess hold on to it?"

"Yes. He can also blow it out for us, along with all its cousins. If it really came from Tom, maybe it needs his substance to continue its life."

So they had Tom blow his nose into a handkerchief,

hard enough to produce substance, and Burgess added the germ to it. Forell took it away with him.

Nona was radiant. "Oh, Tom, you had what he wanted."

"I never thought anyone would want *that*."

She kissed him. "Somehow you generally do manage to do the right thing, in your modest way."

Now they had time on their hands, for Colene, Darius, and Pussy had not yet returned from the other city. Colene's parents picked up on that. "We should show you some of what our region has to offer," Garret said. "As friends of our daughter, you deserve it."

"We prefer not to impose," Cat said.

"You're not imposing," Morna said. "You're our guests. The truth is, our lives have become dull without vices and without Colene. Let us take you to a movie."

Cat was the one with social judgment. "Thank you. Burgess will remain here, but the three of us can go. We have some money Colene left with us."

"This is our treat," Garret said. "You have saved us money by providing us with free food."

"It has been such a pleasure, eating any exotic food we can think of," Morna said. "You are spoiling us with your magic."

"But you must remember that once we depart, that magic will be gone," Nona said. "Only Amos Forell knows of it, besides you. You must not speak of it elsewhere."

"We know," Garret said. "We'd get committed if we did."

"But seeing it ourselves enables us to truly believe in our little girl," Morna said. "That means a lot to us."

"She is a remarkable girl," Nona agreed.

They went to the movie. It was a romance story, shown as a series of rapidly changing pictures on a large screen. After a while Tom was able to ignore the flickering and follow the story as if it were genuine. He was sitting next to Nona, so the pictures hardly mattered anyway.

"Take my hand," Nona said. Tom did so. They had seen that couples in the theater were doing this.

In the movie, a handsome young man encountered a pretty young woman, and they suffered a number of mild misfortunes together and came to love each other. Then there was a misunderstanding that was plainly avoidable, and they quarreled and separated. It was sad.

"Put your arm around me," Nona murmured. Tom obeyed. She put her head against his shoulder, in the manner other women were doing elsewhere in the theater. They wished to appear quite normal. This was wonderful.

There was a crisis, and the couple reconciled. The movie ended then, in a satisfying way. Nona kissed Tom's ear.

The lights brightened. The viewers filed outside, where it was brighter yet. There was the usual traffic and people going busily in several directions. The mood of the movie faded, to Tom's regret. He had almost been able to imagine that he and Nona were the romantic couple.

They returned to their structure in the yard. Nona was in the process of making a decision, but her feelings were complicated and masked. As evening came, she addressed Cat. "Can you accept it if I take Tom from you?"

"In the circumstances, yes."

"Tom, if I asked you to come with me to my home Mode of Julia, to stay, would you wish to do so?"

"I will do what you require."

She smiled. "I require an expression of your feeling."

"I would wish to do your bidding, whatever its nature."

"You will never change, will you!"

"I am not capable of change."

She considered. "I think I would like to have you with me. I am not certain this is fair to you."

"There is no issue of fairness to a null."

"There is with me. If I return to my Mode, I will be

one of the ruling women, because of my magic. I will have a certain notoriety, because I am the ninth of the ninth, the one who ushered in the revolution. If you were with me, you would be another subject male, and some would seek to influence me by influencing you."

"I will never do other than your will."

"I know that, Tom. You are incorruptible, because you are what you are. I can trust you for that reason. Any man of my own world would be vulnerable to corruption, being unused to such affluence or power. You will always be exactly as you are now, with no ambition for anything other than serving me implicitly. You *can't* change."

"That is true," Tom agreed regretfully. "I wish I could be what you desire me to be, but I will always be a null."

Her emotion remained beyond his fathoming. "I understand that, Tom. But I am not sure it would be right to confine you in my feminist Mode."

"You must do what you feel is right."

"Perhaps." She let the subject lapse.

But when they lay down for the night, she addressed him again. "I think I must return to my Mode. I do not know whether I will take you with me. I want something to remember you by. Make love to me."

Now Tom hesitated. "I must ask whether this is your true will."

"Why should it not be?"

"You have shown consideration for my feelings. You may be catering to what you believe should be my will instead of your own."

"I may be," she agreed. "But it is my prerogative to do what I choose, for the reasons I choose. I may indulge your will if I choose, and perhaps that is what I am doing. But it may also be my own will. I am not sure of the ratio that governs my feelings. I thank you for calling this confusion to my attention."

"There is no need to thank me."

"I know it. That much I am certain is my own will: thanking you. Now do it."

Faced with the direct command, he set about indulging her in the manner of a mistress. He kissed her and stroked her breasts, just so, with the technique required to excite the passion of a mistress.

"Not that way, Tom," she said gently. "Do it so that you enjoy it."

"But I can enjoy only obeying your will and giving you pleasure."

"Ignore my pleasure. Take yours."

He was at a loss. "Nona, I can not do that."

She smiled in the darkness. "You can if I tell you to. Do not make me tell you again."

He was faced with another direct command. He tried to obey. But for the first time in his life, he found himself impotent. He was unable to consummate it.

"What is the matter?" she asked.

"Mistress," he said with great regret. "I am failing you. I am unable to obey your directive."

"Why?"

"Because I can have no pleasure without yours. I must know that what I do gives you pleasure, or I can do nothing. I apologize abjectly for disappointing you."

She was silent a time. Then she spoke. "No, Tom. The apology must be mine. I tried to force you to be what you are not. But maybe I can fix that. Be guided by my actions, bearing in mind the original directive."

"I will try," he said, confused and ashamed.

She clasped him and kissed him, fiercely. She stroked him and rolled over with him. She hugged his head and pressed her breasts into his face. She rolled with him again, and wrapped her legs about his waist. "Love me!"

Everything changed. Suddenly he was potent, and mad with desire. He couldn't help himself. He kissed her and stroked her, and plunged into her. She met him with equal passion and abandon. She closed her body about him and squeezed. Any remaining reticence he might have had was destroyed. He thrust again, erupting with a force he had never before known. The shelter, indeed, the planet, indeed the entire Mode seemed to spin around the focus of his unutterably intense pleasure.

Slowly he recovered awareness of his situation. Nona was holding him close, somewhat in the manner of a lover, and somewhat in the manner of a mother Feline. "That is how it becomes mutual," she murmured, stroking his head. "I do not want you to service me, I want you to love me. There's a difference."

"Oh, Nona, I know it now!"

"I think you do, because I shared your mind. Now we can sleep, and if you desire me again I will oblige you—but only if you ask."

"I must not ask."

"Even if you might give me more pleasure by doing so, than if I asked you?"

This put him in a quandary. "Are you directing me to ask?"

Nona hesitated. "Tom, I don't want to require you to do what you are constitutionally unable to do. But just as your greatest pleasure comes in serving your mistress, so mine comes in doing what I feel is right. I want you to be a man in a fuller sense than you are. That means you must show some initiative. It would please me very much if you could learn to do that. I realize that you are and will always be a null, and I am prepared to accept that, but I would like you to be as close to the verge of independence as you are capable of being."

"But suppose I do something you do not wish?"

"Then I will tell you to stop."

"I will try," he said.

"Sleep." But she did not let him go. He slept in her

arms, and knew that if there was such a thing as selfish happiness for a null, this was it.

He woke before her again, before dawn. Once more he viewed her in the darkness, absolutely lovely. He loved her, and desired her, and wished he could be with her for the rest of his life. But of course that could not be, and not just because he was a null.

Yet, if it could even be possible, he had to make it happen. By being what she wanted him to be, to the very limited extent he was capable of. He wanted so much to be what she desired him to be!

He struggled, and finally managed to speak, faintly. "I am asking." He thought she would not hear, otherwise he would not have been able to get the words out. But he had forgotten again that she could read his mind, and that such thoughts alerted her to his interest.

Her eyes opened. She spoke. "Yes, Tom."

For a moment he was transfixed. Then he realized that he *had* pleased her by asking, however faintly. She was waiting for him to follow through.

He kissed her, and she kissed him back. He stroked her, and she stroked him back. Then he loved her, and she clasped him to her tightly. "But we will not do this by daylight," she murmured as he ebbed, and kissed his ear. That little gesture of hers gave him as much joy as all the rest.

Thereafter they got up, cleaned, and joined Cat and Burgess for breakfast. Cat of course knew what they had been up to, but did not comment. Cat had no interest in sex one way or the other, but did want the trio and the hive to function harmoniously.

Nona got a thought. "Colene is returning," she said.

Cat looked at her. "I understood that the series of treatments required two weeks. Only one week has passed."

"Colene thinks one week is enough. The treatments have been effective, and she feels better than she has in years. She wants to return immediately to the Virtual Mode."

"This seems impetuous."

"That's the way Colene is. Evidently the treatment affects her mood, not her nature. That's just as well."

Tom agreed. Colene was special as she was, and it would be a shame to change any more of her than was necessary to enable her to find her joy.

He became aware that Nona was looking at him. Fathoming what she wanted, he expressed his opinion without being directly asked: "I agree. Her dolor is all she should lose."

Nona smiled. Tom knew that his effort wasn't much, but it pleased her. That was all that mattered.

"No, it *isn't* all, but it will do," she said.

Knowing Colene's wish, they set to work taking down their shelter and restoring the yard to its normal state. Tom and Cat dismantled the structure beam by beam, and Nona deconjured each beam in turn. She didn't try to abolish the whole structure at once because her magic, formidable as it was at home, was only partial here, and she might trigger an awkward collapse. But she could handle it in stages, as she had the assembly.

By the time Colene, Darius, and Pussy arrived, the yard was in order. Nona hugged Colene, then Darius. Tom hesitated, then hugged Colene.

Surprised, she kissed him. "Nona's been working on you," she said. "I can tell."

"She wants me to be more assertive."

"She's right. She wants to keep you, if she can."

Then Colene was greeting Cat and Burgess, and Tom was greeting Pussy. "She humped you!" Pussy said. She of course could read him without telepathy. "It must have been glorious."

"It was."

Colene and Darius went to the house to tell the parents

of their departure. Nona conjured knapsacks full of food
for their journey, including one shaped for Burgess to
carry, so that he would not have to depend on the substance of the Virtual Mode.

Amos Forell showed up. "I'm sorry to see you go
again," he said. "But it was great while it lasted."

"Even if we didn't get to kiss you to death?" Nona
inquired, kissing him.

"Even then," he said with mock regret. "Meanwhile,
that microbe you found for me is baffling the local schol-
ars. I think it has a fair chance to make me known, in my
own little obscure realm. I want to thank you for that."

"Thank Tom," Nona said. "He provided it."

Forell turned to Tom and shook his hand. "Thank you,
Tom. You have given me a gift of incalculable value to
me: my niche in the annals of science."

"It was an accident."

"Some of life's greatest discoveries are accidents."

Nona glanced at Pussy, who was wishing she could
greet the man the way Nona had. Like Tom, she couldn't
ask. *Do it* Nona thought at her, making it a directive.

Pussy stepped in immediately. "May I have a kiss too?"

Forell laughed. "I thought you'd never ask!" He took
her in his arms and kissed her. Her delight spread out to
all of them.

Colene and Darius emerged from the house. "Unhand
that poor man!" Colene called cheerfully. "It's my turn."
She flung herself at Forell and planted a passionate kiss
on his face.

He drew back and stared at her with muck horror. "Colene! What has happened to your dolor?"

"The magnet sucked it away. I feel great now. It's as
if I've been carrying this thirty-pound bag of sand on my
back all my life, and now it's gone, and I'm about ready
to float into the air." As she spoke, her feet actually left
the ground; she was floating. "Nona!" she cried, surprised.

Then she sank suddenly back to the ground as they all burst into laughter.

"I'd give almost anything to go with you," Forell said.

"You'd have to hold one of our hands to cross each Mode," Nona said. She glanced at Pussy and Colene. "The three of us would have to take turns holding you and kissing you, and you couldn't escape."

"Anything but that," he said ruefully.

"Oh, it might not be so bad. We could assign Pussy to keep you warm at night. She would take special delight in that."

He backed away, feigning reluctance. "My wife would never understand." And that, of course, was true.

Then they donned their packs and marched as a group to the anchor site. Colene paused at the brink. "Amos, that magnet treatment works. I set it up so that Mom is next for it. But I'll be gone. Could you sort of keep an eye, to be sure they don't renege?"

"I will keep an eye out," he agreed.

Then Colene stepped across the boundary, giving herself no time to dawdle. The others followed. Forell and the house vanished. They were on their way.

"No mind predator," Colene said, satisfied. "But I think we'd better move right along, in case the magnet wears off. No telling what delays we may encounter on the Virtual Mode."

The others agreed. They formed a column, with Tom and Nona at the rear. They moved rapidly through the Modes, seeing the town and its streets change. Tom found the shifting architecture intriguing.

They encountered a building that blocked direct forward progress, so they had to walk along the street to the side, remaining in one Mode. It didn't matter; there would be a cross street soon.

A door opened and a dog emerged. It stared at the

group. It was wearing a neatly tailored vest. Colene and Darius halted.

"Uh-oh," Colene said as they caught up to her.

"There is a problem?" Cat inquired.

Who are you? the dog demanded in their minds.

Tom realized that this was a Mode with telepathic animals. He should have realized that the horse Seqiro would not be the only one.

"We're a party just passing through," Colene said politely.

You're wearing clothing. Remove it at once.

Colene sighed. "Sorry; can't do. We'll just get on out of your way."

Insolent bitch! There was a flare of pain, as of a club striking a backside, and Colene fell against Darius.

Tom leaped forward, going for the dog. But it hit him with a ferocious blast of energy that dropped him to the ground, stunned.

Then a bolt struck the dog, and it too fell. Tom knew that Colene had channeled it from Seqiro. "Cross!" Darius said, half carrying Colene away from the fallen dog. Nona and Pussy caught Tom under the arms and dragged him in the same direction, while Cat and Burgess moved too.

They remained on the street near the building, but the dog was gone. They were in the adjacent Mode.

"It's like this," Colene said as Darius held her steady. "We're in the telepathic animal Modes. They don't like uppity humans. Seqiro can help us some, but it's best just to stay out of trouble."

"We understand," Cat said, speaking for the three Felines, who surely counted as humans in this region. Burgess wasn't human, but neither was he animal in that sense.

"Let's keep going. The faster we get beyond this region of Modes, the better off we should be. The stun effect should wear off soon. We can help each other walk."

Darius put his arm firmly around Colene, and they walked toward the next cross street. Nona and Pussy hoisted Tom's arms up across their shoulders and supported him as he feebly made his feet work.

They reached the intersection and turned, immediately passing into the Mode they had just left. The same dog was down the street, now joined by another.

There!

They plunged on, crossing the next boundary before the dogs could strike again. There were dogs here too, but these were now ones who were astonished by the appearance of this freakish caravan. Before they could make demands, the group was into the next Mode.

They continued rapidly along this street, passing different breeds of dogs, then cats, then cows, then horses. "Seqiro!" Tom said. "Is he here?"

"It doesn't matter," Nona said. "He's not an anchor now, so he couldn't come with us."

Tom recovered full use of his body, and saw that Colene was also walking alone. At one point, as they jogged sideways to get around another building, she spoke to him. "Thanks for trying to help, Tom."

"I didn't succeed."

"Oh, I think you did. You distracted that mutt so the rest of us could organize."

Finally they escaped the telepathic animal Modes, fortunate in their ability to cross boundaries before the animals could assert themselves. They came to a plain covered by brush, as if it were at the edge of the city, but actually a new class of Modes.

As they continued crossing boundaries, the brush became larger, formed into small trees, then medium trees and then large trees. The forest continued to grow, as if on an accelerated course of life, but it was actually merely the difference between clustered Modes. The trees became giants, towering into the sky, shutting out the sun. Their spreading root-bases became formidable obstacles, forcing the party to detour and detour again to get by them. The sky disappeared and dusk seemed to fall, though it was only midday. They were like ants walking by normal trees. Burgess had increasing difficulty, because he could not readily float over irregular surfaces.

They tackled the problem methodically. Nona conjured masses of solidifying foam, which the others shaped into ramps that Burgess could float along, with the help of the others hauling from the sides. It slowed the party, but progress was still good.

At one point they encountered a beetle the size of one of the cars in Colene's Mode. They hastily backed away, through the boundary they had just crossed, and the big bug was gone. It was the kind of creature one would expect to associate with trees this size.

They came to a river. Now it was Burgess' turn to help, ferrying them one by one across it. It lasted several Modes. Then the giant forest resumed. Thereafter it slowly diminished, until by evening they were able to make camp in an approximately normal forest. They located a streamlet for drinking and washing, and made a shelter from Nona's conjured substance.

"Know something?" Colene remarked. "I like the Virtual Mode. Here I can be something other than myself." She stripped off her shirt and trousers. "Coming, Darius, or do I have to wash myself?"

Darius smiled and joined her by the stream. Pussy took a position by a tree trunk and watched them without joining in. They had camped so that it was in the same Mode as they were; it was better to stay together, because if something happened to one person in another Mode, the others might not know of it immediately. So the forest resounded with Colene's shrieks as Darius splashed cold water on her.

"She's getting closer," Cat remarked. "Her loss of dolor helps."

"But she's not there yet," Pussy said. "She can play, but she can't perform."

"Unlike Nona," Cat agreed.

Pussy looked at Nona, lifting an eyebrow. She knew, of course, but would not speak openly of it unless Nona did.

"It's true," Nona said. "I seduced Tom."

Tom had not been asked to speak, so he did not. Certainly he would not correct her statement. Nulls were not seduced, they were used.

"Will you keep him?" Cat asked.

"I don't know. I think I want to return to my home Frame of Julia, to fulfill my duties there. It is governed by women; men have no magic other than illusion. I'm not sure Tom would like it there."

"His preference has no relevance," Pussy said. "You know that."

"Yes it does. I don't want a servant, I want a man."

"How do men differ from servants, there?" Cat asked.

Nona laughed. "Not by much, actually."

"How does Tom differ from one of those men?"

Nona looked at Tom. Her smile seemed somewhat pained. "Not by much. It's a very restrictive environment. He might indeed fit in. But there's something else: if I took him, your trio would be broken."

"It will be broken anyway," Cat said. "I alone will return to the DoOon Mode."

Nona's gaze continued. "Tom, I think I would like to have you with me. But I remain uncertain it is right, and I can't ask you, because you have no will apart from mine. I need an objective way to judge."

"Then ask me," Cat said.

"What is your verdict?"

"I have no verdict, merely a view. Our trio is doomed;

were we to return together to DoOon, we would be recycled because our usefulness is done and our knowledge
might cause embarrassment to Ddwng. Therefore it is better to place Tom and Pussy elsewhere, as compatibly as
is feasible. I can not long endure apart from my trio, but
Tom can endure with a woman he loves, and Pussy with
a man she loves. She can surely find a man to love. The
question is whether you have sufficient use for Tom to
keep him."

"This is not the way I think!" Nona protested.

"That is why the decision must be yours. I simply point
out that you would be doing Tom no disfavor by keeping
him. If you do not take him, we will try to find a woman
for him at Darius' Mode."

"But what of romance? What of love?"

"That, again, is entirely yours to give or deny."

Nona shook her head. "In my home Mode, I will be
one of the few elite. Every man will seek my favor, and
will obey my least whim without question. We do not
have telepathy there. I will have no way to know whether
he cares for me personally at all. That is part of what
drove me away from it." She looked at Tom again. "At
least I know, with Tom. He doesn't care about my status
or my powers of magic."

"Neither does he resent them," Cat said.

She looked at Cat. "You have made a significant point.
I want to be loved, not obeyed. Tom is perfect in that
respect. *But is it right?*"

Cat considered a moment before answering. "Right is
a concept determined largely by emotions I lack. It is right
if you believe it is. If you want it to be. Considering what
I know of your nature, I believe it would be right if you
came to love Tom."

"And there's the key," she agreed. "Colene loves Darius but can't have sex with him. I can have sex with Tom,
but I don't know whether I can love him."

Darius and Colene returned, naked and dripping. "We forget to get towels," she said.

Nona conjured voluminous towels, and they wrapped them around themselves. Then Nona stood, disrobing. "Our turn, Tom," she said.

Tom went with her to the stream. "Don't you resent being ordered about?" she asked.

"No. I am made to be directed."

"And you can't do anything on your own unless it is directed, or you know it is desired."

"Yes."

"I feel I am taking advantage of you."

"That is your prerogative."

"Nevertheless, it bothers me. Tom, if you could be free of your nature—if you could be fully human, with no obligation to serve anyone, or to do anyone any favors, what kind of life would you choose?"

"I would choose to be with you."

She stamped her foot in the water, making a splash. "Damn it, can't you say anything but that?"

Tom was mortified. "Mistress, I will say anything you wish me to. I want never to cause you distress of any kind. I apologize for not better comprehending what you wish of me."

There were tears in her eyes. "Tom, I'm sorry. I'm railing at you for being what you are. You can't change. I'm the one who has to change."

"Nona, you are already perfect. Any change in you would be for the worse."

"That's not true!"

Tom was silent. He could not directly contradict a mistress, but neither could he agree that she had any imperfection.

"Get down here in the water with me," she said. "Splash cold water over me."

He did so. She screamed with the shock of it, as Colene had; it was very cold.

"Now with that reminder of reality," she said, "I can do at least one thing halfway objectively. You have told me I am perfect. That I could not change for the better. I say that's false. Let's see whether I can prove it."

He continued splashing water on her, as she had not asked for a reply.

"Tom, I care for you, but I do not love you. If I came to love you, that would be an improvement, wouldn't it?"

Now he had to answer. "I am irrelevant. You are perfect regardless whom you love."

"You're being evasive. We're discussing your opinion of me. Wouldn't I be better for you if I loved you?"

Tom continued to kneel in the water, unable to answer. It was Cat who did so. "Nona, you are posing a question Tom is not competent to answer. You will do him damage if you persist."

"Then *you* answer it!"

"Tom would like to have you love him, but he is not permitted to request it, even by implication. It is also true that to the degree you loved him, you might become limited by his horizons, and therefore be less than you are. He does not want to diminish you in any way. You may love him if you choose, but that must be entirely your decision, not his. If you keep him, you must accept this limit in him. He is not and will never be a free man."

"And I must always tell him what to do?" she asked somewhat bitterly.

"That is true. If that disturbs you, perhaps it is better to send him away."

She shook her head. "This is theoretically every woman's dream: to have complete power over a man. It repels me. I want an independent man."

"Then send him away," Cat repeated.

She opened her mouth, but did not speak. She caught

water in her hands and splashed herself. Then she spoke. "I can't."

"Then perhaps you have the capacity to love him, not yet realized."

"Perhaps I do," she agreed. She turned to Tom. "Throw me down in the shallow water and make love to me."

Tom hesitated. "I am uncertain this is your true desire."

"So you *don't* have to take my commands literally."

"He does not," Cat agreed. "But he does have to obey his understanding of your will."

"Then I'll do it to you," she said. She put her hands on his shoulders and pushed him back. He could not resist her, and fell into the chill water. Then she fell on top of him, her bare breasts against his chest. "Do it, do it, do it!" She brought her head down and kissed him.

She did want it. He responded, clasping her and finding her warm interior. Her mind sought his as he climaxed, and she rode his pleasure into her own, extending it for him. Now he realized that in their prior couplings she had not actually climaxed; she had shared his. This time she had completed it. He had never before experienced a female climax. It was less intense than his own, but it lasted longer, and there was a broader pleasure in it.

They lay there in the cold water, sharing the lingering rapture. There was a sound.

He looked up, past Nona's head. Darius, Colene, and Pussy were applauding the performance.

Nona lifted her head. "Get out of here!" she cried, furious.

They retreated. Nona looked at Tom and laughed ruefully. "We have no privacy, mentally; they shared our passion. But it's traditional in my culture that most sexual acts be private. I got carried away."

"I love you."

"And you didn't have to say that," she said, and kissed him. "Tom, I think Cat is right: I have the capacity to love you. Can you settle for that? No, don't answer; it's rhetorical. You have no choice. But I believe I will keep you. Maybe, to avoid subjecting you to the rigors of my Mode's culture, I will go with you to Darius' Mode to stay."

Overwhelmed, he lifted his head and kissed her. He felt her surge of pleasure: he hadn't had to do that either. He was learning a little bit of initiative even as she was learning a little bit of love.

"Maybe we'll meet in the center, your initiative and my love," she said, and flattened herself against him. "Now I know we could keep right on doing this, because you are crafted for chronic performance, but let's finish our wash-up and get dry and warm. I promise, at some more convenient time I will make trial of your endless potency."

"There is no ne—" But she cut him off with another kiss.

They got clean, and she conjured towels, and she insisted on drying him even as he dried her. Then they rejoined the others.

"God, I wish I could do that!" Colene exclaimed.

"Well, I suppose I could lend you Tom."

"Please do not," Tom said quickly. Then he was chagrined; he had spoken out of turn. But it hardly mattered; they were all laughing. It had been a joke.

They ate supper from their provisions. Conjuring ramp material and towels and firewood was fine; they did not need to cross the boundaries with them. But food was best from an anchor.

Colene joined them and spoke quietly. "I'm sorry about snooping. I guess I just had to make a joke of it, so I wouldn't cry. I'd give anything to be able to have sex like that. But even in the throes of it, listening in, I felt myself wincing. My dolor is gone, but not my hang-up about sex."

"I'm sorry I reacted as I did," Nona said. "I was wrestling with my own indecision, and was caught by surprise."

"That's okay. We were pretty crude." Colene returned to Darius.

Nona conjured plenty of warm blanket material, and they retired for the night. "Is it all right if we just clasp without more sex?" she asked in a whisper. But before he could answer, she laid her forefinger across his lips. "I know anything I want is all right with you. But I really *don't* like taking advantage. I will make you this deal: let me sleep this night, and just before dawn you may do what you want with me, even if I remain asleep."

"Oh, Nona, I would never—"

She touched his mouth with her finger again. "Wrong answer, Tom. I have in the past, long before I met you, dreamed of just such a liaison, and it intrigues me. If I wake and find you in me, I will know you made a decision of your will, and it will please me. Do you understand?"

"You want me to—"

"I want you to make your own decision, knowing that I will approve it regardless of its nature. I am not telling you do to anything; I am telling you that you *may* do it."

"I understand," he said doubtfully.

They slept. He did wake before dawn, and considered what she had said. Yet to do such a thing with a mistress without a direct order—that was painfully daunting. Still, he did desire her. But he had no right to impose his will. Though she had asked him to do just that. How could he decide?

Pussy, nearby, lifted her head. "Do it, idiot!" she snapped. "You're ruining my sleep. I haven't been humped in ages."

Apologetically, he clasped the sleeping woman with infinite tenderness and slowly, carefully, delicately, made his way into her. He did not want to disturb her repose, so he remained quite still. Then he was overtaken by a rush of urgency, and though he did not move his body, he put his essence forcefully into her.

Nona's eyes opened. "Well done," she said, and kissed him. Had she been awake throughout? She was much better at reading his mind that he was at hers; he generally received only those thoughts she chose to share with him.

Nearby, Colene spoke. "Darius, maybe if you did it that way, I'd be okay."

"You would not," Darius responded. "You are not receptive in the way she is."

"Still, it was nice," Pussy said.

"Even I can appreciate the tenderness and satisfaction of it," Cat said. "This is a truly caring relationship."

Everyone had been tuning in!

Nona laughed. "In my Mode, there is no telepathy," she reminded him. "Won't that visit be a blessing!"

Tom was inclined to agree.

They were all awake, so they got up and dismantled their camp by dawn. Soon they were on their way.

"Uh-oh," Colene said. "It's back."

"But you have no dolor," Pussy protested.

"Maybe we were wrong about that."

"Perhaps it regards your present state as a temporary aberration," Cat said. "It knew you would emerge at some time from the anchor Mode, and it knows your mental trace, so it checked this region periodically and now has found you. If you are not in dolor now, its siege seems likely to put you there."

"You got that right," Colene said, putting her hands to her head. "Damn damn damn!"

"We can help you," Pussy said. "Ride Burgess, and Cat and I will flank you."

"Gotta do it," Colene agreed.

"We remain too far from my Mode," Darius said. "Which Mode is closest?"

"Mine," Nona said. "We were heading for it anyway."

He nodded. "So we were. Lead us there."

Nona took the lead, and Tom accompanied her. "At least you will get a good look at my realm," she said. "If you truly don't like it—"

"How can I dislike your home?"

"We'll see."

As it happened, there were no bad obstacles intervening, and they moved rapidly toward Julia. That was fortunate, because Colene's suffering could be felt by all of them. The siege of the mind predator obliterated her prior cheerfulness and put her into a maelstrom of horrors. Some were physical, some mental, but the worst were sexual. Their specific natures did not manifest, but their emotional burdens did. The girl's recent cheer was indeed mere gloss over an abyss of awfulness, and that was what the predator was feeding on.

"We could never have done it, if that had been in our minds," Nona murmured. Tom could only agree.

They came to some eerily odd Modes. Their landscapes seemed normal yet subtly abnormal. Strange threads of elusive substance extended from odd projections on the ground.

"These are fractal Modes," Nona explained. "We are approaching my home realm."

Tom did not know what she meant, but she was too busy orienting on her anchor to clarify it for him. Soon they came to a grassy hill, and the Modes stopped changing.

Colene lifted her head. "It's gone."

Thus suddenly they were in the new anchor Mode. "Oh, I never thought I would be so glad to be home!" Nona exclaimed. She hugged Tom and kissed him. "I will make you happy too."

"You are already doing so."

There was a village at the base of the slope, and a castle beyond it. They made their way toward the castle.

"I should explain for the Felines that red-cloaked Amazons now govern this planet," Nona said. "We brought them across during our last stay here. Each of them has magic similar to my own, but they may defer to me because I am native."

Tom made an effort, and asked a question. "Why did you bring the Amazons, if women already rule?"

"Oops, I omitted something. My world of Oria was governed by men when I grew up; they were the ones with magic. But I was the ninth-born of the ninth-born, and therefore had magic too, the only women to possess it. With the help of Colene and Darius and Seqiro, I succeeded in reversing it, so that the men lost their magic. But that did not immediately give women magic; that has to wait for a new generation to grow up, possessing it. So there was some civil disturbance. To quell it, we brought in magic women from a larger planet, who now govern and keep order. They are the Amazons, larger than those of Oria, though small for their own world."

"Her Mode has many fractal worlds," Colene explained. "All different sizes. Some are huge, and some are microscopic, but they all have people on them, sized according to their worlds."

"This is a strange Mode," Cat said.

Nona laughed. "It is indeed. But perhaps we will not be remaining here long."

"I had understood that you intended to remain here," Cat said.

"I thought I should, but now I think I would prefer to remain with the group. I think Tom would prefer it there."

"We'll be glad to have you," Colene said.

There was a swirl of air before them. A carriage formed, with a black-and-white-robed driver. "Regent Tulip recognizes the approach of the ninth of the ninth, and welcomes her to the premises," he said, bowing.

"I will walk with Burgess," Cat said.

The others got into the carriage, which then floated toward the castle. They stepped out at the front gate, where a red carpet spread itself out before them.

They walked inside, where the carpet guided them to the audience chamber. There was the Amazon, a tall woman in a bright red tunic. She rose immediately and went to greet Nona. "Gracious lady," she said, bowing her head. Tom realized that she was not speaking any language he knew; Seqiro's telepathy made it intelligible.

"Regent Tulip," Nona replied. "Thank you for your courtesy. This is my companion Tom, and my friends Darius, Colene, and Pussy. Two more are on the way."

"We remember Darius and Colene, and of course Burgess."

"Are there facilities for a temporary stay?"

"There are, of course. But you, lady, I hope are returning to stay."

Nona shook her head. "I'm not sure I am. Are things not in good order here?"

"They may be," Tulip said. Then she changed the subject. "You are surely tired, and wish rest and refreshment."

Actually they were in good shape, but Nona took the hint. "Yes, we would like to relax for a while."

They found themselves in an elaborate three-room suite. Nona had the primary room. "I do like the notion of a hot bath," she said. She glanced at Tom. "You have a question?"

He did. "If there is no telepathy here, how can I understand this language?"

"Seqiro's mind does reach here, though his power is limited in this Mode. It is Colene's expanding mind that makes it possible. Were we to remain here, while they left, you would not be able to understand local speech. That's one reason I think it better that we not remain here."

"You may keep me here if you choose," he said. "Or send me away. You may be better off unfettered."

"Or I may go with you to another Mode," she said. "Now let's have that bath."

It was a fine big tub with plenty of soapy foam. They washed each other, dried, and donned the tunics that appeared. Nona's was red, Tom's black.

They found the others similarly cleaned and garbed. Cat and Burgess had arrived, and were ensconced in an adjacent chamber. There was also a message from the regent: she wished to confer privately with Nona.

Nona went, but she took Tom along. He stood behind her when she took her seat, and neither moved nor spoke thereafter. He just listened.

"Nona," the regent said. "You must stay. Oria has need of you."

Tom felt Nona's concern. He knew what the regent evidently did not: their whole party was telepathically linked, and heard what Nona heard. They might separate physically, but they remained a group mentally. "Things are not in good order here?"

"They are now, but already there are signs of future problems. We Amazons never anticipated an assignment like this. As you know, we were of little account on our own world. We have no experience in governing. Rivalries are developing, which may in time lead to conflicts. There is no way to prevent it, unless we have a queen we all respect."

"A queen," Nona said, feeling a chill.

"You, Nona. You are the ninth of the ninth, the only native woman with magic. The people will follow you—and so will the Amazons, because we all owe you everything. You alone can be queen—and you must be, to preserve the order of the planet."

"I have no desire for such status or power. I left Oria to avoid it. I brought you Amazons here instead."

"You have no moral choice," Tulip said grimly. "You must do it, for the sake of Oria."

"I do have a choice! I brought the anima. I brought the Amazons. I have no further obligation."

The regent looked at her. "It must of course be by your own choice."

"I choose to leave! I will do so tomorrow."

Tulip looked down. "If you can leave, perhaps that is best."

Nona stood and turned away. The dialogue was at an end. Tom followed her back to the suite. As they walked, Tom heard the dialogue of the others, in his mind.

"What did the regent mean by that?" Pussy asked. "That it is best if Nona leaves?"

Cat replied. "She means that if Nona has the ability to desert her world in its hour of need, she lacks the quality of character the position requires."

"She doesn't have to do it!" Colene flared. "They have no right to demand it."

"She does have the obligation," Darius said. "It is not a matter of her choice. It stems from what she is."

"She's a woman who wants adventure and love and freedom!"

"She is the ninth of the ninth. That defines her role. The regent knows it—and so does Nona."

"She has a right to her own happiness!"

"Perhaps."

Tom and Nona arrived at the suite. "We were thinking about you," Colene said.

"So I thought," Nona agreed.

"Darius is a creature of duty. I'm a creature of feeling. I guess you have to decide what you are."

"I never sought notoriety or power. I just want . . ." Nona paused, uncertain of her true will. "Do any of you know what I want? I don't think I do."

"You want a family," Cat said. "Just as each individual

Feline needs its trio, you need the group you have formed. You are unable to abide living apart from it."

"Yes!" Nona cried. "When I joined with Darius and Colene and Seqiro, and then with Burgess and with you, that became my family. I want to stay with you!"

"Yes!" Colene echoed. "I'm with you. I need love, and that's Darius, but I also need family, and that's this group." She got down and kissed one of Burgess's contact points. "You included, BEM. We're your hive."

Burgess responded. Tom heard his thoughts as if they were his own.

It was true. But more than Burgess, she needed Seqiro, whose telepathy truly unified them, breaching the barriers of language and kind. The only way for the group to recover Seqiro was to free an existing anchor. Then the horse could form a new anchor, and be back with them. They also needed to change anchors to change the Virtual Mode, losing the mind predator for long enough to allow Colene to reach Darius' Mode. So Burgess would have to return to his Mode and free his anchor, making that possible.

"No!" Colene said. "I want Seqiro back, but not that way. You're one of us, squirtface."

"Yet it is feasible," Cat said.

"No," Darius said. "Colene cannot go on the Virtual Mode at all until an anchor changes. Therefore we are unable to cross the Modes as a group. Burgess is also unable to cross them alone. He can't reach his home Mode to free his anchor, however generous his gesture."

"And he has no more future alone in his home Mode than Colene has in hers," Nona said. "That would not be an option, even if we were at his Mode." Then she did a doubletake. "Oh, no!"

"*This* is the only anchor that can be freed," Cat said.

Tom felt Nona's grief. "I'm the one who has to do it. I have to free my anchor, and remain here to be queen."

There was silence, physical and mental. Nona crumpled, and Tom took her in his arms. She was caught, and they all knew it. Her pain was everywhere.

"It is not necessarily permanent," Cat said. "When I return to DoOon with the Chip, my duty will be done, and I can free the anchor. Then Nona can recover hers."

"That, too, is a generous motive," Darius said. "But there is a complication. As I understand it, the DoOon anchor is multiple-person: the three Felines, the three Caprines, and perhaps four humans we don't know about. A majority of them must make the anchor-freeing decision. I think you will not be able to do it."

"This is an interesting point," Cat said. "But I believe there is another way. Once I have delivered the Chip, your commitment is complete, and you can terminate the entire Virtual Mode, stranding the other anchor people where they are at that moment. Then you can establish a new one to include the Mode of Julia."

"And you will die," Nona said.

"This is my destiny."

"There may be another option," Darius said.

"What would that be?" Cat asked.

"We can leave this Virtual Mode in place, so that you can return. To rejoin your trio."

"My trio will be scattered across Modes."

"Not if we shut down the Virtual Mode after you return, and establish a new one that includes the Julia anchor. Then Tom will be able to rejoin Pussy and you."

"I could not leave Nona," Tom said.

"I would go with you, to rejoin the group," Nona said, her grief lifting.

Cat nodded. "There are options. Then perhaps it becomes feasible to free the Julia anchor."

Nona crossed the room and kissed Cat. "Feasible," she agreed.

The remaining day passed pleasantly. The regent served

them a fine banquet, and Nona told her of her intention to remain temporarily as queen. Tulip nodded, not entirely pleased.

When evening came, Nona took Tom on a walk outside. "What do you see?" she asked.

Tom looked around. "I see strange glowing patterns in the air, gossamer threads connecting odd designs."

"This is the nature of my world and my Mode," she said. "It is fractal. At its simplest, a fractal design is a simple variation of a pattern. Like a triangle with a similar smaller triangle set on each side. Then smaller triangles on each side of each smaller one, and so on indefinitely. Each iteration is both smaller and more complicated in detail than the one it is based on. Some regard a fractal pattern as half a dimension, since its extension is infinite and its final form unknown."

Tom's surprise grew. "These glowing strands continue infinitely?"

"In their fashion, yes. They contain other worlds like this one, with inhabitants like ours, but much smaller. And this world is part of a larger pattern we call Jupiter, whose inhabitants are enormously larger than we are, but fully human. The Amazons came from a world on a parallel thread, slightly larger than ours, with female magic."

"The regent is taller than you," he agreed.

"And she is very small for her world. Normal women there are a head taller than she. But here on Oria she is not only tall, but magical in a way that only our next generation will be."

"This is beautiful," he said, as the nocturnal patterns intensified. They had come to a small pavilion with a couch, and were looking out across the landscape.

"It is," she agreed. "I do love my home. But the idea of ruling it appalls me."

"If our group could be with you—with minds linked— then you could handle it."

"I suppose I could."

"If the minds could be linked across the frames—?"

She nodded. "I think so. With the family I could do anything."

"Can Seqiro do that?"

"Yes, I think he could. He has learned to reach across the Modes with his mind, and if he rejoined the group physically, he could do that much more."

"Then maybe you can have it all, after all, without remaining physically with the hive."

"Maybe I can." She considered for a moment, then impulsively hugged him. "Oh, Tom, thank you for your clear vision!" Then she kissed him, and drew him down on the couch, and they made love. This time she didn't let him go after the first climax, but held him for a second, and a third, until at last her overflowing passion was sated.

They lay clasped on the couch, savoring the aftermath. "I cannot at this moment say that I love you," she murmured. "But I think it will not be long before I do. I think I can stand being queen, with you always near me. I want to marry you, Tom."

"Oh, Nona," he said, and such was his surge of gratitude and passion that she was caught up in it, and they loved again.

Then they returned to the castle to tell the others, but of course they already knew.

SEVEN

Horse

Seqiro was growing increasingly apt at tuning in to Colene's mind, and with it the minds of her group. But it was a strain, especially now with the party in the Julia Mode, where his power was somewhat dampened. If they did not return to the Virtual Mode soon, he would have to draw back to recover.

He relaxed his mind and returned his attention to his physical environment. Maresy was there beside him. She was brown and healthy. She had been mind blasted by Seqiro's enemies, but Colene had restored her mind by shaping it into the semblance of the fantasy mare she had imagined before discovering the Virtual Mode. Thus Maresy was Colene, in a manner, and that made her ideal for Seqiro. He loved Colene, and this was that girl in equine form.

In fact, Maresy had proved to be more like Colene than even Colene had realized before she left. Maresy was depressive, a vessel of dolor. She was also given to spot visions of the future, and could do a little bit of magic. She had led the way in the quest for Colene's mind, and oriented on it first. Thus she had added materially to Seqiro's power, enabling him to reach farther and stronger through the Modes. He had never been aware of her before as a mare, but as an equine emulation of Colene she had become invaluable. She was his fitting mate.

Except that there, too, Maresy had come to resemble Colene. The girl was unable to breed with her man, because she had suffered rape. She wanted to do it, but her aversion would not allow her to indulge voluntarily. Maresy liked being with Seqiro, but when she came in season she avoided him. It seemed that only when Colene managed to bypass her fear of this interaction would Maresy do the same.

I regret this, Maresy thought. *But it is true. All that I am now, I received from Colene; my original self is gone.*

But overall she was a good companion, and Seqiro wanted to keep her with him. When he traveled with Colene, he had prepared to leave Maresy with reluctance, preferring not to lose the companionship of the girl. When the mind predator had proved to be lying in ambush for her, Seqiro had had to free his anchor to enable her to proceed along the Virtual Mode. It seemed that the shifting of the Virtual Mode confused the predator, so that it took some time to locate its prey again. Unfortunately it had also confused Seqiro, and he had taken time to locate her himself. Both he and the predator had been balked at first by Colene's continuing presence in the DoOon Mode, where they could not reach. But even after she traveled the Virtual Mode, her trace had been slow to coalesce. Had she not come to the environs of her home Mode, which was familiar to him, the search could have been longer yet.

Now that predator had found her again, and she had fled to the Julia Mode. But the predator was lurking, and would catch her the moment she departed that Mode. Seqiro could not detect the predator directly, but felt its influence in Colene's mind—and in Maresy's mind, to a lesser degree. The monster was there.

Yes.

The travelers were sleeping now. They had decided to vacate Nona's anchor, so that Seqiro could reclaim his anchor. He would do so. Then they would be here, and he could rejoin them. That had always been his desire.

Beside him, Maresy maintained mental silence. He knew why. She did not want to be left behind. The difficulty was that only the anchor persons could freely cross the Modes. Other residents of the anchor Modes could cross only when in contact with an anchor person, and could be stranded if such contact was lost. That made such travel dangerous.

Do you want me with you?

Yes, he did. It had been a difficult decision before, leaving her, and would be worse now. But was she was willing to come with him, giving up the Horse Mode?

Yes. I am much of Colene. I want to be with her too.

Then there was a way. At times Colene had ridden on Seqiro's back, especially when they wished to make it appear that he was a pure animal. If one of the anchor persons rode Maresy's back, that person would remain in constant contact, and Maresy would be able to cross freely. But if that person should lose balance and fall off, as might happen if a sudden change in Modes put them into a discontinuity, Maresy would be isolated, and perhaps unable to rejoin the anchor person. Seqiro did not care to risk that.

There is another way.

There was? What was it?

We can become co-anchors.

Seqiro realized that it was true. The DoOon Mode had set up about ten co-anchors, so it was possible. They would do it. Then there would no danger of isolation. Maresy had gained some of Colene's human intelligence, and thought of something Seqiro had not.

Maresy nudged him. She was pleased.

Then they grazed and slept, maintaining only nominal awareness of Colene and her group. When morning came, they would be ready. It was important that no other person on any other Mode have the chance to take the anchor. If that happened, Seqiro and Maresy might never have another chance.

Morning came. They had their lackeys load them with supplies, as for a long trip into the wilderness, keeping their minds closed about their real intentions. Seqiro had assumed a position of leadership since defeating his rival Koturo. He had not desired it, but his choices had been limited: dominance or death. His departure would allow the next most dominant stallion to assume power, and that did not bother Seqiro. He much preferred the excitement of the traveling group. He was like the woman Nona in that respect, preferring what Burgess thought of as the hive to separate power elsewhere.

So do I. Colene is headstrong and gambling by nature, and this is what I now like. Life will never be dull in her company.

But Colene wanted to settle down with Darius and be his true wife and bear his children. Surely that would be dull.

When she does that, I will bear your foals.

That seemed to be a sufficient answer.

Morning came, and they tuned in on the travelers. The party went to the anchor, and stepped across. Immediately the mind predator struck, savagely, bearing Colene down. Her present seeming joy was not match for it; it knew her true nature.

Darius carried her beyond the anchor. They had verified what they expected. The anchor had to be changed.

They bid farewell to the two who would remain in the Julia Mode. Colene hugged Nona, and Pussy hugged Tom. Then Nona tearfully freed her anchor.

Seqiro and Maresy grasped it, reaching jointly with their minds.

And the party stepped out into the Horse Mode.

"Horseface!" Colene cried, running up to hug his neck and bury her tearful face in his hide. Then she went to Maresy. "And Maresy! How I missed you both!"

In a moment, Darius performed introductions: "These are Cat and Pussy, whom we picked up in the DoOon Mode. They are anchor persons." He indicated Maresy. "And this is Maresy, Colene's dream mare."

But of course they already knew each other, because of the increasing linkage of minds.

"I see you're ready to travel," Colene said. "Both of you?"

Both of us, Maresy thought. *We are both anchors.*

"Great! You've taken care of things here? Nothing to stop you going on the Virtual Mode now?"

That was the case.

"Then let's go! I don't know long it will take the mind monster to find me again, so I don't want to dawdle."

I share your sentiment.

They stepped through the anchor. The adjacent mode was similar to the home one, differing only in minor detail. Colene looked around, verifying that there was no mind attack, and was relieved when there wasn't. A change in Virtual Modes had been effective before, but this could not be taken for granted.

They continued crossing Modes, and the landscape changed a bit more with each one. The horse sheds and fields vanished, and were replaced by something more ominous: chewed-up ground. Something large and perhaps fierce had done that.

"Can you range out and find a local mind?" Colene asked.

Pig, Maresy thought immediately.

Pussy jumped, alarmed. "Are the Swine on our trail?"

No. These are native hogs. But they are telepathic.

" 'Cause we're in the telepathic animal zone, again, because that surrounds the Horse Mode," Colene agreed. "So they're dangerous. But we should be able to avoid them by skipping across boundaries."

"Let's hope that is the case," Cat said. Seqiro found the neuter Feline's mind to be eminently rational.

They drew their group more tightly together and continued. Darius and Colene led the way, but stepped cautiously across each Mode boundary, ready to step back immediately if live pigs were spied.

We can do better, Maresy thought. *We can range mentally ahead, and discover where the pigs are.*

Seqiro realized that this was true. He and Maresy had learned to reach across many Modes with their minds, joining forces to increase their power. This was not true of other telepathic horses, or of other telepathic animals. It required a special discipline that Seqiro had developed only when confined, before first meeting Colene. He had reached out, seeking a companionable entity, and discovered Colene. It had been mutual love at first contact, a natural affinity between horse and girl. He had the physical and mental power, she had the hands and the intellect. Together they had escaped his Mode and traveled widely. No other telepaths had had reason to do such a thing. So they could surely spy on pigs, who would not be aware— or if they were, they would be unable to do much about it.

Colene turned back to join them physically. "But if you lead the way you could step into a physical hole and break a leg. We need light-bodied folk to go first."

We can range ahead from within our group, Maresy thought.

Colene nodded, mentally and physically. She liked the way Maresy thought. "Got it. We'll go first, but we'll go faster if you keep us posted about pigs."

They did so. Seqiro tuned in to Darius and the right side, while Maresy tuned in to Colene and the left side.

There were pigs to the right, about a hundred paces from their crossing point. Seqiro warned Darius.

Got it, the man's thought returned. He moved on, knowing that the pigs were too far away to interfere with the crossing.

They didn't try. They looked up, startled, as the horses passed, and did double-takes as Burgess followed. Then they were gone with the next boundary.

Pigs left, close, Maresy warned Colene.

Colene hesitated, but the local terrain was restricted, with prickly brush on one side and a lake on the other; they were threading through the slightly marshy break between them and lacked room to maneuver. *Maybe we can cross before they do anything,* she thought.

She and Darius did cross, but then two ugly boars recovered from their surprise and ran across to block the next traveler, Pussy. *Mode travelers,* one thought. *Capture them.*

A Swine mind caught Pussy's mind, and she was helpless. But then Seqiro and Maresy crossed. Coordinated, each of them delivered a mind knock to a boar, causing the pigs to back away, half-stunned. But they still blocked the way physically, jerking their tusks around.

They're now beyond the boundary, Seqiro told Pussy. *Walk right into them.*

Frightened, Pussy obeyed—and disappeared just before reaching the boars. The boundary affected the travelers, not the residents. Seqiro and Maresy spread out as much as they could, she setting her hoofs in the water, he treading down some brambles. They were making a channel for Cat and Burgess, guarding the way.

But the boars were tough, and of course they were experienced telepaths. They erected mental blocks against the horses and marched back into the narrow section of the Virtual Mode. *Here to us!* one broadcast to others in that Mode. *We have modies to catch!*

Cat and Burgess appeared from behind as the boars closed the gap in front. But they had been warned. Burgess set his body and sucked up water with his fore trunk. He jetted it out from his aft trunk, scoring on one boar. The jet was not strong enough to bowl the pig over, but it did surprise both boars, and they retreated a few steps. Burgess and Cat crossed the next boundary and were gone. Then Seqiro and Maresy crossed too.

The path continued, and they encountered no more close pigs. Instead they came into a broad forest where the air was swirling strangely.

The explosive plankton! Burgess thought, analyzing it as it passed through his system. His thoughts did not have the straight-line focus of the human thoughts, because his hive mind differed, but Seqiro had learned how to recognize them.

"But aren't they confined to water Modes?" Cat asked.

Burgess feared he had carried some across Modes, in their prior travels, and now they had infected the air of the forest.

Darius and Colene stepped back, as they now had room to form a group within a single Mode slice. "If so," Darius said, "this is a lesson in contamination. We thought it was impossible to carry the substance of one nonanchor Mode into another, but we hadn't thought of the microbes existing in the air we breathe and the water we drink. Any of us could have done it. Some specks might be partly assimilated, and then ejected across a boundary."

"Tom carried a germ from DoOon to Earth," Cat agreed.

"Traveling the Virtual Mode may be as dangerous for the Modes as for us," Colene said, chagrined.

"But this is mere conjecture," Darius concluded. "It seems more likely that any contamination we bring will soon die out in an alien Mode."

"Let's hope so," Cat said.

"What's the forest doing here?" Pussy asked. "It wasn't next to pigs before."

"Each Virtual Mode is a different slice across Modes," Colene said. "The effect is to shuffle them. Anything can be anywhere. We could next cross Julia, the fractal Mode, for all we know."

The Modes slowly changed, until the group was in a desolate region. Volcanoes erupted in the distance, and clouds of choking vapor clung to the land. They tried crossing quickly, but the adjacent Modes were similar; they could not escape the fumes.

"Nona could conjure voluminous scarves to wrap around our heads," Colene said. But of course Nona was no longer with them.

However, Seqiro and Maresy carried blankets. Darius, Colene, Cat, and Pussy wrapped light blankets around their heads, swathing mouths and noses and, to a more limited degree, eyes. Burgess needed no protecting; he could handle the fumes. That left the horses.

"Burgess can guide you," Cat said. "He can focus on the ground and choose a route that is firm for your feet. You can wrap your heads and follow him."

They did it. The humans wrapped a blanket around each horse's head, and the horses followed Burgess. As it turned out, they weren't blind, because they could see through Burgess' six stalked eyes, two of which obligingly looked back to focus on the ground at their feet.

After several Modes, the fumes eased, but now the

ground grew hot. They removed the blankets, and Burgess scouted ahead to locate the coolest continuing ground. Then the others charged across to reach cooler terrain before their footwear heated too much. Cat and Pussy lacked shoes, so had to ride Seqiro and Maresy.

In time, with cooperative effort, they passed the volcanic Modes and reached pleasant fields and forests. But these turned out to have their own challenges. When Seqiro set a foot on a grassy section, the blades of grass whipped around, hacking at his hoof. When Maresy took a sip of dark liquid in a pool by the roots of quiet trees, something invisible booted her in the rear. What was going on?

Actually Seqiro and Maresy could read the minds of plants as well as animals, though plants did not think in the same way. This grass was aggressive because it didn't like getting stepped on. They would try to avoid doing that hereafter.

"We'd better camp," Colene decided. "We've had a hard day and we're all tired. Maybe tomorrow we can figure these Modes out better."

They found a pleasant glade, whose plants actually fruited with baked pies. Of course the travelers didn't eat any those, but they did smell delicious. Seqiro read the minds of those plants, and discovered that the pies were their offerings for human beings. They hoped that the humans would protect them in exchange for the food, and it seemed that humans generally did. The party spread blankets to quell the militant grass, and settled down for the night.

Seqiro woke in the night, aware of a foreign presence. It was strange but did not seem inimical, so he remained quiet. He wanted to study it before rousing the others; it might be a passing innocuous animal.

The others were asleep, in their fashions. But Darius woke as the odd entity approached him. The creature was female, and mischievous, and curious. Her mind was like a shadow, never fully formed but not blank. She lay down beside Darius, moved in close, and kissed him.

Colene? he thought. Which was surprising, because this creature was nothing like Colene.

She moved in closer yet. Through Darius' perceptions, Seqiro formed an impression of the thing's form. It was lushly female in the human manner, with large bare breasts and expansive tresses. The body made its way up against Darius' body, and the firm bare belly and thighs sought contact with his own.

Not Colene! Darius thought. *But surely not Pussy either; she is barred from me.*

It had to be a native of this interim Mode. But why was she attempting to seduce Darius?

Seqiro, Darius' thought came. *Who is this woman?*

Seqiro had not thought to advise Darius that the person was something strange. The Felines tended not to initiate speech or actions, awaiting human directives. Seqiro tended to await human insight. *She is some kind of alien female, neither friendly nor hostile. She seems curious whether she can tempt you into copulation.*

Darius had the wit not to leap up physically. *This is neither Colene nor Pussy?*

Correct. They both remain sleeping.

What kind of woman would get into bed with an unknown man?

A mischievous one.

Darius considered. Now Seqiro picked up his incidental thoughts. This was a female of this Mode they had parked on, and she had picked the lone human male to approach. This was not like most women, who were far more choosy about sexual liaisons. Why would such a well endowed woman do such a thing? Darius' scientific curiosity was rising. *You are sure she is not dangerous?*

She does not intend you harm.

Darius made a mental laugh. *That is not the same thing. Would she be dangerous if rudely surprised?*

Seqiro tried to assess this possibility. *It is possible.*

I think we need female input. Can you wake Colene quietly?

Seqiro sent a thought to Colene. *Wake quietly. Something odd is occurring.*

Colene woke partially. *What is it, horsehead?*

A female is seducing Darius.

Suddenly she was totally awake. *Darius!*

I am here.

What are you doing?

I am the object of the seductive approach of a shapely woman.

Well, kick her out of bed right now!

Seqiro interceded. *We do not her know her nature. Her mind is strange. She might be dangerous if too abruptly repulsed.*

Colene was quick to appreciate the potential for trouble. *Then play along until you know it's safe to break off.*

There was a smile in Darius' thought. *May I pretend she is you?*

Sure. But keep me online.

Darius had been lying still, allowing the mysterious women to kiss him and rub her body against his. Now he became active, putting an arm around her and stroking his hand down her back and across her bottom.

Colene read his impressions: lush breasts touching his chest, smooth skin, plush posterior, and ultimately sexy overall. A body it was sheer delight for a man to touch. *Hey—you're supposed to pretend it's me!*

You feel like this to me.

Colene had to bite her tongue to keep from laughing, but there was envy and sadness too. She wished she could feel like that to him, with a body like that. But the plain fact was that she lacked the sheer mass of female attributes this creature sported.

Your body is perfect, Darius thought. *It is, I think, smaller than this, but as delightful to me. If you ever try to seduce me, you will succeed in an instant.*

And his feeling was sincere. He did like her as she was. *Stroke her some more.*

Darius did, and now Colene seemed to feel his hands on her body, playing the game of pretend sex so that she would not freeze up. His fingers cupped her buttock, shaping and being shaped by it.

The breasts, she thought. *Do the breasts too.*

He shifted position, and put his head down to the ample bosom. He kissed the upper breast. Colene writhed under her blanket. *The nipple.*

He kissed the nipple. Colene's breath came faster. *Darius! Do me!*

But this is not you, he reminded her.

It's close enough. Do me—through her.

Realizing that this was a breakthrough, Darius considered, and decided to proceed. If Colene could do it vicariously, maybe next time she could do it directly, and that was what he wanted.

He shifted position, laid the woman on her back, and got over her. She cooperated lithely. He made ready to enter her—and suddenly she froze.

He paused, more than familiar with this reaction. "No?" he asked aloud.

"No!" the woman agreed. "I can't do it!"

Darius rolled off her, resigned.

Shocked, Colene stifled her thoughts.

"What is going on?" the strange woman demanded, abruptly sitting up.

"I thought you were seducing me," Darius said.

"I was! I am! What came over me? I've never balked

before, and I've done it thousands of times. Did you hit me with a balk spell?"

Then Seqiro caught on. *I linked your minds—hers included. She became truly like Colene.*

"Truly like me," Colene said, disgusted. "I couldn't even do it vicariously!"

"You are frozen?" the woman asked.

"Frozen?"

"Cold, icy, chilly, frosty, freezing—"

"Frigid?" Colene asked.

"Whatever," the woman agreed crossly.

Now the others were waking, as early light filtered into the glade. "Who is this person?" Cat asked.

"Who are *you*, whiskerface?" the woman retorted.

"I am Cat Feline, of the DoOon Mode."

"Oh. Well, I am the Demoness Metria of the Demon Mode."

"There are demons here?" Colene asked. "This is a magic Mode?"

"Of course there are, and it is. What did you expect—drear Mundania, where everything is serious and there is neither magic nor much humor?"

Darius made a connection. "Those cutting, slashing blades of grass—is that a pun?"

"I suppose. This land is mostly made of puns."

"I suppose there were bound to be humorous Modes along with the serious ones," Darius said. "Metria, why were you trying to seduce me?"

"Because you are male. Did you want me to seduce a pulchritude?"

"A what?"

"Lovely, beautiful, attractive, charming, comely—"

"A pretty woman?"

"Whatever," she agreed crossly. As the light brightened, her body was increasingly visible, every bit as shapely as Darius' touch had indicated.

"But you can't just go around seducing any man you find," Colene said, frowning as she gazed at that body.

"Well, of course not. Too many are ugly or pot-bellied, and some are canny about relations with demonesses."

"Whyever would they be canny?" Colene asked with mixed feelings.

"They're afraid I'll fade into smoke and laugh just as they are at the point of climacteric, horribly embarrassing them."

"Point of what?" Darius asked.

"Never mind," Colene said quickly. "We know what you mean." But her curiosity remained. "So *would* you fade right then?"

"Of course. I wouldn't want to annoy my husband." She laughed and dissipated into a small cloud of smoke.

There was a silence, as both Darius and Colene realized that the supposed seduction had been a cruel tease throughout. A married demoness?

But Cat remained interested. "Are all the denizens of this Mode like you, Metria?"

The smoke had been floating away on the faint breeze. Now it expanded back into the lush female form and solidified. "No, only the demons. The humans and animals and plants are relatively unsharpened."

"Relatively what?" Darius asked.

"Dull," Colene said quickly. "It's a good thing you're not wearing anything, because clothes would just make you more attractive."

"Really?" A frilly dress with a tightly laced bodice formed round the demoness. Unfortunately for Colene's ploy, it did make her look even more seductive. The bodice had lacing but no material, and the skirt was extremely brief.

"I think it's time for us to move on," Colene said, as cross as the demoness when corrected on a word.

Darius agreed, smiling. This demoness was intriguing, but Colene's temper was wearing thin.

"I'll come with you," Metria said.

"I don't think so," Colene retorted as they picked up the blankets and packed them back on the horses.

The demoness looked prettily ornery. "I do think so."

Colene didn't answer. But when they resumed their trek, they passed through the boundary, and the demoness vanished. For all her mischievous magic, she was confined to her Mode. She was surely most frustrated. Colene's expression was smug.

"I believe I would like to know more of that Mode," Cat said.

Now Pussy laughed. "I'd like to see that demoness try to seduce *you*!"

They came to a river, where they paused to wash up. No dirt from the Modes clung to them, because it could not cross the boundaries, but their natural sweat did.

Then they saw the dragon. It was flying toward them, literally breathing fire. It was large enough to scorch them with a single exhalation.

They hastily picked up their clothing and waded as a group across the next boundary. The dragon vanished. It, too, was surely surprised. They completed their wash-up, dressed, and settled down on the far bank for breakfast. Then they resumed their trek across the Modes. They were not far from Darius' anchor; his sense of home was sure.

And the mind predator located Colene.

"We can make it," Darius said. "Shield her, carry her, and we'll hurry."

Pussy embraced Colene, shielding and sharing. Darius and Cat heaved her up onto Seqiro's back. Then they moved forward as rapidly as was feasible.

Seqiro felt Colene's pain. This siege was more sudden and worse than the others; once the predator located her, it bore right in. This time it meant to consume her. She cried out with the horror of the invasion. This was rape of the mind.

Seqiro continued to carry her, and Pussy continued to walk beside him, her hand on the girl's leg, making sure she did not fall. They would get her there.

They were indeed close to their destination. Darius led them there with sureness, and they came to a region where the terrain gradually turned crystalline. The land itself seemed to be formed of crystals, forming gentle hills encrusted with increasingly sharp projections. Pussy and Cat had to wrap their feet in blankets lest they be cut, for there was no place to step that was not barbed by the sharp stone points. The horses' hoofs were tougher, but were sustaining some damage. Darius' boots did well enough, but Burgess' floating was slowed by the crystals, because they interfered with his cushion of air.

The hills grew into mountains. Then the mountains turned flat on top, becoming mesas. Their route wound around their bases, growing narrower. Seqiro was not sure they would be able to continue much farther.

Darius stopped. "Here," he said.

Where? Maresy thought.

"There. The anchor is on the mesa." He pointed up the almost vertical slope of a canyon. "There is a ladder." Then he paused, and Seqiro understood why. How were the horses and Burgess going to use a ladder?

"Take Colene through first," Cat suggested. "Fetch a harness and ropes for the others."

Darius nodded. "I must carry her. Tie her on me."

They did so. The limp girl was fastened to his back, her arms bound around the front of his neck, her legs around his waist. It was awkward and uncomfortable— Seqiro could feel that directly—but it left the man's arms and legs free for the ladder. Fortunately Colene was a small woman, hardly half Darius' mass, and he was a healthy man.

Even so, it was not easy. He started up, but the girl's arms and legs required him to hold himself out from the ladder, making climbing more difficult. He would soon tire.

"We can help," Cat said. "Pussy from above, me from below."

Pussy climbed the ladder, then hooked her legs through the rungs athletically and hung down to grab Darius' shoulders. She pulled him up one rung, then let go and mounted the next herself. Cat helped from below, putting his hands under Colene's bottom and boosting her. When Darius got high enough, Cat climbed below, and continued boosting with one hand. It was not polite or pretty, but it did the job.

When Darius tired, as he had to, Seqiro projected strength and control, giving him more power. This drew on resources not normally available to a human body, and would deplete it for a longer time, but was necessary now. They had to get Colene through the anchor and away from the mind predator.

Rung by rung, they ascended. It was tediously slow, but it was steady. At last they reached the flat mesa and disappeared onto it.

Then the pain of the girl's mind faded. She had passed through the anchor, and the siege on Colene abated.

She fainted. Seqiro felt her unconsciousness. It was a relief; she was now able to start the process of recovery.

After a time Darius returned, climbing down the ladder. He was tired, but reluctant to relent. He carried a mass of rope. "This is a harness," he said, amplifying the concept in his mind so that they could understand. "We will first haul Burgess up, as he is the lightest of you three. Then we will haul each of you horses in turn."

They understood. Darius laid the rope harness on the ground over the crystals. Burgess floated over it. Darius closed the net over him. It tied into several ropes hanging from a tripod and pulleys at the edge of the mesa. Seqiro knew they had anchored it securely, and that Cat and Pussy were operating it from above.

They hauled on the ropes, and the pulleys magnified their strength. Burgess rose into the air, bumping against the ladder. Fortunately that held him out from the canyon wall, so that he was not cut by the crystals. In due course he rose above the floor of the mesa, and they swung him onto it. He disappeared.

After that they did the same thing for Maresy. She was in touch with their minds, so had confidence, though her four legs dangled below the harness and the ladder chafed her hide. They used a large translucent crystal as a counterweight; as she went up, it came down, so that they were not actually hauling more than Burgess' weight.

Finally it was Seqiro's turn. He was the heaviest, but the hoist was strong; they merely geared it with a larger counterweight and further pulleys, so that it was very slow, but he did rise.

At last he crested the top and swung to the mesa. It seemed precariously small. They removed the harness, and guided him to a spot on its center. He crossed it— and it was the anchor, and suddenly he was in Darius' Mode, with no ropes or pulleys or structures behind him.

Now Seqiro looked around at this Mode, from this height. He had seen it only from below, before. It was interesting. It seemed to be entirely crystalline, with some crystals the size of mountains, covered by smaller ones, all of them reflecting the light of the sun. Above were clouds of many colors. It had not seemed pretty from below, but from this height it was beautiful.

Pussy stepped through the anchor behind him. "It's lovely, isn't it," she said. "Now that we don't have to walk on the crystals."

They didn't? Seqiro had been concerned with the rope hauling, and had not tuned into the minds beyond. Now

he read in her mind that the folk of this Mode used conjuration to move themselves from mesa to mesa, seldom
bothering with the treacherous paths below.

"Like this," Pussy said. "It's fun." She produced a little
figure of a cat-woman. "This is mine. It has my solid,
liquid, and gas. When I invoke it, and move it on a map,
it takes me where I indicate, by sympathetic magic. I'll
go with you, because now I know the way."

Seqiro found this confusing. Where was Maresy?

"They have a nice pasture plateau reserved for us," she
said. "They do have horses here, but they're not telepathic, really not your kind. Anyway, we want to keep
the hive together, for Burgess' sake. So we'll go there, at
least for now." She brought out a figurine resembling a
horse. "Now we need to tune this to you. I'll need five,
no six of your hairs for the solid. Is it all right to snip
them off?"

It was. Seqiro stood while she used her extendible nails
to cut off hairs from his shoulder. She fastened them to
the four legs, tail, and head of the figure. "Now the liquid:
a drop of your saliva will do." She brushed the figurine
across his tongue. "And your gas: breathe on it." He did
so.

"That's good. Now you need to hold it and—" She
paused. "I keep forgetting you don't have hands! Very
well; I'd better sit on you and handle it for you, along
with mine. But I'd better explain about the map."

She kneeled on the ground before him. "Do you see
the lines here? This is a map of the local terrain. Each
little circle is a plateau, a mesa-top. Everything's on mesa-
tops. We're on this one." She pointed to a circle. "We're
going to this one." She pointed to one some distance
away. "Our icons will take us there. But it's somewhat
jolting when you're not used to it, so be prepared. Do you
have the 'here' and 'there' in mind?"

He did, though he still did not properly understand the mechanism.

"You really don't need to, Seqiro. It'll happen. Now let me get up on you." She leaped and scrambled, and got herself ensconced on his back. "Now invoke your icon." She held the horse figure down where he could fix an eye on it.

He focused on it, willing it to be invoked. *You are Seqiro.*

"And I'm invoking mine. Now we're ready. Icons, we are stepping from here at the anchor to there at the pasture." She moved the icons in the air. "Here—to *there*."

There was a gut-twisting wrench. Seqiro did not like it; it felt like a torsion, which was a lethally serious matter for a horse. The scene changed. Now they were on a broad plateau, with many trees growing, and tall grass. The trees had green trunks and foliage of different colors. The grass smelled nutritious.

Maresy was there. She trotted over to nuzzle him. *You took your time, Seqiro!*

She liked to tease him. She had gotten that from Colene, of course. Sometimes he almost expected her to call him horseface.

"Don't forget to render it inert," Pussy said, sliding to the ground. "Otherwise it might take you somewhere else when you least expect it."

Seqiro willed the icon inert, and Pussy took it away.

Burgess likes this land too, Maresy thought. *We can stay here as long as we want, or go to other pastures.*

Cat and Darius appeared and deactivated their icons. "We have the afternoon to relax, while Colene recovers," Cat said. "Then we'll meet her friends here."

Seqiro was glad to relax. He and Maresy grazed companionably on the excellent grass, and Burgess hovered nearby, tasting the different flavors of the air. It seemed that each passing cloud was a different color, and the light that passed through them carried different nourishment. The closer to the clouds a mesa was, there more nourishment it got. The deep valleys between mesas got little, so were largely barren.

When evening closed, Colene appeared. "I'm better now," she said. "That last was a bad siege. Thanks for getting me here, horsie." She came to hug his neck.

She was welcome. He loved her.

"And I love you, hoofer. You and Darius. Now that both of you are here, I should be really happy."

But she wasn't. Her joy had been wearing down, and the siege of the mind predator had depleted more of it. She was coming to rest at her natural level of dolor. Unfortunately, Maresy's mood echoed Colene's.

"I'm no good for you, or anyone," she said. "I'm an emotional drag. I hate that."

How quickly her joy of the small reunion descended to her dolor of perceived inadequacy.

"Yeah, that's me," she agreed. "The vessel of dolor." She brightened marginally. "But they can handle it. I've asked four of my friends here to come meet you folk, to learn about the hive. One is Kublai, who filled in for Darius as Cyng of Hlahtar while he was gone. It's a really important position, but now Darius has to take it back so Kublai can retire again and marry his sweetheart, Koren. You'll like Koren, horsehead; she's like me, only she'll be naturally happy once she recovers."

Had something bad happened to her?

"You might say so. I'd better explain this for Cat and Pussy and Burgess too." The others were gathering around. "It's like this: the King of Laughter—that's how I translate it—marries a woman who has joy. Then he goes on tour, and takes the joy from her, multiplies it a thousandfold, and broadcasts it out to all the people nearby, making them all happy. Including her—but there's always a slight loss, so she's not quite as full of joy as she was before. With each performance he gives, at each village, she loses a bit more, until after a year or so she's too depleted to do it any more. Then he divorces her and marries another woman, and starts over. She gets a good retirement, but she can't enjoy it much until she slowly recovers her natural joy. That can take years, decades even, because it takes about as much joy to abolish her dolor as has been given out to others. It's that thousandfold factor, working the other way."

"Darius took from me only a few times," Pussy said. "It was horrible."

"Fortunately, Darius rescued Prima, a woman who can also multiply feeling," Colene continued. "She should have been Cyng, but the sexist elders wouldn't let a woman have the job. It's a bad scene, but for now Prima is satisfied to marry the Cyng and let him take from her. Because she can multiply it herself, she is able to maintain her level of joy, so she can do it indefinitely. So Koren no longer has to do it, and actually she's almost recovered now, because not much was taken from her. But until Kublai retires, she can't marry him. You see, here love and marriage and sex are three different things. A Cyng can have a wife he doesn't love, and another woman he does love, and a mistress he uses in bed." She glanced at Pussy. "That's a different usage: it means just sex, not dominance."

"I understand," Pussy said.

"But Kublai wants to have all three in one woman—and now that Darius is back, he can. He can marry Koren, and love her, and have sex with her too. But Darius—"

"Give it time," Darius said.

"Darius will marry Prima, in this Mode," Colene continued doggedly. "And love me. And have sex with Ella or Pussy. Because I can provide him with neither joy nor sex."

"Love suffices," Darius said.

"The hell it does! I want to do it all for you!"

They were all quiet, feeling the flare of frustrated love. Colene could not provide joy because she was a vessel of dolor, and she could not provide sex because she remained blocked by her bad memories. That made her furious—and miserable.

After a moment, Colene shrugged, physically and mentally. "At least until I figure out a way to fix myself. This is the way it is now, but not the way it'll stay."

Darius embraced her and kissed her. "You will find a way."

She melted. "I just love having you believe that. Now if only I could find that way."

She was indeed the vessel of dolor; it colored her expectations as well as her moods.

"But it's great having you here with me, Seqiro," she said. "That eliminates the language problem, and I know I feel much better than I would without you. It'll just take me a while to make paradise perfect."

Then four other people appeared: a larger man with a red beard, and three women. The women wore colorful tunics that bulged somewhat at their midsections. Colene had explained about that before: they wore diapers, to conceal their primary sexual parts. It was the fashion of this culture. When a woman removed her diaper in the presence of a man, it was normally for sexual purpose.

"Greetings, Kublai," Darius said. "I thank you for taking my place these weeks. Now I will resume my office, and marry Prima." The man nodded. So did the oldest of the women. She was not pretty by human standards, being lean of body, plain of face, and of middle human age. But she had an almost regal bearing. She was a woman of power, though her culture refused to recognize it.

The second woman was a few years older than Colene, and very pretty, with lustrous black hair. She was the one who could now marry Kublai, since he would no longer need to draw joy from his wife. Her feelings were mixed: she liked the situation no better than Colene did, but she liked Colene very much for sharing that situation and being just as angry about it. She was grateful to Colene for bringing Darius back, thus freeing Kublai.

The third woman was Ella, who was young, bouncy, buxom, pretty, cheerful, and not phenomenally smart: the ideal bed companion for a man alone, as it was not hard to get her out of her diaper.

Prima approached Seqiro. "You are telepathic?" she inquired quietly.

He sent her a thought: *Yes. So is Maresy.*

"I would like to come and commune with you, when I am not busy on tour. Special minds appeal to me. So do folk who have powers equivalent to my own. That is, of other types, but of similar range and impact. You are definitely one such."

Seqiro found himself liking her.

She picked up his reaction, and her own was pleased. "I lost my chance for love with my own kind. I had a bad experience with dragons, being their captive for twenty years, and now my youth is gone. But the sort of mental and emotional community you enable is attractive. Perhaps some day I will be able to join your hive."

Burgess reacted to that. He found her mind compatible, and was impressed by its power. She was indeed a lot like Darius, and could probably enhance his own power if they ever tried to coordinate.

"Exactly," Prima said. "Some things are worth doing for their own sakes. I think we shall get along."

Seqiro thought so too. So did Maresy and Burgess.

The visitors departed. "It is settled," Darius said. "Tomorrow I will marry Prima and start the tour."

"There is one detail I am not quite clear on," Cat said. "Are you not already married to Colene?"

"In her Mode, yes. But marriage here has a different meaning. She understands."

"And what of the Chip?"

"Tomorrow you will meet with the Cyng of Pwer, who will prepare you for that delivery."

"Then I shall soon part from your group."

"Perhaps."

They had their various meals and settled for the night. There was a pleasant cabin on the mesa for the humans, and the field and trees were fine for the horses and Burgess. This was a pleasant Mode, and would become more so as they became conversant with the manner of traveling by conjuration.

Colene, having achieved safety from the mind predator and unification of their group in this Mode, was nevertheless unsettled. The horses felt her distress. She wanted to be Darius' wife, love, and sexual partner. Instead she faced the prospect of being only his love. She understood about the marriage, because she could not handle the donation of joy, but the sex truly riled her. Nothing was barring her from that except herself, yet she could not overcome that barrier. *Damn! Damn! Damn!* she thought.

"It will pass," Darius murmured.

"It's *not* passing. This hang-up has become part of me. Take Pussy."

"She is barred from me."

"Not anymore. Her mission is done."

She was right. But Darius was not ready for this aspect. "Some other time," he said. "Still, as you know, my power will not be complete unless I do indulge within a day of my performance."

"I know," she said miserably. "You made that clear from the start. You've been fair. I'm the one with the problem."

"I do not see it that way."

"Take Ella. You've used her before."

"True. But now—"

"*Take* her! When I get so I can do it with you, then I can afford to be possessive. Until then I have no right to interfere with your job."

"Colene, it grieves me to distress you. If there were any way—"

"Take her!" she repeated. "Go now! Just—just come back to me, after."

Darius did not argue further, because they both knew it had to be. He got up, stepped away from her, and conjured himself to the mesa of the Cyng of Hlahtar, where bouncy Ella waited.

Colene buried her face in the pillow and sobbed, hating herself for her incapacity. Seqiro sent her a wave of emotional encouragement. "Thanks, horsie," she murmured.

Cat wanted a clarification of this also. Seqiro relayed Cat's concern as dialogue so that Colene could hear it. "You suggested that he use Pussy, and he demurred. Then you suggested that he use Ella, and he acquiesced. Why was that? Is Pussy in some way deficient?"

"Oh, hi, Cat. It's that it's part of the Cyng of Hlahtar's ritual. Marriage, love, and sex are three different things, but he needs them all, or his performance will suffer. So he has to have someone. Sure, Pussy could do it, and no, she's not deficient. That's the problem. She's pretty, healthy, smart enough, and willing. If I tell her to. She could go far with Darius; he could fall in love with her if he tried. But Ella is, well, a nice place to visit, but not to stay. He'll never fall in love with her, no matter how hard he might try. So she's safe; she's no threat to me."

"But Pussy is no threat to you," Cat protested. "She exists to do your will."

"She's a threat because Darius *could* love her, just as he could love Doe Caprine. This is an emotional thing with me; if I have to let Darius get his sex elsewhere, I want to be sure that that's *all* he gets."

Cat nodded in the darkness. "Now I understand. Thank you for clarifying."

"Oh, you're welcome, Cat. But I still hate having to give even that much away. Damn, damn, damn!" She relapsed into tears.

But well before Darius could rejoin her, she cleaned up her face and assumed a semblance of equilibrium. She was not going to burden him with her petty jealousy. *Hide that*, she thought to Seqiro.

Within the hour Darius returned. He joined Colene where she lay, and kissed her tenderly. No word was said. Then he embraced her and held her close until she fell fitfully to sleep.

But Seqiro knew that nothing was settled. Colene wanted it all, and would not be satisfied until she had it all. But this seemed impossible.

Colene woke in the night, restlessly. She did not want to disturb Darius, who needed his rest for the morrow, but the issue would not let her go. *Seqiro.*

Seqiro knew her question, of course, and answered: *He pretended Ella was you. That was the only way he could do it.*

Colene's distress became wonder. *Really?*

He loves only you. He has lost his taste for other women. He faced the prospect of impotence.

Gee. So he was still true to me. Did he tell Ella?

No. He felt it would not be kind.

She was halfway thrilled. *Right. Ella's a sweet girl. Why hurt her feelings?*

True.

It'll be our secret. Then, gratified, she returned to sleep.

In the morning Cat went to see the Cyng of Pwer. This was an older man of regal bearing and humble costume. "I cannot say that I am pleased by the compromise Darius made," Pwer said gravely. Seqiro linked their minds so that there was no problem of language; that was really his function in this Mode. Thus he was party to whatever any member of their group—their hive—indulged in.

"I am not pleased either," Cat said. "I do not understand why he agreed to deliver the Chip to Ddwng of the DoOon Mode."

"Yet you serve that monarch."

"Yes, and I must complete my assignment. But Darius is no creature of DoOon, and his will is unbreakable. He allows others to think that he compromised to save Colene and the group from harassment or destruction. But I do not believe that."

"Neither do I. There must be something he knows that we do not."

Cat was uneasy, but had to speak. "I am obliged to deliver the Chip in good conscience. If there is some way in which it is defective or dangerous, I must discover that and advise Ddwng of it. I must not be party to deception in this respect."

"I understand, and not merely because your equine associate allows me to fathom what is in your mind. We do not deal in subterfuge here. At the same time, Darius may not be obliged to clarify the details of his motive."

"Perhaps we should ask him."

Seqiro sent a signal to Darius, who was with Prima, preparing for their tour of joy. *Cat has a question.*

Darius nodded. *Let me do this,* he thought carefully. *Let me explain my decision privately to Prima, who has no part in this. If she concludes that I must advise Cat, I will do so. Otherwise I shall feel justified in declining to answer.*

Cat looked at Pwer, who shrugged. They both knew that Darius would deal honestly with them. *Agreed,* Cat thought.

Seqiro deleted them from the circuit, and waited. While Cat and Pwer discussed other details of the transaction, Darius and Prima conversed verbally.

Soon Prima's thought came. *I love joining your mind, Seqiro. I want to join your hive.*

But the hive was Burgess' concept. On his Mode all civilized creatures merged in hives. He had been denied his hive, and would have perished if he had not discovered a new one on the Virtual Mode.

Then join me with Burgess.

Seqiro signaled Burgess, and connected their two minds. It took Burgess very little time to appreciate both the power of her mind and the sincerity of her desire to belong; she was, despite her importance to the Cyng of Hlahtar, a lonely person. He welcomed her, and with that the comfort of the hive mind gained significantly for them all.

Now I will answer for Darius, Prima thought. *He believes that the Chip will not benefit Ddwng. Rather, it may destroy him. Therefore it may be delivered to him without ill effect on other Modes.*

Why will it not benefit Ddwng? Cat thought. *I must deliver a good Chip, and explain its use so that it is safe and effective.*

The fault is not in the Chip, but in Ddwng, she thought. *That is all Darius cares to say. I understand his rationale, and agree; he is not required to clarify Ddwng's fault to Ddwng, and neither are you.*

Cat smiled grimly. *As it is, I will be abolished when my mission is done. Were I to comment on the emperor's character, my passing could become unpleasant.*

Now Darius sent a thought: *Cat, the hive would prefer to have you back. Should you decide to return, we will help you do so. All you need to do is ask.*

Thank you, Cat thought. *But I am prepared for my end.*

Darius and Prima faded. The Cyng of Pwer spoke. "This has import. Darius is important, one might say vital, to our community, and we are prepared to provide him with whatever support he requires. This is why his other-

Mode associates are welcome here. He has indicated that he would like to maintain contact with Nona of the Fractal Mode, and therefore also with your friend Tom. As I understand it, this would complete your trio."

"It would," Cat agreed, surprised. "I thought it finished."

"Only if it loses you. I suggest you consider carefully whether to return after completing your mission."

"I shall. My hesitation is not because I lack desire to return, but because I may be unable to do so."

The Cyng nodded. "Now I must explain that there is more than one mechanism for traveling to other Modes. The Chip facilitates the Virtual Mode, as you have experienced. It sends out four lines of force, to reach four other Modes, and these must be caught by special folk in those Modes to fashion anchors. But it will not be feasible for you to carry the Chip itself to another Mode, for it is fixed at the Mode of origin when a Virtual Mode is established. Therefore the Virtual Mode will be shut down, and you will carry Chip to DoOon by another route. This is the Key, which establishes a connection between just two Modes. You may invoke it in the manner of an icon, and render it similarly inert. Your trip back to DoOon will thus be instant, and also your return here, if you choose."

Cat was interested. "Does it anchor to specific sites and people, as the Virtual Mode does?"

"No. At its origin it anchors to a site, but at the other Mode it is the Key itself which determines the connection. You may thus travel from place to place in the DoOon Mode, and still return immediately to the site in this Mode, as long as you retain the Key. If you lose it, there is no return."

"And I can carry the Chip to DoOon using the Key?"

"Yes. You can also transport others with it, provided you touch them when you invoke it. The Key is a simpler device than the Chip, far more limited, but for this purpose superior. It will take me a day to prepare it, and to shut down the Virtual Mode and free its Chip, but then you will be free to take both."

"I appreciate your cooperation."

"Darius made a deal. Ddwng completed his portion when he allowed your party on the Virtual Mode. Your delivery of the Chip will complete Darius' portion."

Cat had one more question. "If I am terminated after delivering the Chip, what happens to the Key?"

"I think it best that we attune it to you, so that you alone can invoke it. If you die, it will be permanently inert. No one else will be able to use it to come here." Pwer reflected, then thought of another aspect. "If you choose to return, and to bring some other person or persons with you, you must be aware of two additional cautions. First, you will be unable to return them to their point of origin, because the siting of a Key is not precise. When the Key is in another Mode, its anchor site in this Mode remains; this destination is fixed. But when it returns here, it will have no remaining fix on your particular Mode, and if reinvoked would most likely orient on one of the adjacent Modes of that region of existence. It is not a device for casual use."

"I understand. I can see that the Chip is necessary for repeated excursions."

"Yes, with all it's complications. The second caution is perhaps more difficult. It is that the Key is unable to transport any person or thing that has future significance in its Mode. The analogy we use is that it is in this respect like a rock: you can't casually take away part of it, unless that part is a fragment that is about to separate anyway. Modes cling to their own substance."

"But the anchor people of the Virtual Mode have had no trouble traversing it," Cat protested. "Only nonanchor folk need assistance in crossing Modes. My trio came without difficulty."

"That is true, for the Virtual Mode. It is a more substantial, more interactive construction. Even so, it resists those who are bound to their Modes by future significance. Normally only those whose cases are so desperate that they face extinction are able to fix an anchor on a foreign Mode. This was the case with the girl Colene, who was soon to die by her own hand. I believe the creature called Burgess was also about to perish."

"And for our two trios," Cat said. "Once chosen for service in connection with the Virtual Mode, our usefulness was limited to that. This confirms that we have no future apart from it. But what of Nona, the magic woman, who has returned to be queen of her planet?"

"I believe her future in her home Mode was ending," Pwer said. "When she later decided to return, it was as a changed individual, or perhaps a changed situation, with your associate Tom. It may simply be that the Virtual Mode knew that this was a necessary portion of her experience, and accepted her on a temporary basis. We do not know all the intricacies of Modal interaction. There was also a woman called Provos, who lived backwards. She had a mission to perform via the Virtual Mode; she performed it and returned. But such cases take advantage of the greater potential of the Virtual Mode. Such folk might not have been able to use the more limited Key. So if you elect to bring any person back with you, you may find this unfeasible, unless that person has little or no future in that Mode."

Cat nodded. "I thank you for this clarification. I doubt that I will be returning, or bringing along any other party if I do, but this helps me to understand the limits of the device."

Their dialogue ended, and Cat returned to the hive mesa, conjuring itself there. Seqiro focused his attention on Darius and Prima, who had traveled with a professional conjurer to a neighboring village and were about to perform there. Seqiro had seen Darius exert his magic on occasion, but never in his home Mode.

They were on a floating disk with three other people. It seemed that conjuration included slow floating as well as instant jumping. The land was lovely, highlighted by the crystals glowing in the colored sunlight that descended after passing through the clouds. There were patterns in the crystals between mesas, making circles and squares, triangles and hexagons, in many hues. Reflected beams of light intersected in the air, to form three dimensional figures of red, yellow, and green that blended into realistic images of illusory gemstones.

They floated toward a very large low mesa whose surface had been cleared for crops. The houses of the villagers were around its edge, with paths leading in to the center. Quadrants were fenced off for farm animals. Some of the structures were for artisans who made clothing, weapons, and tools. This was where the sustenance of this culture originated: in the work of the farmers and laborers. Seqiro realized that it was wearing, and they tended to become depressed. But they looked forward to the visits of the Cyng of Hlahtar, for good reason.

The villagers were gathered all around the central stage. The disk floated down to land on it, and the people stepped off. First came the preliminary entertainer, a juggler and joker whose antics made the tired villagers smile. But they did not laugh; their joy was too low.

Next came the dancer, a lovely girl who made her diaper move most suggestively. The villagers watched closely, but still were not roused to enthusiasm. She finally removed the diaper entirely and danced naked. This should have whipped them into a frenzy. They looked, but were not much aroused. Seqiro realized from their thoughts that this was standard: had they been more excited, it would have indicated that they were not in sufficient need of the Cyng's service.

Now Darius stepped forth, leading Prima by the hand. Interest quickened. Darius embraced Prima, and drew joy from her—and Seqiro realized what the villagers did not: she was not depleted. She had multiplied even as he drew, retaining her level. Thus she suffered no loss, and could serve this function indefinitely. That made her invaluable among women.

Darius multiplied and broadcast the joy to all the villagers. Immediately they were happy; their slowly depleted joy had been rapidly restored. This would last for many days, slowly dissipating with use, until it was time for another boost.

The juggler stepped out again. This time he was widely applauded, and even his lamest stunts brought gleeful laughter. The dancing girl, now fully clothed, performed, and was similarly applauded. In a moment she was joined by exuberant village girls. None of them removed their diapers. The scene dissolved into a celebration.

Darius, Prima, and the others of their troupe stepped back onto the disk. Their job here was done, and they had other villages to do this day. The villagers would hardly miss them; their party was just commencing.

Prima turned to Darius. "This is the part I like," she said. "Spreading joy."

"I like it too," he said. "Now that I have you."

She knew what he meant: he could use her without depleting her. It was too bad that she was not allowed to be the Cyng of Hlahtar herself, but now she had much of the reality if not the status. They were doing good for the land, bringing much-needed joy to the masses.

They floated on toward the next depressed village. Seqiro turned his attention to Colene. She was with Pussy, at the Castle of Hlahtar, visiting with Ella. Colene had been here before, but it was new to Pussy. At the moment they were in one of the castle's several pleasant gardens, waiting for Ella to return from an errand. "It will probably be easier if we live here, and let the horses and Burgess remain on the guest mesa," Colene was saying. "You are supporting me now, emotionally, but when Cat leaves I may have to support you."

"But I will always serve you," Pussy protested.

"Maybe. What I mean is, you need your trio, and it's being broken up. We hope Cat comes back, but if it doesn't, you'll need emotional help. The hive will embrace you, and with Prima joining in, it can do a lot. Still, it may be rough."

"I hope Cat comes back," Pussy agreed. "I hope we can visit Tom, too. I know he loves Nona, and maybe some day I will love a man too, but there is no substitute for our trio."

"If—if I can't get my act together," Colene said carefully, "and you lose your trio, maybe you can love Darius."

"I must not!"

"Times change. If I can't do it, and he needs it, you may have to. But somehow I'm going to get past this thing, so I can be with him myself." She spoke with seeming confidence, but beneath was the dreadful uncertainty. "In which case we'll find you a good man, Pussy. But first things first: Cat's got to deliver the Chip to DoOon and return."

"Yes," Pussy breathed.

Seqiro returned his focus to the pasture mesa. *Sometimes I think you are more interested in human concerns than in horse concerns,* Maresy thought as she grazed beside him.

Aren't you?

I'm different. I was made by Colene. I am more of her than I am of me.

They all were made by Colene, Burgess thought in his different way. But for her, none of them would be here.

With that they had to agree.

But I wish she would conquer her fear of breeding, Maresy continued. *Then I would be able to breed with you.*

Seqiro wondered whether it would be possible for Maresy to conquer her aversion, and cause Colene to do the same, reversing the connection.

No, Maresy thought firmly. *The problem is in her, and must be resolved there.*

That was surely true.

The next day Cat was ready to return to the DoOon Mode. Pussy hugged it, and so did Colene. "Come back if you can, furface," Colene said. It was the first time she had used such an endearment for Cat.

Cat bid farewell to Burgess. The two had been especially close ever since meeting.

"Remember," Darius said. "You have to ask." Then he removed the chain from his neck and set it around Cat's neck. "I have acquitted my obligation."

Cat nodded. Then it invoked the Key, which was a small disk. It was set to orient on the DoOon anchor of the Virtual Mode, just before that was closed. The Chip Cat carried was not actually the same one, but its powers were similar.

Suddenly Cat was gone. But Seqiro retained contact with the Feline's mind. Seqiro knew where the DoOon Mode was, and knew Cat's mind, so was able to follow. He broadcast that mind to the other members of the hive, so that they all could share the experience.

They could not, however, communicate directly with Cat. The Modal distance was too great. Seqiro had zeroed in on Cat's mind, with Cat's acquiescence, but at this range that enabled him only to track that mind, not to communicate with it. That was why Cat had to ask, if it wanted help: the asking would mean that Cat contributed from that side, establishing a two-way connection. If Cat did not ask, the hive could not act in the DoOon Mode.

Cat arrived at the site of the former Virtual Mode anchor on the capital planet, though it had not used that device. This was not intended to deceive anyone about the method of travel, but to provide a known spot for the Key to orient on. Otherwise the Key would have been unlikely to fix on the precise Mode necessary.

No one was there at the moment. However, the moment Cat appeared, the observer spheres gave the alarm.

"Inert," Cat murmured, closing the aperture. Then it swallowed the Key. The act seemed like a mere brushing of the face, in response to the alarm.

Swine guards appeared. They recognized Cat immediately. "The Feline is back from the Virtual Mode," Pig reported.

"Bring Cat to me." It was Ddwng's voice from the spheres.

Boar caught hold of Cat's hands and held them out from its body. Sow ran her hands over that body, checking for anything on it. Pig took Cat's pack and checked through it efficiently. There was not a lot there; in fact it was almost empty, as if depleted from a long trek. But it did contain a special package.

"What is this?" Pig asked, holding up the package.

"The Chip. I must deliver it to Ddwng."

"Delivery to me is equivalent."

Cat did not answer. The Swine was surely correct. Ddwng would not accept anything directly from outside; his minions examined it thoroughly first.

Pig carried the package to another chamber. Boar and Sow marched Cat to a private suite where Ddwng waited. "The Feline has brought the Chip," Boar said. "Pig has it now."

The Emperor nodded. "Describe it in context," he said to Cat.

Cat was prepared. "The Chip is an irregular spheroid which needs to be mounted in a suitable frame and provided with magnetic power to enable it to operate. When invoked by a series of mental commands, it sends out four lines of force across massed Modes, which can be tapped by other minds to fix anchors. When four additional anchors are established, they secure a Virtual Mode crossing myriad others. Only the anchor persons can travel freely on a Virtual Mode, though they can conduct others from the anchor Modes to intervening Modes. Neither persons nor things on intervening Modes can cross the Mode boundaries, unless they are assimilated by anchor persons. The Virtual Mode changes in its pattern when any anchor is changed, but can be terminated only by the anchor person at the Mode of origin."

Ddwng nodded. Of course he already knew this. He was verifying that the Chip Cat brought was the type demanded. Now he knew it was. "Where are the others of your party?"

"Darius, Colene, Burgess, and Pussy are at Darius' home Mode, together with two horses from the Horse Mode. Tom and Nona are at the Fractal Mode. The change in personnel occurred when the Fractal Mode anchor was freed, allowing the telepathic horses to recover their prior anchor."

"Why did the other members of your trio not return with you?"

"They preferred to break up the trio, rather than be recycled here."

"Why did Darius agree to deliver the Chip?"

"He wished to enable his party to return to his home Mode, and he believed that the Chip would not benefit you, but rather would destroy you."

"The Chip is defective?"

"No."

Now it comes, Colene thought. *Ddwng will make Cat answer, and then he will be angry.*

Seqiro and the others knew it was true. But they could only watch.

"Why then will I gain no benefit?" Ddwng asked.

Cat did not flinch. "Darius believes that there is a fault in you that will make you unable to use it effectively."

The Emperor scowled. "Clarify this fault."

"I am unable to. I have no knowledge of any such fault. It is merely Darius' belief."

Ddwng considered. "The Chip requires merely a suitable source of power, and a mental command? There is no complication that might render it inoperative?"

"That is correct."

An Ovine female appeared. "Message for Ddwng," she said.

"Speak, Ewe."

"The Virtual Mode the travelers used has ended." Ewe departed.

Seqiro realized that they must have made regular checks to verify the continuing existence of the anchor and the Virtual Mode. A check had been made, and they assumed that the Virtual Mode had been shut down just after Cat's arrival. The particular timing hardly mattered, and Cat did not need to clarify the matter.

Ddwng paused, then nodded. "Terminated from the other side, where its Chip resides. Correct, Cat?"

"Correct," Cat agreed. "There is no further use for that Virtual Mode."

"What of the operatives I had on it?"

"Any person there would be stranded on the particular Mode he occupied at the time it was terminated."

Ddwng considered again. "I am not satisfied with the rationale you express for Darius. The man was incorruptible. If he believed there was a fault in me that would deny me the benefit of the Chip, he had reason. I must know that reason."

Cat waited; it had not been asked to comment.

"I believe that more intensive interrogation is in order."

"I have told you what I know of this matter."

"We shall see. We shall commence by torturing your associates who are presently on Planet Chains. We shall start with Goat, and carry through Buck and Doe and the four human nulls, in your presence. If you have not provided the information I require when they expire, we shall try more persuasive techniques on you."

It was clear that Ddwng would not relent; he never did. All of them faced horrible torture—for nothing. *I am asking.*

Seqiro threw the power of his mind to Cat. Cat forwarded it to Ddwng. It was a memory stun: all that had happened in the past hour was blocked from the emperor's awareness. He sank in his chair, looking dazed.

Boar and Sow stepped forward. "Ddwng," Boar asked. "Are you well?"

"He is well," Cat said. That was true, as Cat was unable to hurt the emperor. But it would be some time before Ddwng pieced together what had happened. "Take me to a ship immediately."

"By what authority?"

"His." Cat turned to Ddwng, and relayed a spot directive.

"Approved," the emperor said. Again, this was not harming the emperor, whose quest for further information was futile. It was merely enabling Cat to save its friends.

Boar and Sow escorted Cat from the chamber. They were trained never to question a directive from the ruler.

All other nulls on the capital planet were subservient to the Swine. No one questioned their progress to the ship. The door opened and the three boarded.

"Take us to Planet Chains," Cat told the captain. "By order of Ddwng."

Ddwng will message the ship to stop, Colene thought.

Seqiro sent Cat another thought. Cat spoke.

"Incommunicado—neither accept nor send any messages during this mission."

The ship departed. Now Boar recovered some initiative. "I heard no such order."

"You did not need to. I am the one whose service is required there. Obtain a stateroom and sleep; you are off duty for the duration."

Boar plainly wanted to challenge this. But in the absence of Pig, and the presence of a nudge from Seqiro's mind, he elected to obey. He and Sow retired.

In due course the ship arrived at Planet Chains. Cat directed the captain where to land. "Take off and orbit the planet until I signal you," Cat said, taking a signal flare. "Remain otherwise incommunicado."

The captain nodded. Cat stepped out near the Feline village. The ship floated away, and disappeared into the sky.

He'll send another ship, Colene thought.

Cat was aware of that. There was probably a ship already approaching the planet. Cat had to act swiftly.

A village Feline came out to meet Cat. "What is required?"

"Bring the Caprine trio and the four human nulls to me immediately."

"They are with the dragon."

Cat turned and ran through the forest toward the dragon's lair. Seqiro lent it strength, and it made good time. But then there was a shadow in the sky. Cat looked, and saw a ship descending toward the village. That would be the second one sent by Ddwng. There was less time than anticipated.

Cat's not going to make it before that ship gets its bearings, Darius thought. Darius had once had a mission on just such a ship.

You can give it super strength, the way you did me, once, Colene thought.

But that was useful only for very short duration. It drew on the reserve strength that living bodies maintained as a cushion. An extended use of it could be deleterious to health.

So how's Cat's health going to be if that ship catches it? she demanded. *What about the health of the Caprines and Human nulls?*

She had a point. Still, it was not a kind decision. *I could kill Cat, by pushing it too hard.*

The hive held a quick consultation. *Risk it,* Colene decided.

Seqiro took over Cat's legs, propelling it onward. But this was depleting the Feline's resources rapidly, and Seqiro felt the damage to the Feline.

Tiring despite Seqiro's boost of strength, Cat staggered to the dragon's lair. All seven nulls were there, holding a dialogue with the dragon. "Caprines!" Cat gasped. "Nulls! You must—"

But the expense of energy was too much. Cat collapsed. Seqiro was able to remain in touch, and to hear through Cat's ears, but could not revive the Feline.

"Trouble!" Goat said. "This is the Cat who went on the Virtual Mode. How has it returned without its trio?"

Two ships have come, the dragon thought. *This is surely mischief.*

"But we don't know what kind!" a Dar null said. "Is the mission done?"

Doe knelt beside Cat. She put her mouth to its ear. "You must tell us what to do," she said. "We don't know."

But Cat was almost unconscious. The stress had been too much.

Damn! Colene thought. *Cat can't tell them—and they need to act fast, before the troops get there.*

The troops were not long in coming. The ship reappeared, floating over the group. They could see it through

Cat's bleary eyes. There was no place for it to land, but it didn't need to. Its portal opened and bodies jumped out. Parachutes opened, and they dropped toward the trees.

"Swine!" the Dar null said. "Armed!"

I believe they are after you, the dragon thought. *The mission must be done, and you are to be destroyed as superfluous or inconvenient. Retreat into my cave. I will balk them.*

There seemed to be no choice. The two Dar nulls carried Cat, and the others moved into the dark cave.

"We must ascertain the situation," Goat said. "Perhaps the Swine are here merely to fetch us in for a reunion."

"Battle Swine?" the Dar asked. "They are used only for carnage."

Indeed, now they heard it outside the cave. The dragon was fighting the Swine. The dragon was a formidable predator, but it would be overwhelmed by their numbers and weapons.

A boar appeared at the mouth of the cave, carrying a shielded lamp. He also had a sword.

A sword? Colene thought.

No power weapons are allowed on Planet Chains. Pussy explained. *It is kept deliberately primitive.*

A second boar appeared. They advanced on the group. "Stand forth!" one cried. "By order of Ddwng!"

They hesitated. They had always obeyed that authority, but did not trust this.

Doe got down beside Cat again. "You must tell us," she said desperately. "Why do they want us?"

Seqiro sent power, and Cat was able to respond slightly. "Must escape," it whispered. "Torture. Gather round me."

"Torture!" she exclaimed. The others stared at her, shocked. They had done nothing to deserve this.

The two boars charged. Buck leaped up to intercept them. The first one cut him down with a single chop of his sword. Doe screamed.

"They mean to torture and kill us!" the Dar null said. "We must fight them."

The two boars stood before them, one with gore on his sword. "Surrender, miscreants. Now!"

All four human nulls ran at them, the Dars swinging their fists, the Cols their hooked fingers. The swords came up, skewering the two Dars, but the Cols landed on the boars and scratched at their eyes.

More Swine appeared at the cave entrance. They had evidently dispatched the dragon and were coming to finish the business. The situation was hopeless.

Doe tried once more. "Cat! What can we do?"

The boars were crowding in toward them. Twin screams sounded the end of the Cols. Goat charged, head down to butt, and brought down one boar, but another sliced through Goat's head. Doe screamed again, hugging Cat protectively in a pathetic attempt to shield it from the savagery.

Invoke! Cat thought. That was all that was required for this specialized Key.

Cat and Doe appeared at the mesa, tangled together. Doe was sobbing and Cat was unconscious.

Pussy dropped down to hug them both. "You are safe now!" she cried.

Doe stared wildly around. "What is this?"

"This is Darius' Mode. The Swine can't reach you here."

"But what of Buck and Goat?"

Pussy looked up at the others appealingly. But they had no suitable answer. "Help her," Pussy said.

Seqiro sent a mental command that rendered Doe unconscious. That was the best he could do for her, for the moment.

EIGHT

✦

Monster

Pussy looked up. "Thank you, Seqiro. Now we must see to Cat." She spoke as if this were routine, but it could never be that. She had seen and heard, though Cat's senses, their friends the Caprine and Human nulls brutally slaughtered. Cat had acted to save them, but in the end had been able to save only one, and that after witnessing horror.

Darius picked Cat up and carried it to a comfortable mat. Pussy and Colene took Doe by shoulders and knees and hauled her to another chamber. Pussy saw that she still wore the chain of paper clips Darius had given her.

"But the alternative would have been worse," Colene said, answering Pussy's prior thought. "They each would have been slowly tortured to death, to try to make Cat tell what it didn't know. Ddwng's paranoia wouldn't let them go. At least now they're out of it."

"True," Pussy said. "But what will I tell Doe?"

"I don't know. Maybe it wasn't kind to save her." She

paused reflectively, gazing at the chain. "And she loves Darius."

That made it even more complicated, Pussy realized. The last thing Colene needed was another pretty female loving Darius. What made it worse was that of all the nulls, Doe was the one Darius liked best. If it had been Buck saved, or Goat, there would have been no such problem. In fact, Buck could have paired off with Pussy, to mutual satisfaction. Nulls understood each other. Instead it was Doe, feminine and decent and horribly bereaved. What were they to do with her?

"What, indeed," Colene said.

They sat by the bed, pondering the awfulness of it. Instead of getting better, things had gotten abruptly worse. Ddwng could not reach them—yet—but they had problems enough regardless.

"I think we must decide what is to be, before she wakes," Pussy said. "She—I am an animal null, and I know how she will feel. We Felines made a deal with the Caprines, to support each other and not to betray each other, and we honored that, but we never anticipated this pass of events. I separated from my male component, and I endure because I know he is fulfilled. I thought my neuter component would die, and I am relieved that it survived and returned. But most of all, I am satisfied because I can continue to serve the one I love." She looked down at Doe. "But she has seen both her male and her neuter die horribly. Her closest attachments are lost. She will not survive, unless—"

"Unless she serves the one she loves," Colene finished. "And that is Darius—the one *I* love."

"Yes. So if you do not wish that, it may be better to kill her."

"Kill her!" Colene's shock was a blast of feeling. "I couldn't do that."

"You don't have to. Seqiro can do it with his mind, just by—"

"No! No killing anybody! That's not an option."

"But she may die of emotional neglect, if not allowed to be with her only remaining emotional tie. Just as I would, in that situation. I dislike speaking this way, for it smells of betrayal, yet I know what kind of anguish she will suffer. She is a fine and loyal creature, and does not deserve such torture. Deprived of her trio, she must serve the one she loves."

"But she loves *Darius*!" Colene cried.

"Yes. So it may be kindness to put her down before—"

"No!" Again the hard wash of emotion as Colene's tears of frustration flowed.

Pussy was hurt. "I apologize for offending you." Her own tears were threatening. Death was kinder than what Doe faced in life.

Colene reached across the bed and took her hand. "No, it's not that, Pussy. It's that you're facing me with a choice I can't make. I can't kill Doe, or let her die in grief. But neither can I give her to Darius. He likes her too well."

"I understand. When a null loves, there is usually some mutuality."

"Some what?"

"Some return of emotion. Not on the same scale of course, or necessarily of the same type. But the master or mistress generally does like the null. That is of course all that is to be expected, for the duration of the master's interest. Then the null is reassigned or recycled."

"Darius is not fickle like that. He would never throw her away, and I wouldn't want him to. That's the problem."

"Yes. He would not. He would be the ideal master, from the null's perspective."

Colene pondered for a while. Then she looked at Pussy

again. "Something you said—about serving the one you love. Whom do you love?"

Pussy was surprised. "Why, you, of course. I have served you from the start."

"Me!"

"I thought you understood. The way we nulls are made and conditioned, we must be devoted to those we serve. When I served Darius, before—"

"You were eager to serve him fully. I remember." In fact, in the guise of giving him a massage, Pussy had attempted to seduce Darius, and would have succeeded but for a fortuitous appearance by Colene on the video screen. Pussy had believed that was what he wanted, and had not been seriously mistaken. He was, after all, a man.

"Yes. Now I serve you, and will not touch Darius."

"But I'm no lesbian!"

Pussy was blank. "I do not know that term."

"It's a woman who is turned on by other women, instead of by men."

Pussy was still confused. "Women must not be friends with women?"

"Friends, sure. Sex, no. Unless they're gay."

"I have no sexual interest in women. I want to be humped only by a man. Of course I would have no choice if a mistress required it, but it is not my nature."

"But you said you loved me."

Pussy was set back. "Perhaps I misused the term. I was speaking of emotion, not sex."

Colene's relief pervaded their space. "Oh, you mean as in a sister or friend."

"Yes. I mean one I want to be with, to support and assist, whose companionship provides me with pleasure, and whose loss would devastate me."

"Oh, Pussy—that's the way I feel about you!"

"I am glad, Colene. I think that even if you were not

my mistress, I would value your nearness. You have so much power."

"I'm a fouled-up kid! A vessel of dolor."

"You are also a great woman."

Colene shook her head. "And you believe that."

"I know it. I feel the power in you, though it shows only occasionally. But I think that you do not know it."

"You bet I don't know it! I mess up everything, especially my own life."

"I am thinking of the way you read minds, and sometimes anticipate the future, and sometimes have magic."

"Oh, that. Seqiro links me to those who can do such things, and I pick up a bit of them. But that's not really me."

"Perhaps." Pussy would not argue long against a mistress, but she knew that Colene sometimes showed powers that could not be accounted for by mere telepathy.

"I'm nothing. That's what I know."

"Yet because of you, we all are here and well, and Tom is happy and Nona is queen of Oria in the Julia Mode."

"In spite of, not because of. Still, I'm glad we got your feeling clarified. You love me like a family member, not a lover."

"Yes. Now, with Seqiro's help, I comprehend the distinction in uses of the same word."

Colene suddenly sat up straight. "Doe! Is that the kind of love *she* has?"

"Of course. Only since Darius is male, she will gladly serve him sexually if he wishes it. Nulls are made for just such interaction."

"But she doesn't *have* to."

"Well, if he required it, she would have to. She would not be dismayed. His desire would immediately become her desire. We live to please our masters."

"And if he doesn't require it, what then?"

"Then she has no need of it. She can be humped by

any man, as I can, without affecting her relationship to her master. As long as the master wishes it to be that way."

"So it's the same as it is in this Mode," Colene said, brightening. "Love, sex, marriage—three different things."

"Yes. Tom, I think, has all three with Nona, but love is what sustains him. She could have married elsewhere, and indulged sexually elsewhere, and he would have been satisfied, as long as he could continue to serve her. I have no jealousy of your other relationships, marital or sexual, so long as I can be your friend."

"And Doe can survive the loss of her trio—if she can just be close to Darius, and serve him, even if I am his wife, his lover, and his friend."

"Yes, of course. Just as I will be well satisfied to be with you when you achieve these things with Darius."

"And she will not try to seduce him?"

"Not if he tells her not to, as he did when they traveled together." Pussy paused, then concluded that an amplification was appropriate. "If given leave, she and I could go out and develop sexual relationships with ardent young men for our own pleasure. That would make it clear to all that neither of us serve master or mistress in that manner, for sex tends to inspire jealousy."

Colene was deeply gratified. "Pussy, I know you and I trust you. Doe's another null. I should be able to trust her similarly. I know she won't do what Darius doesn't want her to do. So I guess it's between me and him. I have to make sure he doesn't want her to do it. And that solves one problem, and points up another. We can save Doe— but how can we save *me*?"

Pussy hesitated. "I am not certain you wish a candid response."

"Forget what I wish! Say what I need to hear."

"Colene, you must overcome your sexual inhibition.

Darius is a sexual man, and he desires you. It is only his supreme power of will that keeps him from you. Now, with the mission over, and other desirable females available, you can not afford to balk him longer."

Colene nodded. "That is exactly what I wish I didn't have to hear. If he came to you and wanted sex—"

"Not without your directive."

"And if I can't get over my own hang-up, I'll have to give you that directive. Or send him to Ella again. Or Doe. That really kills me! Pussy, how can I change? I have tried and tried, but I just can't *do* it."

"Again, I am not certain—"

"Damn it, *tell* me!"

"I think you must defeat the mind predator."

Colene stared at her. "Pussy, that's the one thing I can't possibly face."

"No. It is the other thing."

The girl was thoughtful. "Sex—and the monster. You think they're connected?"

"I am sure of it. Because our minds have been much related, especially since Seqiro joined our party, I have received your emotions along with your thoughts, as they occur. I know you well, Colene, because I have been feeling what you feel, including your balked passions. Maresy is the same, and so she is unable to accommodate Seqiro, until you resolve your issue. This is what you call the downside of such powerful telepathy: those around you receive your negatives as well as your positives. The entire hive is suffering. You *must* resolve your problem, for the sake of all of us. Your deepest horrors, perhaps even your deathwish, are sexual in nature. The mind predator merely animates your weakness in order to consume you. I think that if you could conquer your sexual aversion, the predator would no longer have much power over you. Conversely, if—"

"If I could defeat the mind monster, I would lose my

sex problem," Colene finished. "It's possible. But you know, that mind predator could destroy me."

"I know," Pussy agreed. "But if you should lose Darius because you can't—"

"It would destroy me too," Colene agreed. "I think you're right. I've got to tackle one or the other, and beat it back, or I'm doomed anyway."

"I believe this is the case."

"I'll think about it. Meanwhile, no need to let Doe suffer. We'd better wake her and tell her, and assign her to Darius."

"Perhaps if he were here—"

"This is something I'd rather handle myself. Seqiro—let her wake."

The horse's mind was always present, though never obtrusive. Burgess brought the concept of the hive, but Seqiro brought the reality of it. The sleeping Caprine woke.

Doe's eyes opened. "Pussy—Colene," she said.

Colene took her hand. "Doe, Cat returned and delivered the Chip to Ddwng. But then Ddwng wanted to torture all of you, thinking there was more to learn. So Cat went to Planet Chains to try to rescue you before that happened. Only the Swine troops were too close behind. They killed everyone but you, because Cat managed to bring you to this Mode to be with us. We know this is a terrible shock for you, and we wish it hadn't happened that way. But there is one saving grace. You can serve Darius, and be with him constantly, and that begins now."

Doe's horror had been building as Colene spoke, but now there was a counterforce. "Darius." They felt the outflowing emotion.

"I know you love him. Now you can serve him in any way he chooses. He likes you, and will be glad to have you with him. Pussy and I will be near too. In fact, I think you should join the hive."

"The hive?"

"This is Burgess' way of conceiving of a group of close friends. Seqiro joins us mentally, and so we can share thoughts and emotions. It's a great comfort, and it will help you. In fact we can merge you now, so that you can adjust before you go on a tour with Darius and Prima."

"I do not understand."

"Seqiro," Colene said.

Seqiro brought the minds of the hive to Doe: Burgess' alien but friendly nature, the two horses, Pussy, and Colene herself. Darius and Prima, who were preparing emotionally for their next tour of joy. Everyone except Cat, who remained unconscious, slowly recovering from the depletion of almost all its body resources. The minds embraced Doe, lending comfort and support. Her anguish was not abolished, but it was made more bearable by its sharing. There was group stability and sanity in the embrace of the hive, apart from the stress Colene's conflicted emotions brought.

"And when you go with Darius, it will be that much better," Colene said. "You will feel his mind in yours, and know that he cares for you. This will give you strength to endure your terrible loss."

"This—this is amazing," Doe said.

"It gets better," Colene said. "Pussy will take you around to meet the others, and see what this Mode is like. It has bright crystals, and pretty colored clouds, and magic—you'll like it."

Doe was not quite reassured. "Darius—he told me not to let him—"

"That's right. But you don't need sex in order to love him, do you?"

"Of course not," Doe agreed, exactly as Pussy would have. "But if he desires—"

"You will do what he tells you. He will tell you to be with him in all other ways but that. You will in due course find a separate boyfriend to make deliriously happy in fifteen-minute doses. Do you have a problem with that?"

Doe smiled. "No."

Colene nodded. "Take her, Pussy. I have to get by myself for a bit and do some heavy thinking."

Pussy obeyed immediately. "Come with me, Doe. You have met several members of the hive mentally. Now you can meet them physically."

Doe followed her, still dazed by the presence of the other minds. Pussy glanced back, to see Colene lying on the bed that Doe had vacated. She did indeed have heavy thinking to do. She had solved everyone's problems except her own.

Doe was properly amazed by everything. Pussy understood, being another female null. She was especially impressed by the horses, having had prior experience only with the Equines of Planet Chains, which were not at all similar. "You're so big!" she breathed, standing before Seqiro.

It's my nature, he thought tolerantly.

"I like you. And Maresy."

Girls do, Maresy thought. *We will always be with you.*

Pussy felt the emotional reassurance, and knew that it was having significant impact on Doe's bereavement. The hive was replacing her lost trio. It would take time for that process to be complete, but it was happening.

Then Pussy brought her to where Darius sat with Cat. Prima stood near. "Cat saved me!" Doe said. "I was trying to shield Cat, but Cat saved me."

"Cat will recover in time," Darius said. "Its life force is depleted, but we will see that it returns to full strength." He stood. "Come to me, Doe."

She stepped close, and he embraced her. Her pleasure suffused the hive, making everyone feel joyful. "Master, I apologize for my weakness."

Darius glanced at Pussy. She nodded, mentally guiding

him in what was appropriate. "Be weak," he said, giving Doe leave.

She dissolved into tears. He held her, gently patting her back, glancing again at Pussy as he sent a thought of appreciation for her role. He understood Doe's situation, having seen what Cat saw, and had been in mental touch with Colene, but was vague on the exact protocol of the moment. He was offering Doe full comfort during her grief.

Pussy looked closely at Cat. She took Cat's hand. The pulse was there. Cat would survive. That was enormously reassuring.

Darius released Doe, and she looked down at Cat. "I lost my neuter. Cat saved me, as Goat would have. May I—"

This was Pussy's prerogative, as the female member of her trio. "We are missing our male. Another null will help."

Doe dropped down, half hugged Cat, and kissed it on the face. Again her emotion spread out: gratitude and need, of the kind that only a null could feel.

Cat stirred. Some of Doe's life force was infusing it, giving it strength for recovery. They were, in an ad hoc fashion, a trio again.

Then Pussy left Doe with Darius and Cat, and returned to be with Colene. Prima went with her, responding to the need within the hive. The girl was lying on her back, her body still, but her mind in turmoil.

"You're right, Pussy. I've got to tackle the mind predator. It may be the death of me, but it's the only way. Only I don't know how to fight it."

"Maybe I could help."

"You're not the one with the sexual hang-up. What can you do?"

"Perhaps I could hold your hand."

Colene laughed. Then she sobered immediately. "No

offense, Pussy, but this is wa-ay beyond the hand-holding stage."

Prima spoke. "When all other bearings are gone, the hand of one not under attack may be the best guide. Darius held my hand physically to get me across the Modes and bring me here. There may be a mental component."

Colene looked uncertainly at the woman. "I guess you should know."

"I also know that you are another female multiplier."

Colene laughed. "Oh, I don't think so! I can't even hang on to my own scant measure of joy."

"The power is independent of joy. It can multiply any emotion. Yours multiplies dolor—but it could do the same for rage, or love, or joy, were it not internally conflicted."

"That's me, all right," Colene agreed. "So what do *you* think I should do?"

"I think you should face the monster—with Pussy's support."

"I was able to shield you a little from it before; maybe I can be of some help," Pussy said. "But of course it is your decision."

"Maybe you're right again. I know that the mind monster overwhelms me. I'm going to be spinning in the wind something awful. If you can steady me, okay."

"I will try."

Colene sat up, then stood. "This terrifies me. So I'd better do it before I lose my nerve."

"But I wasn't thinking of right now," Pussy protested. "Just that at some time, when it seems right, to do it."

"The time will never seem right."

"One other thing," Prima said. "I suspect that the first thing the predator will do is try to cut you off from the hive. It will want to make you more vulnerable."

"Yeah. It tried before."

"This time you should let it."

Both Colene and Pussy stared at her. "Let it?" Colene asked.

"This is I think a battle you must fight alone, apart from Pussy's limited support. Only then can your victory be complete."

"Or her defeat!" Pussy protested.

"Yes. What is required is total decision, positive or negative. Of course I may be mistaken."

"I don't think so. I've been leaning on the hive too much already. Maybe that's why I haven't done what I need to." Colene walked from the chamber. Pussy followed, troubled. Prima walked behind, having had her say.

They came to where Cat lay, with Darius and Doe sitting near. They were holding hands with each other and with Cat. "I gotta go back on the Virtual Mode," Colene said. "Now."

Darius was surprised and dismayed. He had evidently not followed their separate dialogue. "But the mind predator will still be lurking. And we shut down that Virtual Mode. It no longer exists."

"Fire up a new one. It's the Mode monster I'm looking for."

"It would destroy you."

"Maybe so. But I'm no good to you as I am, Darius. I've got to change, and if I can't change, you're better off rid of me."

He saw that she was serious. "I love you, Colene. In time things will work out."

"I don't think so. Not on their own. I've got to fix them now."

"But if you brace the monster, and are lost, what will I do?"

Colene smiled grimly. "You can love Doe. She knows what loss is like. In fact she knows what rape is like. She'll understand."

Doe looked up. "I wish you would not do this, Colene."

"I have a suicidal nature. This is my greatest death-flirting challenge. If I can take the Mode monster, I can survive life. And sex. And have it all. So I'm going for triple or nothing." She looked at Darius. "Get the Cyng of Pwer to set up another Virtual Mode, just for me. And Pussy. For better or worse."

Darius considered for a moment more. Then he stood, stepped to Colene, embraced her, and kissed her with fierce passion. Pussy knew that he feared for Colene's sanity, perhaps even her life, but that she had also pleased him by deciding to address the problem between them. He turned her loose and left the chamber.

Colene took his chair. "How's Cat doing?"

"Cat is slowly recovering," Doe said. "It is conscious now, and should be ambulant tomorrow." Indeed, Cat's eyes were open.

"I meant what I said," Colene said. "If I don't make it, and I think maybe I won't, you take care of Darius. I want him satisfied. He's got Prima for the tours, but he needs a home life too. You can handle it."

"I will do as directed," the Caprine said. "I do love him."

"And he needs that," Colene said.

Darius returned. "The Cyng of Pwer will do it. It seems he is not surprised. The Virtual Mode will open with you as the prime anchor in a moment."

"Good." Colene hesitated. "Darius, in case I don't make it, I want you to know I do love you, and want you to take Doe for your home life."

He stood, evincing an indecision unusual in him.

"Colene—"

She stood on tiptoe, reached up to catch his head, pulled it down to her level, and kissed him. "But if I do make it back, I'm all yours, Darius. Really all yours. And you'll be mine. All mine."

She disengaged, took Pussy's hand, and looked around. "Where's the anchor?"

"Where you stand," Darius said. "Step through it."

Colene stepped, and Pussy paced her. The chamber remained, but Darius, Doe, and the supine Cat disappeared. They were in the Virtual Mode.

"Monster, where are you?" Colene called, sending out a mental wave of summoning. "Here I am; come get me."

There was no answer. "You're still protected by the hive," Pussy said. "That shields your nature from it, for a while."

"Yeah. Okay, 'bye, hive." Colene concentrated, shutting out the mental connection. It was like throwing off a warm jacket. "Okay, monster: I'm naked now. Are you coming after me, or do I have to go after you?"

Pussy felt the distant pulse, rapidly intensifying. Colene had called it, and made herself vulnerable, and it responded. The monster was indeed coming to get her.

Colene turned to Pussy. "Hang on, Puss," she said. "Hell is on its way." She spoke bravely, but she was terrified, and so was Pussy.

Hell arrived. Suddenly Colene was screaming, and Pussy with her, as the horror of the invading mind encompassed them. It drowned them, burned them, pulled them apart, impacted them, and washed them in a tide of emotional filth. They were carried away on a fierce current of nothing, flailing uselessly. It was a maelstrom of confusion and uncertainty.

Fight it! Pussy thought. *Don't let it take you without resistance.*

But I'm supposed to go without resistance.

No. Without hive help. To fight it yourself. To beat it yourself.

Colene tried to fight, but her limbs had no purchase. Her eyes had no sight, her ears no sound, and her body no breath. Pussy was stifled too, her life force suspended by the terrible tide. They were utterly helpless before it.

We are lost, Pussy thought despairingly.

Like hell! It was Colene, her resistance solidifying. She oriented on the mind predator. *If I'm going down. I'm taking you with me, creep!*

That was more like it. Pussy added her faint force. It seemed pathetically inadequate. Yet they felt the swirling forces around them easing. The horror was diminishing slightly, becoming marginally less intense.

Encouraged, they fought harder. Their descent slowed; the vertigo ameliorated. This thing could after all be opposed. Yet they were deeply buried in its awfulness, with no way to escape. The horror still stalked them.

Vague sight returned, and fuzzy hearing. They stood on a shifting mound of slime, surrounded by the smell of carrion. Putrid clouds wafted across, making them gasp and gag. "We're in the belly of the beast," Colene said, wild-eyed. "It's digesting us."

They tried to walk, clinging to each other's hands, but their feet slid without effect. The mound was slowly sinking into a bilious morass. Bubbles forged slowly up through the muddy flow, popping at the surface to release puffs of yellow gas. The fumes intensified. "We can't stay here," Pussy said. "We'll be dissolved."

"But where can we go? There's nowhere."

"That's what it wants you to think! So you can't orient and maybe escape. There must be somewhere."

Colene looked around again. Hideous clouds of roiling vapor surrounded them. "Nowhere I want to go."

"It's all illusion! We haven't really moved. If we step back one or two paces, we'll pass back through the anchor and be out of it."

Colene looked at her. "You may be right. But I came here to beat this monster, or die in the attempt. You're not suicidal; you can go back. I won't."

Their environment was awful, but Pussy liked the girl's

emerging fighting spirit. "I won't leave you."

"Then we'll go forward." Colene strode, and this time her feet had purchase. They plunged into the noxious cloud before them. "You know, when I act as if I had guts, I almost feel courageous. It's weird."

"You *are* courageous. You just don't believe it."

They were moving, but there was no indication where. In a moment they emerged from the cloud—and found themselves on the same mound of slime they had thought to leave. It was the cloud that was moving past them, rather than them walking through it.

Colene paused again. "We're getting nowhere fast."

"Maybe we need a destination."

"Maybe we do. But where?"

"Your fear!" Pussy cried with sudden inspiration. "We must find your fear. Or your loathing. Whatever it is that animates this cesspool we're in."

Colene paused thoughtfully. "I hate it when you tell me things like that. Especially when you're right."

"I'm only responding to your mind. You know where you are going even if I don't."

"Maybe so. Now that I'm here in hell, I'm not nearly as afraid. It's as if I just cut myself, and it stopped the pain."

Pussy was perplexed. "Wouldn't it *cause* the pain?"

"That's what's weird about it. It makes the mental pain go away for a while."

"So challenging the monster is like cutting, and now you're not hurting?"

"Yeah. But the effect is limited. I have to keep challenging, or it will get me as I try to flee. What's my worst fear?"

"Sex."

"Damn." Colene took a moment to nerve herself. "Then let's go for it before I realize what I'm doing and turn into quivering green jelly." She moved forward again.

This time a wan light showed ahead, guiding them. They advanced through thickening mists until their footing became firm and the light expanded into a large bulb mounted on a bending pole. It illuminated a house.

Colene halted. "Oh, no!"

"You know this place," Pussy said.

"I remember it. I've tried to expunge it from my mind, but it never would go. I don't want to be here." She turned away.

"What is it?"

"You don't want to know." Colene strode back toward the stinking morass.

"I have to know. It looks like an ordinary house in your Mode. What's wrong with it?"

Colene turned on her. "It's the house where I got raped!"

"The rape! That's what you have to conquer."

"I can't conquer it. It's already done. All I can do is try to forget it."

"But you can't forget it," Pussy said. "It remains in your mind, preventing you from being sexual with Darius. You must expunge it."

"Oh, sure, just like that," Colene said witheringly. "It destroyed my whole innocence and made me suicidal, and I have to just get rid of the memory? I want no part of it."

"Doe came to terms with her rape after the rapist was punished. What of yours?"

"We punished them," Colene said grudgingly. "The time before, on Earth. Seqiro made them confess, and they were going to trial. But not for what they did to me. That was lost in the welter of what else they did. I was never really satisfied."

"Maybe that's the key. You are not satisfied, so you can't let it go."

"Why the hell *should* I let it go?" Colene flared. "Those

turds raped me! They destroyed my innocence with my virginity. They crippled my soul. I'm supposed to forgive them for that?"

Pussy realized that even in the throes of facing the mind monster, their dialogue could have problems. "I hesitate to argue—"

"Argue!" Colene said. "You've been right so far, damn you."

"When Doe was raped, she had to let it go, not for the rapist, but for herself. His power was over her until she dealt with it. When he was killed, she was able to let it go. But at that point neither her acceptance nor her forgiveness could do the rapist any good. It was only to do *her* good."

"I know the theory," Colene said bitterly. "It's like religion: all those churches and faiths don't do much to obtain justice, they just find ways to forgive sin. That doesn't do it for me. I don't want forgiveness for anyone, I want justice."

"I don't think you do."

Colene whirled on her. "What are you talking about?"

"Those rapists have been brought to justice, but you remain tormented."

Colene stood still. "Maybe so. Because I'm the victim. I'm the one who lost it. I can't just say okay, that's all in the past, and it's okay now, it wasn't that big a deal. It *was* a big deal. I tell you I hated being raped. I HATED it. I hate it now. You tell me I'm supposed to figure it's all right now, just because they maybe serve some piddling time in jail? I'd rather seem them fry! I want their eyeballs to heat up and pop as the current goes through them. I want them horribly dead—and I want them to know it's because of what they did to me."

"I don't think you do," Pussy repeated.

"Okay, femme Feline. What do you think I really want?"

"To be free of the memory."

"I don't want to forget what happened! I want vengeance."

"Would vengeance undo what you suffered?"

"That's not the point. They did it, and they should pay. If not with their lives, then with castration, so they suffer as I do."

"How would it help you if they suffered that?"

"It would satisfy me that they have been served as they served me. *That's* justice."

"But wouldn't it be better if it had never happened?"

"Yes! But it *did* happen, so it has to be settled. And it hasn't been. Not as far as I'm concerned."

"If you forget it ever happened, wouldn't that restore your innocence?"

Colene stared at her. "Pussy, where the hell are you getting these questions? You sound like a damned psychiatrist."

"From the other side of your mind," Pussy said. "They are your own doubts, open to me now that we share the ambiance of the mind monster."

"Trust the monster to torpedo me," Colene muttered. "Okay, already: if I forgot all about it, sure, I'd be innocent again. Mentally, if not physically. But it wouldn't be right. It would be papering over a chasm. It *did* happen, and it messed me up something awful, and now I can't even be with the man I love."

"So what you need is not to forget it, but to be able to handle it. To put it in perspective so that it no longer cripples you sexually."

"You got it, sister."

"So what happens to the rapists doesn't matter. What matters is how you handle it."

Colene raised her hands in mock surrender. "Okay, okay! It's me who counts, not them. But they are part of it, because without them I wouldn't be suffering. I can't just forget them and still be a victim."

Pussy nodded. "I wasn't at your rape. I really don't know anything about it. Let's look at it. Maybe there's something you haven't considered."

"Look at it! It's past and done, Puss. No way to see it happen."

"It is there in your memory. Open that chamber."

Colene quailed. "Shit, Pussy! That's the last thing I ever want to do."

"That's why you have to do it. We can't do surgery on your damaged innocence without exposing the injury to it."

"Surgery!" But Colene became thoughtful. "That's a nice concept. You do surgery to fix something wrong. The surgery cuts you open and hurts your flesh, but it fixes the problem. Then you slowly heal until you're better than before."

"Yes, that is the concept. We must do it to free you of the monster's hold."

"Not to fix my relationship with Darius?"

"The monster feeds on emotional conflict. That conflict bars you from Darius. So they are the same."

Colene considered that. "I thought it was dolor the monster wanted."

"I don't think so. Not now. In your mind is the memory of Provos, the woman who lived backward. She was not dolorous, but the monster attacked her first. She must have had a conflict."

Colene nodded. "Maybe she did. She risked everything to travel the Mode with us. She finally rescued two people from my Mode of Earth and took them home with her, and they were really fouled-up folk. I think she adopted them, and they lived happily ever after."

"So the conflict was in her relationship with those from whom she was separated. Once she got them back, the conflict ended. Then the monster had to search for another mind to feed on."

"You know, it could be something like that. Sure as hell I've got conflict!"

"Yes. So you need the surgery. When the monster loses its power over you, you will be free to be with Darius."

"I guess I knew that. Otherwise why would I have come here? But, lord, that surgery scares me."

"I know. That is why I am holding your hand."

"And thank you for that, Pussy."

"Open that chamber."

"Damn." Colene looked around. "I'd rather face the monster. It's hardly bugging me right now."

"That's because it uses your own horrors to defeat you, as you figured out. When you address your horror, the monster loses force."

"But this—Pussy, this is ugly."

"Open the chamber."

"This'll kill me!"

"It is killing you already."

Colene sighed. "I guess this *is* what I came for." She turned and walked to the house. She put her hand to the doorknob. She turned it. She hesitated, nerved herself, and opened the door.

Pussy was watching, but had no body. She was an invisible ghost in the air, focusing on Colene at age thirteen. The girl was on a date with a boy she liked but knew only slightly. She was wearing a party dress with a bow, dowdy in her opinion but racy by her mother's standards. But her mother was drinking, so her caution had been successfully brushed aside for this date. Colene was looking forward to some real fun for a change. Getting this date with an older boy was a real prize.

As they entered the house, she hesitated. "Where is the party?"

"Inside," he said. "There's rare entertainment."

Intrigued, she suppressed her doubts and moved on through a short hall. They came to a pleasant living room, where three other young men stood to greet them. Bottles of beer sat on a low table.

"Where's the party?" Colene repeated, looking around.

"Right here," her date said. "Have a drink." He picked up a bottle and opened it for her.

She hesitated. "I'm not supposed to drink that."

"No, it's okay. This is a private house. You can do anything you want."

She had heard that. Wickedly tempted, she accepted the bottle. She sipped it. The stuff tasted foul, but she didn't want to show her naïveté, so continued sipping. "Where's the entertainment?"

"It'll be soon," her date said, taking his own beer. "Have a seat."

She sat where he indicated, on a plush couch. It was very soft, and she sank down so far that her knees were higher than her bottom. Her shirt rode up along her thighs. She tried to restore it with one hand, but it wouldn't go. So she settled for keeping her legs together. She took another gulp of beer. Her mother was alcoholic, and that was no good, but of course Colene herself would never be that way. Anyway, this was only beer, not the dangerous stuff. She could handle it.

They talked about this and that. Colene kept hoping that some other girls would appear, but they didn't, and after a while her head got pleasantly dizzy and she didn't care. When she finished her beer, she was immediately given another. It didn't taste as bad now. She saw at one point that her knees had fallen apart, and the boys were looking, but who cared? If they thought there was anything there worth seeing, that was maybe a compliment. She just didn't have the kind of figure some girls did.

But this was getting dull. "Where's the entertainment?" she asked again.

"Oh, that's in the bedroom," her date said. "Here; I'll help you up." For she, in the deep couch and burdened by the bottle of beer, was having trouble getting to her feet.

"The bedroom! I'm not going in there!"

"Sure you are," he said, smiling. "Here, maybe you've had enough beer." He took the bottle from her hand, then reached down to put his hands under her shoulders.

"Hey!" she said as his hands missed her armpits and landed on her breasts.

"Sorry." He got them placed correctly and hauled her up. The room whirled around her and she would have fallen, had he not caught her. This times his hands passed around her back and took hold of her buttocks through the dress.

She tried to pull away, but was so unsteady she couldn't do it. He half carried her to the bedroom and pushed the door shut behind them. Then he let her fall onto the bed.

"Where's the—" she started. But as he sat beside her and ran his hands up her legs, the chilling truth penetrated: *she* was the entertainment. They had looked; now they were touching.

She rolled clumsily over, trying to escape him, but he put one hand on her back to hold her down, and explored her bottom with the other. "Hey!" she cried, trying ineffectively to crawl away. She felt his fingers hook into her panties and pull them down. "Stop that!"

But he didn't stop, and she knew it was hopeless. She could hardly walk straight, and even if she got away from him, she would have to go through the other room where she would be intercepted by the other three. If she fought, they could readily overpower her. She could get hurt.

So she stopped trying to resist. She just lay there as her date took off his trousers and joined her on the bed. But she didn't cooperate; she remained on her stomach, her legs spread to brace her that way, so he couldn't actually have sex with her.

He covered her. His weight squeezed her breath out of her. "Hey!" she gasped. Then he eased up—but something else happened. Something hard and hot was pushing into her bottom from below.

He was doing it from behind! In her naïveté she had thought that impossible. Now, too late, she knew it wasn't. Indeed, she realized she should have known, because she had read of different positions. She had been willfully blind, to her cost. She was caught in a worse position than otherwise. He found the place, her quivering vulva, and wedged painfully into the crevice. "Hey!" she cried once more, but there was no stopping it. She felt something tear and give way, and the pain surged, but she lacked breath to scream. He impaled her on his huge hard penile stake, and it rammed up into her belly so far she thought it would never stop.

Then he shuddered, and she felt hot fluid inside her. She knew what it was: he was ejaculating. He had reached her secret inner core and was jetting his passion there. She was disgusted; it was the last thing she wanted in that region. She wished she could spit it out, blow it out, get rid of it like noxious garbage.

After an eternity he withdrew and got off her. At least it was over. She struggled to roll onto her back, too confused and distracted to do more. She had been raped, and she hadn't done a thing to stop it.

She was vaguely aware of the door opening. Thank God he was leaving! But then she saw that one of the others was there. "Hey, what—?" she started. And saw that he was taking down his pants.

She tried to get off the bed, but he caught her and held her easily on her back. He came down on her, and she saw his erect penis. She had never seen that before, and was appalled. It was huge and ugly and horribly menacing, but she didn't know what to do, so she did nothing.

He got his member lodged and thrust in and up. Her raw crevice stung, but he covered her faint scream with his face, kissing her open mouth. She tried to turn her face away, and succeeded, but meanwhile his member was deep into her, thrusting repeatedly. It jetted inside her, like a huge hypodermic, filling her with its septic discharge.

He got off her, and she thought it was over, but then there was another man, and this one squeezed her breasts through the cloth of the dress as he lay over her. Then he jammed inside her. At least this time there wasn't much new pain, because it was thoroughly wet and slippery down there. The first two had poured in dirty hot grease, and now her cleft was a river of slime. She didn't protest at all; she just waited for it to be over.

The fourth man wasn't satisfied to have her lie hopelessly sprawled out. He turned her over and made her get on her hands and knees. She cooperated, just wanting to get this dirty business over. He told her to say she liked it. "I like it," she said obediently, hating herself. Then he flipped her dress over her back, squeezed her bare bottom, and thrust from behind, his hands on her hips holding her in place. "You like it!" he said. "I like it," she echoed. "You just love to have it in you." "I just love to have it in me." "Do it harder, Joe." "Do it harder, Joe." Satisfied he did it harder, almost knocking her over, and climaxed. "Good doggie," he concluded, laughing. "Good little bitch." She felt like dying.

After that they were done. But she wasn't. She crawled off the bed, got her feet on the floor, pushed herself up, and stood unsteadily, loathsome gunk squeezing down one leg. She saw that there was a connected bathroom. She made her way to it, using bed, chair, and wall for support. She put her head over the sink and vomited out what remained of the beer in her stomach. She heave and heaved, but what she really wanted to get out was not in her stomach. It was in her belly.

She sat on the toilet and used a sponge to clean her legs and bottom. She was revolted by the gelatinous fluid with its streaks of red, but she had to get it out and off. She rinsed the sponge repeatedly and used it until nothing more showed. She wished she had a water jet she could jam in there and use to blast out every bit of egg white at high pressure. Then she stood, looked in the mirror, and used the sponge to wash her face. What difference did it make? She was filth all over.

Pussy broke in. "Filth? That was sex." The scene dissipated; she had ended it with her intrusion, but she had seen enough.

"Same damn thing. I never got that foulness off me after that. I never told; I was too ashamed, and knew nobody would believe me, and anyway I didn't resist, so it was my fault."

Pussy had been drawing most of her thoughts from Colene's mind, but now she didn't. "Sex is not dirty. I have done the same thing you did, with multiple null males, and loved it all. They forced it on you when you didn't want it; *that's* what makes it wrong. Why do you think it's dirty?"

"It just is. Sex is filthy business. Every child knows that. It's why it's kept secret from them as long as possible. I wish it had been a secret from me longer. I washed and washed, I practically scoured my vagina raw, but it's still foul."

"I don't believe it. Your culture differs from mine, but not by that much. Sex is a gift for adults, perhaps life's single greatest pleasure. It has nothing to do with dirt."

Colene looked at her. "Boy are *you* from a different planet! It's even in our literature. The Bible shows how God kicked Adam and Eve out of the Garden of Eden for discovering sex. Plenty of religious folk will tell you that the naked human body is obscene. Everyone knows it."

Pussy was puzzled. "DoOon does not have a god, but I have the concept from your mind. Did not your God fashion your body as it is?"

"Yes, of course. God made everything. What of it?"

"Yet that body, as God made it, is obscene?"

Colene halted with her mouth half open. "I never thought of it quite that way. I guess you'd have to go to a Biblical scholar to answer that one. But maybe it's that using it for sex is what's obscene."

"Didn't God make sex too?"

"For procreation, not just fooling around."

"We nulls can't procreate. We are all sterile. Yet we enjoy sex. Are we obscene?"

Colene paused again. "No. It's natural for you. It's the way you're made."

"And if you love Darius, and want to have sex with him, but don't want a baby yet, that's obscene?"

Colene looked at the ground. "My mind says no. But my emotion says yes. If those four kooks had just kissed me, or peeked into my bra, or even felt me up some, I guess I would've been annoyed, but not devastated. It's what guys do; they're chronically hooked on peripheral sex. But they *raped* me. They got into my pants and pumped their sewage into me. I can't forgive that."

"Sewage," Pussy said thoughtfully. "There's that filth theme again. I never thought of it that way when Buck humped me. I loved making him spurt. I made him do it over and over until he was worn out. We had a great time."

"Well, you're animals." Then Colene reversed. "I didn't mean that, Pussy!"

"It's all right. We're nulls, which are mock human animals. Maybe we are different. But I still don't see dirt in semen."

"Well, maybe it's because it's so close to the dirt."

"What do you mean?"

"Well, like what that poet, William Butler Yeats, said. I always liked to check into what the teachers didn't recommend, and I found this poem he wrote, "Crazy Jane Talks With the Bishop." It tells how this old hag Crazy Jane met the Bishop, and he told her to get out of the foul sty and live in a heavenly mansion. I think he meant she was going to die soon, so she should purify herself so as to be ready to meet God. And she wouldn't have it; she said that fair and foul are near of kin, and the one needs the other. And when he tried to argue, I guess about how far apart they are, she said "But Love has pitched his mansion in the place of excrement." I guess that fractured his cross! Because she's right: look at a man: he pees through the same penis he uses to have sex with. And look at a woman: her vagina is right between her urethra and her anus. So fuck is between piss and shit. The place of excrement. How much uglier can you get? Isn't it like some huge cosmic joke, that if you want to make a baby you have to put your excretory organs together? If you want to have sexual fun, you have to get close to urine or feces. Some dirty fun!"

"Is it worse than eating?"

"Eating?"

"The same mouth we use for kissing we use for eating. For chewing up food and making it into a formless wet mass. For vomiting. Is urine worse than vomit?"

"Well, we keep our mouths clean, most of the time. We don't vomit when we're kissing."

"We don't defecate when we're having sex, either."

Colene spread her hands. "Maybe so. But that business I went through—it still ruined me. I can't just reason that away. Maybe for you it would have been fun, but it sure as hell wasn't for me."

Pussy had an idea. "Let's replay that scene, and fix them."

"What?"

"This is like a lucid dream, isn't it? We can choose what happens in it. Come on; let me handle it this time."

"I don't know what you're talking about."

"I'll show you. We'll go in again. This time I'll be the girl and you can watch invisibly. Life is dynamic, and this is an animation; we can play out the alternatives."

"Okay," Colene agreed dubiously.

The house reappeared. Pussy stepped up to the door, wearing the dress Colene wore before. The same young man was beside her. They opened the door and went in.

It started with the same deceptive quiet. Pussy accepted the beer.

"There was my first mistake," Colene said, speaking with her mind so that only Pussy heard her. "That beer! I never should have taken that. I should have known better. I *did* know better! But I thought I could handle it. They got me drunk so I couldn't fight. I should have just poured it on his head."

Pussy got lithely out of the couch, lifted the bottle high, and poured it over the young man's head.

He reacted angrily. "Bitch! This's a good suit!" He swept the bottle out of her hand and took hold of her, ripping at her dress. She fought him, punching him in the eye. Immediately the three others closed in, grabbing her by the arms and legs. She tried to kick and bite, until one of them closed his fist and smashed her nose. Then, while she was distracted by the pain and blood, they ripped off her dress and underclothing, and took turns holding her by the neck and breasts while they raped her vertically. When they were done they let her slump to the floor, unconscious, her face a mass of blood.

"Maybe you're right," Colene said, wincing. "Dumping the beer on him would have just made it worse, faster. But at least I could have gotten out of there at the start."

The scene dissolved and re-formed. Pussy and her date

entered the living room. She saw the three other men. "I don't trust this," she said, and turned around.

"Hey, where you going?"

"Home. This isn't my kind of party." She stepped toward the door.

"The hell it isn't!" Her date grabbed her and hauled her back into the living room. She screamed and kicked, but the others caught her legs and stripped her. This time they gave her no chance to bite or kick. They hauled her into the bedroom, threw her down on the bed, and two held her down spread-eagled while the third licked her breasts and the fourth raped her. Then they changed places, so that they could all have their turns.

"I guess not," Colene said. "I guess I was lost the moment I got to that house. Even if I'd gotten out the door, I was far from home, and didn't know how to drive. They'd have had me."

"So the way you played it was probably about as well as you could have," Pussy said. "They had lured you there for sex, and they were going to have it, gently or harshly. You were never at fault."

"Maybe not," Colene said, beginning to believe. "Still, if I'd had an effective way to fight them—"

The scene re-formed. This time when Pussy turned to depart, and the man grabbed her, she reached into a sheath on her thigh and drew a knife with a wicked blade sharpened on either side. She slashed at the man. He fell back, but the others, outraged, charged at her.

Pussy whirled, fencing with the knife, making them pause. Then she saw an opening and lunged. She scored on a throat. It opened like a mouth, and blood poured out as he fell, his face surprised. While the others stared, aghast, she turned on the next, and cut his throat too. The two remaining men plunged out the door and jumped into the car. In a moment it roared away.

"And there I am, a murderess," Colene said with appalled resignation. "And they haven't even raped me yet."

The gory scene dissolved. "I think there was no better way out," Pussy said. "You were caught in their trap, and you had no way of anticipating it. It was not your fault."

"I guess not," Colene agreed. "It was just one of those things. It could have been any girl; it just happened to be me, that time. It wasn't because of any fault in me, other than in being a naïve girl."

"And thereafter you were less naïve," Pussy agreed. "It doesn't matter whether they wanted to rape you or murder you or just embarrass you; you were stuck. You were blameless. And what they did to you did not make you blameworthy or unclean. The blame was theirs. The dirt was theirs. You should not carry it with you to spoil your life."

Colene nodded. "I guess it's like a broken leg. If you knew it was coming, you'd do whatever led to it differently, and save yourself a whole lot of pain and trouble. But if you didn't know, you could still get it reset, and wait for it to heal, and in time you'd be almost as good as new."

"Yes. And you would not have to be afraid of running or jumping. You'd just be more careful."

"Yeah, I guess so."

"And you can go with Darius, knowing you are not unclean, and do whatever pleases you both. It wasn't the sex that was wrong, it was its coercive nature. Sex without force is not evil."

"Not evil," Colene agreed.

"Now let's go back."

They turned, but Colene balked. "I can't."

"What?"

"I can't go this way. The monster's holding me back." Indeed, her feet were moving without purchase, as before.

"But we beat back your nightmare. It's gone."

"It's not gone."

"But you know that you should have no guilt for what you couldn't help. You can be free of it, now."

"You have shown me that my worst nightmare was not my fault, and that I should be able to have sex with Darius without guilt. I admit it, logically. But that's intellectual. Deep down inside, I still know better. Sex is dirty, and I can't do it."

Pussy considered. "We're not out of here, then. There must be another level."

"I don't need any more levels!"

"What do you think it is? What are you still afraid of? It shouldn't be sex."

"Maybe not sex itself. But it's part of a larger thing, and that's what gets me. The associated feelings."

"You're afraid to like sex?"

"Maybe."

"It's just an act, like kissing or hugging. No reason to fear it, as long as it's voluntary. You know that. There must be more. What about the pleasure of it?"

"That's closer."

"The sensuality of it?"

Colene thought for a moment before answering. "I'm not afraid of sensuality itself, but of the emotions that come with mine. I want someone to touch me, and yet I can't stand the thought of some man touching me like that. I want to kiss his lips and break his fingers. I want to touch his cheek and slash his throat. I want to stop seeing rape where I look when someone gets friendly with me, or says he's attracted to me. I don't see someone attractive when I look in a mirror. It doesn't have to mean anything, but the panic flashes to my throat, and I have to resist the urge to punch *his* throat. I am not ready. Where maybe there once was beauty, I see calluses and flesh and things dying, flawed. I see the human ugliness, and there is nothing I want from him. Or her, if it's a woman. Not that I'm not flattered when a woman says she'd like to get up with me, but I don't go that way."

"And you thought—when I said I loved you—"

"Yeah. Sorry about that."

It was Pussy's turn to consider. "I guess we're not through here yet. The mind monster doesn't bother you when you go deeper into it. It strikes only when you try to get away. It must be feeding on those conflicts, and won't let you go till they're all gone. Then maybe it will have no further power. You have given it a good meal, I think, but we have to find what else there is."

"There's nothing else!"

Pussy knew better. "Then maybe we'll find an empty room. Let's go see."

"I hate this," Colene muttered, but she turned and went with Pussy in the other direction. Now her feet had ample purchase.

They came to a large building. "That's my school!" Colene exclaimed. "That's no site of buried horror."

"Then let's go inside."

They went inside. Classes were in session, and there were few people in the halls. "We're going toward the cafeteria," Colene said. "Nothing bad there except the food." She laughed. "Not really. Everybody hates the food; it's mandatory. But it's actually no worse than it is anywhere else."

They entered the cafeteria, and came to a table where several girls were eating. Most were finishing, but one was a little late. "Oh, shit," Colene breathed.

"What is it?"

"It's what I can't handle. I'm getting out of here." Such was her determination that she actually made progress. Right through a wall. The school dissipated as she forged through; she had destroyed the vision. They were back outside.

But now huge insects appeared. Each was the size of a house, with barbed hairy legs and enormous mandibles.

They surrounded Colene and Pussy, closing in. One reached down with a long thin snout. It was a gargantuan mosquito, about to suck out all of Colene's blood in a single pull.

But Colene stood her ground. "Get out of here, freak," she said. "I know you aren't real, because of the square-cube law. If you were that big, those spindly legs would collapse and you'd die before you even got started."

Pussy watched, amazed, as the insects retreated. But then dragons appeared in their places: huge winged snake-like things with crocodile teeth. They dived, orienting on Colene.

"Same for you," the girl said. "You'd never be able to fly if you were physical. You need a wingspan ten times what you got. Go!" She waved her arm, and the dragons were swept back as if blown away by hurricane winds.

"But this is all in the realm of the mind predator," Pussy said. "How can you banish its dreams?"

"Because they're borrowed from the monster movies I've seen. I always knew they were impossible. It's *entertainment*. I like pretending I'm scared that way."

"But you came here to face what does scare you, to reveal it and abolish it. Colene, you have to go back to that school scene."

"*Damn* you, Pussy! You're supposed to be helping me."

"I am. Colene, if you fight your way out of here now, will you be able to be all things with Darius?"

The girl stopped. "Damn you," she repeated. She turned around, and the school building was there. They walked inside again, to the cafeteria. "Oh, I really, truly hate this!"

Then Colene's body sailed ghostlike and merged with the late girl. Pussy saw that she was Colene, perhaps two years younger, or three. Her hair was shorter and her features less mature. She was just on the verge of physical maturity, and rather pretty in her shy way.

Pussy watched as the girl ate her soup. Then someone passed and threw something. It landed with a splash in Colene's soup. Pussy was unfamiliar with the object, but got it from the girl's horrified mind. It was a tampon. A cylindrical wad of cotton or some absorbent substance whose purpose was to fit inside a girl's vagina and soak up her menstrual flow. That enabled her to maintain normal daily activities without soiling her clothing or otherwise embarrassing herself.

But Colene was just reaching menarche, and was not at all comfortable with such paraphernalia. She understood the necessity, but the whole business made her feel unclean. She wished it would all go away. She wanted to banish it from her body and her mind. Menses were unclean. Everyone knew that. There were endless jokes.

And here in her face, floating in her red tomato soup, was this *thing* that reminded her of everything she wanted to forget. The bowl seemed to be filled with blood, and the tampon was trying to eat it, in the process slowly swelling. The whole thing was obscene.

She couldn't move. She was transfixed, frozen with that horrible vision dominating her contracting world. She couldn't escape it.

There was laughter around her. The girls thought it was a funny joke, and some of the boys were noticing too. Colene received it all, in her larger awareness, as though she were looking down at the scene and seeing the whole cafeteria, herself in the middle, a vessel of utter shame. She was crystallized in place, her boundaries fixed, congealed, set. Her body was vacated while her spirit fled the overwhelming humiliation. She wanted to die. In fact, she *was* dying, and rigor mortis was setting in.

The others left, but Colene's husk remained, locked to the awful bowl and its appalling content. She knew she should have gotten up and left, but she hadn't, and now she couldn't. She should have laughed, pretending it was nothing, but she hadn't, and now it was too late. She couldn't do anything, so she did nothing. She had freaked out, and the whole world knew it.

A teacher came. "Colene, go to your class." But she didn't react. She couldn't break the bonds that had coalesced around her, making her a statue. She would stay here forever. There was no other way.

Someone took away the bowl, but that didn't change anything. It was still there in her vision. She was petrifying, slowly changing into stone, like a buried sequoia tree.

Hours passed, and she didn't move. Finally her father came. He must have been notified and taken time off from work. He had never done that before.

He could have yelled, or registered disgust. Instead he was oddly understanding. He took off his jacket and put it over her shoulders as though she needed protection from the weather. The oddest thing was that it helped. "Come on, honey," he said. "Let's get out of here."

He helped her up, and put his arm around her. She hid her face in the jacket, and let him guide her out. He brought her to the car and set her in the front seat.

"De gustibus non carborundum," he said. "Do you know what that means?"

She shook her head.

"Don't let the bastards grind you down."

That was all. But it was enough. She sealed over the incident, like an archaeological artifact covered by new foundations, and next day returned to school, and no one spoke of it. Oh, they were surely thinking of it, and she was a marked girl, but soon there were other gossipy mini-scandals, such as who got pregnant by her best friend's boyfriend and had to quit eighth grade, and Colene's freak-out receded into nonentity.

"But you remembered," Pussy said.

"How could I forget?"

"And you didn't let the bastards grind you down."

"Not externally. I concluded that the best defense was a good offense, and resolved never to allow myself to be freaked out by anything gross again. I was sharp with the cutting humor when I put my mind to it, and I discovered how easy it was to make friends by complimenting people, even when I didn't mean it. I became popular. But that hole in my core remained. I can still close my eyes and see that red-soaked tampon floating there."

"But you know what it was. Everything in that scene was ordinary, just inappropriately juxtaposed."

"Sure. I should have looked up immediately, caught the girl who tossed it, and yelled so the whole school could hear: 'Susie, take back your bloody tampon!' That would have turned the tables and made *her* the laughingstock. Instead, I freaked out. That's what so disgusts me. I let the bastards get me down. It was as though someone yanked off my skirt and panties and left me bare-assed before the multitude: I was stuck exposed for what I was, an innocent kid who couldn't handle it. I hate myself for ever being that naïve."

"But everyone starts naïve."

"But not everyone gets her tender little ass bared in public."

Pussy sorted carefully through this. "We nulls of course don't have monthly cycles. We never bleed. Sometimes we wish we could, because it would mean that we could bear our own babies. But we can't. We are never plugged by anything but a man's ardent member, by design. There is never a time when we are not completely ready for sexual expression. So I have no experience of this nature. But if I understand your concern, it was that this tampon was an object that belonged in your vagina at a time when you felt unclean. So its appearance in public suggested that your most shameful secret was exposed for all to see."

"You got it. A girl's supposed to be pristine, and never give a hint of her unclean condition. That's why they developed tampons. The other way is to have a pad covering the whole works, and she can't wear a bathing suit because the pad makes her crotch lumpy, and for sure she can't swim, because the water would soak through it. The tampon's a whole lot more private. But also more specific. It goes right *in*, the same place the penis does, so it's like she's having this dirty secret sex with a cotton dildo. So when one of those comes out in the open, it's as if everyone sees right into her hole, and knows her most intimate secret."

"Is that the way other women see it?"

"No. It's the way *I* see it. That's what counts."

"But you know there is no evil in it. Nothing to be ashamed of."

"I know."

"Then let's leave this monster and return to current life."

But when they tried to go back, a flying saucer appeared. From it piled weird-looking alien creatures with huge bug-eyes and colorful pistols. They aimed these weapons at Colene. "Cheap sci-fi," she muttered. "More junk mined from my childish mind." She forged on, ignoring the aliens, and sure enough, their laser beams didn't hurt her.

"The predator is still trying to hold you. You have to face whatever else it has."

Colene nodded grimly. "I guess I'm not done yet." But she didn't turn around.

Pussy refrained from sighing. "I suppose the dirt is still there. You felt that the tampon and what it signified was dirty, and you were ashamed."

"I did, and I was."

"Yet you now know better."

"I do. It's an idiotic hang-up. So I was mortified at the time. So now I know better."

"So what is still holding you back?"

"Whatever convinced me that sex and everything remotely associated with it is dirty or evil. I guess it predates even the tampon. Because I still know I can't do it with Darius, though I want to."

"You humans are more complicated than we nulls. We never have a problem of performance, when a master or mistress expresses desire."

"Well, Tom did, at one point."

"That was really a case of conflicting requirements. It passed."

"I think I envy you your simpler psyche, noncycles and all."

"You did not have sex before the rape, because you bled then. That's another complication nulls lack. But then what secret could you have had, so young? Or were you simply taught that sex is bad?"

"No, not directly. I had the same education everyone else did. Girls my age were getting into sex from the time I was eleven or twelve, and I guess I would have too, if there'd been love. But now I feel it: there's a deep guilt, and it's sexual in nature. I must've done something I managed to forget about, but it lingered."

They turned and walked on into the awfulness of unknown guilt. And came to another house.

"Why, that's my neighbor's house, early-on," Colene said, surprised. "My friend Buffy lived there. I'd almost forgotten; they moved later and we lost touch."

"Buffy?"

"Short for Elizabeth. She was my age, seven, when— oh, no!"

"You found something."

Colene tried to turn around. "I'd really rather leave it alone."

"So it must be what we seek."

"Oh, yeah. Oh, damn."

"You must explore it."

Colene gritted her teeth. "Yeah."

The front door of the house opened. A little girl ran out. She wore a flouncing blue dress with matching blue ties for her pigtails. "Lene!" she cried gladly, as if they had not seen each other in weeks. "Come in and play!"

Colene went with her. Colene was in a similar outfit, her dress being green, her hair tied back with a green ribbon. The two girls were of similar height and build, and both seemed carefree. It was a deliberate emulation of each other, as though they were twins, a game of identities.

"We got a new game today," Buffy said brightly. "With Dad. Mom's away."

Colene knew Buffy's father, a friendly and pleasant man who was often in the vicinity when they played. She thought it was because he wanted to be sure that no harm came to his little girl. But he had never actually played with them before, and she wasn't sure what game would interest an adult. "What is it?"

"He wants to lick your crack."

Colene was at a loss. "My what?"

"You know, between your legs." Buffy pulled up her dress and drew aside her panty to show her clean little cleft.

Colene wasn't sure about this. She had picked up the news, by the osmosis of family indirection, that no one other than her mother or another girl was ever to see that part of her that was covered by her panty, let alone touch it. "I don't think so." She wasn't saying no, just that she was uncertain of the propriety.

"It's okay, Lene. He does it all the time, to lots of girls. It doesn't hurt. It's fun."

"Fun?"

"Sure. It feels good. And he gives gifts."

Colene liked gifts. Christmas was her favorite time, because of the presents she got then. "What kind of gifts?"

"Nice dolls. Come on, I'll show you." Buffy hauled her to her bedroom, where she had a fine collection of dolls. "See? I got this one for a good licking." She picked up a fine big teddy bear.

"But isn't it wrong?"

Buffy looked at her with surprise. "What's wrong? It's fun. Only we don't tell Mom. It's not her kind of game."

"Mine neither," Colene said, knowing that her mother would Not Approve.

"So it's secret. That makes it more fun." Both girls loved secrets, and shared them constantly.

Still, Colene was uncertain. Secret hideaways, secret codes, secret stories—these were the stuff of joy. But to let a man put his face in there—that was a shameful secret. "I'd better not."

"Oh, c'mon! It's fun. I bet he's got a really nice doll for you. 'Cause he likes you. He said so. He said you're really cute."

"He did?" Colene was inordinately flattered. She wanted to be pretty and popular, but suspected that she was nothing of the kind.

"Sure. He said he'd really, really like to do you. So he must have a really nice gift. C'mon, let's see."

They went to the bedroom of Buffy's parents, and there was her father, sitting at a desk in the corner. "Hey, Dad, whatcha got for Lene?"

He gazed at them. "That depends. Does she want to play?"

Colene didn't answer, being more uncertain than ever.

"Show her what you got," Buffy said.

The man reached into a drawer and brought out the most beautiful doll she had ever seen. It was a horse, a mare, velvety black, standing about six inches tall at the shoulder. The long tail just touched the ground, and the mane flared back and fell to the right. Colene fell in love with it, that instant.

"See?" Buffy demanded. "She's real pretty!"

Colene reached toward it, then hesitated. If she took it, she would be agreeing to the game.

"Go ahead," the man said encouragingly. "See how she feels." He put the doll into her hands.

Colene held the mare doll, and stroked her back. She had never before felt such silkiness. The mane and tail were made of real, individual hairs. The face looked wise. This was a heaven doll.

"Keep her," the man said.

Reluctantly, Colene handed it back. "I can't."

"Oh, c'mon," Buffy said, exasperated. "It's nothing. I do it all the time."

"You do?"

"Sure. Like this." Buffy jumped up on the edge of the bed, swung her legs up so that her dress fell almost across her face, ripped off her panties, and braced her feet against the edge of the bed so that her knees were high and spread. What she called her crack was completely exposed. She let her back flop on the bed. "Watch."

The man kneeled on the floor, then leaned forward and put his face up against that open crevice. He licked it. "See?" Buffy said, completely undismayed. "It feels real good."

The funny thing was that it did look like fun. It obviously didn't hurt. And there was that horse doll. She truly wanted it. "Okay," she said at last.

"Good. Get beside me, like this. You got to do it right."

Colene got on the bed, removed her panties, braced her knees up and apart, and let her head fall back on the bedspread. She was wide open in a way she was sure was wrong. But she so much wanted that mare!

Buffy got up and put her panties back on. She looked

at Colene. "Gee, yours *is* real pretty," she said enviously.

Colene closed her eyes, not wanting to see anything. She felt the man's breath on her thighs, and willed herself not to move. If she didn't move, it wouldn't be her doing it. So she couldn't be blamed. She concentrated on the doll, desiring it intensely. She felt the mouth touching her cleft, kissing it, licking it. She focused on the doll. The tongue stroked the length of her slit, and nudged into its center, and it did feel warm and good. She thought of how wonderful it would be to have the doll. Her body felt increasingly good as the man's lips and tongue caressed the crevice. She imagined riding the horse, in some dreamland where it was full size. The pressure against her thighs and bottom felt divine. She hated it, yet wished it would continue forever. She drifted into a semi-dream state. It was as though that wonderful horse were carrying her away to some perfect other world, where everything felt so good.

"Okay, Lene," Buffy said. "You did real good."

Colene realized that it was over. The man was gone, and the doll was on the bed beside her. She had earned it.

She got up and put her panties on. She hugged the doll.

"Whatcha going to call her?" Buffy asked.

The name came without thought. "Maresy."

Buffy laughed. "Great! Let's go have some pop."

Colene never told anyone else how she had won the doll. It was just a gift from Buffy's dad. No one questioned it. She never did the act again, but that once was branded on her memory. At night she would lie with her bare knees up, and hug the doll. Sometimes she touched herself, feeling illicit pleasure, but also enormous guilt. She knew she shouldn't have done it. But she loved Maresy.

"Oral sex," Pussy said. "You had oral sex as a child. Why do you feel guilty?"

"Children are not supposed to do it," Colene said. "They just aren't. I knew I had done something horrible."

"But you liked it."

"I hated it!"

"You liked it."

"I hated that I liked it."

And here it was: her guilt was only partly for the act, and mostly because the act had felt good. She had sold herself for a doll, and maybe it would have been all right if she had hated the act, but she had liked it. The warm wet tongue had brought her a peculiar pleasure she never found anywhere else.

In time she managed to forget the act, but her love for Maresy Doll remained, though with a mysterious tinge of guilt. Maresy became her confidant for her most sensitive secrets.

Pussy shook her head. "We nulls do that sort of thing all the time. We always did. It *is* fun. Why did it make you so ashamed?"

"It just *is*," Colene said. "Children aren't supposed to know anything about sex."

Pussy shrugged. "Well, you did what you had to, to earn your doll. It didn't make any difference whether you liked it or hated it, it was what you had to do. So there's no point in feeling guilt, then or now."

"But I do feel guilt, then and now."

"Look, Colene. You were a child. You weren't expected to know everything that was right or wrong. The girl set you up, and the man took advantage of you. If there was guilt, it was theirs. You have no business feeling it."

"I went against my culture. That inspires guilt."

"You're no longer in your culture."

Colene nodded. "I guess you're right."

"It's not what you did, but how you feel about it that

counts. You let your culture foist guilt on you. You don't have to keep it."

"But I was only seven!"

"Too young to know better."

"But I liked it."

"Does pleasure equate with guilt?"

Colene thought about that. "I guess you're right. I shouldn't have done it, and I knew that then and know it now. But I was led into it, and made a mistake. I shouldn't have to pay for that all the rest of my life."

"Exactly."

"When something else happened, like that tampon, that original sin came back to lend it force. I was paralyzed again, trying to avoid blame."

"And you were helpless when you were raped, and felt the guilt again. It was a continuing current, because you had never dealt with it. But now you have. You don't have to be a patsy anymore."

Slowly, Colene nodded. "I think I feel something letting go. The guilt's beginning to leak away."

"So now that you have explored the guilts that paralyzed you, you can return to Darius without inhibition."

"I wonder. Maybe there are other layers."

"We can find out. Let's go back."

They turned, and tried to walk back the way they had come. They made scant progress.

"Damn it, enough already!" Colene flared. "I was fooling about more layers. There *isn't* any more guilt. I've used up my deepest inner conflicts."

"Then why won't the monster let us go?"

"Because it's cheating!"

Pussy laughed. "How do we deal with a monster who cheats?"

"We force it to obey the rules."

"*What* rules?"

"Okay, then we bluff it back." Colene turned around in

a full circle. "Monster, I'm done with you! I have fed you all I'm going to. If you don't lay off, I'm going to start feeding on *you.*"

The only answer was a shifting of the foul clouds surrounding them. The clouds changed course to converge. Pussy wanted to urge caution, but saw that the girl was determined. There was something subtly different about her. She had weakened the dreadful bonds of her guilt, and now she was emerging as a qualitatively different person.

"Okay, you asked for it," Colene said. "I'm fed up with your crap, and I'm not going to take it any more." She stood and concentrated.

The clouds hesitated. They were responding!

Then they closed in again, faster.

"I warned you," Colene said evenly. She concentrated again.

This time the clouds were flung outward and blown apart. Could Colene have done that? This was something new.

"Let's get the hell out of here," Colene said.

But a ring of light formed around the horizon. It contracted, turning out to be fire. The flames burned high, surrounding them, drawing closer and hotter.

"Forget it, monster," Colene snapped. The flames abruptly melted and seeped into the ground harmlessly.

"How are you doing that?" Pussy asked, amazed.

"The monster works by animating the spooks of the mind. I can do it better, is all."

"But how, when you couldn't before?"

"I was internally conflicted before. Now I'm not. I may have some lingering hang-ups, but I know they'll dissipate, now that I've dug out their roots. I've had my surgery, and I'll be healing. Meanwhile I'm tired of getting hassled by this thing."

The ground shook rhythmically. Something huge was

coming. It turned out to be a giant dinosaur. It spied Colene and changed, lowering its head and opening its mouth to reveal enormous teeth.

"Get out of here before I hurt you," Colene said, undismayed.

The predator lowered its head to snap her up. Colene snapped her fingers, and a phenomenally large head swept down and caught the entire dinosaur in its mouth. It chomped and gulped, and the dinosaur disappeared down its gullet, the long tail switching frantically behind.

"This is magic!" Pussy breathed.

"No, it's all illusion. Let's go."

"Now you can destroy the mind predator."

"No. I took its measure when it was taking mine. The thing is eternal. But I'm no longer its prey. It'll have to go after some more troubled mind. What it really seeks is renewing stress. I had an ongoing bundle of that, but I'm done with it now." She lifted one hand in a wave. "Bye, Monster!"

They started walking, and now they had traction. "So facing your buried guilt worked," Pussy said.

"Yeah. Before, I was fighting myself, and that limited my ability to handle an external enemy. Now I'm all together, and can do what I was made to do."

"Made to do?"

"I'm a magical mind. That's why Darius oriented on me in the first place. It wasn't a mistake after all. All the anchor people are special, or they can't make anchors. Darius is the Cyng of Hlahtar. Nona has fantastic powers of magic. Seqiro has similar powers of telepathy. I really am one of them. I can be magic, once I learn how. But I was crippled by my cultural conditioning and my ignorance, not to mention my layers of misplaced shame and guilt. Now I'm finally free of all that, thanks to you, and can realize my full potential."

"What is that?"

"I don't yet know the limits. I never believed in magic, before I got on the Virtual Mode. There's a lot to discover." Colene paused, her eyes dilating. "I can be all three to Darius! I can multiply joy, now that I'm not locked on dolor. I can do it all!"

Pussy had been encouraging her all along, but now she was afraid of overconfidence. "Are you sure? Could it be a trick of the monster, to lure you into a worse trap?"

"No. I know my own potential, now. I can see the future, and I *am* all three. Only it will take a little time, sexually, because I'm not there yet. I've fixed the problem, but still need time to heal. But the rest of me is unbound. I know where I'm going. Maresy will be better much faster. The whole hive is going to grow and prosper; Burgess loves it. And you and Doe will have virile boyfriends who really appreciate how you're made. We're all going to be happy."

This had the ring of conviction. "But what of Ddwng and the DoOon Mode?"

Colene looked into the larger ambiance. "Say, wow! So *that's* why Darius agreed to take the chain. He saw it long before I did."

"Saw what?"

"Ddwng! He's another magical mind. Terrific power, but he's hung up twice as bad as I ever was. He's fighting himself all over, and he keeps renewing it. He's paranoid, and he won't let go for anything. That's why he was going to torture the Caprines to make Cat talk: he couldn't believe there wasn't a dastardly plot. But what Darius said is true: the flaw is in Ddwng himself. He's a monkey with a jar."

"I don't understand."

"It's how they caught monkeys in India. They put out these anchored jars with trinkets or food in them, with the narrow openings just big enough for a monkey's hand to get in. But when the monkey grabbed what was inside, it wouldn't let go, and its closed fist was too big to get out the little hole. So it was caught. Ddwng wants power so bad he just can't let go of any piece of it. So he's finished."

"How can he be finished? He's the emperor."

"He's finished because he is what he is. He can't trust anyone else to possess the Chip, especially after the way Cat seemed to betray him, so he'll make himself the anchor, and go on the Virtual Mode himself. Then—"

"The monster!" Pussy exclaimed.

"Right. The mind predator will be waiting for him. In fact it's waiting now, because I've just clued it in. I don't like emperors who try to push me around. Ddwng's doomed. I see it happening. I had you to help me get through, but Ddwng has no one. Darius knew. When he strikes back, he really makes it count. How I love that man! Now come on, Puss; we've got lives to fulfill."

Colene forged onward, and Pussy hurried to keep pace. The monster made no further effort to stop them. In a moment they found the anchor and emerged from the Virtual Mode.

The others were standing there. "What happened?" Darius asked.

"As if you didn't know," Colene said, hugging him. Then she collapsed.

"Colene!" Pussy cried. But already Seqiro was reassuring her. The girl was well, just tired after her great mental and emotional effort. She would be all right after a few hours of rest. More than all right, in time.

In fact, all of them were going to be more than all right. The hive was strong.

Author's Note

I wrote the first novel in this series, *Virtual Mode*, in 1990, and in the two following years completed the sequels *Fractal Mode* and *Chaos Mode*. My literary agent got me a very good contract, but—well, when we called a bookstore to inquire how the hardcover edition of *Virtual Mode* was selling a month after publication, the man said, "You mean that's in print? Why didn't they tell me? I've been waiting for it." It seems the book salesman for that area hadn't even made his rounds that month, and rather than clean up that act, the publisher simply cut the print order. It had to rush back to press twice in the month of publication, because of demand as readers discovered the book, but of course had forfeited the real chance the novel had had to make the bestseller lists. Since publishers typically limit the print order for the following novel to the early sales of the first one, it virtually guarantees that each will do worse in hardcover. Paperback printings tend to be a function of the hardcover printings, so this series was doomed, and folded after the third novel. Ever since, readers have been asking where the next novel is. I have had to tell them that a series that has readers but not a publisher has little chance. There was no point in writing a novel I couldn't get published. I hate having the corporate bottom line be in charge of the arts; as I like to put it, the money changers have taken over the temple. But this is reality, and not just in novels.

Then came the Internet. Because I do feel that readers should have some say in what is made available for them, and I also feel that the myriad hopeful writers who are essentially shut out of the system because there is room for only one in a hundred novels written should have their chance. So though at this writing I haven't been on the Internet myself—just email, which I learned while writing this novel—I have supported Internet publishing. In fact, I invested in two Internet publishers, Xlibris.com and Pulpless.com, and gave each one of my novels: my World War II historical *Volk* and the science fiction *Realty Check*. Whether these publishers will be successful I don't know at this writing, but at least I have done what I can to make it possible. Xlibris enables any writer to self-publish for a nominal fee, which is different from the notorious vanity publishing, where hopeful writers get taken for huge amounts. Pulpless is trying to "sell" its books to readers free, supported instead by advertising, in the manner of so much of the Internet. Both publishers produce physical copies identical to those of regular publishers. This is the sort of thing that I hope will open up publishing, and enable writers to have a better shot at realizing their dreams. I think that regular commercial publishing should continue, but that there should be this alternative for those who need it—which means the great majority of hopeful writers.

(Note: In the interval between the writing and the publishing of this novel, much changed. Pulpless.com folded, and Xlibris became Global Publishing Service. I developed an ongoing Internet publishing survey at my site, *www.Hipiers.com* and also have a bimonthly column there.)

So while I was writing this novel, my involvement in Internet publishing became significant. If this novel does not find a regular publisher, it well may go to one of these Internet publishers. You, the reader, have the benefit of seeing the future in a way I can't: check the title page to see what kind of publishing this novel achieved.

Otherwise, my life while writing this novel has been routine. I started it in Dismember after catching up on jobs such as reviewing thirty years of writing accounts and updating my accounts database: what a chore. I also clipped back the foliage and pulled down long grapevines encroaching on our three-quarter-mile-long drive, in the process twisting my left knee so that I limped for three days. Those grapevines do fight back. The Christmas season also slowed things; think how much more efficient life would be if there were no holidays. Then in Jamboree I went to autograph copies of *Dream a Little Dream* with my lovely collaborator Julie Brady, who has also contributed to this novel. In FeBlueberry our new 450 MHz Pentium II computer system arrived, with a scanner so we could start scanning my old novels into the system for Internet republication. Naturally the system fought us at every step, and at this writing still refuses to recognize the scanner. It is evident that the computer industry has little concern for the convenience or welfare or peace of mind of those who try to use the infernal machines. In Marsh we did manage to get the system grudgingly performing on email, and I learned how to receive and send such letters. In Apull I expect to start cruising the Internet; I have read three good books on the subject and believe I can do it without making too much smoke pour out of the system. So in my time of writing this novel, I have come to the very verge of the Internet, and that I think is significant. It means I am lagging behind much of the rest of the world by less than a decade.

My wife and I and our dog Obsidian live on our tree farm. Six days a week the dog gets to ride in the car with my wife to fetch in the mail, and she loves that. Sundays I take Obsidian for a walk through the tree farm; she loves that too. Have you any idea how much there is to smell in a forest? On the day I wrote most of this Author's Note, we followed the path I have cleared from the house to the lake—our property is a peninsula in the marsh, shaped rather like Florida—around to the pines, and across one of our myriad sink holes. My wife was nervous about our excursion, because there are feral pigs in the neighborhood. They can get to be several hundred pounds, and the boars can have tusks and attitudes. But this day we saw no fresh signs of pigs, which was a relief. I may buy a spear—no joke—to carry in the forest, to fend off a boar if I have to. I'm a vegetarian, because I don't want to hurt animals, but that does not mean I want any animals to hurt *me*. The pigs chew things up so badly that we fear other wildlife will suffer, and we do regard this property as a wildlife sanctuary. So our neighbors have our permission to catch and kill any pigs they spy; they're not vegetarians. Thus an innocent dog walk in the forest begins to assume ethical complications. Life at times seems barely simpler than computers.

I now use two bicycles, which I alternate for trips out to fetch the newspapers or close the gate. One I call the AweCycle, because I bought it at Awesome Cycles. It is a recumbent bicycle, which feels like a moving deck chair with a big wheel behind and a little wheel far in front. It took me a while to learn to keep my balance on it, because the reflexes for a regular bicycle don't match those for a recumbent, but it's a nice machine. Nevertheless, I sometimes take a spill; my last one occurred on Ogre Drive when a tire skidded in sand and I couldn't correct course because sand destabilized the bike, then a tree was in the way, and then the wheels skidded on leaves, dumping me. No damage done except that I sprung my left knee. That knee just seems to be the one to get it. My other cycle is the RowBike, which is propelled by emulation oars. It was developed by the same man who invented the inline roller skate. It's actually a traveling exercise machine, but I use it just for traveling. That one took me about six months to get used to, and I had my spills, but now I like it well. During this novel a part broke; I phoned to order a replacement, and they said there was a lifetime warranty and sent it to me free. That's an attitude I like.

I exercise regularly, mainly by jogging and with dumbbells and by archery. I have two bows, one a compound bow set at a sixty-pound draw weight, meaning that my arms must be able to pull that hard. The other is a left-handed reverse curve bow I bought from an obliging reader in Kiss-Mee. Twice a week I shoot arrows at a target, right handed and left handed so as to exercise evenly, and the other days I simply draw the bowstring twenty times without firing any arrows. Thus I combine exercise with fun, and possible self-defense if it ever came to that. My aim has gradually improved so that now I seldom miss the target at fifty or one hundred feet. That saves having to use my metal detector to locate lost arrows. So I hope to stay healthy a while yet, even if I do keep injuring my knee.

Actually my mouth is my other weakness. I know, I know: my critics are falling over themselves to agree, this one time. But what I mean is that I have had enough work done on my teeth over the years to finance a college education: sixteen onlays, and I think nine root canals, and some oral surgery. I take good care of my mouth, but this mischief seems to be genetic. A tooth was bothering me, so finally I went to have it checked: sure enough, it was another thousand-dollar item. Decay had started in *below* the filled root canal. So while editing this novel I had my second apicoectomy. Specifically, the endodontist cut open the gum, cut off the tooth root, filled in the affected area, and sewed the gum back into place. So for a couple of days while editing I was on soft foods, took a few pain pills, and had the right jowl of a dour Scotsman, until the swelling subsided. Anyone who wants some advice about what to avoid should bear this in mind: stay clear of decay below the tooth roots.

In this period also my father was declining. My mother died in 1991, the time of the original Mode novels, and that was an ugly surprise that caused me to pay closer attention. Thus I have had a monetary and social involvement with my father, who is at this writing just shy of his ninetieth birthday. I have found aspects to be both expensive and emotionally painful as his capacities diminish, not least in their possible foreshadowing of my own future decline. This is of course what most adult children encounter as the eldest generation passes, but that does not make my turn comfortable.

Let's conclude on a small positive note: in the period of this novel we planted one of the fringe trees that were given out locally free; for almost three months it sat there like a dead stem, but then suddenly sprouted and is growing rapidly. I also spied a small hanging nest in the little magnolia tree I stopped the bulldozer from razing a dozen years ago; now it's a medium-sized tree, doing well, and the nest appears to be that of a white-eyed vireo. We see the tip of her beak as we pass, as she sits on her egg. So the tree I saved is helping to bring forth new life.

Several people contributed to this novel. Colene, of course, was derived from a melange of suicidally depressive girls I heard from over the years, but she quickly enough assumed her own identity. As I have done in the prior volumes, I'll list them alphabetically by first names, and not identify what they contributed, with one exception. This is because some of the material is sensitively personal in nature. Most of it I invented, but not all. Some derives from material in *Virtual Mode*.

Adam Boenig—the microscopic energy creatures
Anne Valley
Julie Brady
Robyn Johnson

And so at last the Mode series is complete. I will be moving on to other projects, wrapping things up as I move into the final segment of my life.